Praise for Jenny Oliver

'Brilliantly written, this is packed full of
humour… A perfect holiday read.'
The Sun

'This book made me want to dance on the beach with a
glass of sangria in my hand. The perfect summer read.'
Sarah Morgan

'This is a real treat. A touching story of love, loss and
finding out what really matters in life. I love it!'
Julia Williams

'Jenny Oliver writes contemporary women's fiction
which leaves you with a warm, fuzzy feeling inside.'
Books with Bunny

'Intelligent, delightful and charming! The writing is exquisite.'
What's Better Than Books

'A perfect summer read.'
This Price Is Usually Right

'A sprinkling of festivity, a touch of romance and a
glorious amount of mouth-watering baking!'
Rea Book Review

'…it was everything I enjoy…I couldn't find a single flaw.'
Afternoon Bookery

'I didn't want to put the book down until I had
reached the very last word on the last page.'
A Spoonful of Happy Endings

Jenny Oliver wrote her first book on holiday when she was ten years old. Illustrated with cut-out supermodels from her sister's *Vogue*, it was an epic, sweeping love story not so loosely based on *Dynasty*. Since then Jenny has gone on to get an English degree and a job in publishing that's taught her what it takes to write a novel (without the help of the supermodels).

Also by Jenny Oliver

The Parisian Christmas Bake Off
The Vintage Summer Wedding
The Little Christmas Kitchen
The Sunshine and Biscotti Club
The Summerhouse by the Sea

The House We Called Home

Jenny Oliver

ONE PLACE. MANY STORIES

HQ
An imprint of HarperCollins*Publishers* Ltd
1 London Bridge Street
London SE1 9GF

This paperback edition 2018

1
First published in Great Britain by
HQ, an imprint of HarperCollins*Publishers* Ltd 2018

ISBN: 978-0-00-821798-3

MIX
Paper from
responsible sources
FSC™ C007454

This book is produced from independently certified FSC paper
to ensure responsible forest management.

For more information visit: www.harpercollins.co.uk/green

Printed and bound in Great Britain by
CPI Group (UK) Ltd, Croydon, CR0 4YY

To Emily

CHAPTER I

She stood at the cliff edge looking out at the rolling summer surf. The house towering behind her, solid grey stone and slate, bursting pink rhododendrons, white garden furniture that needed a paint. The image, like closing your eyes after glancing at the sun, almost indelible on her retina, beams of light dancing in the dark.

Out ahead, mountains of cloud hovered on the horizon, a windsurfer made painful progress in the non-existent breeze while paddleboarders cruised on water that glistened like a million jumping fish.

Moira balled up her fists. Tight so she could feel her nails in her palms. If she could she would have rattled them like a child throwing a tantrum. If she could she would have screwed her eyes shut and stamped her foot and shouted down at the bloody picture-perfect view, 'Graham Whitethorn, you god-damn pain in the arse.'

But she couldn't. Because from inside the hoody of the teenage boy standing beside her she could just glimpse big worried eyes, and see the wipe of snot on his frayed baggy cuffs.

So, instead she took a deep invigorating breath of salty sea air, pushed her hair from her face, and said, 'Come on then,

Sonny. Let's make some breakfast and call your mother. Tell her what silly old Grandpa's done.'

They turned back towards the house. The beautiful house. The image on her retina fitting the outline exactly.

CHAPTER 2

'What do you mean he's gone missing?' Stella frowned into her phone, then almost without thinking pointed out of the car window and said to her seven-year-old, 'Look, Rosie – Stonehenge.'

'Missing...?' Jack, her husband, mouthed from the driver's seat.

Stella made a face, unsure.

Behind her, little Rosie had no interest in Stonehenge, deeply imbedded in YouTube on the iPad, happily powering through their 4G data with her gem-studded headphones on. Usually Stella would have clicked her fingers to get Rosie's attention and pointed out of the window again to make sure she didn't miss the view, but the phone call from her mother trumped any tourist attraction. 'I don't understand, Mum,' Stella said. 'How can Dad be missing? Where is he?'

Jack was frowning. Traffic was backing up from the roundabout up ahead.

'Well darling, that's what we don't know,' said her mother, her voice tinny over the phone.

Stella felt strangely out of control. Thoughts popped into her head that she wouldn't have expected.

She and her father did not get along well. They barely talked. Hadn't for years. Past anger had morphed into silence, and silence into habit – the threads tethered firmly in place, calcifying solid with stubbornness and age. Yet as her mother spoke, Stella found herself overcome by unfamiliar emotion. She worried suddenly that she might start to cry. God that would be embarrassing. Jack would probably crash the car in shock.

'How long has he been missing?' Stella asked, turning towards the window, eyes wide to dry the possible threat of tears.

'Since yesterday,' said her mother. 'Although I'm not altogether sure what time he left because we were at Sainsbury's.'

'Since yesterday?' Stella said, shocked. 'Why didn't you call before?'

'Well, I knew you had a long drive today and I wanted you to get a good night's sleep. And I thought it might be a good idea to give him a chance to come back without worrying everyone.'

This seemed very odd behaviour from her mother, who had never been the kind of person to suffer in silence.

'So you've been worrying on your own?'

There was a brief silence at the other end of the phone.

'Mum, are you OK?'

'Yes darling, I'm fine,' her mother said. And she sounded fine. Too fine. Almost drunk. Stella would have anticipated much more drama. A little more sobbing and neediness when actually she wondered if that was the kettle she could hear being flicked on in the background.

Stella frowned. 'Is it something to do with Sonny? Is that why he's left? Has Sonny been a pain?'

'Not at all. Your father and Sonny have got on very well actually. I only told Sonny he'd gone this morning too – teenagers need their sleep, don't they?'

Stella scrunched her eyes tight. The idea of her son and her father getting on well was too much at this point.

'And have you rung Dad?' Stella asked.

'Yes. Straight to answerphone. He's left a little note telling us not to worry.'

Stella pressed her hand to her forehead. She was really tired. They had left at five to avoid the weekend holiday traffic down to the Cornish coast but had stopped once already for Rosie to be sick in a Starbucks cup after secretly shovelling all the sweets meant for the five-hour journey into her mouth in the first twenty minutes. 'Look, Daddy – a whole Haribo bear,' she'd said, quite gleeful. The traffic report on the radio suggested that this current tailback was because a caravan had jack-knifed further up the A303. 'What does the note say?'

'Just that he's gone away for a bit.'

'But where?'

'To be honest darling, I haven't the foggiest.'

Something really wasn't right in her mother's reaction.

'Mum, is there something you're not telling me?' Stella said, glancing across at Jack who was doing all sorts of faces back at her trying to get the gist of what was going on.

'No darling, nothing.'

Stella nodded, wary. Disliking the feeling of uncertainty that had settled over her. 'OK, well we'll be at yours in about three hours I reckon.'

'Don't drive too fast,' said her mother.

'Unlikely with this traffic,' Stella said, then added a goodbye.

When she hung up the phone Jack said, 'Where's your dad gone?'

Stella shook her head, chucking her phone into her bag. 'She doesn't know.'

Jack half-laughed. 'That's absurd. He doesn't go anywhere.'

Stella held her hands wide. 'Apparently he does.'

Jack looked like he was about to say something else but was cut off by the car behind beeping when Jack didn't immediately move forward to fill the gap as the traffic rolled forward a car's length.

'I knew we should have taken the M4 route,' he muttered.

Stella shook her head, incredulous. It had been her suggestion that they take the A303 and she couldn't believe he hadn't held in that comment in light of the whole missing-dad fiasco.

They drove on in silence for a while, the car warming up as their dodgy air conditioning failed to compete with the rising sun.

She and Jack had already had a row after she'd admitted being a bit nervous about seeing Sonny.

The reason they were currently driving down to Cornwall was to pick up their thirteen-year-old son, who, at the end of her tether, Stella had sent to stay with her parents for a fortnight.

Jack had sighed and replied, quite haughtily in Stella's opinion, 'Well, it should never have got this far in the first place! We should have dealt with it at home.'

'You can keep saying that, Jack, but you weren't there. You're never there to see what a pain he is. You waltz in the door at seven thirty when it's practically bedtime anyway.'

'I do not waltz in the door.'

Stella had wanted to say that he very much did waltz in the door, but they'd been over this a thousand times already. That was how her and Jack's relationship had been for the last few weeks. She'd tried countless times to explain to him the unrelenting frustration of every night trying to force their thirteen-year-old to get off his phone and do his homework, Stella's own deadlines pressing down on her, stress mounting. Until the evening that Sonny had sworn he was doing his physics project but was just hiding his phone behind half a papier-mâché Vesuvius. Furious, Stella had whipped the phone off him, deleted the game he was playing and every other one and changed the password to her iTunes account so he couldn't download anything else.

'You stupid bitch!' Sonny had shouted at her and then he'd looked immediately at the floor, his face rigid.

'I beg your pardon?'

Silence.

'Apologise. Now!' Stella said, hands on her hips, eyes wide.

Still silence.

Time hung paused in the air.

'Apologise.' Nothing.

She could feel her heart rate rising. 'If you don't apologise, Sonny, by the time I count to three—' The words came out of her mouth almost on instinct. As if she was so tired and stressed her brain had resorted to a time when she was guaranteed control. To when Sonny was a little kid and more than happy to apologise if it meant he'd get to keep his chocolate buttons.

Right now, Stella had no idea what she would do when she got to three. She should have used the deleting of the apps as bait but such strategy was easy in hindsight, all she could do now was start counting. 'One.'

Sonny's eyes stayed fixed on the ground.

Please just say sorry.

'Two.'

His jaw clenched.

Stella took a breath in through her nose. She contemplated 'two and a half' but knew she was putting it off for her own benefit.

'Three,' she said.

Sonny looked up, stared her straight in the eye. Then the corner of his lip turned up in the smallest hint of a smirk, his expression saying, 'What you gonna do now, Mum?'

For the first time ever, Stella had felt the urge to slap him round the face. She hadn't. But it had crossed her mind that in that moment she didn't like her son one bit. Nor did she know what to do with him. So she had walked away, hands raised in the air, and said, 'Do you know what, I don't need this.' A flash of her own childhood had popped into her head. She imagined what would have happened if she'd looked at her father the way Sonny had just looked at her. It was unthinkable. The thought made her pause and turn, look at Sonny still grinning smugly down at the carpet, and say, 'You can go to Cornwall. See what a few weeks with Granny and Grandpa does.' Her father had certainly never taken any crap from her growing up.

So here they were, driving down to Cornwall a fortnight later to pick up Sonny. The morning sun was shimmering like dust in the air, tension thrumming through the car.

Stella glanced across at Jack's profile. His eyes were fixed on the crawling traffic ahead. She hated that he'd cut her down when she'd mentioned feeling nervous about seeing their son because Jack was who she talked to. He was the person who made her feel better, who helped her think straight. Her wingman.

They didn't usually fight over things like this, Jack usually took her lead on parenting. But they seemed so busy at the moment, both of them distracted with work, the kids being particularly kid-like, and with the start of the summer holidays they hadn't had a proper chance to talk it all through. She had thought maybe they might on this five-hour journey, but now it all seemed rather overshadowed by the sudden and strange disappearance of her father.

Stella stared out of the window, repeating the fact over in her head, 'Dad's missing.' But it wouldn't really lodge properly in her brain, like a moth on a light bulb fruitlessly knock, knock, knocking to get inside. She didn't want to acknowledge it – there were too many questions to know where to begin.

The traffic started moving again.

Stella felt completely off-kilter. She got her phone out to try and distract herself but immediately remembered the emails on there about a looming work deadline that she couldn't bring herself to open. Work felt like another life. If she thought too much about it she could sense her normal balance of organised chaos teetering precariously into overwhelming. She stared at her phone. The screensaver was a picture of Rosie and Sonny posing over giant milkshakes piled high with whipped cream and a load of Cadbury's flakes and Oreos shoved in the top – an after-school treat on Rosie's birthday. It had all gone a bit pear-shaped after the photo was snapped because Sonny had accidentally on purpose nudged Rosie's face into the cream, but it was rare to get a picture of the two of them smiling for the camera. Stella clicked the phone off and put it back in her bag. It scared her that she didn't know if she wanted to see her own son. She had a vision of him at her parents' house, would he even come down to greet them? Then she thought of the empty sofa cushion where her dad always sat and felt herself go a bit dizzy. Like her brain couldn't hold all this stress. She pressed her palms to her temples.

'You OK?' Jack asked, glancing Stella's way.

'I'm not sure.' Stella took some deep, calming breaths.

Jack frowned. Stella was always sure.

'Are you going to be sick?' he asked, panic in his voice. 'Do you need a cup?'

She had to laugh. 'No, I don't need a cup.'

Then from the back seat Rosie shouted, 'I need to go to the toilet.'

And Stella was back in the moment. Her momentary lapse shaken off by the sharp immediacy of parenting. 'OK there's a service station just up here,' she said, glancing round to reassure Rosie and then back to Jack. 'I'm fine,' she added, to dispel his look of nervous concern. 'Absolutely fine. Dad can't have gone far. As you say, he doesn't go anywhere so it won't be that hard to find him.' She got ready to undo her seat belt as Jack pulled into the Little Chef.

'We find him. We get Sonny. We go. It'll be fine.'

CHAPTER 3

Moira was nervous about her daughter arriving. She always got a little nervous around Stella, wrong-footed, feeling ever more the neurotic mother as she tried to make too many plans for their stay. Did the kids want to go to the new model railway, for example, because tickets were hard to get hold of and the queue without them snaked round the block. Stella's replies of, 'Don't worry, it'll be fine. We'll decide when we get there,' would leave Moira wound up like a spring – should she get tickets or not? When they arrived, Stella's family would breeze into the house in a cloud of barely controlled pandemonium, eat everything in the fridge, traipse sand on the carpet, and uncork more wine than Moira and Graham drank in a month. Quite often Moira would escape to the kitchen to tidy up because the energy of them all was just too much. How many times she'd cleared up the plates at Christmas to the sound of one of Stella's stories, loud and confident, secretly wishing she had a fraction of her daughter's strength.

Now, as Moira stood in the kitchen making herself a cup of tea and glancing up at the driveway every time she heard a noise, convinced it was them, she thought how the memory of the few holidays Stella had with them existed in a short, loud blur. Like a rollercoaster – pause for too long and it would all fall from the sky.

She unhooked one of her Emma Bridgewater mugs from the Welsh dresser. It was a collection she'd amassed over the years – everyone buying her one of the decorative pieces for birthdays and Christmas after she'd once expressed a passing interest while flicking through a *Country Living*. Now she was almost overrun with the stuff, it was hard to know how to tell them to stop. When she'd had the kitchen done, Moira had considered packing it all away but couldn't face the questions, imagining their faces, almost accusing about why she didn't like it any more – if indeed she ever had. She wasn't sure, it had just become who she was to them: 'Mum, that's the china you like.' There would be too much hurt confusion to deal with if she changed.

The kettle clicked off. She poured the water three-quarters full, squished the teabag just so and added a long splosh of milk – far too much for Stella's taste, which Moira would have to remember.

The day was warming up. She leant over and opened the kitchen window, filling the room with the heady, teasing scent of the jasmine that climbed up a trellis from a big pot by the front door. She stood, inhaling the perfume, her hip resting against her beautiful new rose marble kitchen worksurface – a recent, very expensive addition that Graham had huffed was change for change's sake, but Moira adored. The smell of the jasmine was intoxicating. It made her want to pack up all that china immediately and go and buy the snazzy hand-thrown cups she'd seen in the local gallery with gold handles and bright turquoise stripes.

Graham would hate them.

Stella would mock them.

Or maybe she wouldn't. Moira paused. Maybe Stella would like a gold-handled mug. Moira sipped her tea and thought briefly about whether she actually knew Stella at all nowadays. The telephone conversation asking them to have Sonny to stay for a fortnight had been the first time Stella had asked for anything in years. Moira had felt a momentary flutter of flattery but knew better than to ask Stella what had happened. 'Of course, darling. I can meet you in Exeter if you like, save you the full trip. I've just repapered the spare bedroom – a lovely Zoffany gold, did you know they did wallpaper in TK Maxx now? – so he can sleep up there. Have his own little space.' Waffling on in a nervous attempt not to pry.

But my God, she had wanted to know what was going on. The desire had tickled her insides like beetles. This type of thing didn't happen to cool, confident Stella. Or 'Potty-Mouth' as anyone who read the *Sunday News* knew her as, one of the genre originators of the slummy-mummy brigade. The worst example, according to the *Daily Mail*, of resentful, neglectful motherhood with her gin-soaked, laissez-faire attitude to childrearing.

While Moira had tutted over a few of the expletives in Stella's columns she'd always been quietly proud of her daughter's success. Stella had worked her way up with no help from anyone. It had been an old friend of Moira's who'd posted the copy of the local magazine where Stella's first ever article had appeared along with a tiny headshot, 'Is this *your* Stella?' she'd scrawled on a Post-It, and Moira had had to lie when she'd telephoned her friend back, saying she knew all about it. Then soon followed by-lines in the national papers – Stella texting to say when and where at the request of her mother – and then full-page editorials in the colour supplements. Then came 'Potty-Mouth', as divisive as it was loved. But however controversial some elements, Moira would often allow herself the odd snigger when a straight-talking anecdote about the frustrations of motherhood touched a nerve.

But right now she couldn't help wondering if all was quite as it once was. She'd noticed a slightly more acerbic tone to a few of the columns recently. Nothing too bad, just a touch less light-hearted. Poor little moody Sonny, who was currently upstairs locked in some battle on his laptop computer, hadn't fared so well in a couple of them. She'd almost rung Stella to say something but hadn't quite had the nerve.

She thought again of monosyllabic Sonny, sulkily slamming the door of Stella's car at Exeter Services, trudging over in the torrential rain, hood down so his hair got soaked in a seeming deliberate defiance of his mother, and barely scowling a goodbye.

Moira went over to the bottom of the stairs and called, 'Do you want a cup of tea, Sonny?'

'No,' he shouted back. Then a second later, 'Thanks.' As if remembering that he wasn't in his own home and couldn't quite get away with his desired level of moodiness.

Moira was still getting used to the open-plan nature of the entire bottom floor of the house. When she and Graham had first bought the place, full of youthful exuberance, it had been part of their grand renovation plans but they'd never got round to it. Then after Christmas Moira had insisted. Determined to get Graham up and doing something, she'd thought it was the perfect project. But never had she heard someone grumble and gripe quite so much and, in the end, she'd put Graham out of his misery and taken over the project herself mid-way. After it was done Graham had complained of a draught from the front door. At the time Moira couldn't have given two hoots about a draught, high on the fact she'd overseen the renovation almost single-handed – with a lot of help from Dave the builder. But nowadays, while she still adored the light and space, she missed the fact she could no longer shut herself away in the kitchen, imagining herself alone. And, if pushed, she might concede to a slight draught, on a chilly day.

Walking back across the beautifully sanded wooden floorboards, she remembered the look of terror on Sonny's face when on Day One of his Cornish banishment Graham had stood in the centre of the living room and barked, 'No hoods up indoors, no stomping on the stairs, and we say "please" and "thank you" in this house.' Graham had marched over to the bottom of the stairs, glowering across at Sonny who had, a second before, been head down, hood up, stomping up the stairs ignoring an offer from Moira of a toasted teacake, and said, 'Got that, young man?'

Moira had been standing in the exact same place she was now and had been as shocked as Sonny to see Graham unfurl himself from the sofa and stride across to the hallway to issue his orders.

The new layout had proved an unexpected bonus from that moment. It gave Moira the perfect vantage point to view the gradual development of the Sonny and Graham show, something she would have missed had the great big wall still been in place separating the kitchen and the lounge. She would stand, chopping, mixing, sometimes just pretending to do either, and watch the pair of them in bemused fascination.

It had started after an almost silent evening meal – not uncommon in their household lately – when Graham was back firmly in front of the TV and Sonny slumped in the armchair opposite. Graham had muttered, 'Bloody phones. Do you ever look up from that thing?'

Sonny had glanced up, eyes narrowed, looking the spitting image of Stella and said, 'Do you ever look up from that?' gesturing towards the TV.

Moira, who was drying up her Limited Edition Emma Bridgewater mugs to commemorate the birth of each of the Duke and Duchess of Cambridge's children, had held her breath, waiting to see what might happen. Whether Graham still had it in him to rage at insolence. She'd seen it flit across his face, but Sonny didn't flinch, just sat, eyes locked with his. The stance intentionally designed to provoke, as if Sonny had gone upstairs after that first telling off from Graham and drawn out his battle plans.

To Moira's surprise, Graham had reached forward for the remote, turned the TV off and said, 'Come on then, show me.'

And they sat for hours, Graham having gone to get his glasses then watching as Sonny scrolled through miles on his phone. Moira couldn't believe there was enough in there to look at. At one point they'd watched something that had them both in stitches. Moira had squashed an urge to go and look at what it was that could make Graham laugh like that nowadays. But just as much she didn't want to know, she'd wasted enough of her time trying to fathom his moods. Instead she had made herself a peppermint tea in her newly washed-up Prince George mug and considered how much cheaper it was getting Sonny to stay as a way of piquing Graham's interest than knocking down the entire ground floor.

Now, just the thought of Graham made her furious. Made her wipe down the rose marble with frustrated vigour. Made her slam the window shut, annoyed with the bloody jasmine and its sickly overpowering smell. She thought of him sitting on that sofa barely moving except to come and sit silent and grumpy at the dinner table and chew infuriatingly loudly, scoff at the newspaper, or sigh at building costs and plumbers' estimates. For the last two years they'd lived under a grey cloud – longer than that if she was honest – and then suddenly he ups sticks and disappears.

Furious was an understatement. In Moira's opinion he'd gone missing in order to be missed. She paused in her wiping and stared out at the giant hydrangea that lined the gravel drive – pink when she'd have preferred blue, someone once advised she plant a rusty nail in the soil to make it change colour, fat lot of good that had done – and wondered if they could just not find him. If he was old enough to leave, he was old enough to find his way home.

Wouldn't that teach him a lesson, she thought as she went over and started cleaning the hob, for taking something that for the first time in her life was hers, taking it and stealing it for himself.

It was too hot. Moira walked over to the dining room area and threw open the big French windows, welcoming the deafening sounds of the sea and the unfailingly calming view out over the cliff to the beach.

There was a glimmer of a breeze. Moira fanned herself with her hand considering how, before she had discovered

Graham's note the previous afternoon, she had spent most of the week – rehearsing as she lay in Stella's old bedroom where she now slept – plucking up the courage to tell Stella when she arrived, 'I'm leaving your father. I'm starting a new life.'

But Graham had beaten her to it. Stolen her thunder. Kept her firmly where she was, unable to leave while he was missing. Hence why the thought of ignoring his little sojourn teased her so, danced around in her head like an excited imp too wily to catch.

As she stood there smiling, behind her came a great yawn from the sofa. She turned to see Frank Sinatra – the dog – stretch and look up, eyes knowingly guilty as he nestled comfortably in Graham's usually off-limits seat. Moira watched with no intention of turfing him off. Instead she went over and gave him a little scratch behind the ears.

Frank Sinatra was hers. He had absolutely no interest in Graham. Christened by its previous owner, it was a ridiculous name for a dog. In the past she would never have had a dog, let alone one that made her feel like a fool calling him on the beach. But in retrospect it felt like a symbol. As her friend Mitch said, if she could hold her head up high and shout, 'Frank Sinatra, come here boy, here!' she could do anything.

She wondered what Mitch would make of all this. Then she shuddered at the idea of Stella meeting Mitch. She would think him a cliché.

But Moira didn't have time to dwell on the thought because the sound of gravel crunched outside and there they were, a big black Nissan Qashqai cruising in like a stag beetle.

Moira took a deep breath in through her nose and out through her mouth.

She'd started doing a yoga class at the church hall. Her breath was meant to ground her.

She went over to the window and watched Stella get out of the car, lift her sunglasses up a fraction, narrow her eyes out towards the sea, then put the sunglasses back on again.

Moira felt a shiver of nerves coupled with the gentle fizz of adrenaline. She itched to present her new more confident self but was all too aware of how easily one simple glance from Stella could shatter it to the ground.

What would Mitch say, she wondered. Probably something about taking strength from the grounding force of Mother Nature. Moira looked dubiously down at the Ronseal varnished floorboards.

Sonny appeared beside her at the window, his hair swept heavy across his forehead, his eyes narrowed to the same slits as Stella's.

'All right?' Moira asked him, placing her hand on his shoulder, wondering perhaps if she could take strength from him.

But Sonny just shrugged in a gesture as much to get rid of her hand as an answer.

Moira straightened up, smoothing down her new skinny jeans she wished suddenly that she'd stuck to her old slacks then berated herself for such immediate loss of courage. Doing one more yoga breath, she walked solidly round to the front door, clicked the old metal latch and the wood creaked open.

CHAPTER 4

Stella stood in the driveway, tired and hot. The house towered above her, grey and imperious, like an old teacher from school unexpectedly soothing in their authority. Usually she barely gave it a passing glance, distracted by the dread of the stay, too busy unloading the car, chivvying in the kids, listening to her mother wittering on about such and such's nephew's horrendous journey down from London the previous day that had taken a million and one hours and weren't they lucky that wasn't them. Today, however, she almost drank in the view: the great solid stone slabs, the white jasmine dancing over the windows, the bright red door cheery as a smile, the seagull squawking on the chimney, its mate squawking back from the wide green lawn. The Little Shop of Horrors giant gunnera was just visible between the house and the old garage that looked more dilapidated than ever but was still standing, the black weather vane stuck permanently on south. The neat little almond tree next to the cherry, the two wind-ravaged palms, and the rusty bench a few metres back from the cliff edge with an uninterrupted view out across the blanket of sea.

Somehow the sight made her father going seem less

free-floating, tethered the whole debacle to reality, to familiar bricks and mortar. Looking back to the house it was a relief to know that not everything had changed.

But then the front door opened and Stella was momentarily baffled by the sight of her mother standing in the porch. She'd never in her life seen her wear a pair of jeans let alone this skin-tight pair with a trail of embroidered ivy down one leg. She'd had her hair done as well and seemed to have had lessons in exquisitely flawless make-up.

Her mother looked completely different. Why hadn't Stella noticed a fortnight ago when she'd dropped off Sonny? Because it had been pouring, she realised. Moira had had her cagoule buttoned up tight, and Sonny had refused to go inside for them all to have a coffee, storming away to slump in the passenger seat of her mother's Volvo.

Looking at Moira now, Stella didn't quite know what to do, how to greet her. She tried to think about what she usually did but came up short, realising how little notice she usually took of her. How much her mother normally just blended in like the white noise of her chat.

In the end it was Moira who took the lead. Crossing the gravel drive to give Stella a little squeeze on the arm and a kiss on the cheek. She smelt of something expensive and zesty. No more quick spritz of whatever from the Avon catalogue. 'Hello darling. How was the journey?'

'OK in the end,' Stella said. Then, looking her mother up and down, added, 'You look very well. New jeans?'

Moira's cheeks flushed pink as she replied. 'Well, just – you know. They're a bit of fun.'

'Any news about Dad?' Stella asked.

Moira shook her head, flame-red highlights bobbing. 'Nothing more than I said on the phone.'

Stella was on the verge of asking why her mother didn't seem more worried when she caught sight of Sonny hovering in the shadow of the doorway, head down. She swallowed. He looked up, pushing his overly long fringe out of the way. Stella took a couple of steps forward and pulled off her sunglasses to get a better look. Sonny's eyes were all pinched and worried-looking, his skin ashen.

She got up level with him, 'Are you all right?'

He nodded.

'Are you sure?'

He nodded again.

She had missed him over the last fortnight but now as they stood in front of one another she wasn't sure what to do. Whether to apologise for sending him away, whether to demand an apology from him, whether to hug him or to stand as she was, fearing rejection. She knew after all these years that that was the bit a parent was meant to rise above. There could be no external show of fear regarding a shrugging-off from one's child – they could sense it, like horses. So she forced herself to wade through it, to not care, and putting her arm round his shoulders she pulled his cardboard-rigid frame into her side and kissed his greasy-haired head. 'Hello, you idiot.'

He grunted.

He didn't pull away.

He reached his hand up and touched her arm. Gave it a quick pat.

Then he pulled away.

It was enough for Stella, for the moment. 'Why do you look so pale?' she asked.

'I'm worried. About Grandpa,' he said, like she was a fool not to realise.

'Oh.' She was taken aback that he would have such a reaction. Stella was pretty certain the only thing Sonny had been emotionally wrought about in the last year or so was when Rosie trod on his iPhone and the screen cracked.

She looked up to see Jack watching, all the bags he could possibly carry weighing him down like a packhorse. He kept moving as soon as he saw her see him, and said, 'Give us a hand with these, Sonny.'

Sonny took the biggest bag, then could barely lift it.

Jack and Stella shared a look, as if asking how they had managed to raise such a nincompoop, then kissing Moira on the cheek as he went past, Jack said, 'You look well, Moira. Sorry to hear about Graham.'

'Hello, Jack darling. Yes, it is a nuisance. How are you? Work going well?'

'Same as always. Can't complain,' Jack said, straining under the weight of luggage.

'Let me help you with some of these bags.'

'No, no.' Jack waved the fingers of his hand holding the suitcase handle, refusing to let her take one. 'I can manage.'

'He likes to feel the weight of burden,' Stella joked.

Jack didn't find it as funny as she thought he would and walked away with a simple raise of his brow.

'I was only joking,' Stella muttered, and went back to the car with her mum to get Rosie who was still sitting strapped in, glued to the iPad, oblivious to their arrival.

'They must be a godsend for a long journey,' her mother said, gesturing towards the iPad.

Stella nodded, thinking how she would have killed for a similar distraction in the car growing up. Stuck in the back of their maroon Vauxhall Cavalier trundling all over Europe, banned from asking, 'Are we nearly there yet?'

The engine overheated one time just outside Madrid, the bonnet getting stuck, her dad ranting, and Stella unpeeling her skin from the hot plastic seat and going to sit on the grassy verge with the midday heat beating down in an attempt to escape his furious tirade. She'd ended up with sunstroke, making him even madder and them even later for a race he was determined not to miss. Growing up, their holidays always coincided with wherever the World or European Swimming Championships were, depending on which athletes her dad, ex-Olympic swimmer and GB Team coach, was training. Not a weekend or a holiday went by without it having something to do with swimming. 'If there's 365 days in the year, that's 365 training days.' And so to spend any time with him, they would go with him, even though he was always busy and in a bad mood for most of it. When his athletes would moan about being over-trained and tired he'd glance up with his infamous mocking, hooded gaze and say, 'Sleeping is cheating.' Which, as a kid, Stella always secretly wanted to say back to him when he packed her off to bed of an evening. She could still feel the childish rush of adrenaline at the idea of ever saying it, the punishment never worth the risk of such liberating impertinence.

Above them now the afternoon sun disappeared behind a stripe of cloud in the otherwise blue sky. Stella could hear the drone of bees in the lavender and a tractor thundering down the lane as she wondered what it was that had kicked off such reminiscence of her childhood. A time she tried to give very little thought. She could blame it on the heat of the car combined with the scent of sweets for the journey and the faint whiff of stale sick, but she knew it was simply the strangeness that her dad wasn't there. His absence, the element of wrongness, forcing Stella to pause.

It made her uncomfortable. The last thing she needed was the distraction of unwanted memories. 'Rosie!' she said, a little too snappily.

Rosie looked up from the iPad screen, almost surprised to see that they had arrived. 'Granny!' she yelped, unclicking her belt and launching herself across the seat into a giant hug with Moira. For a second, Stella envied Rosie's ability to take everything at face value, to throw herself carefree into people's arms and assume they would hug her back. She watched them trot together towards the house, Rosie's hand in Moira's as she said, 'My Barbie has jeans like those, Granny.'

Stella stifled a laugh as she watched Moira blush again. The outfit fascinated her. Her mother's black and white striped blouse was definitely still Marks & Spencer but it looked like she might have ventured out of Per Una and into the Autograph section. There was a ruffle around the collar and the silk hung heavy and expensive. This was no sale-rail purchase. And her hair, still red but now somehow even redder. Sparkling. Stella tried to inspect it as she followed her back into the house. The sun picked out various shades of copper highlight – it was no Nice'n Easy, head over the bath dye-job. It was hard to imagine her mother handing over what she'd deem ludicrous money for a cut and colour. Yes, Stella had seen her mother be lavish but only at times Moira considered appropriate – a swanky new dress for her annual summer party, a sapphire ring for her big birthday. Things that, if she were ever stopped in the street and questioned about, her mother would feel she could justify. Hair, clothes, and make-up would usually fall into the spendthrift category. The price of a lipstick in a department store elicited a disapproving click of Moira's tongue.

And it wasn't because she didn't have the money. In Stella's opinion her mother notched up things to disapprove of in order to give herself something to do.

It was only when Stella stepped inside the front door that she realised the makeover extended beyond her mother's wardrobe. Gazing incredulously at the newly knocked-through ground floor, she began to wonder if it was more a case of what hadn't changed. 'Wow!' she said, taking in all the space from where she stood – the point which had previously been the door of the kitchen. 'I knew you were having this done, but I don't think I realised it would be quite like this.' In front of her was the living room with its wooden ceiling beams now exposed and a flash log burner in place of the open fire. The walls which had once been magenta and Harrods green had been given the Farrow & Ball treatment, licked with Elephant's Breath. Light flooded in from the wall of windows that lined the old dining room, no longer obscured by heavy velvet drapes but a flutter of white muslin and a wraparound sea view.

Moira frowned. 'But I sent you pictures?'

Stella nodded. 'Yeah, I know.' Had she even looked at them? Messages from her mother were so easy to ignore.

Stella looked down at the floor. The cream 'no red wine in

here, please!' carpets had gone to reveal beautifully varnished floorboards overlaid with a huge sisal rug. And next to her the old pine kitchen cupboards had been given a Shaker-style makeover alongside some slightly garish marble surfaces. It was all achingly on-*Country-Living*-trend. Certainly the image of her father sitting silently in his seat staring at the snooker on the muted TV felt a touch outmoded.

'Sonny!' Rosie squealed, letting go of Granny's hand to hurl herself at her brother who was standing in the centre of the living room, head down on his phone, the baggy cuffs of his hoody yanked out of shape. He took the hit like one of those wobbly toys that refuses to keel over. As Rosie wrapped her arms tight around him, Sonny managed to pat her on the head with the one hand that wasn't on his phone.

Stella paused in the hallway. She blew out a breath, wanting to rip the damn phone out of his hands. Hug your sister, she wanted to shout. Sonny caught her eye and Stella raised a brow at him, he made a face. It was like they lived on repeat. Always the same. He looked away from her, put his phone in his pocket, and made a show of giving Rosie a little, not particularly enthusiastic, hug.

She thought about her last Potty-Mouth column, when she'd written,

The problem is with motherhood that sometimes you don't want to be selfless. Sometimes you want to tell your son that you actually just don't like him very much. Then immediately after the thought appears it's countered by an annoying inner voice that says, this is your fault. It is you that created this behaviour. You who has failed him by not giving him the right tools, you should have nipped it in the bud. At this point sanity must prevail to remind you that he's a teenager and that, yes, it really is his fault! Sanity can be found in many forms. And that's why God invented white wine as well as ovulation.

Stella watched little Rosie, undeterred by Sonny's unwillingness to show affection, drag him by the floppy cuff as she spotted a black and white Border collie's head poking up over the side of the great grey sofa. 'Frank Sinatra!' she cried.

Stella couldn't help but smile. She wondered if Rosie even knew there was a namesake. The pictures her mum had sent of this new dog Stella had opened and looked at, more out of disbelief, because Stella couldn't imagine ever being allowed a pet growing up – she remembered having to watch TV sitting on an old throw as a kid so as not to ruin the sofa, the bare cushions saved for guests only. Everything was always for show, even behind closed doors her mother would never just flop on the couch after dinner, seemingly always on guard in case someone popped by. Never off duty for a second.

It always felt to Stella like her mother had invented this all-consuming lady of the manor persona, spinning off from her dad's sporting notoriety – nine-time Olympic gold medal winner and nominated for Sports Personality of the Year – to make up for his never being home. As if by raising him up on a plinth it was OK to excuse him anything. Her mother was always on edge waiting for when he eventually did come home, constantly polishing and tidying like a manic bee buzzing about the place, forever straightening corners, always so very uptight. And it was all wasted on him anyway because he only had eyes for the day's swim times – reams and reams of paper that caused even more mess.

Now Stella watched as the dog licked Sonny's face and Rosie giggled, feeling a tiny twinge of jealousy at such relaxed freedom existing in this living room.

She went over and sat on the arm of the sofa, giving the dog a little pat on the back, all the time watching Sonny, almost reabsorbing him after their time apart, remembering his stubby little nose and how his eyes could twinkle on the rare occasions that he laughed. She didn't dislike him. She loved him. She would, as one of the annoying NCT dads had once said, 'take a bullet for him'. She just found herself constantly exhausted by him. Angry when he did something that she knew he knew better than to do. Frustrated by him for wasting his potential on the cliché of his phone and PlayStation. Disappointed when he did exactly the annoying thing she expected him to do. And he always seemed to know how to infuriate her further, like an angry mosquito bite. For half a minute there would be calm and then there it was again: itch, itch, itch.

Like right now. He wasn't letting the dog lick Rosie's face – not that Stella could think of anything more disgusting than having a dog lick one's face – but Rosie was desperate for a share of the licking and Sonny was having it all to himself.

'Sonny, let Frank Sinatra lick Rosie!' There it was. One of the first proper sentences she'd said to her son since she'd got there. Not only was it the stupidest sentence she'd ever said, it stuck fast to their usual rules of communication – her having to constantly tell him to do something differently.

Jack came down the stairs, eyebrows raised at Stella as if questioning whether there was seriously going to be conflict already, and took a seat on the other side of the dog. Then he reached forward and squeezing Sonny on the shoulder said softly, 'All right son?'

Sonny looked up at him and nodded. 'Yep.'

Jack smiled.

Stella almost rolled her eyes. That was part of the problem; it was so easy for Jack and Sonny because Jack was allowed to take the path of least resistance. He was good cop. He'd effortlessly bagsied that role early on. Which meant Stella was bad cop, and she had been OK with that – when the kids were still young enough to always relent to a hug. But now, with Sonny, it was a whole new role, like graduating from police academy into the real world – the hits were painful and never let up.

Jack joined Sonny and Rosie in the showering of attention on the dog. 'Aren't you lovely? Who gives a dog a name like Frank Sinatra?' he said, giving him a generous rub behind the ears.

'Mitch's dad called him it,' Sonny said, showing them a trick with the dog's front paws that Rosie thought was hilarious. They looked the picture of a perfect family.

'Who's Mitch?' Jack asked.

'Granny's friend,' said Sonny. 'He's a hippy.'

Moira shut the fridge with a clatter.

Jack looked up and caught Stella's eye. He raised an intrigued brow. Stella made a similar face back.

'Does everyone want tea?' Moira called, all matter-of-fact, lining up her dotty mugs as she deflected attention from this Mitch character.

There was a chorus of Yeses punctuated by a breathless

request for hot chocolate from Rosie who was squealing delightedly as the dog licked all over her face. 'Can we have a dog?' she laughed.

'Mum won't let us,' Sonny said without looking up from where he and Jack were rubbing Frank Sinatra's tummy.

Stella sighed. Jack stayed silent. He'd always wanted a dog, Stella always said no. She thought they smelt and she couldn't think of anything worse than picking up its giant poos. The question of why they didn't have a dog had become, 'Mum won't let us.' As if having the dog was the given and she was the one taking it away. Which she was. But then it had never been a given in the first place. See, bad cop.

Hating herself for feeling like the outsider, Stella pushed herself up to go and help Moira make the tea. 'So, are you sure you're OK, Mum?' she asked.

'Oh yes, I'm OK,' Moira said, pressing buttons on the microwave to warm the milk for Rosie's hot chocolate. Then she paused and sighed. 'Just pissed off really – what does he think he's doing, gallivanting off without telling anyone? His note's on the table,' she added, nodding towards the dining area as she shovelled some custard creams out on a plate. Stella wondered how great the tragedy would have to be before they could eat them straight from the packet.

Moira led the way to the dining room table carrying a tray of cups and matching milk jug, the plate of biscuits balanced precariously on the top. She gestured for Stella to follow with the teapot, adding, 'So you like the new layout?'

'Yeah, it's very nice, very airy,' Stella replied, still expecting her mother to be quite a lot more upset about her dad's disappearance. She hoped she was just putting on a brave face, otherwise it felt too tragic – that he could slip away and the finding of him be secondary to thoughts on the new decor. How the mighty had fallen.

The dining room table was one of the only things that hadn't changed. But instead the dark varnished wood had been sanded down to give it a scrubbed driftwood look. Stella wondered who'd done it, whether they'd found all the things she'd scrawled when she was meant to be doing her homework. Defiant teenage graffiti where she'd jab at the underside of the table with her biro after a dressing-down from her dad about her split times for her swim that day. Or when he'd wordlessly leave a graph of her heart-rate calculations on the table, dips in effort marked with just a dot from the tip of a sharpened pencil.

Stella put the teapot down and picked up her dad's note that was pinned to the table by the edge of a tall white jug – unusually not part of her mother's treasured Emma Bridgewater set – filled with freshly picked cuttings from the garden. Stella wondered if they had been snipped before or after her father had disappeared.

'Gone away for a while. No cause for alarm. Graham/Dad/ Grandpa.'

How odd that he'd signed it all three names. She glanced back at Sonny, remembering his pale look of worry, and wondering at this sudden relationship between the two of them. She felt a touch of suspicion at the thought of it, immediately wanting to protect Sonny from any sights her father might have set on his grandson's swimming ability, but also a strange niggle of envy at their apparent closeness. She looked away, across at the dog occupying her father's seat, and tried to remember the last conversation she'd had with her dad. One that wasn't him nodding his thanks for the jumper she'd bought him for Christmas, the gift receipt in one hand, the plain grey sweatshirt in another. 'Great, yep, thanks.' Did that count as conversation?

Her mother started pouring the tea.

Stella walked over to the window to get a bit of space. Out ahead, past the strip of mown lawn and the patio furniture, was a view of the beach, the water as blue as the sky, light flashing like sparklers off waves rolling gently on the sand. She rarely looked out this way when she came to stay. Not for any length of time anyway, maybe a quick glance to check the weather. In the past she had stared at the sea for hours. Especially in winter, mesmerised by the giant breakers, the harsh angry froth of icy white water. As she stared now, the noise of the kids and the yapping dog loud behind her, she could suddenly feel the burning sensation in her lungs of the 6 a.m. swim. It made her put her hand to her chest, the memory was so sharp. She looked down at her fingers almost expecting to see raw pink skin like whipped flesh or the sting of the salt in her eyes. She felt like she was going mad. The sound of her heart in her ears as strong as the beating of the waves. Like the stress was oozing out of her in strange long-forgotten flashbacks.

Jack came and stood next to her, her dad's note in his hand. 'So where do you think he's gone?' he asked.

Stella swallowed, unable to believe he could saunter over and think her completely normal, that how she was feeling wasn't radiating from her body like disco lights. She glanced across. He was waiting, casually expectant. She turned her back on the sea view in an attempt to regain her normality. 'I have no idea,' she said, 'but things here are clearly not quite right.' She nodded towards where her mother was handing hot chocolates to the kids, and added, 'And I wouldn't be at all surprised if this Mitch character has something to do with it.'

Jack turned as well, taking in the scene. 'Do you think he might have something to do with those jeans as well?'

Stella laughed. Relieved at the joke.

Jack put his arm around her. 'We'll find him,' he said, all solid and sure.

Stella didn't reply. She couldn't. She had the same rising sensation she'd had in the car, that it was all too much, like she might suddenly burst into tears which was not something she could let happen. Especially not in front of her mother. Or Sonny for that matter. And what would she be crying about anyway? Certainly not the disappearance of a man who'd basically cut her out of the family photo album. She was just tired.

A phone beeped in the kitchen. Her mum went over to read the message. 'Your sister's train arrives at about six she says.'

'Oh God,' Stella looked up, eyes wide, caught completely unawares. 'I'd forgotten about Amy.'

Jack wrinkled up his brow as if the workings of her mind continually baffled him. 'How could you forget about Amy?'

CHAPTER 5

'No, I just can't find it.' Amy rummaged through her bag for the umpteenth time. 'It's not here. I did buy one though. I did, I promise. I just ...' She trailed off, searching through her bag, her hair straighteners, her phone charger, her teddy. She pushed that hastily to the bottom of the bag.

She could feel Gus next to her, watching.

The ticket inspector loomed above her seat. 'Sorry madam, failure to show a valid ticket for a journey means I'm going to have to charge you a penalty fare.'

'No, you can't.' Amy shook her head. The flicks of blonde catching on her cheeks. She pushed the short hair back behind her ears, she was no closer to getting used to it. Why in films they always showed someone getting a haircut to start a new life was beyond her. It was a bloody pain in the neck – learning how to style it, straighten it, stop it from being a giant fluffball on her head. She hated it.

She leant forward for another rifle. The hair flopped forward. She held it back with one hand. 'Honestly, you can't charge me again. My father's gone missing,' she said, pushing pairs of pants out of the way.

She thought she heard Gus scoff and looked across to glower at him but his expression was innocently bemused.

'Are you going to help me?' she hissed under her breath.

He shook his head. 'What can I do?'

'I don't know? Talk to the man.'

'You seem to be doing a very good job of talking to the man. He says you have to pay a penalty fare.'

'But I bought a ticket.' She sat back in her seat. 'Seriously, I did. I could get my bank details up on my phone and show you.'

'Sorry, madam, I'm being generous here. Last month it was zero tolerance – would have had to escort you from the train at the next stop.'

Amy put her hands up to her head.

'Just pay it,' said Gus, one hand holding his tiny takeaway espresso cup, the other some obscure-looking comic book.

'No.' Amy felt suddenly like she might cry. Gus was looking at her all superior through his big black glasses like he couldn't understand why anyone wouldn't just do what the man had said. 'No.' She looked up at the ticket inspector. His face possibly kindly. His bald head reflecting the strip lighting. 'Please,' she said. 'Please, I did buy a ticket. This is a nightmare day for me. I'm going home because my dad's gone missing. I'm not thinking straight. My emotions are all over the place,' she sighed, pushed her stupid short hair back, 'because I'm pregnant. And,' she sighed again, 'well, you don't need to know everything about it, but let's just say it's not ideal and I did buy a ticket, I promise I did, because the man at the counter I remember thinking looked like Father Christmas and he gave me a toffee.' She reached into her pocket, eyes welling up.

'Look, see here,' she held up the shiny wrapper of the Werther's Original. 'See, this is the wrapper.' She nodded, trying to elicit a response. She could see the people around her shifting in their seats as they uncomfortably tried to listen and not listen at the same time. 'Do you see?' she said, brandishing the tiny crinkle of gold. 'And I nearly threw it away but I didn't because I liked that he'd given it to me.' She put her hands up to her eyes to wipe away the first spill of tears. 'Do you see?' she said again, voice plaintive, nodding at him and wiping her face while also trying to find a tissue in her jacket pocket.

The ticket man seemed to think for a second, then reaching into his own pocket brought out a brand new Kleenex. 'That would be Geoff,' he said. 'Santa Claus with the toffees.'

Amy blew her nose. 'Yes,' she said. 'Yes, Geoff.' She had no idea what his name had been.

'OK,' he said, tapping something into the machine that hung round his neck and handing her a replacement ticket. 'Just this once.'

Amy put her hand on her chest. 'Oh thank you, thank you so much.'

He nodded. 'I hope you find your father.'

Amy nodded.

'And that everything works out with the baby.'

She nodded again, wiping her eyes, clutching the new ticket.

The ticket inspector walked away down the aisle and into the next compartment.

'Bloody hell,' said Gus, flopping back in his seat, shaking his head, dumbfounded. 'That was unbelievable.'

'What?' Amy said, blowing her nose.

'That you just managed to get away with that.'

'I don't know what you're talking about.'

'Yes, you do. That— That little-girl-lost routine. That was unbelievable. How old are you?'

Amy looked at him affronted. 'You don't ask a woman that question.'

'But you ask a little girl.' Gus raised a brow.

'Why are you so horrible?'

'Why are you so like that?' he said, gesturing to the tissue and the ticket and the blotchy face. 'Normal people just pay the fine when it's their fault they lost the ticket. Look at what you put that poor guy through.'

'He was kind to me,' Amy snapped, feeling like she was under attack.

'Yeah, and you made him feel really awkward.'

'I did not.'

'You think it wasn't awkward? You crying about your whole life history?'

'I don't want to talk about this any more with you.'

'Oh, that's right.' Gus snorted a laugh. 'That's your answer. Very mature. I'm delighted that you're about to be the mother of my child.'

Amy gasped. 'How dare you?'

Gus blew out a breath. 'How dare I?' He shook his head, turning to look out of the window, closing his eyes for a second longer than necessary.

Amy felt a rush of resentment, it made her want to do something to him – flick his coffee over or maybe pinch his arm. But she sat seething instead, trying to get her hair to stay tucked behind her ear. Gus took a slurp of espresso and went back to his book all aloof.

'Well at least I don't read picture books,' Amy s
immediately regretting the comment, immediately realising
she'd made herself look even more of a fool.

Gus turned his head slowly as if deigning to address her.
'What, you mean this Eisner Award-winning graphic novel?'
He rolled his eyes. 'You stick to your *Grazia*, Amy.'

'There is nothing wrong with *Grazia*.' Amy wanted to take
her new ticket and stab his eyes out with it. 'It's very issue-led.'

Gus smirked. 'I'll look out for it on the Pulitzers.'

'I'll look out for it on the Pulitzers,' Amy repeated, all whiny
and childish.

'That's very grown up. Again, mother of child, very glad.'

'I hate you.'

'Rest assured, the feeling is mutual.'

CHAPTER 6

Just pulling up in front of the house in the taxi made Amy feel better: the sweep of purple sunset like smoke out of the chimney, the sparkle of the solar-powered fairy lights wrapped round the almond tree just visible in the early evening light, and the big hydrangea flowers like perfect pink balloons. The gravel underfoot gave the same comforting crunch as it had her whole life. She just had to block out the crunch of Gus's feet next to her. As she put her key in the lock she could already picture the dark cosy hallway, smell the roast dinner from the kitchen, see the flicker of the TV, and a fire in the front room.

Except it was summer and there was no fire. And she'd forgotten her mother had had the entire ground floor demolished. When Amy left last it had still been a building site. Now, as she opened the door, she saw it was all pale and grand and open. She swallowed. Everyone was looking up from where they sat in the living room, watching. There was no time to take a breath in the hallway any longer or peek her head round the door and beckon her mother over.

'Er, hello,' Amy said, conscious of the presence of Gus next to her and everyone staring. 'Have you found Daddy?'

Moira stood up. 'No darling, not yet. We're about to
a plan.'

Amy nodded. She felt suddenly on the verge of tears, like
she wanted to throw herself at her mother and sob about
everything, but in defiance of Gus and his already derogatory
opinion of her she stayed rooted where she was.

'Hi.' Gus raised a hand.

'Hello,' Stella said back from where she sat at the table, watching intrigued and looking all cool and relaxed in a loose black
sleeveless shirt, the plainest gold hoop earrings, skinny jeans and
bare feet. Amy saw her glance across at Jack. Jack raise a brow
back at Stella. Their silent language asking, 'Who the hell is he?'

'This is Gus. My—' Amy paused by mistake because the
word friend got stuck in her throat.

'Just a friend,' said Gus, which sounded so ridiculously
unnatural that it made Amy want to cover her face as she
blushed scarlet under her hastily retouched contouring. Stella
was clearly holding in a smirk.

'Hello darling. Hello Gus, lovely to meet you. You must
be exhausted from the journey, it's such a long time to sit on
a train. Come in, sit down, have a drink.' Moira stood up,
glossing over any awkwardness regards this stranger in their
midst, and came over to greet the pair.

Gus dumped his bag by the stairs and went to take the beer
that Jack was pouring like he'd never needed anything more
in his life. Moira gave Amy a kiss and a hug and whispered in
her ear, 'Will you be sharing a room?'

'Absolutely not,' Amy snapped.

'Righto,' said her mother. Then turning back to Stella said,
'Rosie and Sonny are OK to share, aren't they?'

mny moaned.

They're fine.'

d.

t and sat down at the table across from Stella,
o meet her eye, even when Stella kicked her under
the   1e.

'Beer, Amy?' Jack asked.

'No, I'll just have water. I'm really thirsty,' she replied.

After some pleasantries about how warm the weather was, the length of the train journey, and how long it had been since they'd all seen each other – how terrible it was that someone had to go missing in order for them all to make the journey – Jack cleared his throat and said, 'Right, shall we get started on a plan of action?'

Stella nodded.

Jack opened the pad that was in front of him then looked up at Amy to explain what had been discussed in her absence. 'We thought it might be a good idea to note down all Graham's usual spots. Places he goes most often. Then tomorrow go round and have a word with people. See if he mentioned where he was going, just get a sense of how he was. That kind of thing. Yes?'

Amy nodded. 'Have you rung his friends?'

'A few,' said Moira.

'Why not all of them?' Amy frowned.

'I've been busy.' Moira shifted in her seat.

Amy glanced perplexed at Stella, who just raised a shoulder to show she knew and agreed with whatever it was Amy was thinking but who knew what forces governed their mother.

Gus watched.

Amy said, 'Mum, you've tried to ring Dad, haven't you?'

'Of course I've tried to ring him. And I've sent a text asking where he is.'

'A text? I rang his phone twenty-three times on the train,' Amy said.

'It's not a competition, darling,' Moira muttered, turning away to top up her wine with obvious affront.

'OK!' Jack held up his hands to try and take back control. 'We talk to his friends, see what he's been doing and if anyone noticed anything out of the ordinary. Good. Right. Moira, have you checked your bank account?'

'I don't see when you think I've had the time to do all these things.' Moira shook her head.

Stella leant forward. 'No one's accusing you, Mum. Jack's just asking.'

'I know.' Moira crossed her arms over her chest, then through pursed lips added, 'I can pop into the bank tomorrow.'

'Could you do it online now, Mum?' Stella asked.

'No, I can't.' Moira blushed. 'I don't know how. Graham does all that.'

Jack said, 'Well we can help, do you know the passwords?'
Moira hesitated.

Amy said, 'Don't worry, Mum, I never know mine either. That's why I have them all written down in my phone.' She saw Gus shake his head at what a stupid thing that was to do. She made a face at him which she instantly regretted when she caught Stella looking.

Moira was getting flustered. Smoothing down her silk blouse, she said, 'I know I should know them. It's just something I haven't quite got round to. There is something written

43

down in the kitchen, though, I think. Hang on, let me have a look.' She got up to go and rifle through a flowery Cath Kidston box file on the counter.

Jack wrote 'Account activity' down as the first point on his list.

Amy leant forward and said, 'Shouldn't we be calling all the hospitals and the coastguard and things? We need to be certain he's not hurt.'

'Amy, he left a note,' Stella said, one mocking brow arched, 'I don't think he's hurt.'

'What if he was made to write the note?' Amy replied, brows raised back at Stella, defiant.

Stella scoffed. 'Like a hostage? Please.'

Amy refused to be ignored so easily. 'Don't look at me like that, someone might have taken him. It's a real possibility. I think it should go on the list.'

'Seriously?' Stella shook her head. 'It's not *Murder, She Wrote*, Amy! It's Cornwall.'

Gus snorted into his beer. Stella looked up, appreciative of his finding her funny. Then sat back with her wine, giving her long fringe a smug little blow out of her eyes.

Amy huffed.

'Here they are. The passwords. I knew I had them somewhere,' Moira called from the kitchen, brandishing a scrap of notepaper covered in numbers.

Amy pulled off the thin sweater she was wearing, feeling hot and bothered from the stand-off with her sister.

'I have that top!' shouted little Rosie, pointing excitedly at Amy's Primark vest top patterned with different emojis. 'Mummy, don't I have that top?'

Amy watched Stella nod as she sipped her wine. 'You do have that top, Rosie,' she said, as if of course Amy and a seven-year-old would have the same fashion sense.

'We're T-shirt buddies,' Rosie said, coming over and draping her skinny little arm round Amy's shoulders, then peering closer to inspect her face said, 'I like your make-up. You're so pretty. You look just like Zoella.'

Amy felt the conflicting rush of both embarrassment and pride at what she considered a compliment. In the past she would have just snuggled Rosie up close and relished the adoration. But now she had Gus smirking under his breath at the end of the table. And something made her want Stella not to perceive her as quite such a child. Perhaps because Amy knew at some point she was going to have to tell them all about the baby. And she couldn't face the accompanying looks of pity and the 'Oh Amy!' tone. But most of all she dreaded their lack of surprise that she would do something so stupid. It had made her contemplate just WhatsApping the news: 'It was a one-night stand! Can you believe it? And when I told Gus he was like, "You're not having it, right?" [crying laughing emoji]'

But it wasn't funny.

It was terrifying.

It was hard to say if it was more terrifying now or earlier today when she had been standing on Gus's North London doorstep delivering the news. She'd only remembered where he lived because it was above a Nando's. He had winced when she'd told him. His expression as if it were possibly the worst news he had ever heard in his entire life. She had thought he might react badly but not like that. She had presumed he would usher her inside, make her a cup of tea and ask what he could do to help. Not stand in the hallway, his expression somewhere between panic and disgust and say, 'Do you need money? How much is an abortion?'

'I am not having an abortion.' Her phone had rung as she'd spat out the words. 'Oh, hi Mum!'

Then her already trembling bottom lip had gone into full-blown wobble as her mother told her about her dad going missing. Meanwhile Gus was pacing the tiny, hot hallway, rolling his hands as if hurrying her to wrap the conversation up so they could get back to more important matters.

'I have to go,' she said to Gus as soon as she'd hung up.

'Oh no you don't. We have things to discuss.'

'Well I have to go home.'

'I'll come with you.'

'It's in Cornwall.'

'I won't come with you.'

'Good.' Amy had stormed out of the dark poky little flat onto the high street, taking in deep breaths of warm sunshine air and traffic fumes. She made her mind up she would never ever see Gus again. Good riddance. She'd block him on any dating app or social media if he tried to contact her.

'Wait!'

She paused. Turned. Deflated at the sight of Gus jogging lankily towards her in his stupid bright green shorts and old Levi's T-shirt. 'What?' she snapped.

'I'm coming with you.'

'No.'

'Yes!' he said. She now noticed the bag slung over his shoulder. He narrowed his eyes. 'You can't just turn up, tell me you're pregnant and then leave.'

'I can.'

'And what if you decide not to come back. I know nothing about where you live. How would I find you?'

Amy shook out her hair, stood with her hands on her hips. 'I will come back,' she said, haughty expression on her face, internally glossing over the fact that permanently avoiding Gus had been her very intention.

'I don't trust you.'

'That's not very nice.'

Gus laughed, incredulous. 'You gave me a fake number the night we went out.'

Amy paused. 'You rang me?' she asked, unable to help feeling a little smug.

'No,' Gus scoffed. 'I just know how many digits are in a phone number. You don't, clearly.'

Amy swung round, incensed, and started to stomp away. To her annoyance he followed her a few paces behind all the way. No matter how many times she stopped and tried to plead with him to go home. He sat opposite her on the tube. Made himself at home at her kitchen table as she packed. Walked beside her in the smoggy heat to get the Hammersmith and City line to Paddington. 'Please go away,' she said as the train pulled in. 'Please?'

'No chance.'

'You don't even want the baby.'

'No, I don't want the baby. But I don't want you to have said baby and me not know.'

Amy screwed her eyes tight. 'You're muddling me.'

'Well, let's stop talking then.'

Now, as she sat round the dining room table, Amy took

a covert glance at Gus and immediately had to look away with displeasure. He ruined being back here. The sight of him brought her previous life into stark relief: the parallel path when she would have run into the house shouting that she was pregnant at the top of her voice, grinning gorgeous husband by her side holding their clasped hands aloft in triumph. A path long gone.

She had to swallow down a rise of sadness. Close her eyes for a second and think of a really complicated times table – her grief counsellor's tip that had done wonders for her maths. When she opened them she was looking down at her T-shirt, at the three little monkey emojis – eyes, ears and lips covered – and knew how they felt.

Moira had got the laptop out and was waiting for it to crank to life. Gus next to her was wide-eyed at how old and slow it was. When finally the NatWest page loaded, Moira clearly didn't have a clue what to do.

'Here, do you want me to do it?' Gus asked, unable to stop himself. Pained by the slowness, he angled the laptop towards himself.

'Oh Gus, darling, yes please,' Moira said, relieved.

Amy winced. She didn't want Gus to speak. If he was going to be here she wanted him to sit mute. She watched as he keyed in the passwords. Under the table Stella bashed Amy's leg again, clearly trying to get her attention as Gus and Moira were distracted with the website. But Amy stayed resolutely looking away.

Out of the window the sun had spread pink and orange across the horizon, a bonfire of light that made the room glow amber.

Oh, why wasn't her dad here? Amy wanted him sitting on that seat on the sofa so she could curl up next to him, her feet tucked under the furthest cushion, his arm around her as they drank tea and he watched the snooker while she put her headphones on and caught up with all her favourite YouTubers. She had prayed he might be back home by the time she and Gus arrived. And that perhaps he would stand at his full six foot two height – her vision of him more from when they were kids, strapping, scary, and heroic rather than in his old Edinburgh Woollen Mill cardigan and slippers – beckon Gus to one side, pull out his chequebook and say, 'Come on then, how much will it take for you to disappear?'

Her fantasy was interrupted by a loud gasp from Moira.

Amy glanced across.

Her mother was peering close to the screen where Gus was pointing at a withdrawal.

'A thousand pounds?' Moira said, outraged. 'What the bloody hell does he need a thousand pounds for?'

Gus cleared his throat, clearly a little unsure about whether it was a rhetorical question or whether she was in fact looking to him for an answer. 'It's … er … most likely so he doesn't have to take any more out, the bank would be able to tell you where he was if he did.'

'Oh.' Moira sat back in her chair, only slightly mollified. 'Yes, I suppose so.' She crossed her arms and legs, and added sourly, 'I didn't know Graham was so forward-thinking.'

'Mum!' Amy's voice was a little harsher than she'd intended, but she felt like her mother was being far too cold about the whole thing. 'Why are you not more worried about all this? He's missing. Dad's missing!' she said, looking accusingly round the table. She had envisaged a lot more drama, more police popping round, more notices taped to lampposts and front page head shots in the local paper.

'Yes, with a thousand pounds of our money!' Moira said. 'I am worried, Amy,' she added, more because it was what was expected of her than with real emotion, 'but he's a grown man with enough money to get by and a phone if he needs any help.' Then Moira paused, as if she'd had a brainwave. 'His phone. He was on his phone a lot more, wasn't he Sonny? You taught him all that fancy stuff with that Instabook.'

'Instagram,' mumbled Sonny.

They all turned to where Sonny was slumped at the end of the table on his phone.

'He speaks!' said Amy.

Sonny glanced up and when he caught Amy's eye she winked at him. He blushed and half-smiled beneath his mop of hair.

Amy thought Sonny was great. He styled himself like a little grungy One Direction, which made him even more sulkily adorable. He wound Stella round the bend. She remembered last Christmas Eve, the house pre-open-plan all garlanded and twinkling. The huge tree by the fireplace tied with red bows and gold baubles, the fire crackling. The heavy curtains blocking out the drizzle that should have been snow. The waves thundering on the beach. Amy had sat helping Stella wrap all the kids' Christmas presents, both of them a bit pissed on the Aldi Prosecco their mother had rushed out to buy in bulk after it got voted Top Tipple in the *Daily Mail*: 'I've never been in an Aldi before. It's quite something.'

Earlier Sonny had got a bollocking for pressing Rosie to explain why she thought some of her friends at school got more

Christmas presents than her – especially the ones she didn't like. Was it because Santa preferred them to her?

'He's just such a pain,' Stella had said as she curled ribbon with scissors. 'I'm like, "She's six years younger than you! Stop being so mean to her!"'

'I think you said stuff like that to me when we were younger,' said Amy.

'I did not,' Stella gasped with affront.

'You did. You told me that Jackie down the road had seen her dad scoffing the mince pie and sherry for Santa, and signing the card she'd left out.'

Stella snorted into her Prosecco glass.

Amy raised her brows. 'Yeah? Remember? You're basically just the same as him.'

'Rubbish,' said Stella. 'God, I would never have got away with half the stuff he does. Dad would have throttled me.'

Amy had been unable to disagree. If the analogy was right then Amy was the equivalent of little Rosie. Dancing through life unencumbered. Her only discontent coming from the fact she had been almost invisible to their father for the first fourteen years of her life. But that had been more than made up for by being completely doted on by her mother. And her dad had been pretty terrifying so being overlooked had often felt like a blessing. But then Stella had left – her dad erasing practically all trace of her – and Amy had got them both. Her dad subdued, like a tranquillised lion, a soft cushion for his youngest daughter to curl up into.

Now, as Amy looked across at sullen little Sonny, she felt a bit sorry for him – all eyes on him as they wanted to find out more about Grandpa's sudden interest in Instagram.

'I thought he hated his phone?' Stella said.

Sonny shrugged. Then when he realised that wasn't going to be enough he said, 'He really liked Instagram.'

'Why didn't you say this before?' Stella asked.

'You didn't ask.' Sonny glared at her.

'Instagram?' Amy leant forward, deflecting from the mother-son bickering. She smiled, this being the first positive thing she'd heard about her dad since he'd disappeared. 'Did he post anything ever?'

Sonny shook his head. 'No, never. He followed everyone, though.'

Around the table phones came out.

'Even me?' Rosie piped up.

Sonny nodded. 'He's Neptune013.'

'I wondered who that was,' said Jack, who had about fifteen Instagram followers and barely ever posted anything. 'I thought it was someone who'd followed me by mistake.'

Everyone was scrolling through their list of followers, Amy was quietly satisfied that hers was taking the longest. 'Here he is,' she said finally and clicked on the avatar picture of waves on the shore. 'No followers.' She looked up. 'That's really sad.'

'I've just followed him,' said Rosie.

'Me too,' said Jack.

'Yep,' said Stella.

Amy nodded. Pressed Follow.

'And so have I,' said Gus, his voice taking Amy by surprise that he was even still at the table. She wanted to tell him to immediately Unfollow. That he had no right to be Following. But she didn't say anything, just had a really quick skim of her Timeline before putting her phone back down on the table.

Sonny looked quite pleased. 'He'll like that.'

Amy glanced across at him. 'You think?'

'Maybe,' Sonny said, a little more noncommittal since revealing a smidge of enthusiasm. He was about to go back to his phone when he mumbled, 'You could put the fishing lake down as well. On the list.'

'Fishing?' said Stella.

Moira shook her head. 'He hasn't been fishing in years.'

'We went.' Sonny shrugged a shoulder. 'Last week,' he added, before flicking his fringe in front of his eyes and burying himself back in his screen.

Amy realised that both she and Stella were watching Sonny. Both of them seeing a relationship that had developed that they didn't know about. Amy wondered what Stella felt about that: Sonny and their dad.

'Good, right,' said Jack, scribbling Instagram down on his pad. 'OK, so what else did Graham's day look like?'

Everyone turned to look at the sofa.

Jack tried again. 'Where did he go when he went out?' This was not how things worked at his office, Amy thought. At Christmas she remembered him saying that they'd introduced five-minute stand-up meetings at his firm. She'd thought that sounded dreadful, the best thing about a meeting, in her opinion, was the catch-up chat at the beginning and the free croissants.

Stella said, 'He drinks at the Coach and Horses, doesn't he, Mum?'

Everyone turned to look at Moira who was cradling her wine glass while looking uncomfortable with all the attention. 'Yes, I think—Yes.' She nodded, more committed this time, 'Yes, on a Friday.' She said, definite.

Amy wondered what had happened in the months since she'd left. Her mother didn't seem sure at all what their father had been up to. And what were those jeans she was wearing?

'OK, what else?' Jack asked.

Moira seemed to visibly wrack her brain, before saying, 'He sometimes chatted to the cashier at Londis, I can never remember what her name is.' Her expression showed she was clutching at straws and to save embarrassment quickly changed the subject by saying, 'Would anyone like anything else to drink? I might put some crisps out, if anyone's feeling peckish.'

Amy tugged at her emoji vest, embarrassed for her dad's life. Embarrassed that this was what Gus was hearing about him. She wanted to go and get the photo albums from the bookshelf or drag him into the upstairs loo where all the trophies were kept and say, look this was him, this was him in his heyday. He was a champion. A star. People used to stop him for autographs.

Gus seemed quite oblivious to any awkwardness, or was doing a good job of hiding it, and said, 'I wouldn't say no to another beer.'

'Oh yeah, me too,' said Jack.

'Lovely.' Moira jumped up to go and get some more bottles from the fridge.

Amy watched Gus, unable to quite accept that this guy sitting calmly drinking Budweiser was going to be related to them all for the rest of his life. She wondered how she would have behaved were the situation reversed. She couldn't even imagine it. She simply wouldn't have gone. If his family wanted to meet the baby they'd have to come and meet it. She didn't even want Gus involved, let alone the rest of the— She paused.

What was Gus's surname? He must have told her. She tried to think. No idea.

Jack wrote Londis as the next item on his pad.

Amy cringed again at the mention of it. Suddenly wished for that parallel life again. The one where she was happy about the baby with her husband, Bobby, sitting next to her. His arm round her shoulders – he would have given her a squeeze at the Londis comment. Bobby would have known that she thought it denigrated her father and said something to counter it, something good like, 'Lucky Graham's so friendly. I've never chatted to the cashier at Londis.' Even though everyone would know that was a lie because Bobby chatted to everyone because everyone wanted to chat to Bobby because he was so golden and glowing that people couldn't help flocking to him. The number of people who used to stop them when they were walking around to ask if they knew Bobby from somewhere, if they'd seen him on the TV, which of course they hadn't. He just looked like a celebrity. Amy would always get a little flutter of pride.

She closed her eyes and tried her times tables again but just got muddled. She felt a wave of nausea creep over her; whether from the memory of Bobby or a side effect of the pregnancy she didn't know.

Her mother was pouring Kettle Chips into a bowl. Amy reached over for a handful.

'Since when did you eat carbs?' Stella asked, surprised.

Amy didn't eat carbs, she infamously hadn't touched them since a modelling stint in her teens. But since the pregnancy anything went to quell the sickness.

'Well, you know me,' Amy said. 'Can't stick at anything!'

She'd said it to try and sound funny, deflect attention by taking the piss out of herself, but it obviously came out less carefree than she'd imagined because Stella was really watching her now. Gus too, come to think of it.

The nausea rose.

Her mother glanced across at her, expression concerned. 'OK?' she asked.

Amy nodded. 'Yeah,' she said, quick and slightly too sharp.

Then she felt the sympathy of everyone round the table. Like they all knew what she was thinking. Like they were all suddenly thinking about Bobby. Everyone except Gus, who was completely oblivious to the network of undercurrents, unknowingly dangling, like it was *Mission Impossible*, above a hundred infra-red beams that could set off any number of deep-rooted family alarms. He was just frowning like he'd missed something and had no idea what.

But they didn't know what she was thinking. Because while she was thinking about Bobby, she wasn't thinking of him in a, 'Oh God, he's dead,' way, the blank all-consuming way she had two years ago. The way she had when she'd wandered around this house in her pyjamas unaware what day it was, knowing only that time was slower than it had ever been before. But instead she was thinking of him in a, 'Oh God, why can't he be alive,' way because if he were this would all be so much easier. So different. She doubted her father would be even missing if Bobby were still here. And if he was, well, Bobby would at least whisper that everything was going to be all right. He'd make sure of it.

'I've just got to go to the loo,' Amy said, pushing her chair back and walking quickly to the stairs, trying not to hurry too much so as not to draw more attention to herself but desperate to get out of the room and up the stairs where she sat in the bathroom, the loo seat down, head in her hands, trying to think of nothing. Trying to be mindful. To let the thoughts swish past – Bobby laughing, big white grin as he jogged with his surfboard, her sitting in the sand with her arms wrapped round her knees, wind whipping her hair. Sometimes she wished she'd gone shopping instead of sitting on the beach to watch him surf because it could get very boring at times, but then he'd catch the best wave there was and people strolling on the sand would pause and watch and point and Amy would get high on a rush of pride. She saw them eating popcorn snuggled on the sofa in their little cottage. Laughing down the Coach and Horses. Their wedding barefoot on the beach. The noise of the lost ambulance, like a distant fly buzzing against the window, unable to find the dirt road of the obscure beach where the best surf hit on the high spring tide. Her dad trying to swim closer but the rip current yanking Bobby's body away, limp like seaweed on the surface of the water. The waves gobbling him up. The watch on the shelf in the bathroom when she got home.

Amy sat up. Pressed her fingers into her eyes. 'You're OK,' she said. Then she said it again and stood up only to be brought back down by another rush of nausea. This time she sat with her hands on her stomach, waiting for it to pass. Knowing there was a baby in there. Knowing it but feeling like she was watching it from afar. That it was someone else's baby. A kangaroo's baby in a nature documentary or that woman's in the pamphlets who was just a faceless cross section.

CHAPTER 7

It was ten o'clock, and Stella was in her room with Jack. Amy had sloped off much earlier, almost the same time as Rosie. Gus had made polite chat for a bit after dinner before offering to walk the dog for Moira, who'd seemed a little reluctant to hand over the duty but accepted when Gus got close to pleading for the task, clearly the more desperate of the two to escape. Sonny had played computer games while Jack and Moira washed up and Stella did some work. Then Gus had come back and everyone had called it a night.

It was hot and sticky in Stella's bedroom – the stone walls unable to stave off the humidity. They didn't usually visit in the summer – too many tourists, too much traffic – popping down at Christmas or occasionally Easter instead and so it felt odd to be here in the heat. With the window open Stella could smell the sea, reminding her of when as a kid – a big swim the next day, Trials or Nationals – she'd lie on top of the bed, buzzing with nerves, eyes wide open as the heat pressed down, inhaling the calm familiarity of the salty air. But other than the occasional memory there was nothing in this room that would mark it out as ever being hers. The bright yellow walls had been neatly papered over in cream patterned with green parrots. Her mismatched furniture was long gone, now a French vintage wardrobe and chest of drawers sat next to a huge white bed with scatter cushions the same lime tones as the parrots that soared over the walls. It was like a hotel.

She sometimes wondered where her stuff had gone. To charity if her dad had had anything to do with it. She'd never given him the satisfaction of asking though. The first time she'd been back to visit after she'd left she'd just pretended it meant nothing that all her belongings had gone – all her trophies and medals disappeared while all his still lined the shelf in the bathroom, mocking her every time she went to the loo.

Stella sat at the dressing table. Jack was lying on top of the bed in his boxer shorts and a T-shirt, reading the news on his phone, the duvet had been pushed into a heap on the floor.

'I think it's hotter here than at home,' he said, not looking up from his screen.

Stella nodded. She was inspecting her skin in the mirror. Lifting up one side of her eye. Peering at the lines around her mouth. There wasn't a chance in hell of Rosie comparing her to Zoella. It made her think she shouldn't have been quite so disparaging of Amy when she'd looked at teenage Stella all brown from her sea swimming and said, 'You'll pay for that.' At the time Amy's fledgling modelling aspirations meant she was drinking a litre of water a day, eating mainly cucumber and celery, and constantly applying Factor 50. Stella had scoffed that Amy's career wouldn't last longer than the *Just Seventeen* photo-story she'd been scouted for and was right. Amy stuck at nothing. Except the application of Factor 50. When she'd turned up today – hair all newly bobbed in choppy layers – Stella had, for the first time, found herself jealous of Amy's youth. Or maybe it was her freedom.

She sighed.

Jack put his phone down and looked at her over his new reading glasses, a move that she hated because it made him look so old. 'Why are you sighing?'

'Do you think my skin looks old?' Stella asked.

Jack inspected her reflection. 'No older than mine.'

Stella frowned. 'That was not the answer I'd been hoping for.'

'Why – do you think I look old?'

Stella paused for a second too long. 'No.'

Jack laughed. 'Damned by slow praise!' Then he sat up and went to sit on the edge of the bed nearest to Stella and stared at himself in the mirror. 'Christ, I do look a bit tired around the edges.'

'I don't think I've ever imagined us getting old,' she said.

'How have you imagined us?' Jack looked perplexed.

'I don't know. I suppose, whenever we've talked about holidays just the two of us when the kids have grown up, I think I've always thought of us young, like in those photos of us on the train in Rome. You know? I've never thought that we'll be old.'

'I'll have no hair.'

'I'll be all wrinkly,' she said, lifting her eyelid up with one finger then letting it drop again. 'That's the problem with parenthood. Half of it is spent waiting it out till it's done and you can go back to the people you were before, but you don't realise that the older your kids get the older you're getting. Those before people have gone.'

Jack glanced at her in the mirror. 'That sounds very much like the start of a column.'

Stella thwacked him on the leg. 'I'm serious.'

They were conversing via the mirror still.

'As am I, that's the kind of thing you write about, isn't it? When you're not bashing Sonny.'

'Thanks for that, Jack.'

He laughed. 'I'm joking,' he said. 'But you need to talk to him. The longer you leave it the harder it will be.'

Stella nodded.

They stared for a moment, side by side in the reflection. The heat of the room making their skin glisten.

Jack was the first to look away. 'You look as young and vital as the day I met you.'

She sighed a laugh. 'That's just a blatant lie.'

Jack went back to sitting up against the headboard scrolling through his phone.

Stella stared at herself a moment longer. Seeing in her face the features of her mother. Swallowing when she thought of the simmering animosity her mum was currently showing towards her father. It made her pluck up the courage to turn to Jack and ask, 'Is everything all right between us?'

'Fine,' he said, looking up with a frown, bemused as to why she was asking the question.

Stella nodded.

Jack put the phone down. 'Stel, we're fine. Just a bit tired, probably.' He scooched over the bed and gave her a kiss on the cheek, ruffling her hair a bit. She swatted his hand away with a half-smile.

'All right?' he checked.

'Yes.'

That was the reassuring thing about Jack. Whatever happened he'd soldier on through, pick you and everyone else up who might be floundering without a moment's pause to question.

But as she watched him go back to his phone, she knew it wasn't fine. The car journey had proved as such – like a condensed version of their current relationship, normal one minute and bickering the next. Both of them too quick to react, like they knew each other so well there was no point plodding through the benefit of the doubt.

A couple of weeks ago, her editor had asked her if she'd wanted to write a piece called MOT Marriage for an upcoming edition of the magazine. They wanted it written as Potty-Mouth, picking up on the current trend for critiquing the minutia of stuck-in-a-rut long-term relationships with a list of tasks and questions for the married couple to complete. Stella agreed, and while she knew she and Jack had precisely the kind of long-term relationship that most of her readers had – a bit stuck in a rut but getting through the day-to-day via Netflix and the anticipation of mini-breaks – she had fully intended to make up the content. Nowadays, fierce competition in the Slummy Mummy marketplace had pushed the Potty-Mouth brand to be much cooler and far more exciting than Stella, like an older sister she was constantly trying to impress. Stella already had it plotted out: Potty-Mouth and her fictional husband were going to throw the questions out of the window and do it their way – going to a host of exciting erotic workshops, flamenco dance classes, and a bit of swinging with another set of parents at the fictional school gate. She'd researched it all, the article was practically written and in the bag.

Now, however, she stared at the face in the mirror, as she thought of the clear disintegration of her parents' marriage and the strain on her own relationship since the Sonny incident, she wondered if maybe she should do it, for real.

She swivelled round on the bed to face Jack, feeling a nervous warmth creep up her neck.

Outside the sound of the waves rolled gently in the darkness. Jack looked up. 'What?'

'Do you want to help me with an article I'm doing?'

He narrowed his eyes, uncertain. Stella never asked for any involvement in what she was writing. He usually just read about their souped-up life over his Shredded Wheat. 'What's it about?'

'It's called Marriage MOT,' she said.

'Oh Jesus, Stella. We just said everything was fine.'

'Well, then it should be easy.'

Jack tipped his head back against the wall. 'What do we have to do?'

'You know the type of thing: are you having enough sex? Are you listening enough to each other? Harbouring any grievances … blah blah blah.' She tried to spin it all casual.

Jack sighed. 'I'm not harbouring any grievances.'

'Great,' she said. 'We'll tick that off the list.'

Jack thought about it and frowned. 'We have enough sex, don't we?'

'Well that's what we test. You think you're fine but you can never be completely sure until you check. Like when we had the car done and he said the brake pads were worn out.'

'Would the sex be the brake pads?'

'Maybe?' Stella smiled.

'There's nothing wrong with my brake pads,' said Jack, puffing his chest out.

'I'm not sure that analogy makes sense.' Stella shook her head.

There was a pause. Jack bit down on his lip. 'I don't know, Stel. Seems all a bit forced.'

'Yeah but maybe it'll be fun. At the very least it might stop us from becoming like them,' she said, angling her head towards her parents' bedroom. 'I don't want you to go missing.'

Jack looked at her, his eyes softening. 'I don't want you to go missing either.' Then he shook his head like he couldn't believe what he was about to say. 'All right, fine.' He slid his phone onto the bedside table. Stella did a little cheer and came round the bed to get in next to him, the beautifully ironed sheet crisp and momentarily cool. 'So, what's the first step of this MOT?' he asked.

'We have to start having loads of sex,' she said.

'Really?' Jack looked sort of intrigued.

Stella nodded, the pillow soft beneath her head.

Jack nodded.

There was a pause as they lay in the sticky humid heat.

'But I'm really tired,' Stella said.

'Thank God for that.' Jack exhaled with relief. 'Me too.'

CHAPTER 8

Moira caused quite a stir in the morning – while everyone else was either clearing up the breakfast things or, in the case of Sonny and Gus, playing on their phones while Rosie was watching TV – by hoiking her bag onto her shoulder and saying as boldly as she could, 'Righto, I'm off to my book club.'

Glances had been exchanged.

'What about Dad?'

'There's enough of you to cover all the bases,' Moira said quickly before adding, 'Sonny, can you look after the dog?' and leaving the house without really waiting for an answer.

She didn't know the protocol of going to one's book club while one's husband was missing but if she was quite honest, Moira just had to get away. She loved her children but when they were all in the house together sometimes it just got too overwhelming. She felt herself retreat like a snail; every comment about her clothes, her hair colour, her plans of action, her dog's stupid name – every one left her edging away, till she hurried out to book club without even thinking about the propriety of it.

It was another bright, hazy day. She wove her way through the back lanes to the village, the sun piercing through the overhanging canopy of leaves to banks of lush ferns, the car clipping the odd wayward frond in her haste. In the past Moira would never have dreamed of joining anything like a book club. There was a twinge of shame now when she thought back. She'd always seen herself as rather above it all. She'd happily indulge in a bit of village gossip but always with the aloof air that she was humouring them all, donating a little of her very precious time. Her husband was an Olympic hero.

She had to touch her face now as she coloured at the cringing memories. Every summer Moira was renowned for throwing a party, a lavish summer bash – strings of Venetian lanterns bobbing across the garden, long tables laid with glasses and drinks served by kids from the private school dressed up as waiters, candles lighting the drive, a gazebo with a band. One year she'd made the marquee men pause their work to help her trail an extension lead all the way over the cliff edge to the beach in order to floodlight the sea. It had been magical. Now, it all seemed a bit too showy-off – done for herself rather than the guests. Her moment in the spotlight. She hadn't thrown a party since Amy's Bobby had died and she knew she would never reinstate the tradition. In the past she had viewed herself as the aspirational hostess. Now, she wondered if people had perhaps scorned her behind her back, enjoyed but ridiculed the ostentation. Pitied her even. They knew how often Graham was away. She hadn't consciously done it for the attention but in retrospect it seemed so wincingly obvious.

She knew Stella would say not to worry about what people thought, to just live as you liked, that at the end of the day no one cared. But they did care. Moira knew they cared. She knew because she cared. She judged Joyce Matthews in the village for having a cleaner – how hard was it to clean your own home? She judged the mayor's wife for having her Waitrose shopping delivered – get out into the community, for goodness sake. She judged the Adamses for having a monstrous new extension that looked like an alien invasion to house a live-in nanny so they could work all hours – those little children needed to see their parents. She knew what Stella would say to that as well. Tell her that the parents had a right to be happy too. And Moira would have to bite her tongue to prevent herself from snapping back, 'Did I? I gave up everything for your father and you kids.'

It was her new friend Mitch who had called her on it. Walking the dogs one day on the beach, he had told her she was jealous when she had been muttering about the cleaner.

Moira had felt herself bristle. 'I'm not jealous.'

He'd laughed. Easy and carefree. Not looking her way. 'Yes, you are. Bitching is jealousy. It always is.'

She'd gone to say something but hesitated. Feeling both astonishment and affront at being called on her behaviour. Graham never called her on anything, just nodded along at her stories.

'It's not bitching, it's an opinion.'

'It's a judgement,' Mitch had said, his smile irritating. His chin raised to enjoy the wind in their faces. 'And not a very nice one. Why shouldn't she have a cleaner? She's busy. She has other focuses for her time.'

'It doesn't take very long to run a Hoover about the house.'

'Moira.' Mitch had stopped, his bare feet in the sand, his mutt that was humbly just called Dog on a long piece of faded orange rope, yapping at the surf. 'If you could go back in time and have a cleaner and a live-in nanny, keep your job, and go for a drink on a Friday night guilt-free, would you? Do you think the kids would have turned out any different?'

'Well, I don't know.' Moira felt herself getting defensive. 'Yes, I think they probably would.' Would they? She wondered. Amy might be a bit less dramatic. A bit more self-sufficient. Stella would be much the same. She paused, or perhaps if Moira had had something else to focus on, their relationship would have been completely different. Moira wouldn't have been quite so envious of Stella: of her easy camaraderie with Graham, or her unequivocal natural swimming talent, of the ease with which she laughed at her mother's neuroses.

'Would you and Graham be happier?'

Moira had swallowed.

Mitch laughed again. 'You don't have to answer that. Bitching, judgement – Moira, they're all jealousy. And jealousy, well, that's just fear isn't it? Fear of taking the leap yourself.' Mitch had started walking again, his brushed cotton tartan trousers like pyjama bottoms getting wet in the surf. 'I think you actually quite enjoyed your life. It's just now your boxes are empty.'

Moira stopped abruptly. 'Excuse me!'

Mitch laughed. Then jogging to the shoreline to pick up a driftwood stick he drew two boxes for her in the sand: 'If all your life is taken up with these two roles' – he'd written MOTHER and WIFE in two separate boxes – 'then that's what your whole life becomes. It's as simple as that.' He'd stood there in his cheesecloth shirt with a lump of jade round his neck on a black thong, freshly tanned from a meditation week on the Algarve, and stared at her directly until she'd got embarrassed by the eye contact and had to look away. 'You need more boxes, Moira,' he'd said, pointing to the two in the sand with his stick then drawing lots more all around them. 'You need more elements that create you, that we can write in these,' he said, gesturing to the new, empty boxes, 'otherwise your life just gets smaller and smaller.'

Moira had wanted to say, 'I have Frank Sinatra now.' But luckily she'd run the sentence through in her head before saying it and realised how pathetic it sounded, on so many levels.

And so she had joined the book club at the library. Where she was sitting right now, with an AWOL husband, in a fancy pair of jeans, next to Joyce Matthews (of cleaner fame), looking about guiltily to check no one was watching because Joyce had tipped a slug of brandy from a hip flask into her cup of lukewarm Gold Blend.

'Don't, it's half past ten in the morning, I'll be pissed as a fart. I shouldn't really be here.' Moira waved the brandy away.

'Nonsense,' said Joyce, pouring a dash into her own. 'Your husband's gone missing. Sometimes you just need to escape.'

Moira thought of her house filled up with her children, the view like one of those funny optical illusion pictures – look at it one way and they're all as close as close can be, squint your eye and it's a room full of strangers.

'I haven't read the book,' she said.

Joyce shook her head. 'Neither have I.'

Moira gave her a sideways look. 'You never read the book.'

'Shall we escape?'

'I couldn't.'

Moira could see the librarian walking over. She had her slippers on. She always put them on for book club – she wanted to relax apparently. Moira hated it. Why couldn't she wear shoes like everyone else? That was judgemental. Surely she couldn't be jealous of the librarian's hideous pink moccasins? Maybe she could. Maybe she was jealous of her audacity, or her desire for comfort above all else. Maybe she was jealous that this lady's husband had not gone missing and all she had to think about was slipping on her slippers to happily chat about what might well be, had she read it, a very good book.

'Come on.' Joyce gave Moira a nudge.

'I can't. It's bad enough that I've escaped to come to book club. I can't escape book club as well.'

'Oh Moira, if you can't escape now when can you? Come on, let's go for a coffee. Or to the pub.'

But Moira said no. Propriety got the better of her. She couldn't bear the idea of the slipper-clad eyes of the librarian watching her back as she retreated, going home to tell her husband or her cat about the terrible woman who lived in the big house by the sea who skived book club when her husband had disappeared. She couldn't bear the eyes of the locals in the pub – 'Is that Moira? Moira, good to see you! Take it Graham's back then?' 'No, no, still missing.'

She pulled the book out of her bag and sat with it on her knee as the librarian started flicking through her own copy to the book club questions printed at the back.

As Moira hadn't read it, the whole chat went straight over her head. So she sat staring at all the people's shoes in the group and thought instead about Graham. About what a relief it was to come downstairs this morning and not find him sitting on the sofa.

She hadn't minded Graham's numb passivity when Bobby

had first died. She understood that it was a bit like losing Stella all over again. Bobby had been the first athlete since Stella that Graham had got excited about. Bobby was a star in the making. An ace little surfer when he first met Amy. He just wasn't strong enough, didn't have the killer instinct. And so Graham had taken it upon himself to train him up. He had him swimming every morning at six, in the gym every evening on the free weights, constantly pushing him to better his maximums. It was Graham who gave him his pep talks and made his competitive acumen sharper and stronger with visualisation and meditation. It was Graham who got him his first big win. And when Bobby moved into a league higher than Graham could take him – not being a surfer himself – they would still train together, still swim those early mornings. Just like he had with Stella.

But Bobby had died over two years ago. And still Graham sat. To the point that it felt like he'd almost forgotten why he was sitting. The grief subsiding while the hopeless lethargy remained. He seemed to shrink away from life, getting grumpier, angrier, and more annoyed with the world he barely ventured into – bar the occasional trip to the pub but even that he muttered about – too far, TV too loud, beer not cold enough. It had been OK when Amy had moved back in. Her sadness after the accident enough to consume all their lives. It had given Moira back her familiar sense of motherly purpose, like having a baby bird to look after: feeding it, caring for it, keeping it safe and warm until it was strong enough to fly the nest again.

Unfortunately, when Amy did get strong enough she showed no intention of flying the nest again. And the two of them – Amy and Graham – just became a permanent fixture in the house, a morose little team staring zombified at the TV flickering in the corner. Moira had started to worry she might go mad. Even getting the builders in had barely shifted them, after Graham had absolved himself of project management duties they'd just decamped to a makeshift living room upstairs for a couple of weeks. That was why Moira had got the dog – an excuse to get herself away from them. And that was when she'd met Mitch. When she'd found joy in life again. When she'd started, for the first time in almost forever, to see herself as a person in her own right. When she'd plucked up the courage to give Amy a gentle nudge out of the house – which Amy had taken very badly and flounced off to London in an impetuous show of defiance, leaving Moira worried sick that she'd done the wrong thing, hardly hearing from Amy the whole time she was there. She'd only been able to console herself recently when Sonny showed her Instagram selfies of a perfectly happy-looking Amy eating brunch overlooking the Thames.

But with Amy gone, it just left Moira and Graham in the house. The gulf between them ever widening. She thought of the silent dinners, the two of them on either side of the table, when just the sound of him chewing made her body tense with irritation. The sighs when she'd make him lift his feet for the Hoover. The noise of his incessant snoring. It saddened her to think he had become just a litany of annoying noises, that there was no spark left between them. But she had tried to help him and she was exhausted from trying. At some point enough had to be enough.

In the book club circle a small row had broken out which the librarian was ineffectually trying to quash by steering the discussion back to the official book club questions. Moira glanced over at Joyce who rolled her eyes and then gestured towards the door with a tilt of her head, trying again to get Moira to make an escape.

Moira shook her head.

Then she sat annoyed with herself for staying. She couldn't even leave book club – what hope did she have of leaving Graham? She had thought she was getting braver. Fiddlesticks. That was before the children had arrived, before she saw herself through their eyes as well as her own. Now it all felt a bit silly, the idea of her leaving. Like a flying dream, when you get hooked on the adrenaline of soaring free then wake up to find yourself lying boringly in bed.

The determination she had felt to leave was forever being tempered by propriety, like a game of ping pong, always batted back. But she hoped it was still somewhere deep within her, simmering, because now she was trapped, trapped till the stubborn old fool decided to come back, where she had been poised ready to jump. Ready to soar.

And her fear was that as time ticked, her children – just their raised brows at her jeans was almost enough – and the comforting pressure of respectability, the omnipresent fear of judgement, of being gossiped about as she had gossiped, of being pitied should she fail, would kill her little sliver of courage, and she'd wake up, boringly, in bed forever.

CHAPTER 9

While Moira was at book club, two teams set off to find clues as to Graham's whereabouts. The decision as to who was on which team essentially came down to the proximity to ice cream. When Gus and Amy were handed their list of places to check, including Londis, Rosie peered at the piece of paper and squeaked, 'Ooh, they sell Twisters at the Londis. I'm coming with you.'

'I like a Twister,' Amy agreed, searching the living room for her sunglasses.

Gus, who had been ready for the last hour and was waiting at the door, made a face. 'They're vile.'

Rosie came to stand by Amy and said, eyes wide with disbelief, 'They're like the best ice lolly in the world.'

Sonny sloped over to stand by Gus, 'I'm going to have a Calippo.'

Gus nodded. 'Wise choice.'

Stella had been rummaging in her bag for the car keys, only to discover Jack was holding them, and when the ice cream chat had finished said, 'So, I take it you four are going together?'

Amy and Rosie looked disparagingly at Gus and Sonny. 'I

74

suppose so,' said Amy, putting her sunglasses on and poofing her hair. Then she looked down at the list again. 'So, we've got the pub, John and Sandra's house … Oh, that's going to be awkward – what am I going to say? Have you seen my dad?'

Stella raised a brow. 'Sounds about right.'

Amy sucked in a breath and went back to the list. 'Post office, other shops, Londis. OK.' She nodded, grabbed her bag, and said, 'Come on then.' Rosie trotted after her like an adoring puppy, dressed today in her own emoji vest, while Amy was wearing skin-tight white jeans and an acid yellow T-shirt. Sonny and Gus followed a little less enthusiastically, both now checking their phones.

The easiest walk to the village was across the headland. They walked the road part of the way then Amy paused by a gate and started to climb the stile, lifting her legs over it really high so she didn't mark her jeans.

Gus watched, thinking of when he'd first seen her profile picture online. In it she had long blonde hair in high pigtails, dressed up like Britney Spears for – hopefully – a fancy-dress party. Gus remembered all his friends passing it round the pub table sniggering because it was clear she was a bit of a dimwit, but also mocking because there was no denying she was good-looking and well out of his league in the looks department. That was why, when he'd seen them the next time, he'd sat down all cocky and full of it, making the fact he'd slept with her unmistakable. They hadn't believed him at first, but when he didn't back down, didn't crack a smile and agree that he was winding them up, his best mate had blown out a breath, held up his pint and said, 'Gus shagged Baby Spice. Nice one.'

Baby.

He felt suddenly woozy.

The air seemed to get muggier and more humid. Above him a gauzy layer of clouds locked in the heat, smothering them all like a huge white duvet.

The kids followed Amy over the stile. Rosie tripped and in the process trod in a cow pat. Sonny laughed. Rosie slapped him on the stomach. Sonny laughed even more and called her Cow Pat Rosie, which made Amy have to hold in a laugh as she told him not to call his sister names while Rosie cried.

It made Gus think about his own family. About the near constant bickering with his siblings – all five of them – and his own parents' house on a farm in Suffolk, crammed full of stuff and people and kids. There were always more babies, more cats, more dogs, more tiny chicks in the airing cupboard; everything mismatched, spotlessly clean but worn and tired. He couldn't imagine anyone going missing other than because they'd got lost on the land somewhere. He had spent his life appreciative of it but desperate to escape it. He had lain on his triple bunk bed dreaming of one day having his own space. A place where he and he alone would be in control, where he could do as he pleased, where it would be silent. And now he had it. He cherished his independence, barely had long-term relationships, and shuddered inside when a girlfriend tried to make him commit to a holiday a couple of months in advance. Yet here he was, on the verge of being permanently tied to this Britney Spears wannabe because of one stupid, drunken mistake. He had to make her see sense.

They walked single file down the side of the field, the footpath jagged with stones, the air scented with cows and wild garlic, and the barbs of the blackthorn bushes clutching at their T-shirts.

'Amy,' Rosie said, idly plucking at the long grass. 'Is Gus your boyfriend?'

Gus snorted a laugh at the back as Amy visibly bristled, her hand fluffing up her hair like a nervous tick. 'No,' she said, short and sharp without turning round.

Sonny turned round though and made a sniggering face at Gus. And Rosie was walking backwards now, eyes narrowed as if she'd been certain she had cracked a particularly difficult code that no one else had yet deciphered.

Gus raised a brow, smug to have outwitted her.

Amy marched on ahead, not speaking, putting herself as far ahead of the group as she could.

Gus thought about the phone call he'd had with his mother last night when he'd been out walking the dog. Needing to talk to someone but unsure who. As soon as she'd answered the phone he knew she'd been the wrong person to call.

'She says she's going to keep it.'

'Oh, Gus, love, that's wonderful.'

'It's not wonderful.'

'Where are you? It's very loud.'

'Cornwall. It's the sea.'

'You could do with a bit of fresh air.'

He imagined her bustling round the kitchen, desperate to envelope him in a big, busty hug. She'd be clutching the cat, probably, to make up for his absence. He'd sighed, regretting the panic that had made him ring in the first place. 'If she has it, I suppose it'll only be every other weekend though, won't it?' he said, almost to himself. 'Isn't that what people do?' He could hear his sister, Claudia, in the background as his mother relayed the whole chat to her, say, 'Overnight usually in the week as well, Gussy!'

'Stop it, the pair of you,' his mother said. 'You don't just have a baby at the weekend, Gus. It's forever. It's in your life, that's it.'

Gus had made a hasty excuse to hang up then walked glassy-eyed after the dog, the word 'forever' looping in his head like the monotonous drone of the waves.

Now the air was getting warmer as they walked. Out the other side of the field they trudged up the coastal path. A maze of brambles on one side, a sheer drop on the other. Gus peered down at the sea, tide in, lapping at the base of the cliff like a hungry dog. There was no shade. No one had thought to bring any water. By the time they got to the Coach and Horses they were all sweaty and sulky with thirst. Amy snapped at Rosie and Sonny to stop squabbling as she patted her skin with a tissue, checking in the window that her make-up was all still in place before they went in. Gus wondered if he had time to get a swift half in but thought he'd better not when Amy opened the door and all the locals greeted her with a big show of sympathetic enthusiasm. Gus thought he'd loiter close to the door instead. An old man by the bar gave Rosie a pound for the fruit machine which kept her and Sonny busy. Gus watched as a group of young surfer-looking guys hovered round Amy, hugging her, draping their arms round her shoulders, kissing her on the cheek and ruffling her hair. It was fascinating to watch. She seemed surprised to see them all and less comfortable with the attention than he'd presumed she might be, breaking the chat short to ask the barman if he'd seen her dad recently or noticed anything unusual.

'Barely been in,' the barman said. 'Last couple of weeks haven't seen him. Sorry, love.'

Amy nodded. 'That's OK.'

Behind her the fruit machine started beeping and flashing. Rosie yelped as coins started clanging into the tray. 'I've won!' she shouted.

The whole place turned to look. Amy's friends laughed, a couple of them swaggering over to gawp at the jackpot. Gus heard them invite Amy to sit down for a drink but she declined, pointing to the door, inadvertently at Gus, saying that they had to go. Gus lifted his hand in a self-conscious wave. One of the guys raised a brow at Amy. She did a little shake of her head, 'It's nothing like that,' then helping Rosie scoop coins into her pocket, ushered them all back out into the sunshine.

'Right, to the high street,' she said, pushing her sunglasses on and pointing up the lane, clearly on edge.

'Race you, Cow Pat,' Sonny shouted and ran ahead.

Rosie sprinted after him. 'Don't call me Cow Pat.'

Gus found himself side by side with Amy.

They walked in silence for a bit.

'Everything OK?' he asked, more just for something polite to say. She definitely seemed a bit odd but then she always seemed slightly odd to him.

'Fine,' she said, without turning his way.

Gus nodded.

A bus trundled by. They walked past a tea room and an antique centre. An old woman with a stick was deadheading her geraniums. 'Oh, hello Amy, love. You all right?' she asked.

'Fine thank you, Mrs Obertone,' Amy said, super polite,

taking her sunglasses off and making a point of checking that Mrs Obertone's children were well, etc.

Gus shuddered. He couldn't bear the idea of everyone knowing him and everything about him again. Visits to his parents' house were always accompanied by wind-ups in the pub about when he was going to take over the farm.

When they got to what Amy had referred to as the high street – a gallery, fish and chip shop, pasty shop, and pharmacy – Gus trailed behind her as she went into every shop and enquired about her father. And every single person enquired about her, a subject he noticed Amy expertly deflected, countering quick smart with questions about all the other person's extended family. For Gus, it was painfully slow going.

Finally, they got to the Londis.

Gus ambled the aisles as Amy queued at the checkout to talk to the cashier whose name nobody could remember.

He found Rosie in the toy section holding a Barbie in a box. 'Don't you think she looks like Amy?' she said.

Gus exhaled as he took the Barbie off her and stared, reluctantly, at the big blue eyes and the big blonde hair. 'A bit.'

'You don't look like Ken,' Rosie said flatly.

Gus laughed. 'No, I know I don't.'

'Your nose is too big,' she said, giggling naughtily to herself after she said it.

'Thanks.'

Rosie looked confused. 'I don't understand why you said thanks.'

'Because your aim was to insult me and it didn't work.'

Her cheeks pinked. 'Will you tell my mum?'

'Yes.'

She looked panicked.

'No,' said Gus, rolling his eyes. 'Why would I tell your mum? How old are you?'

'Seven.'

'Well, you're old enough to learn. Don't say bad shit about people's noses.'

'You said "shit".'

'Yes, I did. Got a problem with that?'

'It's not nice to swear.'

'Are you going to tell my mum?'

Rosie giggled. 'I can't tell your mum.'

'Here,' Gus got his phone out his pocket, 'ring her up, tell her.'

'Noooooo,' Rosie laughed, like he was the silliest person she'd met.

Gus put his phone away with a grin.

Rosie picked up the Ken doll box. 'He actually looks like Uncle Bobby.' She turned to look at Gus. 'He died. Did you know that?'

Gus shook his head.

'Surfing,' Rosie said.

'Oh right.' Gus nodded. 'And Uncle Bobby, that was your Mum and Amy's brother, yeah?' Part of him knew that that wasn't going to be the right answer when he said it, but the part of him willing it to be right had overruled it. Because if, as he suspected, this Bobby character had been Amy's husband then it suddenly added another layer to this person he'd inadvertently slept with. To this person he had intended to persuade to terminate the baby she was carrying. To this person who wasn't really a person but just an airhead Britney Spears WhatsApp avatar.

Rosie made a face at him, a real winner of an are-you-completely-stupid stare and said, 'Mum doesn't have a brother. Bobby was married to Amy. It's really sad. Amy was really sad. Bobby was really handsome—'

'That's enough, Rosie,' Amy's voice cut in on the conversation. She was standing at the end of the aisle, arms crossed.

Rosie jumped and dropped the Ken doll.

Gus bent down to pick it up, slowly, all the time watching as Amy came forward and yanked Rosie over to the ice cream freezer.

Then he stood up and slotted the doll back on the shelf, pausing for a second, his hand resting on a Buy One Get One Free sign. 'Shit,' he muttered under his breath.

CHAPTER 10

Stella and Jack were halfway back from the fishing lake when the car broke down. The petrol gauge had been bleeping on empty since they left the house but a trip to the petrol station was in the opposite direction to the lake, and Jack had assured Stella that the Nissan Qashqai can run 43 miles after the needle hits empty on the dashboard. The lake was only ten miles away. Unfortunately, Jack hadn't factored in a key road on the route being blocked by a lorry pouring concrete for building works and a diversion which then led off into a winding country lane maze outside Stella's jurisdiction and unnavigable because iMaps wouldn't load on either of their phones. When they finally got back to countryside she knew, they were out of petrol.

'We should have got the sat nav fixed,' Jack muttered, slamming the car door.

'Or,' Stella said, standing in the passing point where they'd managed to crawl to a stop, 'we should have got some petrol.'

Jack didn't reply. Just sucked in his cheeks, visibly fuming.

Stella scratched her head, looked around to get her bearings. It had been so long since she'd lived around here.

'Which way?' Jack said, his phone map still just a frustrating grey grid with a blue dot.

Stella shrugged. 'Well, the house is that way.' She pointed slightly to her right. 'But the quickest route would be straight ahead to the sea and then along the cliff path. So up there.' She pointed towards the high verge beside them that flanked the road. Jack looked dubious but didn't argue, clearly still furious with himself about the petrol.

Heat bore down on them as they climbed. The humidity was reaching its peak. Stella slipped on the grass in her flip-flops. Her long blue skirt and white vest were not meant for trudging walks. Midges buzzed round her head.

She felt like she was walking through one of the polytunnels she'd watched out of the window of a coach journey once through the arid wasteland of southern Spain. It was years ago, in the early days of having Sonny when she had no clue how much sun the pale new skin of a baby could handle. Sonny had spent the week squeezed like a fat little sausage into an all-in-one sun protection suit and hat with a white baby-sunblock face. She'd watched other children running about naked. She remembered running about naked herself, but the sun was more dangerous now because of global warming – that's what she'd read on Mumsnet when she'd googled it before they left. But then one of the posts had warned of babies having vitamin D deficiency nowadays because they were overly protected from the sun. She remembered sitting looking perplexed with Jack – both of them, she knew, secretly remembering the holidays when they could lie back for a nap or nip off to the bar for a beer. Jack did actually nip off to the bar for a beer, and alone with the sand-eating sausage baby, Stella had started to write, scribbling in the back of the paperback she had naively taken to read, and Potty-Mouth was born. The first column was called, 'Holiday? What holiday?' The first line: 'I never believed anyone when they said a holiday with kids was "same shit, different place". I thought they were just miserable bastards. They were. They had kids.'

She'd actually quite enjoyed the holiday in the end – staying up eating tapas while Sonny snored in the buggy in just his nappy, watching him giggle at the sea and be cooed over by grannies – and the article had gone full circle, ending on a high note but certainly not scrimping on the grizzle. The Sunday broadsheet magazine that she wrote for occasionally had run it, delighted by the angle – their readers loved a shocked snort with their weekend brunch, a nod of retrospective agreement 'I wish we'd been able to say things like this in my day' or a pass of the page over the table, 'read this, it's like that time it rained in Mallorca every day and the twins got chicken pox'. A flurry of letters arrived in uproarious response – some full-blown thank yous from people just relieved that someone else was finding it all as bad or worse than they were, others who didn't find her funny at all, she tried her best to ignore those, because Potty-Mouth was hired.

Over the years her column had lost an inch to advertising space and a new editor had made it clear that the readers wanted the grizzle. The best of the bad bits wrapped up in a witty package that took just over three minutes to read.

'I'm sweating,' said Jack as he hiked the final few feet up the hill. The verge dotted with spiky gorse bushes and pink heather.

'Me too.'

Jack wiped his brow with his T-shirt. Dark hair pushed up off his forehead. Face still rigid.

They stopped side by side at the top. Below them the scene

dropped into fields of sheep and crops. Rows of cabbages and corn. A tractor was backing into the farm, then further out past a golf course and caravan park was the sea. Glinting and familiar. Pale as the sky. Stella inhaled through her nose, felt her shoulders drop slightly.

Jack shook his head. 'This is madness. We're miles away.'

Stella rolled her eyes. 'It's not that bad,' she laughed, his annoyance working to deflate her own.

'It's pretty bad,' Jack said, sweeping his arm to take in the endless view.

Stella shaded her eyes with her hand. 'Well, look, that's the Goldstone Caravan Park,' she said, pointing at the rows of white static vans in the distance. 'And the leisure centre.' She squinted, gesturing to the right of the vans, to an ugly grey concrete building. 'Once we're there, we're pretty much almost home.' It was the distance between them and there that was the worry. 'We just have to get across all those fields.' She grinned.

Jack blew out a breath, wiped the sweat away again. 'You sure about this? You've never had the best sense of direction.'

Stella mock gasped, 'I have a sense of direction.'

Jack looked at her like she was deluded. The tension broke. She smiled. He came over to walk next to her as she tucked her skirt into her knickers to stop it trailing along the ground and started to stride purposefully ahead. Jack matched her pace, bashing her shoulder with his at one point, when she caught his eye he shook his head with a resigned smile.

They walked on a little in silence. The warm sun slicking their skin. Stella pointed to an overgrown footpath that ran down the side of the sheep field, trees wild and straggly making it dark as a tunnel. Jack held a bramble back so she could pass.

'Thanks.'

'My pleasure.'

In the shade Stella could feel the sweat on her arms cool. Jack wiped his forehead again with his shirt.

Stella pulled a leaf from the side of the path, twirling it in her fingers. 'So, do you want to do the next thing on the MOT list?' she asked.

Jack kicked a stone. 'What was the first thing?'

'The more sex,' she said.

'Oh yeah,' Jack laughed. 'That went well, didn't it?'

Stella glanced around her. 'We could do it now if you want?'

'What? Have sex?' Jack looked shocked. 'I'm not having sex here, someone might walk past.'

'No one's going to walk past, there's no one here.'

'Stella, I'm blushing,' Jack said with a laugh. 'No.' He shook his head. 'No.'

The dark silence of the tunnel closed in around them.

'Why not? Come on, let's live a little.' Stella wasn't actually that keen on having sex on a deserted footpath – what would she do about the brambles? And the initial suggestion had only really been to wind him up, but the fact he was so adamant niggled her. She had thought they were the type of couple who would at least have given it a go, or perhaps she suspected they weren't which made it seem twice as important.

Potty-Mouth and her husband would have had sex on a deserted footpath. They'd probably have done it on a busy thoroughfare if challenged.

Stella didn't want to go that far, but she wanted to know

that she and Jack were game. That they might step out of their comfort zone in order to fulfil what, yes, was a silly magazine challenge, but a challenge nonetheless to prove that they weren't trapped in middle age. That they weren't in the rut she feared more and more that they were. She stopped walking. 'Come on. There's some trees over there. No one will see.'

She didn't want their relationship to have become the type that would never have sex in a field. The idea of it hit her with more sadness than she expected. 'Come on, Jack,' she thought. 'Say yes!'

Jack looked at her. 'Stel, I'm hot. We've had to leave our car in a layby. And we're meant to be finding out about your father. Forgive me for not wanting a shag.'

Stella nudged a broken frond of grass with her foot. She sighed, glanced around her. 'No,' she said begrudgingly. 'You're probably right.'

They started to walk on again. It felt cold now in the shade.

'So, go on then, what was the next thing on the list?' Jack asked, nudging good-humouredly at her silent sulk.

'It doesn't matter,' Stella replied.

'Go on, tell me.'

They came out of the tunnel into a wide expanse of cornfield, poppies and white butterflies like paint splatter against the yellow. Stella put her hands on her hips, staring out at the view. 'We have to say what we most appreciate about the other.'

Jack tipped his head like he was accepting a challenge. 'OK,' he said, 'I can do that.'

Stella started to walk on past the waist-high corn.

Jack followed, catching up quickly. 'I appreciate how funny you are.'

Stella did a little shrug.

Jack grinned. 'I appreciate how young your skin looks.'

'Give me a break,' Stella snorted. 'You don't have to say "I appreciate" before everything you know.'

He laughed. 'I appreciate how much you do for the kids.'

'That's nice.'

'I thought so.'

'I appreciate how good a mother you are. Although I do think you should talk to Sonny.'

Stella stopped walking and swung round. 'And what do I tell him?' she asked, genuinely perplexed. 'That it's OK to call your mum a bitch and spend the whole time killing people on screen all day then fail your exams? That would be good.'

They stood facing each other.

'No, I don't think that.' Jack held his hands out in a gesture of peace. 'Just we're here, we're away from home. Maybe see it as a Time Out,' he said, head tilted to one side, his expression trying to encourage her to see reason. 'Talk to him, man to man, so to speak. Get to know him again.'

Stella looked the other way, out over the corn. Her heart rate slowing as she considered it, knowing he was right. 'OK, fine,' she said, starting to walk again along the side of the field, turning to take a few paces backwards as she added, 'Make a note that one of the things I don't appreciate about you is the use of the term "Time Out".'

Jack grinned.

'Anything else?' Stella asked.

'I'm thinking.'

'About what you appreciate about me?'

'Yeah, it's hard to articulate. Like I appreciate how you look – I think you're really good-looking. But that sounds shallow.'

'No, that's OK with me,' Stella said, a quirk of a smile on her lips.

'I appreciate your strength. Not like weight-lifting strength, but strength of character.'

'You think I have strength of character?'

'Of course.'

'I don't think I do.'

'Definitely you do.' Jack nodded.

They walked side by side in silence.

Then Jack said, 'So, what do you appreciate about me?'

'Nothing,' Stella said flatly.

Jack laughed.

Stella tried not to smile.

The backs of their knuckles brushed as they walked.

Stella glanced across at him. Jack tipped his head, unsure whether she was about to say something. Stella swallowed, she wasn't very good at things like this. Then she said, 'I appreciate that you—'

But the comment was cut off by her phone ringing.

Amy's name flashed on the screen. 'Hi, Amy,' she said. 'Everything OK? Are the kids OK?'

'Fine,' Amy said, but after that her voice kept cutting out, the reception terrible.

'Just tell me quick, I can't hear you.'

'Swimming,' Amy said.

'Swimming?' Stella frowned.

'Londis. The woman. Said he's been swimming.'

'No.' Stella shook her head. 'He hasn't swum since Bobby.'

'At the pool,' said Amy.

'We're right by the pool,' Stella said, raising her voice in a pointless attempt to overcome the bad reception.

Then Amy cut out.

'He's been swimming at the pool.' Stella looked up at Jack, confused.

'So I gathered,' Jack replied. Both of them glanced over to the ugly grey leisure centre building a field or so away. 'Would you be all right going to the pool?' he asked, tentatively checking.

'Me?' Stella scoffed, slipping on her sunglasses. 'I'll be fine.'

CHAPTER 11

The leisure centre smelt exactly as Stella remembered. Like chlorine and feet. To call it a leisure centre made it sound much more impressive than it was. Really it was just a pool, a room with a few free weights, and a café area that was staffed only at peak periods, and at all other times drinks and snacks were supplied by whichever one of the three vending machines was in order.

Standing in the reception, Stella felt almost dizzy. Like she was being attacked by soft air punches of ungraspable, overwhelming recollection. The pattern on the tiles in the foyer was the same – rows of raised beige squares with tiny speckles of black. Two had fallen off the wall, leaving zigzagged lines of yellowing putty. There was the same strip light in the ceiling and the same scuffed swing doors to the changing room.

The only thing that had changed was the fancy new glass reception desk with automatic barriers for entry and exit into the pool. It was an anomaly in the battered, worn-down building. Stella found herself wanting it gone, and the nineteen-year-old surf dude with the sun-bleached, salt-dreadlocked hair behind the counter gone with it. She had liked it when old Peggy had sat at the entrance desk, her cup of stewed tea going cold next to her, her occasional walk round the pool to chat to the lifeguards leaving the desk unmanned so you could sneak in for a free swim, her knitting, her championing, her little nod of acknowledgement that she'd seen you break your record in training.

'Hi,' Stella said to the dude.

He was on Snapchat. Stella did not understand Snapchat – why anyone would want dog ears and a dog nose was beyond her.

He looked up smiling from something he'd read on his phone. 'Yep,' he said, phone down, hands flat on the desk, scooting himself forward on his wheelie chair. 'Two to swim?' he said, already keying the price into his computer.

'No.' Stella shook her head.

'Oh.' He looked up with a cheeky grin. He was painfully, youthfully good-looking. Stella found herself surreptitiously detangling her hair, pulling her skirt out from where she'd hitched it into her pants, wanting to check her reflection. She imagined herself all sweaty, make-up run in the heat.

'Is Pete here?' she asked, feeling unexpectedly nervous at the mention of the name. Suddenly psyching herself up for the possible meeting.

The dude picked up a phone and as he pressed the buttons glanced up and said, 'What's your name?'

She paused. 'Tell him it's Stella.'

She felt Jack place his hand on her back. She half wanted it gone. Wanted to appear strong on her own.

The tone rang loud as they waited for someone to pick up. Then suddenly recognition dawned on the dude as he looked up at her frowning and said, 'Stella? As in Stella Whitethorn?'

'Well, I'm Stella French now because' —she pointed to Jack— 'but yes, I was Stella Whitethorn then,' she said, her explanation seeming awkward and rambling.

The young guy's mouth spread into a smile. 'Cool.' Then the phone was answered and he said, 'Hey Pete, Stella Whitethorn's here for you!'

Two long, fidgety minutes later Pete arrived, the side door swinging open with a bang. His belly leading the way, his arms wide. The only thing he was missing was the cigarette that used to dangle permanently from his lips. Pete was the only person Stella knew who managed to shout and smoke at the same time.

'Well I never. Look what the cat dragged in,' he said, all open arms and wide toothy smile.

The dude pressed the button for the snazzy doors so Stella and Jack could walk through into the corridor. He was watching it all with a massive grin.

'Hey Pete,' Stella said, awkwardly rigid as he pulled her in for an unexpected hug. He smelt the same. Like sweat and coffee. 'You look exactly the same,' she said, surprised by how unchanged he was, like a dusty waxwork pulled out from the basement.

'Less hair.' He patted the wisps on the top of his head. 'And a bit more here,' he added, patting what was now an astonishingly large stomach.

'Need to get in the pool again,' Stella said, because she couldn't think of anything else to say. Blood to her brain had been redirected to her senses that were currently working in dizzying overdrive.

'So do you, my dear.' Pete shot back with a lazy drawl, weathered skin creasing as he grinned.

Stella couldn't think of anything else but to ignore the comment, and said instead, 'This is Jack, my husband,' a little primly.

'A pleasure,' said Pete, holding out stubby fingers.

Jack did his usual solid handshake and charming small talk as Pete ushered them down the corridor, through the changing rooms and out into the wide blue of the pool.

Stella stopped by the silver barriers, overpowered by the scent of chlorine. There was the tingle of familiar adrenaline as she'd walked through the changing rooms, every sound setting off a chain of reaction in her head: the slam of the lockers, the turn of the key, feet against the wet tiles on the floor, the hiss and suck of the filter. She watched an old lady doing achingly slow lengths in the middle lane. It was all so familiar.

'Nothing's changed, eh?' Pete nudged her forward. She didn't want him to touch her. 'We can sit in the office. I've got a lesson in ten.'

'We won't keep you long,' Stella said, unable to stop glancing across at the water – the garish blue, the string of floats, the black-tiled numbers, and the five-metre flags.

'Or you could help me with the lesson?' Pete said, opening the door to the office.

Stella fake-laughed.

The office was just the same. Stacks of paper-filled boxes, rows of lever arch files, chipped trophies, the cork noticeboard, and the casually chucked rescue Torp were all so familiar. Like time here had paused, all of these relics frozen just waiting for her to step back in.

Pete gestured to the chairs opposite his desk, shoving a pile of papers off one of them on to the floor. Stella felt immediately small. Immediately under interrogation. Her palms were sweating and she turned her hands up to look bemused at the layer of moisture, then subtly tried to wipe them on her skirt. She hadn't felt like this for years.

She retied her hair, lifting it from the back of her neck, and adjusted her position on her seat while internally pep-talking herself: you are a grown-up, Pete is your equal. But she remembered flinching as he'd slammed his hand against a wall, bellowing, 'You stupid bitch. I could f'king kill you right now, Stella, I'm so angry!' Her dad standing next to him in stony-faced silence.

'So,' said Pete, leaning back, hands clasped over his belly, his chair squeaking under the weight. 'I take it this is about Graham?'

Stella nodded.

Jack, realising that Stella seemed to have lost her words, said, 'We've just heard that he's been swimming again.'

Pete flipped forward in his chair and shook his head. 'Have you now?'

Stella and Jack exchanged a glance.

Stella found her hands were gripping the edge of the seat. 'Has he been here often?'

'Not often,' said Pete, leaning back in his chair again, taking a moment to look at the two of them, clearly relishing the fact he knew things they didn't. 'Couple of times recently. Once last week,' he added, hard eyes watching Stella.

Stella decided then that this had been a mistake. She hated that she was not only back here but also back at Pete's mercy. She was about to say her thanks and get up and leave when Jack asked, 'And did he tell you anything about where he was going?'

The side of Pete's mouth turned up. Stella internally winced. He would love this. He would love that they didn't know where Graham was, that she had had to search Pete out for answers. 'Let me think,' he said, scratching his tummy. 'Oh aye aye, there's my kid for his lesson.' He nodded out towards the pool, deliberately stringing out his reply to Jack, Stella thought. 'Sorry, duty calls.'

Stella and Jack stood up, watched as a gangly kid in green Speedos hovered nervously by the door.

Pete opened it quickly and went, 'Boo!'

The kid nearly fell over with fright.

Pete roared with laughter.

Stella shook her head. 'You haven't changed, have you?'

'Why mess with perfection,' he laughed, throaty and bold.

The gangly kid was scuttling along behind him to the edge of the pool. He was probably just a bit younger than Sonny.

'Right, ten warm-up lengths. Go!' Pete clapped his chubby hands and the kid jumped in, nervous like a foal.

Pete went to stand by Stella. She could still smell his power over her. It made her want to edge away but she forced herself to stay put, thinking about how Jack had said she had strength of character. She didn't feel strong.

'Ten lengths?' she tried to joke. 'I thought it was twenty?'

Pete shrugged. 'I've mellowed with age.'

Jack made a face behind him like he dreaded to think what he'd been like previously.

Stella watched the skinny boy splashing cack-handedly through his lengths. Her heart clenched.

'Oh, I miss the old days,' said Pete, watching the boy as well. 'Look what they give me now.'

'Well, go and make him better. Stop talking to us,' Stella said with mock reproach, using it as an excuse to back away. 'His stroke's all over the place. What's he doing with his elbow?'

'Do you want to take the lesson?' Pete asked, his voice flipped in an instant, tone questioning, bushy brows raised because she had dared suggest she knew better than him.

'No way,' Stella forced a laugh, like it was all good-natured.

Pete chuckled, as if he'd been teasing her. 'Calm down,' he said, as though she'd been the one to get defensive. Then he stared at the terrible swimmer and blew out a breath, resigned to his next half an hour. He blew sharp on his whistle. 'Elbow up,' he shouted. 'Up!' Then shook his head again.

'Well, we'd better be off, leave you to it,' Stella said, edging backwards. 'I take it he didn't mention where he was going?' she added, just to make sure.

'No.' Pete shook his head. Keeping his focus on the swimmer in the pool, he said, 'Kinda funny that it's you here asking though, isn't it …?'

Stella ran her tongue along her lip, waiting for whatever it was he was going to say next. Pete liked nothing better than a 'kinda funny' followed up by his own musings on why so hilarious. 'Hey Stella, kinda funny that you went slower on that length than the one before, isn't it? I'd like to say it's cos you're tired. But I'm gonna say it's cos you're a pussy. The only thing you're not afraid of is failure.'

Pete turned to look at her, head swivelling like a lion, lazy and lethal. 'I mean considering what you did pretty much destroyed him.'

Stella stood stock-still, staring as his mouth stretched into a broad grin.

Out of the corner of her eye she could see Jack frown. Could see him hovering on the verge of saying something like, 'I think that's enough now.'

In the end he didn't have to say anything because Pete just walked away, blowing his whistle to chivvy the scrappy little swimmer along.

'You OK?' Jack moved closer, arm round her shoulders.

Stella immediately shrugged off his embrace, aware that she didn't want Pete to see her need anyone. 'He's an arsehole,' she said, watching Pete's portly figure hanging over the railings shouting something mocking down at the kid in the water. 'Always has been, always will be.'

'Come on, let's go,' said Jack, touching her briefly on the small of her back.

'Yeah.' She walked with him to the exit at the far end of the pool.

Pete was still at the other end with his stopwatch, and beside them the kid was getting ready to do another length, struggling to hold onto the side and adjust his goggles at the same time.

'Hey.' Stella found herself crouching down so she was level with him, bunching up her skirt so it didn't get soaked in the puddles of water round the edge of the pool. The kid squinted up at her, fluorescent light catching on his goggles.

'Tell your mum to find someone else to teach you,' she said.

The kid made a face like he thought she was crazy. It reminded her of Sonny. 'I'm serious,' she said. 'It's meant to be fun. Not like this.'

'Whitethorn, what are you doing?' Pete's voice bellowed from where he stood at the shallow end.

Stella straightened up. 'Just telling him about his elbow. How to correct it.'

Pete narrowed his eyes.

Stella smiled. Wide and cheek-aching.

Then she turned back to the kid. 'Do it.'

Pete blew the whistle, loud and sharp. Stella flinched. She watched the kid go. Splashing and struggling. He reminded her of Sonny. Then suddenly he reminded her of herself. The endless lengths in her navy blue swimsuit and white swimming cap. Whistle blowing. Orders shouted, all a dull murmur under the water. Tired coltish limbs speckled with goose pimples as she shivered, awaiting instructions.

She had a vision of her dad and Pete: one at each end of the pool. Both with their stopwatches, their shining 1970s Great Britain Team sweat-jackets, their hard eyes. Pete with his cigarette.

'Nope. Again.'

'Nope. Again.'

'No! Again.' Hands raised, incredulous at the slowness.

'You're just wasting time, Stella. Our time, your time. You want to go home? Me too! Believe me. Me too!' Her dad always silent. The watcher. He left all the hard shouting to Pete only to swoop in every now and then with a closed-eye shake of the head or some technical gem that would shave a tenth of a second off her time. He was the one everyone wanted to impress.

Sometimes, at the end of a length, she'd look up and she'd see it. The tight, contained exuberance. Painfully covetable in its rarity. The click of the watch and the blink-and-you'd-miss-it air punch. The barely perceptible pleasure coiled tight. And then he and Pete would confer – they'd stroll to meet midway down the pool, her dad resting an arm on the high lifeguard's chair, eyes languidly glancing at the legs of the female on duty.

Stella would pull off her goggles, panting, waiting. Pete would light another cigarette, walk away and shout, 'Warm down!' He lived by a belief that if you told someone they'd done well, they'd stop trying. But her dad would walk back, tracksuit glinting in the pool light, his hair coiffed and skin tanned from some warm weather training camp, feet always flip-flopped. And just before someone would stop him for a chat, or Peggy from the front desk would bring him a tea with adoration in her eyes, he'd catch Stella's eye and he'd wink. And she would pull off her cap, tip her head back in the water feeling it cool and sharp through her hair, and look up at the fluorescent strip lighting to bask in a wink.

Now, as Stella watched the kid only halfway through his length, meandering off course and hitting the floats, she had the rising feeling that she missed him. She missed her dad. Not who he had become but who he had been. She didn't miss this – this pool, Pete, the hours that she had spent there that seemed so important and now so insignificant. But she missed the man who had winked at her, the one who waited outside the changing room with his classic homemade electrolyte drink and peanut butter sandwiches for her and said, 'Are you warm enough? Put this on,' handing her a jumper he'd packed just in case.

In the pool, the kid finished his length. Pete scoffed, 'Jesus, I thought you'd never finish. It's almost lunchtime.'

'Stella?' Jack touched her arm.

Stella turned her back on the water. Nodding at Jack, she walked out through the changing room with him.

Outside, she gave the pool once last look. She didn't want to miss her dad. She had wasted too much time trying to rationalise how he had allowed all this to be more important than her. She was happily, neutrally detached from him. She didn't want the feelings back – the ones that made her want to punch him in the face and then be hugged by him.

CHAPTER 12

The sky darkened as Stella and Jack hiked back from the pool. The initial novelty of walking through fields was long gone, dissipated further by the first pitter patter of warm summer rain.

Stella was distracted. To silence the confusing thoughts brought on by the visit to the pool she was working out excuses to gather up the kids and their suitcases and flee for home. Her quietness threw Jack off balance. He'd once said that she was the one that talked and he was the one that answered – that was the way their relationship worked. So when she wasn't talking, the balance tipped and Jack was left floundering, to the point that he'd stopped walking as they came to an empty field, hands on his hips, sweat pouring from his brow, and said, 'Come on then, let's do it.'

Stella frowned. 'Do what?'

'Have sex in the bushes.' He'd been all upbeat, trying to cajole her back to normality. He'd even pulled faux-sexily at the bottom of his polo shirt.

Stella felt her shoulders slump. 'No,' she said, as if it were the most ridiculous thing she'd heard, and carried on walking.

After that they had stumbled on mostly in silence. They

arrived back at her parents' house just as the pitter patter morphed into an all-out downpour that sounded like hands slapping on the windows. It was a relief to see the solid stone walls and the glow from the kitchen.

'You were lucky,' Moira said as she opened the front door, an apron with some witty slogan about having no wine left for cooking wrapped round her waist, in the middle of rolling out pastry for a summer berry tart.

Sonny was lying flat on the sofa, arms raised, holding his phone above his face, the dog asleep on his legs. Amy was in the armchair, eyes shut, headphones on.

Sonny sat up when he heard the door. 'What did they say at the pool?' he asked.

Stella shook her head. 'Just that he's been there. Nothing else.'

'I had no idea he'd been swimming,' said her mother.

Sonny looked momentarily crestfallen that there was no more news.

Jack walked over and ruffled his shaggy hair. 'We'll find him, don't worry.'

Her mother said, 'Cup of tea?'

Amy pushed one headphone back and said, 'So, how are we going to find him?'

Stella felt like the walls were closing in on her.

At the table Gus was playing Barbies with Rosie. She had him fashioning a house out of a cardboard box. 'Not like that, Gus!' Rosie sighed all dramatic when he started drawing on a door with glitter glue.

'You OK there, Gus?' Stella asked as Rosie issued strict instructions on how the door should look.

'Having a great time, thanks Stella,' Gus replied.

Stella liked him immediately. In that instant. She didn't think there were many people who would give themselves over to Rosie.

Amy glanced round to see what was going on and scowled when she saw Stella laugh, like she didn't want Gus to be funny, she didn't want him to amuse her family. It made Stella remember how proud Amy had been of Bobby, draped over him as they lolled on the sofa together drinking Diet Cokes. Stella had liked Bobby, he'd been amiably funny but after about five or ten minutes' chat, usually about surfing, she'd never known what to say to him. She'd often wondered what he and Amy had talked about when they were together – how they had spent their time. She'd worried that Amy had spent a lot of it, like their mother had, waiting for her husband to come back, making their cottage beautiful for when he jogged in from the waves. But she and Amy hadn't had the kind of relationship where she could ask her. And what would she have said, 'Are you lonely in your perfect marriage, Amy?'

As if she knew she were the subject of Stella's musings, and wanting not to be, Amy sat up in her seat, pulled off her headphones and said, 'Seriously, what are we going to do now? What's the next plan?'

Stella thanked her mother for the cup of tea that appeared as if by magic and said, 'We have to leave tomorrow.'

Outside the sky was dark as a winter night. Lightning forked over the sea.

'What?' Amy was aghast.

Sonny sat forward. 'We can't, Grandpa's still missing.'

'You go, darling, if you want to go,' Moira said calmly. 'There's no need to stay.'

'I don't want to go, we have to go,' Stella said, knowing that she absolutely did want to go. 'Sonny, your dad's got to go back to work.'

Sonny swung round to look at Jack. 'Can't you take time off? This is a family emergency.'

Jack nodded his head. 'Well, I could certainly ask.'

'No,' said Stella categorically.

'Dad!' Sonny thwacked the back of the sofa when Jack shrugged as if it were up to Stella. 'This is so unfair!' he shouted, stomping over to the table to slump down next to Gus.

Rosie was watching, wide-eyed and hesitant.

Gus leant forward and whispered something that made her giggle, distracting her from the tension. Then they started cutting snazzy crenellations into the top of the cardboard box castle.

Stella looked down at her shoes.

Amy stood with one hand on her hip. 'That's typical.'

Stella licked her lips before glancing up. 'What is?'

'You. Leaving.'

'Oh please.' Stella blew out a breath.

'You always go.'

'I do not always go.'

'You do.'

'Girls!' Moira said sharply.

They stopped, pouting down at various spots on the floor. No one made eye contact. Sonny sat hunched in a sulk, glaring out of the rain-soaked window. Gus and Rosie quietly stuck stickers on the cardboard box. Jack sat with elbows on his knees on the sofa, hands clasped together, head bowed. Moira started wiping down the rose marble counter. The rain hammered, bang bang went the hands smacking the glass. Stella took a sip of her tea and it burnt her mouth.

Above them clouds rumbled with thunder. The dog jumped scared off the sofa and trotted over to the kitchen, winding its way through Moira's legs. Everyone was silent.

Then Stella heard Sonny sniff. And sniff again.

She narrowed her eyes, looking over at him, trying to work out his game.

Gus paused with his glitter glue.

'Can anyone smell poo?' Sonny said, screwing up his face.

'Sonny!' Stella cut in.

Rosie stopped sticking, sat up straight and sniffed loudly. 'I can.'

Moira stopped wiping and straightened up, smelling the air. 'Oh my goodness.' She looked mortified.

Lightning crackled on the horizon.

Amy and Stella shared a look, they knew exactly what it was.

Jack shrugged a shoulder, standing up to go over to where Sonny was making faces as he sniffed. 'Probably just the drains in this rain.'

'No, it's not that.' Stella shook her head.

Gus looked over, intrigued. 'What is it?'

Moira walked over to the sink where water was backing up in the plug hole. She had her hands on the rim, head hanging. 'It's the septic tank.' She turned round to face the family, and announced, 'I think it might be blocked.'

'Urgh, gross,' laughed Sonny, making gagging noises.

'Why?' Rosie squeaked, delighted by the drama. 'What does it mean?'

'It means poo is going to flood the house.' Sonny grinned.

'Sonny, shut up!' Stella sighed.

Sonny made a face at her. Rosie giggled, nervous and excited.

'Well quick, let's call the drain people,' Amy said, holding out her phone for someone else to take it and do the actual mechanics of calling and speaking.

'They won't come in this weather,' said Moira, peering out at the thunderous sky.

'Mum, people work in the rain,' Amy said, then glancing at her phone frowned. 'Oh, I haven't got a signal. Anyone got a signal?'

No one had a signal.

All the lights went out.

'Oooh, a power cut,' Rosie said, gleefully. 'Shall I get candles?' She jumped up to go and search in the cupboard under the stairs.

'Rosie, we don't need candles.' Stella went over to stop her as she grabbed a handful. 'We can still see,' she added, gesturing to the grey afternoon half-light.

Rosie stuck her bottom lip out. 'I like candles.'

Standing on the living room side of the kitchen counter, Amy was pressing buttons on the landline. 'It doesn't work!'

Jack nodded, coming over to have a go. 'Cordless rarely do in a power cut.'

'How do you know that?' asked Gus, bemused and impressed.

Jack shrugged.

'Jack knows stuff like that,' said Stella. 'It's his thing.'

'What?' Gus looked confused.

'Kind of obscure useless knowledge,' Stella said.

Gus laughed. 'Good thing to have.'

Jack made a face of mock offence. 'I like to think it's more on the useful side of the scale. This being a case in point.' He gestured to the phone.

'Can you fix it?' Gus asked.

'No,' said Jack. 'But I know why it isn't working.'

Stella rolled her eyes and went to look out of the window. Gus came to stand next to her. 'So, where's the tank?'

'There.' Stella pointed to the raised patch of grass behind the pink hydrangea bush where the gazebo always used to go at her mother's garden parties. 'There's a manhole cover just by the steps. There's a pipe from all the drains in the house that runs under the drive. See that drain cover there—' she angled her hand down to where water was bubbling up from a drain in the centre of the gravel drive.

Gus had to peer through the rivulets of rain on the window. 'I see it. So, what do we do?'

'We're going to have to go out there, have a look and see what's happening. See whether it's blocked.' Stella shuddered. 'It'll be disgusting.'

Jack came over to join them. They all stared out of the window.

'Well.' Gus shrugged. 'It all sounds quite exciting to me.'

Stella made a face like he had to be joking.

He grinned.

Amy cut in, 'It's not exciting, Gus. We have no power and if someone doesn't do something or we don't call anyone, Sonny's right, the septic tank will literally back up into the house.'

Gus chuckled as if she were being a drama queen.

Amy replied with a death stare.

'Right, no point standing around here talking.' Jack clapped his hands. 'What can we do to sort it out, Moira?'

Moira looked unsure. 'Graham usually deals with it,' she said, sheepish. 'He's got rods and gloves in the garage that clear any blockages, if indeed it is a blockage.'

'Yuck!' Sonny gagged again. Rosie collapsed into giggles. Stella sighed.

'Right.' Jack rolled his shoulders back. 'Good. Rods and gloves in the garage.' He looked a little daunted heading to the coat rack for his anorak, like he was going off to war.

'I'll help,' said Gus, following with a spring in his step.

'Oh, that's terribly kind of you, Gus.' Moira went to search the coat rack for a waterproof. 'Here – wear this,' she said, handing him Graham's old grey fishing jacket. 'I don't know what you must think of us all. It's not usually like this.'

Jack had his dark green anorak on and was tying the cords of the hood around his face. 'Anyone else? We'll need more than the two of us, I think.'

'I'll help but I have to change this skirt,' Stella said, nipping up the stairs.

'There's no way I'm doing it,' muttered Amy, arms crossed.

'Why not, it'll be fun!' said Gus, swamped in the massive grey jacket with a million pockets. 'I grew up on a farm. I've seen a lot of shit.'

'Not a chance.' Amy shook her head. 'It's poo. I don't want to see poo.'

'Probably your poo.' Gus grinned.

Amy gasped. 'That's disgusting.'

Sonny sniggered.

Gus opened the door, still smiling.

Stella returned in jeans and started rummaging on the coat rack for her turquoise rain jacket. 'Mum, are you coming?'

Moira made a face and gave a little shake of her head.

Stella zipped up. 'But you know where everything is better than us.'

'They'll work it out, Mum,' Amy said, coming to stand next to Moira. 'We can stay in here.'

Both Amy and Stella knew their mother would never go outside and deal with the septic tank. That was their dad's department. Moira stayed in and made the tea and toast for when it was all dealt with and then thrust the Fairy liquid at their dad to wash his hands outside.

Amy gave her mum a little in-cahoots nudge, like they'd be able to peer out at the garden together, all cosy inside, quietly chuffed that they weren't getting wet and looking at poo, her mother opening the window every now and then to shout instructions.

But then suddenly, after some hesitant dillydallying, Moira pushed her shoulders back and said, 'Yes. Yes, I do know where everything is.' And marched towards her wellingtons.

Amy looked bereft. Like her mother was acting off-script. She wanted her inside with her by the window not belting up her Joules 'Marine Navy' quilted jacket.

Stella was tying up her hair. 'Kids, you stay inside with Amy.'

'But I wanna see the poo,' Sonny whined.

Stella shook her head.

Then Gus chipped in and said, 'Let the kid see the poo.'

Everyone was momentarily silent.

Gus looked embarrassed, like he'd said something casually that had been taken much more seriously than expected.

But this stranger's voice amongst the mix was enough to pull Stella up short.

'OK, Sonny, get your boots on,' Stella said and Sonny did a celebratory fist pump that he immediately looked like he regretted.

The thunder had rolled into the distance but still cracked loud enough to make Frank Sinatra whimper.

'I'll look after you,' Rosie whispered, kneeling down and hugging the dog's neck.

Sonny yanked on one of the cagoules from the peg and dashed outside.

'You can look after me, too, Rosie,' said Amy, going to kneel by her and the dog, jumping when the thunder clapped again. Rosie put the arm not cuddling the dog round Amy and squeezed her tight.

Then Gus appeared in the doorway, back from the pouring rain. 'Amy, we need torches. Can you get them? I'm soaked.'

Amy sighed, moving away from Rosie's cute little embrace to start opening and shutting kitchen drawers. 'I don't know where they are...'

The rain outside seemed to get louder. The lightning now in sheets across the sky. The heavy heat of the day rising like a volcano in the darkness.

Gus was hopping from one foot to the other, waiting, clicking his fingers. In the garden Jack was swearing as he tried to prise up the manhole, rain pounding.

Amy was panicking trying to find the torches. Feeling under pressure, she rushed about the kitchen and living room, finally finding them in a box under the telephone. 'Here you go,' she said, bundling two heavy Maglites and a head torch into Gus's hands.

'You two all right in here?' he asked, pushing the torches into his pockets then pulling his hood back up again, his jacket way too big, hair slicked in rats' tails on his head.

'Fine,' said Amy, tone curt, as if she was put out by the question.

Gus laughed. 'Enjoy it. It's fun.'

Amy threw him her best disdainful stare before slamming the door shut with a flick of her wrist.

CHAPTER 13

It must have been about teatime. Moira had envisioned herself serving a summer berry tart with clotted cream and maybe doing the crossword, certainly not standing outside with rain-soaked jeans clinging to her legs. The Joules jacket was holding up well, she would write that on the website product review they were constantly chasing her for. Currently, she was getting ready to shine a torch into the septic tank once Gus and Sonny, who were on their hands and knees, managed to lift the manhole cover. Rain was making the task awkward. Jack and Stella were standing in the drive, Jack with Graham's arm-length black gloves on screwing the drainage rods together to make one huge stick that he would plunge through the drain to clear any blockage – or at least that's what Moira had seen Graham do out of the window in the past and presumed it was nothing more complicated than that. Stella heaved the lid off the small drain cover at their end. 'Oh, Jesus Christ,' she turned around and made gagging noises at the floor.

'Is it bad, darling?' Moira shouted, wiping rain from her face with the back of her hand.

'It's disgusting,' Stella coughed, 'it's the most disgusting smell I've ever smelt.'

Gus and Sonny snorted with laughter below her.

'You wait,' Moira said to them, pointing to their manhole cover, 'it'll be here when you lift that up.' She found herself smiling as well. When Graham did this it wasn't a laughing matter, it was all very serious and stressful. He got very annoyed when it didn't go to plan. Gus and Sonny, however, seemed to have lightened the mood for everyone. Gus mainly, she thought. He injected a bit of humour that had been long missing from the Whitethorn brigade. He allowed things to be funny.

She wondered if Graham would be laughing, were he here. No probably not, because they would have had a massive argument about how this could have happened in the first place, and she would have sent him out to fix it alone.

Gus said, 'OK, heave, Sonny!'

'It's like World's Strongest Man!' Sonny panted, rain dripping down his face.

'And what a lame episode it would be,' Gus replied, voice strained with effort as they tried to lift the massive slab of metal. 'Oh God, I think you've frightened my muscles away.'

Sonny laughed and dropped his end of the manhole.

'Don't let it fall!' Moira shouted and, dropping the torch to the grass, helped them heave the rain-slicked metal lid.

The smell was atrocious.

'Oh man!' Sonny buried his face in his cagoule. 'That is savage.'

Gus turned his face away. 'That *is* savage,' he said, but then he turned back to the deep underground well. 'Quite invigorating though. Elemental.'

'No way,' said Sonny.

But Moira found herself inclined to agree, almost giddy from the noxious fumes. All her senses alert. Grounded completely in the soaking-wet present with these two chaps, neither of whom she really knew very well but who were both vastly entertaining.

It angered her if she thought of all the experiences she had missed by so tightly weaving her role in life. She had blamed Graham on more than one occasion, the years of absence as a result of his job and then later his stubborn reluctance to do anything new. She had blamed the children needing her. She had even blamed the expectations the people in the community had of her. And when, on the beach, Mitch standing with his stick, drawing the boxes in the sand, had simply blamed her, she had refused to believe him. She had done her book club, she had even joined yoga, but she still harrumphed that Graham was stifling her life. Her decision to leave him was based on it being entirely his fault. But as she looked down at Gus and Sonny shaking with laughter as they examined the full extent of the septic tank contents with the torch light, she wondered if really she had become as cossetted as Graham. Had found her equivalent of his sofa in her opinions and, as Mitch pointed out, her judgements. In her refusal to use a computer. In her inability to understand social media or the DVD player or know anything about the accounts.

She always thought of herself like a bird trapped in a cage of Graham's making, but now she wondered if perhaps they were both birds and the door had always been open but they had sat there on their perches refusing to fly away.

'Right, what now Moira? Do we just go for it with the rod?' Jack was shouting through the rain. Lightning lit up the sky behind him like a strobe.

'Yes,' she called back. 'Yes, I think so. I think that should do the trick.'

'What does it look like up there?' Stella shouted.

'Like poo soup!' Sonny shouted back.

'Blocked,' shouted Moira.

'OK, here goes,' said Jack and he started to feed the ten-foot rod into the drain in an attempt to clear any blockage. 'Shout if something happens.'

The rain was incessant. Dripping off their noses and eyelashes. The clouds pressed low and dark trapping the heat and making them sweat in their plastic anoraks. Moira had to cover her mouth from the smell. Sonny had his head buried in his raincoat. Gus was watching it all enthralled. 'Nothing yet!' he shouted.

The window of the house opened. Amy peered through. 'What's going on?' Rosie's little head squished in beside her trying to see.

Gus sat back on his haunches. 'You should join us,' he called. 'You're missing out!'

Amy made a face. 'It stinks.'

Rosie called to her brother, 'Sonny, is it fun?'

'Yeah,' he shouted back. 'It's gross but pretty fun.'

Moira looked down at the cavernous gloop of the septic tank and wondered if anyone had ever called this fun before.

Then suddenly the drainage rod appeared at their end of the drain, and along with it a torrent of all manner of disgusting things. Sonny retched onto the grass.

'Jackpot!' Gus whooped.

Sonny wiped his mouth and looked back. 'Wow.'

Gus glanced across at him. 'Now *that* is savage.'

'Properly savage.'

The sound of the window shutting was followed by the crunch of little feet on the drive as Rosie appeared next to them. 'I want to see! I want to see what's savage.'

And then along came a very reluctant Amy. Moira could hardly believe it.

'I didn't want to miss out,' Amy said with a shrug. She was wearing one of the see-through ponchos Moira kept in the box with the torches for emergencies. Amy peered into the tank. 'Yuck! Yuck! Yuck!' She covered her face. 'Yuck.' She coughed and spluttered into the flowerbed. 'You said it was fun!'

'It is fun!' said Gus.

'That is not fun.'

Jack was still going with the rod, Stella helping him. The rain eased up enough for them to wipe their faces and not be immediately drenched again. Gus gave Jack a thumbs-up that the contents of the drain seemed to be moving now, all unblocked. Sonny and Rosie were seeing how long each one of them could lean right over the tank without having to move away from the smell. Amy hovered on the sidelines, occasionally stepping forward to have a look at what was going on then immediately stepping back again, disgusted. The thunder rolled over the sea.

Jack shouted, 'I think we're done! What do you think?'

Moira said, 'Someone has to go in and flush the chain of the toilet.'

'I'll go,' Amy volunteered, clearly keen to be back indoors. She walked tentatively in slippy flip-flops back to the house. A few seconds later they heard the toilet flush and watched the water swish through the drain as it should.

'We're good!' Jack shouted.

There was a collective whoop. Sonny and Gus high-fived. Rosie did a little dance then slipped and was saved from toppling into the tank by her brother.

'I think we need to get the lid back on, pronto,' said Gus.

Amy stuck her head out of the door. 'Did it work?'

Moira nodded, overcome by a rush of pride that they had managed to navigate this task – that she had managed to navigate it. She felt the same thrill as with the downstairs renovation, of having expanded her role.

Gus and Sonny hefted the manhole cover back into place and the smell disappeared. Stella did the same her end with the little drain lid.

The air was muggy and humid. Despite the rain they pulled their hoods down and unzipped their jackets to escape the heat, relaxed now the job was done. All the lights suddenly came on as the power was restored and the inside of the house was bathed in light.

'Good job, team,' said Jack. Then he made a move to try and hug Stella with his dirty black gloves on.

'That's disgusting, go away!' Stella shouted, trying to run from him.

Jack laughed and went after her.

'Get her, Dad,' Sonny shouted.

'We'll block her off this way.' Gus jumped up so he and Sonny could make a human wall.

'Save me, Rosie,' Stella yelped, laughing, trying to escape Jack and his disgusting poo-stained gloves.

'Over here,' Amy shouted from the driveway where she had picked up the lid of a dustbin and was holding it like a shield.

Stella slipped in beside her. 'Nice one.'

Moira watched with a broad smile on her face, laughing at their antics; then she caught herself, for just an hour ago she had blamed Graham entirely for this fiasco with the septic tank and now it was done and dusted she felt a bit guilty that his going had made them experience this jollity. This bonding. All of them expanding into these new roles. Into Graham's role.

She drew in a breath, felt for the first time a wash of sadness that it had come to this. With her head down she scurried back across the driveway to the house, past Jack as he made a sign of defeat and went to wash the gloves at the outdoor tap and then peel them off. Stella ambled over to help him. Amy put the bin lid back. Inside Moira put the kettle on, as if by resuming her normal role – retrieving a stack of Emma Bridgewater side plates from the dishwasher for the summer berry tart – she could make the significance of what they had done less prominent. She could feel less like she had usurped Graham and might in part be to blame for his disappearance.

But then she watched conflicted from the window as the others messed about in the driveway – Gus trying to get Rosie to catch rainwater in her mouth, then the others following suit, even Amy and Stella, heads back, tongues out. Moira would like to be in the garden, carefree in the rain, arms outstretched. Why should she be inside feeling guilty? Where had her anger gone? It wasn't her fault, it was his, she thought, her familiar annoyance returning. One of the dotty plates slipped out of her fingers and smashed to the floor.

Stella stopped catching rain. 'You all right, Mum?' she shouted.

'Yes, yes, fine.'

Moira was on her hands and knees with the dustpan and brush when they all trooped in to see what had happened.

'Oh no, it's one of your favourites,' Amy said, looking at the broken plate pieces.

Moira had to bite back the urge to shout that it wasn't. It wasn't one of her favourites.

But the moment moved on, they were all pulling arms out of anoraks and smoothing back wet hair. Sonny and Rosie wanted their tart in front of the TV but Stella said they had to sit at the table. Jack said he might go upstairs for a shower first. Amy couldn't work out how to fold up the plastic poncho so she just scrunched it up into a ball and shoved it by the boot rack for someone – most likely Moira – to sort out later. Stella edged past the broken plate pieces and started making the tea. Gus bent down to where Moira was laying out a bit of old newspaper to wrap the china in and said, 'Do you want me to do that?'

'No!' Moira said, sharp and loud.

Gus looked taken aback.

Moira didn't know why she'd shouted.

'All right, Mum, he was only asking,' Stella laughed, her expression as if Moira was living up to her usual neurotic self.

But Moira didn't want to be seen as that self any longer. She wasn't that self. She wanted to be the woman who had been outside laughing with the boys. The one who had changed – who had got stronger and braver.

But that would mean being brave. Confronting them.

She looked at the floor, then across at Stella's feet – even those were daunting, slipped into some trendy brand of flip-flop and with pale grey nail polish that only someone like Stella could pull off. Moira's position crouched on the floor

121

suddenly felt symbolic. If it were yoga she would rise from this spot like a tree.

Stella stretched over her to get the teapot from the draining board.

Gus walked away to flop on the sofa.

Sonny asked whether he and Rosie could have chocolate ice cream with the summer berry tart.

Moira swallowed and stood up, leaving the makeshift parcel of newspaper and broken china to unfurl on the floor. She did a little cough, then said, 'I think I'm the reason he left.'

Stella paused, the kettle hovering over the pot.

Jack stopped on the stairs.

Amy glanced round from the mirror.

'Who? Dad?' Stella said. 'Why?'

Moira brushed some imaginary lint from her top, then stood with her hands on her hips in an attempt to brace herself. 'I told him that he had become a burden.' They all edged a little closer.

'He wasn't a burden to me,' Amy said quietly.

'Well, that's fine, Amy,' Moira tried not to snap, 'but for me he was.' She smoothed her hair back off her face. She could see Gus slump further down into the sofa, distancing himself from the family drama that had just a short time ago been all laughs. Moira was suddenly annoyed at herself for ruining it, for thinking she should say something. 'I don't know,' she sighed. 'I'd had enough. He had just shut down so completely. I was vacuuming around him for goodness sake.' She threw her hands up, then exhaled, feeling less brave than her imaginary self had expected her to feel when she finally unveiled all this. 'It wasn't the life I wanted. And I'm afraid I told him I was leaving him.'

Stella's jaw dropped. 'What!'

Amy gasped. 'Why?'

Moira saw Gus raise his eyes and make a face, like he was suddenly on the set of *Coronation Street*, and flinched at the airing of the family dirty linen. But she soldiered on, emboldened by the preceding events. Emboldened by her need to prove she could not only stand on her own two feet but also stand up to her family. She shook her head. 'He had just become so detached from the world. From me. We've been unhappy. I can't really say any more than that.'

She glanced to her left and saw Sonny, head hung, fingers toying with the fabric of his T-shirt. She felt terrible. She should have thought more about who was in the room before blurting out her confession, should have saved it for grown-ups only. She tried quickly to make amends. 'But goodness, I mean, if you say he's been swimming. And fishing!' She gave Sonny a wide-eyed look of surprise when his gaze flicked up momentarily. 'In retrospect I probably should have made him talk a little more, but—'

'He doesn't talk,' said Stella.

Amy started crying.

Moira sighed, wishing she'd never said anything. She searched in her pocket for a clean tissue and handed it to her.

Everyone stood awkwardly where they were.

Moira held her hands wide. 'Well, there you go. Now you know. And it's most probably the reason why he left.'

Amy blew her nose then hiccupped. Wiping her eyes, she said, 'No. I think it's maybe because of me. Because I left. I shouldn't have left.'

Moira closed her eyes for a second. 'Yes, you should have, Amy. You can't be expected to stay at home for your father.'

Amy started crying again, furiously wiping at possible mascara streaks under her eyes.

'Come on,' said Moira, picking up the tart, trying to move them all on from this. She'd said her piece, she hadn't wanted to upset everyone quite so much.

Then suddenly Sonny spoke. 'It was me. I think it was my fault,' he said, looking down at the floorboards, kicking them with his shoe. 'I got really cross with him because he was pressing the iPhone buttons all wrong. He was tapping and it wasn't doing anything.' Sonny re-enacted the movement. 'His fingers were too fat. It was too much pressure on the screen. I sighed at him. I joked that he couldn't do it cos he was old.' He pushed his hair out of his eyes and glanced up. 'Then I got annoyed cos, you know, it was frustrating. I got really annoyed. I'm sorry.' He did a big sniff like he was trying not to cry.

Moira wondered how long Sonny had been holding that to his chest. How long he'd thought that this whole thing was his fault.

'Oh, Sonny!' Moira watched as Stella swept across the kitchen and wrapped Sonny in her arms. His head pressed into her white vest, his hand giving his face a quick swipe. 'It's got nothing to do with the iPhone buttons,' she said, kissing the top of his head. 'Nothing. Do you hear me?'

Sonny nodded and pulled away from her, wiping his face with his sleeve.

She laughed. 'You silly sod.'

Gus leant across from the sofa. 'I know what you mean though, if people press those buttons wrong, phew, it's a killer.' He shook his head.

Stella gave him a look. Gus turned away, deliberately

expressionless. But Sonny laughed. Then he tugged at the hem of his T-shirt, readjusting himself back into teenage Sonny, immediately embarrassed that he'd cried.

Stella stood where she was, crossing her arms over her chest. She looked down at the floor, scuffing the boards with her flip-flop just like Sonny had, then glanced across at her mother. 'I don't think you have to blame yourself, Mum,' she said. 'At the pool Pete made it pretty clear that it was my fault. I was the one that destroyed him.'

Moira frowned. Normally she would have been in sidelong agreement but today she felt an unfamiliar rush of outrage. 'He didn't?'

Stella nodded.

There was silence. No one knew what to say. The sun fringed the black clouds like gold.

Gus said, 'Looks like you're all to blame.'

And Amy said, 'Oh my God, Gus. Shut up!'

But everyone else sort of laughed.

CHAPTER 14

That evening there was a new cosiness to the house. The septic tank ordeal and the string of confessions had brought them all together. Everyone was exhausted but more relaxed, more comfortable with each other. Moira had made a light supper which they ate dotted about the living room – the kids and Gus watching TV, Amy sitting at the kitchen counter, Jack standing forking food into his mouth quickly while his bath was running, Moira and Stella at the table with the French windows thrown open, everyone holding back on questions they were itching to ask, like they'd come in from battle and needed time to unwind.

The thunderstorm was long gone, raging somewhere out to sea. In its place was a gradually clearing sky and finally some freshness. The air warm but no longer humid, a breeze fluttered the curtain of the open dining room window bringing with it the sound of the rain-flattened sea.

Jack went up to have his bath. Rosie got ready for bed. Sonny stayed half-watching TV, half-watching Gus who was on the sofa trying to master a computer game that Sonny had downloaded on his phone. He sniggered every time Gus died.

After putting Rosie to bed, Stella sat with her mum at the long table drinking red wine and talking in hushed voices.

Amy came downstairs having taken a shower. She'd needed a break from it all. Wearing her watermelon-patterned pyjama bottoms and a white T-shirt, her hair wet from the shower, clipped back because it was too short to tie up, she felt a bit calmer. 'What are you talking about?' she said as she took a seat at the table.

'Nothing,' said Stella, dismissive. 'Wine?'

'Yes you were,' Amy felt immediately defensive, hated being shut out of their supposedly adult chats. 'No, I'm OK,' she waved the offer away.

Her mother said, 'We were talking about my decision to leave your father.'

'But you're not actually leaving him, are you? You didn't mean it,' Amy said, looking between the two of them.

Stella just shrugged.

'You can't leave. You love each other. You're our family. This is our family.' Amy felt her heart pound and wondered if it was doing any damage to the baby.

Her mother retied her hair in the tortoiseshell clip she always wore. 'We don't have to be together to be your family, Amy.'

'Yes you do,' Amy said, stubborn.

'It will be weird, Mum,' Stella said, sitting back, arms crossed, sipping her wine.

Moira looked around her to see if anyone else was hearing this. Gus and Sonny were locked to their screens. 'Does it occur to either of you to think about whether it will make me happy?'

Neither girl said anything. Amy toyed with the cord of her pyjama bottoms.

'I just don't want you to do anything rash and regret it,' Stella said in the end.

'Oh believe me, it's not rash,' Moira said, pulling over a copy of *Country Life* and viciously flicking through it.

'What about the house?' Stella said. 'You've only just done it up.'

Moira didn't look up from her flicking. 'Well, it's the perfect time to sell it then, isn't it?'

Amy gasped, her hand went to her chest. She loved this house. It meant everything to her, like a physical manifestation of her stability. It was her family, her childhood. She knew the sound the stairs made at night when as a child she thought it was the noise of monsters and as a teenager how to creep in past midnight, the sound of the grandfather clock ticking like white noise, the waves in summer, the waves in winter – nose pressed to the glass ogling the surfers. She had been bribed by Stella to creep into the dark cellar, she had played tea-parties in the back garden, she had been kissed against the cool grey bricks of the outside wall.

This house was one of them. It had been where she had run to when Bobby died, black tears seeping into the stone. She had sat crippled by the claustrophobic quagmire of grief at the top of the stairs, on the toilet floor, in the spider-ridden garage with her face pressed against the muddy wheel of Bobby's motorbike. There was an essence of Bobby here, an essence of her. It held too much of them to merely pop up on Rightmove and then be gone. But more than any of that, she felt that she would be needing to run back again very soon. Her default vision of the early days with baby were of it crawling across this living room rug, her parents the scaffolding for her unknown foray into motherhood. She couldn't do it on her own, and she sure as hell didn't want to do it with Gus.

'Please don't sell the house,' Amy almost whispered.

Her mother sighed as she flicked the magazine pages. 'Let's not talk about it any more.'

Stella raised a brow and then took a silent sip of her wine, one hand running over the gold S on her chain, back and forth over and over.

Moira looked up. 'Let's talk about something else. Amy, when did you have your hair cut?'

'A while ago,' Amy muttered, deliberately non-committal to punish her mother for deigning to talk to her after unveiling such traitorous plans. She sat pushing sulkily at her cuticles.

'I like it,' Stella said.

Amy looked up and made a face. 'It's awful. It's too short. I look like a boy.'

'You don't look like a boy!' her mum said, shaking her head as if Amy always managed to surprise her with the stupidity of her comments. 'You look beautiful.'

Amy tugged a strand of the hair. She hated it. She hated its choppiness, its fluffiness, and its white blondeness – and more than that, she hated what it represented.

'Why d'you do it, then?' Stella asked.

Amy shrugged. 'Just cos.'

But of course it wasn't just cos. It should have been a major movie moment. She'd been in London a month before she walked into Toni & Guy for the chop.

When she'd first arrived in the city, she'd never have believed she was capable of such a dramatic restyle. She'd moved to London in an impulsive whirlwind after her mum had booted her out. The suggestion that after two years grieving it might be time to start thinking about living a little had felt like a hammer blow. Amy cringed now when she thought of all her flouncing and foot-stamping snot and tears. In retrospect she could grudgingly see that it probably was the best thing for her, but she'd never admit that to her mother.

Answering the Gumtree ad for a flatshare, she'd had aspirations of a glamourous central London apartment. But it had turned out to be a box room in a flat above a cab company in a grotty Hammersmith side street with two girls – Kat and Cath, who had matching pastel pink balayage through their blonde hair and called themselves the KittyCats. She'd arrived with two suitcases, all her other possessions in boxes in her mum and dad's attic. All her married life packed up and labelled. She'd got a temping job in Leicester Square designing in-house promotional materials for an Icelandic shipping company. Her first night she'd wept on her single bed nearly the whole night, listening to the cabbies laughing and smoking outside her window, then she'd been woken up by a tramp vomiting on the doorstep. If she hadn't made such a fuss with her mother she'd have got the first coach straight back to Cornwall.

The KittyCats were hardly ever home, they'd leave scrawled notes to join them at some club, which for Amy, who hadn't been out clubbing since she'd got married and had spent the best part of the last two years snuggled up on the sofa with her dad, was all a bit daunting. It had led to a lonely first week. When quizzed over breakfast – a KittyCat Eat Clean Smoothie Special – about her life to date, Amy lied that she'd just split up from her husband. They weren't the kind of girls you told that your husband had died, smashed on the head by his surfboard in waves that he was more than able to handle. It would have infuriated him, had he known, that that had been the cause of his death. He'd have wanted a freak super-wave not an above-average Cornish spring tide. At the funeral his best friend had stood up and said that Bobby would be happy that he'd died doing something he loved but they all knew that was a lie. If Bobby hadn't have died, his friends would have mocked him for the pathetic wipeout. Amy wished she'd stood up and said so because now it was all she remembered of the day – the whitewashing of the truth to suit the situation. She'd wanted the friend to have been brave enough to say, 'Bobs is up there kicking himself about how shit that wave was!' and everyone would have laughed. But then Amy wasn't in a position to blame anyone considering she hadn't been brave enough to stand up and speak at all. It also occurred to her that maybe Bobby wouldn't have wanted everyone to laugh, he was never very good at being the butt of a joke.

If she'd told the KittyCats any of that they wouldn't have known quite how to respond. They weren't in London to offer sympathy to a weeping widow. They were there for Tinder, #hairgoals, #fridaycocktails, Saturday morning #insanity, Saturday night #partytime.

She was pretty sure they would have rescinded the flatshare had they known about Bobby. It was the decision to lie about her past, however, that altered the course of her future. In the eyes of the KittyCats she went from being boring new house-mate to super-fun #project. They dragged her out of herself. They dressed her in their bulging wardrobes of Primark once-worns. They enrolled her in their Pineapple Studios Freestyle Hip Hop class and then chivvied her into Covent Garden bars for an #aperolspritz! And it had been more liberating than Amy had expected. It had, after a daunting first week, begun to feel like a holiday from herself. It had been the freedom and anonymity to laugh raucously, to wrangle free Prosecco at brunch by pretending they were famous YouTubers, to shop all Saturday and dress up for Saturday night, to loll hungover at her desk, to skive work for a spa day, to giggle with the safety of the KittyCats as she got cornily chatted up in clubs. It had been expectation-less.

In this heady parallel universe she had been given her twenties. A time that she had spent in her little cottage with Bobby, playing at being grown-ups. Planting wisteria to grow up round the door, baking cupcakes in a frilly-edged apron, drinking coffee in huge Central Perk mugs that they'd bought after visiting the *Friends* set on an LA road trip after honeymooning at Disneyland, and watching as Bobby built a chiminea pizza oven in the back garden while she Instagrammed it. All things she was more than happy doing, things she had never not wanted. But things that, now she wasn't doing them, seemed like a totally different world. Things that, if it meant having Bobby back, she would be happy to carry on doing forever. But things that, at moments just before she fell asleep in her London bed, she felt guilty for being pleased she wasn't doing.

The haircut had been a present from the KittyCats. A mark of her new life. They had frogmarched her into Toni & Guy and stayed to sip complimentary Prosecco and take selfies with her before and after the chop.

It was strange the idea of her dad being on Instagram. Watching them all. Viewing their lives from afar. Amy hadn't really put much of her London life up out of fear of looking to Bobby's friends at home like she might be having too much fun – only the odd snap of her smashed avocado #brunch – but it was enough to show that she was starting to move on. The photos the KittyCats had taken – posing with Amy's giant severed plait – had felt too symbolic to post on her timeline. Not least because one of the reasons she had kept her hair long was because Bobby liked it that way.

The haircut had ended up being symbolic for a completely different reason. It was before the night of her first actual Tinder date. Helped along by the frenzied cajoling of the KittyCats and an Oreo martini, that date had been with Gus.

Amy had been so repulsed by him, like she had been forced to scrape the bottom of the barrel having loved and lost the very best and he so clearly felt likewise – which she had difficulty reckoning with since she was so obviously a cut above looks-wise – that they had drowned their sorrows in a conveyer belt of a florid purple cocktail called Unicorn Tears and pints of Camden Pale Ale respectively. In the morning she had left Gus's studio apartment, scampering away while he pretended to sleep, her untameable bed-hair a white blonde puffball, and sat mortified on the tube looking like a scarecrow, silently cringing and swearing off unicorns forever.

Two months later she was knocking on his door.

Now, as she sat at the long bare-wood table with Stella across from her inspecting her hair, taking a sip of wine and saying, 'It'll grow back,' Amy realised that she didn't want it to grow back. From the moment the skinny black jean-clad stylist had held up the mirror so she could see the back, ruffling the choppy layers with insouciant disinterest at her thoughts on his masterpiece, she had wanted her hair back to exactly how it had been before. But her internal recoil at the mention of it growing back now made her realise for the first time that back wasn't where she wanted to go. She wasn't the girl in the cottage any more and this cut might come with its own host of problems but it was nothing compared to keeping waist-length waves under control, especially when your husband liked it when you wore it loose.

She heard Gus swear at the video game. She rested her hand on her stomach. The problem was that where she was right now wasn't where she wanted to be either.

'I'm pregnant,' she said, unable to hold it in any longer.

Gus flinched. The video game made the noise of someone violently dying.

Her mother's hand stilled on the *Country Life*. 'Oh my goodness!'

Stella snorted into her red wine, making it splash up onto her face.

Amy sat very still, watching the expressions around her.

Stella wiped her face with her hand. 'And Gus is the—' she asked, nodding in the direction of the sofa where Gus was half standing up, one hand in his pocket, not quite sure whether he should stay where he was or join the group.

Amy nodded. 'Yes.'

Gus stood up straight. 'Yes.'

A flash of pleasure crossed Stella's face like finally it all fitted into place.

'He doesn't want me to have it,' Amy said.

Gus jumped to his own defence. 'I didn't say that!'

'Yes you did,' Amy snapped.

Gus chewed on his bottom lip for a second. Hands in his

pockets he started to cross the room to where they were sitting at the table. 'OK, yes I did. But I don't want to look like the bad guy here.' His hand went to his chest. He stopped by the armchair, leaning against it, not quite brave enough to join them. 'We don't know each other. It's the most obvious suggestion.' He looked at Stella and Moira to see if they agreed. Neither of them said anything.

'Yeah well, you don't have to have anything to do with it,' Amy said, not looking at him then sitting forward, chin resting on her hands, eyes downcast.

'Oh Jesus, it's my kid. I'm not gonna not have anything to do with it.' Gus scratched his forehead, then glancing at the others sitting at the table, added, 'I feel like we should have this conversation more privately.'

Stella picked up her wine and started to stand up. 'Absolutely. Yes. You do that.'

'I don't want to have it privately,' Amy said. 'I get confused when I talk to you. I want my mum here.'

Gus stood awkwardly, hands still in his pockets. Stella ducked in front him like she was trying to avoid being in a photograph. 'Sonny.' She clicked her fingers. 'Bed. Now.'

Sonny seemed relieved to be given the opportunity to slope away and they both disappeared up the stairs.

Amy sat beside her mother at the table. She wanted her to tell Gus to stop being mean to her daughter. In the absence of her father, she wanted her to help sort it all out.

Moira cleared her throat, glanced down at the magazine for a second, then looking back to Amy said, 'Darling, this has to be a decision you make between the two of you.'

Amy frowned. That wasn't what she was meant to say. Amy glared at her. 'But we can't.'

Moira closed the magazine and stood up. Beside her the breeze ruffled the curtain, she leant across and closed the window then, turning back to her daughter, said, 'Amy darling, I will help you however I can, but this is your life and this needs to be between you and Gus here.' Moira gestured towards where Gus was standing like a teenager, scuffing the wooden floor with his foot. 'And the only way that is going to happen is if you talk to each other, which, let's be honest, I haven't seen you do much since you got here.' Moira picked up her wine in one hand and tucking her magazine under her arm she gave Amy a kiss on the top of her head. 'I'm going to go and take the dog for a quick walk then go to bed.' She paused as if trying to work out how best to say the next bit. In the end she said, 'Thank you for telling us your news.'

Then she walked away, touching Gus briefly on the arm as she went past. The dog, who'd been asleep on the sofa, jumped down and padded behind her as she slipped on some shoes and quietly opened the front door.

Silence filled the room, stretching like bubblegum till it was almost impossible to speak.

Amy was about to push back her chair and storm off upstairs when Gus moved to stand at the end of the table.

'Why did you tell me, Amy?' He narrowed his eyes as he stared at her. 'Why not just never have let me know?'

Amy swallowed. She wanted to open the window again, the air was too warm. 'I don't know,' she said, shaking her head. Why had she told him? At the time the need had been overwhelming. Positive Clear Blue: tube to Gus's door. She had berated herself for it a number of times since. But it had been, she knew, a knee-jerk reaction to have someone else share the burden. She wasn't stupid, she knew full well that she'd spent her whole life with someone else in charge while she cruised through in the passenger seat. It was a sorry realisation that the few weeks she had been in charge she had ended up pregnant.

Gus took her answer at face value and nodded a couple of times, before turning away towards the stairs.

Bobby would have wrapped her in a huge hug, smelling of the Acqua di Giò Homme she'd bought him for his birthday.

The cloud of a sulk was on the cusp of engulfing her. One that would see her sit silently staring at the table until Gus left. But then, a little like Clark Kent changing to Superman, her mind vortexed towards the baby inside her. It was all she could see. She shifted in her seat. She realised that in telling Stella and her mum she had made it real. It was still a problem and a worry and a God-awful mess but it was real – it was a baby with hair and teeth and nails, or possibly not but with the potential to have hair and teeth and nails at some point soon. Right now it was probably something very unglamorous like a bean or a mange tout. The fact she'd thought of a mange tout made her smile. She looked away so Gus wouldn't see.

She heard him walk across the rug and pick up his phone from the table, she turned to watch him slip it into his back pocket and head towards the stairs.

'I told you because I didn't want to deal with it on my own,' she said, frankness a seeming by-product of the sudden radiating power of this mange tout foetus. 'I've never been very good at doing things on my own.'

Gus turned, he pushed his hair back from his face with his

hand. 'I would never make you get rid of it,' he said. 'God, I don't even know how I'd make you do something.' He crossed back to the centre of the room. 'I'll do whatever you want. You may not like me but I am a good person, Amy.'

'I never said I didn't like you,' she said, immediately defensive.

He scoffed, 'Please. We're clearly not in each other's fan club.'

Amy ran her tongue across her top lip, she had to concede to that. 'No.'

He went and sat on the arm of the armchair, held his hair back from his forehead again – it made his face look really thin and his nose really pointy and his eyes really wide. She tried her hardest not to focus on what he looked like, on which one of these less aesthetic elements the baby might inherit. But it made her wish, not for the first time, that this was Bobby's baby. She imagined the glowing, golden child that they had wished for but had never been able to conceive. The mop of blond hair it would have had. The olive skin. The smile. The two adoring parents.

She fished around for something to say. 'Have you ever been a member of a fan club?' she asked, then inwardly cringed at the ridiculousness of the question.

Gus raised his brows in surprise and laughed. He let go of his hair and it flopped back almost over his eyes. 'Actually, yes. Well more of an appreciation society.'

'Oh yeah. What for?'

'Strepsils.'

Amy made a face. 'What, for the cough sweet? There's no such thing.'

'There wasn't until me and my friend Wayne Wilcox set it up in third form.'

She laughed despite herself. 'Why would you set up a Strepsil fan club?'

'Because they're amazing,' he said as if it were obvious. 'They're like the high priest of the lozenge.'

'Why?'

'Everything about them. The roundness, the stickiness, that thing they get where they cut your tongue if you suck them too long.'

Amy shook her head. 'That's ridiculous.'

He shrugged.

'I always preferred a Tune,' she said.

'I'll try not to be offended.'

They sat in silence again. The waves rumbling in the background. The howl of a fox. The timid little yap of Frank Sinatra. Then the door opening and her mother coming back, trying really hard to be stealthy but getting caught up in the plastic poncho that Amy hadn't put away earlier and swearing under her breath. 'Sorry, sorry,' she said, with a quick, embarrassed wave of her hand. Then she grabbed her wine and magazine and ushered the dog quickly up the stairs.

More silence followed.

Gus asked, 'Have you ever been in a fan club?'

'My Little Pony,' Amy replied.

He nodded. 'Figures.'

She didn't even bother to act insulted. It did figure. She ran her nail down one of the wood grooves in the table. 'What's your surname?'

'Andrews.'

Amy nodded.

A car drove past lighting up the kitchen.

Gus got up from the armchair and came and sat in the seat opposite Amy, where Stella had been. There was still a ring of red wine on the table. 'What was that woman's name in the end?' he asked. 'You know, from the Londis.'

Amy frowned. 'Do you actually care?'

Gus shrugged a shoulder. 'I'm intrigued.'

'Ethel.'

'Classic.' Gus laughed.

Amy felt a smatter of pleasure from having made him laugh. 'She wasn't actually called Ethel,' she said. 'She was called Claire.'

Gus looked confused, like he couldn't quite believe she had it in her to make a joke.

Amy raised her brows in challenge of the fact.

Gus looked away, lips downturned, still clearly surprised.

'Why did you play Barbie with Rosie?' Amy asked.

He dabbed his finger in the red wine ring on the table, seeing how far the droplet would stretch. 'Because seven-year-olds are easy company. I don't really know anyone here and it's a fairly awkward situation to come into, so...' He glanced up at her. 'What can I say, I'm a big fan of Rosie's.'

Amy too was a big fan of Rosie's. She found her easier to hang out with than the adults talking about proper things she really should know more about. 'You have brothers and sisters?'

'Five,' said Gus.

Amy was shocked. 'Wow!'

Gus said, 'Yeah. Busy parents,' with a raise of one brow.

'You want a big family?'

'Not particularly.'

It was weird, having to ask polite questions to someone whose baby she was carrying. Someone she had spent a few days with total in her life.

'Do you want a glass of water?' Gus asked, standing up to go over to the kitchen.

If it had been Amy getting the water she knew she wouldn't have offered one to him. 'Yeah, OK.'

He came back with two of the Emma Bridgewater spotty mugs. 'I couldn't find the glasses.'

'They're next to the mugs.' She shook her head in disbelief.

'Oh.' Gus shrugged like he wasn't really that bothered whether it was a glass or a mug anyway.

Amy sipped her lukewarm water. He hadn't run the tap before pouring.

'Amy?' he said.

'Yes.'

'What do you do?'

'What, like for a job?'

'Yeah.'

She reclipped her hair. 'I'm a graphic designer.'

'Really?' Gus looked taken aback.

'What do you do?'

'I work in IT.'

That sounded extremely boring to Amy so she didn't ask any more. Instead she said, 'What did you think I'd be?'

Gus shrugged. 'I hadn't really thought about it.'

Amy checked her reflection in the window, taking the clip out again because it wasn't right. 'Yes, you had,' she said, kirby grip between her teeth.

Gus looked a bit awkward. 'I suppose I er—'

'What?' She put the clip in, checked her reflection again then sat back and stared at him.

His neck flushed red. 'I suppose I er— I suppose I couldn't really imagine you in a job.' He cleared his throat, then he said, 'I misjudged you.'

'Well, there you go,' she said, aloofly matter-of-fact. But the victory was bittersweet considering she had spent the last however many years not working.

When Amy hadn't been able to get pregnant, Bobby had suggested that it might help if she took some time out. Especially as all she did was moan about her advertising agency job being too stressful. He was earning good money through sponsorship, enough to support them both. It had felt, at the time, like a dream come true.

Bobby had a way of making her dreams come true – the surprise birthday flight to Tenerife when he'd packed her bags and everything, the footprints on the beach that, from the cliff looking down, spelt out Will You Marry Me? – he made her feel like a princess. Gus, incidentally, also made her feel like a princess, in a completely different way. She had never felt quite so embarrassed of herself before.

She thought of her job at the Icelandic fishing company back in Leicester Square. Of how, once she'd got over how dull the product was, she'd quite enjoyed the work. Or rather, she'd enjoyed the compliments she had got for the work. They were currently in talks about whether they might alter her contract from temporary to full-time. She realised then that she hoped that they would. She enjoyed the sense of belonging and achievement more than she'd allowed herself to acknowledge. Perhaps because part of her felt a little traitorous, like she was saying that being 'Bobby's girl' wasn't enough.

Gus pushed his chair back. 'Well,' he said, putting his hands back in his pockets, edging from one foot to the other awkwardly. 'That was a good talk.'

Amy half-laughed, unsure that was how she would describe it. 'Yeah.'

'OK, well, I'm going to bed.'

She nodded. 'OK.'

He walked away, across the living room and up the stairs two at a time. Then, when she thought he'd gone, he poked his head over the bannister. 'I'm glad, you know, that you told everyone. It's been really weird them not knowing why I'm here.'

Amy hadn't at any point thought about how that might feel for him. 'Oh right, yeah. Sorry about that.'

Gus shook his head. 'I didn't mean it like it needed an apology, just— It's a relief it's out in the open.'

She nodded. It was a relief. Less a huge weight of secret pressure. Less a mass of anticipated reactions. Just less big. She felt her shoulders relax a touch as she exhaled. 'Night,' she said.

He paused. 'Yeah. Night.'

CHAPTER 15

In Jack and Stella's bedroom it was all dramatic whispers and gesticulations as she told him about Amy being pregnant. Jack was in his dressing gown, having just got out of the bath, sitting on the side of the bed, expression astounded. 'I could safely say that is the last possible thing I thought was going on between the two of them.'

Stella had the satisfied glow of having told someone an awesome piece of gossip. She sat on the other side of the bed to pull off her jeans. 'I know, right.'

Jack shook his head. Then he twisted round, hand on the slightly crumpled sheet, and said, 'It was nice, earlier, to see you with Sonny.'

Stella unclipped her necklace and earrings so she was just in a white vest and knickers. 'I felt sorry for him,' she said, remembering the feel of his head against her chest, the smell of his hair.

Jack looked at her, examining her expression. 'It's not a weakness, Stel – to love your son.'

'I know!' she said. 'I know that.' She walked towards the bathroom. At the door she paused and added, 'But loving someone doesn't mean you let them slump around the house with a massive attitude problem. Jack, he's so sullen, quite often Rosie and I go out to escape him.'

Jack nodded. 'He's a teenager.'

'Yeah, well that only counts so much.'

Stella started brushing her teeth. From where she stood at the sink, she watched Jack go and peer out of the window at the dark sky. Saw him sigh like he was trying but failing to fix things. She rinsed her mouth and walked over to join him. Put her hand on his back.

'There are loads of stars,' he said, opening the window further so they could both get their heads out to see.

She had grown up with those stars, the jet-black sky splattered with a billion dots of white. This was no London sky. This was infinity. A view that in the past had told her it was OK – the world stretched beyond this bedroom, this village, these expectations. That there was more.

Right now, however, the vastness of the universe made her feel uneasy. Small and insignificant. Perhaps she was just unnerved by her mother's confession that she was leaving. At how easily things set in stone could be unset. But as she turned to look at Jack's profile, lit by the bedroom sidelights, she felt compelled to say something.

Stella had never been very good at saying how she felt. At saying good things – maybe it was a side effect of the hard-won praise of Pete and her father, or maybe she was more like Potty-Mouth than she realised. But she swallowed and said, 'I never told you what I appreciate about you.'

She watched Jack smile in profile. 'That's OK, Stel.'

She looked out over the shadowy garden, the moon highlighting the giant gunnera leaves, the cliff edge, frosting the tips of the waves. 'I appreciate the stability you bring to our family.'

Jack glanced across at her.

She caught his eye and half-smiled. 'I appreciate that today you could step in and do all that with those rods and gross stuff. That you just did it. I suppose I appreciate that you're the proper one. But in a good way.' She ran her finger across the back of his hand where it rested on the window frame. 'I appreciate that you're one of the goodies' —she turned so she was leaning against the sill, eyes smiling— 'like in a Western. Like THE goodie. You're John Wayne.'

Jack's cheeks flushed, he looked embarrassed.

'You're blushing,' she laughed, touching his skin where it had pinked.

He put his hand over hers. 'Well—' He coughed, lost for anything to say. 'I er—'

'There's other stuff,' she cut in, 'that I appreciate. That you're considerate, and you don't lie and you don't get angry. And you put up with my family. But that's the stuff right now. That's what today made me feel.'

Jack nodded. Then he moved away from the window. 'That's all very nice to hear.'

Stella felt suddenly embarrassed. Schoolgirlish. Like she'd exposed too much of herself. 'Good,' she said.

He smiled.

She smiled. Then as Jack started to pull back the sheet on the bed, Stella said, 'Maybe we should get on with having some of this sex we're supposed to be having.'

'Remind me how much sex we're meant to be having,' Jack said, hands on his dressing-gowned hips.

She tipped her head. 'It's meant to be every day.'

'Every day!' Jack whistled.

Stella grinned.

'Right,' he said. 'Well, good job I'm the real-life equivalent of John Wayne then, isn't it?' And he yanked her towards him like a cowboy hero. She stumbled on the edge of the curtain. 'Oh sorry, are you OK?' he asked, immediately letting her go and bending to check where she was rubbing her stubbed toe.

'Yes, I'm fine.'

Jack made a face. 'That wasn't very John Wayne, was it?'

Stella shook her head and laughed. 'It's OK, I don't fancy John Wayne.'

'OK good. Good.' He took hold of her hand, gentle and polite. 'Let's get into bed before there's any more injuries.'

It was good sex. Good in-the-bed sex. They had always had good sex – when they had it. This had been a bit odd though – like they were doing it for a scene in a movie. Jack uncharacteristically attentive and tender, whispering to her which made her want to laugh but he seemed really serious so she didn't. It was like learnt-from-the-TV sex. Like he was trying to live up to the person she'd just praised him for being. But even so, despite her stifled giggles, it was good. Made her think they should do it more often. It was always less of a hassle than she remembered.

CHAPTER 16

'Ow! What are you doing?' Stella opened her eyes, disorientated. Jack was poking her shoulder to wake her up. It felt like the middle of the night. 'What's going on? Is it the kids?'

'No, it's not the kids. Don't worry, nothing's going on.' Jack was sitting up next to her, T-shirt rumpled.

'What time is it?' Stella reached for her watch. 'Jack, it's four o'clock in the morning. What are you doing?'

'I have to talk to you,' he said, face set, like he'd been sitting waiting for a while.

Stella squinted at him. Struggled to sit up. She could taste exhaustion. She could even vaguely remember her dream.

'I do lie,' he said, turning to look at her, swallowing.

Stella was confused, still half-suspended in sleep she felt caught on the back foot. 'Let me put some clothes on,' she said, pulling on a T-shirt and pants from her case on the floor. Then, tying up her hair and sitting back next to him, she said, 'What are you talking about?'

'You said I didn't lie and that I was the proper one. But I do lie and I'm not the proper one. I'm a fraud.'

Stella rubbed her eyes. She was awake now. 'Why are you a fraud?' she asked, bracing herself. Preparing for him to ask for a divorce, to admit to an affair, to say he liked wearing her underwear, to say anything. Something that was about to upturn the preceding calm – that wasn't calm at all but now felt calmer in light of this moment.

Jack was looking down, pleating the sheet between his fingers.

She thought about the adoring, whispering sex. It suddenly seemed such an obvious precursor to an admittance of guilt, the joke on her now.

Maybe he knew where her dad was. Maybe they had chatted on the phone, discussed a plan. Maybe it was just that Jack had finally cracked under the weight of subterfuge.

That didn't seem so bad. She could handle that. Yes. That seemed the obvious answer.

'I got made redundant,' he said, letting go of the perfect neat sheet folds.

'When?' she frowned.

'A couple of months ago.'

'Months!' Stella couldn't believe it.

Jack nodded.

'Shit, Jack. Why didn't you tell me?'

He didn't say anything.

Stella rubbed her forehead. 'I don't understand – I don't see why you'd— A couple of months. What have you been doing every day?' She was flabbergasted. All she could see was him making his cheese and pickle sandwiches, packing his apple and Hula Hoops, and heading out of the door at 7.45 every morning. 'Shit. Why didn't I know? How much money do we have? Do we have enough money?' she asked.

'It's tight,' he said.

Stella retied her hair, pulling it right on top of her head in a bun. She thought of their lovely South London house, their nice tidy little life slipping away. She took a deep breath. 'It's OK. It'll be OK. We'll just have to sell the house. That's OK. Did you get a payoff? Have you been looking for other work? Did anyone else go? Was it just you?'

'Stella. Stop.' He held his hands up.

Stella stopped. She closed her mouth. She looked at him, really looked at him. His brown hair – usually perfectly combed and parted – was messy, his eyes looked the kind of tired that she'd only seen before when the kids were newborn, in his T-shirt and boxers he looked under-dressed – without armour, without the turned-out trappings she expected to see him in. He didn't look like the proper one. He looked like the exhausted one.

It was Stella's turn to pick at the sheet. 'Just tell me if we need to sell the house.'

'I don't know. Maybe. Not just yet.' He put his hands on top of his head. 'I don't know.'

Stella nodded. She knew she needed to ask again why he hadn't told her but she didn't want to. All the clues were there that she wouldn't like the answer. That while this was about him, it was definitely about to reflect badly on her.

After a silence she said, 'Jack, why didn't you tell me?'

His hands flopped down from his head to rest on his bent-up knees. 'I don't know.'

It was sort of easier, for now, to pretend that was true. 'Well,' she said. 'We need to come up with a plan.'

Jack nodded.

She looked at her hand and realised it was shaking.

Then Jack said, 'I think that's why I didn't tell you.'

'Why – because I'd make a plan?'

He nodded. 'Because I knew you would make me act on it. Do something. And I didn't want to do anything.' He stared at her, resigned. 'I think I understand why your dad's gone. It's just for—' He exhaled, confused like he couldn't quite explain. 'For the break. For the break from life. From expectation. Stella, you like me because I'm responsible.'

'I don't.' She could feel panic fluttering inside her.

He shrugged like there was no point arguing but he knew it was true.

She looked at her hands and the concertinaed sheet. There was a safety in knowing Jack was the rock of their family. She'd even said it herself. He brought the stability, a regularity of income – she did well but the steadiness of her cash flow was less reliable. He made sure their monetary base was solid. He gave good 'dad-time', he played squash on a Wednesday, he emptied the dishwasher and took the rubbish out, he knew about wine. He was the all-round good guy.

'And you like control,' he said, arms wide, his expression like he'd started this so he may as well go the whole hog. 'You'd have tried to fix it.'

Stella gasped. 'I do not like control.'

'Oh come on, Stella.'

'What do I control? My life's a shambles. I have a whole column dedicated to the fact my life is a shambles.'

'Yeah, and you make half of it up!' he said, voice raised in exasperation. 'Stella, the fact you have a column in the first place proves that it isn't a shambles at all.'

Stella crossed her arms over her chest. 'Name me a time that

I like being in control,' she said, eyebrows raised, expression challenging.

'OK, fine,' Jack snapped. 'With Sonny. You're controlling with Sonny. You completely take over as the parent. So it's basically your way or no way. And sometimes your expectations of people are too high because your expectation of yourself is too high.' He was doing the emphatic hand movements he'd been taught on an away-day presentation course, Stella rolled her eyes, more so she could shy away from his accusation. 'Maybe I don't want to parent the way you parent,' Jack went on, pointing to himself, 'but I get no choice. And to be honest, yes, I'm fine with you as the main parent, but you have to accept the responsibility of fault. Sonny did not need to be sent away – it was too much. We could have sorted it at home as a family. You just jumped in and you couldn't back down.'

When he finished all the words seemed to hang in the air like washing on a line.

'Wow.' Stella blinked. 'So this is all my fault?'

'No, I'm not saying that.' He sighed, looking across at the curtains and then back again. 'I don't know what I'm saying.'

He looked a bit scared. Stella felt a bit scared.

Outside was a dusky darkness, sunrise waiting in the wings.

'I didn't mean all that,' Jack said, immediately backtracking.

It was Stella's turn to stare blankly. She'd been fast asleep not so long ago. 'This is a nightmare,' she said, looking at her pillow, knowing that it was more than likely she wouldn't sleep again tonight. She looked at Jack, huffed a sort of laugh as she said, 'You know the next one on the MOT list was "Air your grievances". You jumped ahead.'

Jack wasn't smiling.

Neither was Stella.

She pulled her hair out of the band. 'Looks like the bloody Marriage MOT finds out we're a write off.'

'I'm sorry,' Jack said. 'I shouldn't have said all that. I'm tired. Stressed.' He rubbed his face with his hand. 'I am glad I told you though. About the job. I wanted to. I just didn't.'

He felt a bit like a stranger. Not her husband and the father of her two kids.

'I think maybe I need to go to sleep,' he said.

Stella nodded. 'OK.'

She wanted to say: You arsehole. This was your problem. Your lie. And somehow now it's all my fault.

Jack had slithered down the bed, his eyes three-quarters closed, trying but failing to stay awake. Stella watched the moment he slipped into sleep, like she had watched Sonny and Rosie as babies.

She sat staring at him. This lump of slumbering human who had just shaken her upside down then left her there suspended.

She too was starting to understand why her father had gone. Her every urge was to stand up and walk away. To leave this mess, these accusations. It was too heavy, too confusing, too unfixable.

The sky lightened through the gap in the curtains. She could hear the sound of the birds alongside the waves. She sat looking at Jack a little longer, unable to believe he'd hidden this double life from her. His arm moved across and touched hers. She moved away. She tried to shut her eyes but couldn't stand the darkness. In the end, she got up, pulled on her shorts, and left the room.

CHAPTER 17

The early morning sky was the pale pink of roses. Mist hovered over the water. The yellow crescent of the sun like butter on the horizon, all trace of yesterday's rain long gone. Stella could feel damp sand squish between her toes. The tide was out, lines of flotsam left in its wake; shells, seaweed, bottle tops, sea glass. She picked up a bright blue piece as she walked, the smooth edges soft in her hand, round like a pebble, then she chucked it as far as she could throw. The cool of the morning chilled her skin, the hairs on her body tingled, the smell of the salt in the air caught her breath with memory.

She walked and walked out towards the water, perfect footprints in a line behind her, only stopping when she was calf-deep in the sea, tiny white horses lapping round her ankles. The cold pierced her skin, raw and sharp, then almost immediately dulled as she acclimatised, a pattern repeated every footstep deeper.

She tried not to think of Jack as she stared out at the horizon. She brought her hands up to her face, over her eyes. It felt almost like he'd had an affair. A double life that made everything they had done the last few months a lie. How could she have tripped through it so blasé, so unsuspecting.

She wondered if this would be the death of them. Imagined packing up her things, Rosie clinging to her side. Sonny would probably choose to stay with Jack. And the gulf between them would widen. It would feel less like her place to run and hold Sonny's head to her chest when he was about to cry. Stella took her hands from her face. She felt grey. Tired. She felt like the sand slipping away beneath her feet with the ebb and flow of the tide. She tried to grab it with her toes but still it slithered away.

She stared out at the white horizon of the sun-bleached sea. The rolling tide had brought with it the sharp memory of standing here every morning at six with her dad. Every day whatever the weather. A Tesco bag of Marmite sandwiches and a Thermos of tea on the shore. Two towels. Two dressing gowns. Standing in the surf, pulling her swimming hat on, spitting in her goggles to stop them fogging, rinsing them in sea water, adjusting them, her dad by her side doing the same. The summer sea calm and languid around their ankles, arms skating over the glassy surface, sun warm on their backs. And then the bitter menace of winter. The press of the waves, the gasp for air, the breathless dive through icy grey waves.

Standing here now she couldn't believe she had done it. The cold of the water on this early summer morning made her want to back away. Her teenage self would mock her – say she was old and cosseted. But Stella could see no benefit to hurling herself into what was no more than a block of melted ice.

Her brain gave her a little test, tried to make her dive but her body stayed where it was.

The feeling bowled her backwards to another time she had stayed put. The British National Swimming Championships, the final selection race for the Olympic team. Another moment she had been poised ready to spring, where she had tried to will her body to dive against its will. She saw the view of the swimming pool as she stood on the blocks. The turquoise of the water, the smell of the chlorine. She could feel the nerves of the people next to her, the girls she'd raced and beaten year in, year out. She felt the nerves of her father on the side. Saw him already visualising the Olympic Stadium, the tour bus, the scoreboard, the medal podium. This was it for him – this wouldn't be any normal coaching job. This would be reliving the Olympic dream. The glory. Reliving it through her. This would be pride born out of blood. His daughter, there in no small part because of him. She could be as good if not greater, that's what people said. And she had been one swim away. One dive into that rippling turquoise blue. Everything they had worked for. Every morning. Every evening. Every nutritionally balanced meal. Every holiday – always Portugal because they had an Olympic-sized pool near good beaches for her mother. Every injury. Every physio. Every training camp. Every weekend.

Stella retreated out of the waves and sat down on the shore. She wrapped her arms around her knees. The sea lapped cold around her bottom.

She shut her eyes. The bright blue of the pool flickered like the sun behind her lids. She remembered the cool absence of any nerves. Nothing. No pre-race vomit, no trembling, no bone-jangling fear. Not a single scrap of adrenaline pumped through her body that day. Which meant that rather than glancing down the course and envisioning the searing pain to come, thriving off it, taut with robotic focus, blinded to the enemies in neighbouring lanes knowing that this would be hers, as it always was, she could instead have turned to the girl on the blocks next to her, head down, quivering with nerves, and gone, 'Hey, why so serious?'

Because Stella had lost the biting, furious desire to win. It had slipped away, in retrospect, gradually during two months off to recover from a rotator cuff injury in her shoulder just before her eighteenth birthday, but at the time it felt like it happened overnight. Waking one morning and finding the impulse gone, she scrabbled around her brain trying to get it back, trying to grasp in the dark for her competitive edge. Pleading with her body to find its desperate want. But coming back empty-handed. Lying in bed trembling with the terrified sinking feeling that she would have to tell her dad. Tell him or else just pretend nothing had happened. Go through the motions, her limbs in every stroke slowed with reluctance like an anchor dragging along behind. Stand in the locker room with nothing but a bubble of nervous laughter. Climb onto the blocks and wait and see what happened.

On the beach, Stella glanced around her, checking that no one else was around to catch her sitting in the waves wearing her shorts and vest. There was nobody. Just a mile of yellow sand and ochre cliffs and seagulls stalking like sergeant majors. She turned back to the water. She swallowed. She felt the bind of so many versions of herself; Stella the daughter, Stella the swimmer, Stella Potty-Mouth, Stella the mother and the wife. And immediately she wanted to be just Stella. Stella with the weight of no disappointments, no expectations, no responsibilities, no let-downs or controls.

Suddenly she was standing. And then she was running,

ungainly and splashy, through the waves. Her brain no further ahead than her body. And then she was diving. Her hands cutting the surface, her face stinging, the freezing water shivering over her like gloss. Hard and tough, painful and exquisite.

Her head throbbed from the cold. Her cheeks pink, her heart thumping. Her muscles on autopilot, carving her through the water – like they had been crying out for this for years, dusting themselves off, fizzing for joy. She swam and swam, right out through the glassy stillness of the water. And then the moment hit, as it did, as she had forgotten, every time, when the cold and the adrenaline made her fly. When she felt the majesty of every wave. When the world became as small as this stretch of sea. When her body burnt from cold and her skin stung from salt and her muscles screamed and her heart thumped and she felt a rush course through her like bubbles in champagne.

She swam and she swam. She thought of nothing. She thought of everything. She saw the look on her dad's face after she hadn't dived in at the start of that race – the flash of worry that something was wrong then the shock and the barely restrained fury. The image of him edging quickly between the plastic seats, trying to get to the selection committee, his hand movements as he protested, the officials coming to talk to Stella. The silent shake of her head. The astonished, nervous faces when the shout of her father's curse echoed round the pool. She heard her mother's sigh of disappointment, her look of what a waste of time. She saw herself slamming the door of her crappy Fiat Uno car packed for university, a last-minute place through clearing, standing on the drive with her father inside the house refusing to say goodbye and her mother telling her softly that it was better if she just went, that she didn't want to make a scene, did she?

Stella swam until she thought her lungs might pop. Then she rolled over slick like a seal, gasping for air, lying on her back, floating with her arms outstretched staring up at the sky, blue and pink like a bag of penny sweets.

She closed her eyes and let herself sink, the water closing over her, hair swirling in tentacles. She remembered when her and her dad would sit, wrapped in their towels, drinking their tea, eating their sandwiches, staring out to sea in silence, gulls drifting in the sky above. A moment of being completely alone but together. The world retreating. And her dad would look at her and say, 'Best part of the day.' And they would grin, high, like they held the secret of life while others simply strolled on by.

She wondered where that feeling had gone. All that love. And why, when it went, did it all have to go. She lay submerged. Why couldn't she have kept this bit – this swimming, this sea, this calm, this elixir. Why couldn't they have saved this?

It made her think of Jack. The man she had married not just because of his stability and his being proper. But for his evenness. His rationality. His calm whatever the storm. That, unlike her father, he would never in the heat of emotion say, 'I am so ashamed of you I can't look at you.' She hadn't married him as an antidote to her dad, she had married him because he had shown her way of living different to the one she had known. A balance, a partnership, an equality.

'Hello there? Everything OK? Need a hand?' Stella was snapped spluttering back to reality by a booming voice on the shore.

She looked around disorientated, treading water and shielding her eyes from the sun to see a tall white-haired man standing on the shoreline in yellow baggy trousers and a black T-shirt, two dogs were sniffing about in the sand and next to him was a woman who looked remarkably like her mother.

'Fine!' she shouted back. 'Thank you.'

He nodded.

'Oh, it's Stella!' she heard the surprise in her mother's voice and got the impression that she and her mum were wanting the same thing – that they should just continue on their dog walk and Stella stay where she was. But the man – Stella presumed he must be Mitch the hippy – did not appear to be for moving. He just stood watching with an annoying-looking smile on his face. Like the sight of her swimming was abundantly pleasing to him.

Stella did not want to be watched. And since he didn't seem to be going anywhere, she had no choice but to swim back in. The distance suddenly quite long and exhausting, the joy lost with this stranger and her mother standing watch.

When she finally got shallow enough she walked the rest of the way out of the water, the pull of the almost non-existent waves against her legs. Self-conscious of the fact she was in her shorts and vest with no towel, the spontaneity of her moment beamed embarrassingly off her.

'Stella, you're in your clothes.' Her mother frowned.

'Yes, I know.'

Mitch was still smiling. The dogs were off chasing a ball he'd thrown. 'Apologies if we ruined your swim, but it's early and I just wanted to make sure you weren't in trouble.'

'It's fine,' Stella said, pulling at her wet clothes. The fabric clung like suction cups.

'Stella, this is Mitch,' her mother said, her cheeks marked with the smattering of a blush.

Stella squeezed her wet hair. 'Hello,' she said, a little wary. This was the guy who had her mother going to book club, divorcing her father, and wearing embroidered jeans.

Mitch thrust out a hand, big silver rings on two of his fingers, leather straps round his wrist and a tattoo of Buddha on his forearm.

Stella inwardly rolled her eyes.

'Your mother and I walk our dogs together,' he said, just as a scruffy mongrel dropped a saliva-covered ball at his feet and next to it Frank Sinatra panted for it to be thrown again.

Stella wanted to ask if they were having an affair.

'Do you not have a towel, Stella?' Her mother frowned, looking around on the beach for where Stella had left her things.

'No, but I'm fine.' Stella waved away the concern in her voice.

'You'll catch a chill,' her mother pushed.

'Moira,' Mitch cut in, giving her mother a look. 'Stella is perfectly capable of looking after herself, remember.'

Her mother inhaled, a deep breath through her nose. 'Yes,' she said. 'Yes, I suppose she is.'

Stella couldn't help the slight upturn of her mouth or the bemused expression on her face as she looked between the pair of them. No one ever said anything like that to her mother, not without getting a shocked harrumph in reply.

The dogs came bounding back. Mitch hurled the ball miles down the beach. 'No word from Graham today?' he asked, as if enquiring whether the postman had been.

Stella shook her head. 'Not that I know of.'

Moira said, 'No.'

Mitch nodded. 'I'm sure he'll turn up soon.'

'Let's hope so,' Stella half-laughed, almost warming to this character. 'Then we can all go back to normal.' She said it before thinking. Her mother walked away a few paces, picking up a pebble from the shoreline then tossing it into the sea.

Mitch was watching Stella watching Moira. An annoying half-smile on his face. 'You'll never get back to normal, Stella,' he said. 'There's no such thing.' The dogs were back, nudging around his ankles, keen to move on. Mitch threw the ball, it landed with a smack in the frothing water and the dogs splashed full tilt into the surf.

Stella didn't reply.

His expression was smug in its knowingness. 'As I've said to Moira, if it's ever normal again no one's saying what they really feel. You're all politely lying.'

Stella was about to scoff at this guru-ish psychobabble, but then she was reminded of Jack's earlier confession and the polite lies of their marriage.

Her mother threw the ball this time. Underarm, high up in the sky, the dogs hovering in anticipation. Stella watched as Mitch briefly touched her on the small of her back. 'Shall we carry on?' he asked. Her mother turned and nodded. Stella felt a bit ill watching the gentle intimacy of their movements. She couldn't remember the last time she'd seen her dad touch her mum.

'There are fresh beach towels in the airing cupboard, Stella.'

'Moira!' Mitch warned, jokey but firm.

'Yes, yes, I know. She can look after herself.' Her mother

shook her head. 'OK, I'll see you later, darling,' she said, giving Stella a quick peck on the cheek.

'Lovely to meet you, Stella,' Mitch said, shaking her hand again, rings clacking. Just before he turned to go, he added, 'Remember, never wish for normal,' with a confident, cocky wink.

CHAPTER 18

Stella stood watching them walk on, the chill her mother had warned of beginning to seep under her skin. Unable to look away she was still watching the figures tiny in the distance, goosebumps on her arms, when she heard a voice call, 'Mum! Mum!'

Stella looked across to see Sonny walking at a pace a little quicker than his normal lope down the beach towards her. He was wearing his stripy pyjama bottoms and a grey T-shirt, his phone outstretched in front of him. 'Mum, take a look at this!'

After the encounter with Mitch and Moira it was a relief to see him, if also a surprise. She walked up the beach to meet him midway. When she got closer she could see that he'd just woken up, his hair standing on end, a line in his face from the pillow.

He handed her his phone.

'What is it?' she asked.

Sonny was a little breathless, more with excitement than exertion. 'It's an Instagram. He's Instagrammed.'

'Who?'

'Grandpa.'

'No way!'

Sonny was nodding, grinning as he stood next to her and tapped in his passcode. 'I took a screenshot as well, in case he deleted it. I don't think he knows how so it's just a precaution.'

'Well done,' Stella said, casting a quick glance at her son.

'Thanks.' He flicked his hair out his eyes with a sweep of his head. Her chest tightened at their camaraderie. Then, almost to undercut his own buoyancy, Sonny added, 'I think he's posted it by accident, so it's well…'

Stella turned to look at the photo posted under the account name Neptune013. What she'd been expecting she wasn't sure; a smiling sun-lounger selfie maybe or a shot of a serene landscape. In reality the image itself was a bit of a disappointment, partly out of focus and taken at the awkward angle of being snapped by mistake. There was a pole in the centre of the shot from a train or a bus, a grey scuffed floor with different pairs of feet, and then a jean-clad leg – pale denim, a touch too short, white athletics socks and a pair of old white Nike hightops – without a doubt, her father's leg. On the floor was a red triangle – the corner of something or a box. She zoomed in to see if she could decipher more but the focus was too grainy.

Sonny peered over her arm at the screen. 'That's his leg, isn't it?'

'Yes, I think so,' Stella agreed.

'And do you see there?' Sonny reached over and zoomed right in close. 'That's a staircase.'

'Really?' Stella wasn't sure.

Sonny shrugged. 'It might not be.'

'No, no, it could be. A double-decker bus, maybe? And what's that red thing?'

'I don't know.'

She blew out a breath. 'How annoying.'

'Well, at least it's a clue,' he said, glancing up at her, hopeful.

Stella smiled, still surprised by how much he cared. Softened that he had come to find her when he'd seen it. Her dad unwittingly uniting them with his accidental Instagram post.

She could feel the weight of Sonny leaning against her arm, she watched his fingers zooming in on the photo and wondered when the last time they had shared an interest was, when the last time they had done anything together that wasn't her sighing up at the ceiling as Sonny wrote gobbledegook numbers down on his maths homework.

'It means he's looking at his Instagram,' Sonny said.

Stella nodded.

'Maybe we need to post something?' Sonny went on. 'Tell him to come home?'

Stella shook her head. 'I don't know, Sonny. He knows people will be worried and still he's choosing not to come back.'

'Yeah,' Sonny took his phone back. 'You're right.'

They walked on a few steps. Stella inwardly quite stunned by their chat. It felt like the first grown-up conversation they had ever had. This was Jack's recommended Time Out, sneaking up on her unawares. And now she'd recognised it, she was desperate to keep it afloat. From the fact Sonny had ceded her point, it felt like he knew it too. The conversation now a game of bat and ball that had reached the hundreds, neither wanting the ball to drop.

Sonny stopped walking. 'Maybe we need to post to show him what he's missing. Rather than that we're missing him.'

Stella paused, she smiled. 'That's a nice idea.' She wondered if she would ever have been able to come up with Sonny's plan – because to Sonny her dad was a person. To her he was an object entitled her 'father'. One she wanted back purely so she could move on, sort her own shit out. Get back to normal – a phrase now ruined by Mitch the hippy. Perhaps their mistake so far had been trying to locate her dad's whereabouts via the practical. All of them too aware of his character to consider any other way. Sonny, on the other hand, had enough youthful hope inside him to aim for the heart, banking on the fact her dad could feel.

The sun was higher now, the sky more blue and less pink. Stella's clothes were starting to dry as they walked. 'So you two got on, did you?' she asked.

Sonny kicked the sand ahead of him. 'Kind of.'

Stella pulled her wet hair back and gave it a squeeze. 'What did you talk about?' she asked, trying not to sound as keen as she was to know.

'I dunno. Stuff,' he said. Then he picked up a bit of drift-wood and chucked it ahead of them. 'Sometimes we talked about you,' he said. 'When you were younger.'

'Did you?' Stella was shocked. 'What did you say?'

'He said you could have won an Olympic medal.' Sonny picked up another stick. 'I didn't realise you didn't dive in at the trials. I thought you just, I don't know, weren't good enough.'

Stella scoffed. 'I wasn't good enough.'

Sonny looked up. 'He said you were.'

Stella crouched to pick up a big blue mussel shell, taking a moment out, annoyed with her dad for still pedalling the myth. 'Thing is,' she said, standing up, running her thumb over the barnacle-dotted surface of the shell, 'to get a medal, you have to want to win. It all has to come together, it's all up here.' She pointed to her head, 'It's not enough just to be good. And I didn't want it as much as he did.' She let the shell fall from her fingers.

They walked some more, Sonny scuffed up the sand with his bare feet. 'I can't believe you didn't dive in! That's mental. Grandpa must have been mad.'

Stella looked across at him, his eyes wide and bright with disbelief, but there was something else there, something she'd never seen before, respect maybe. Or perhaps just interest. It made it all seem much less of a drama. Much less the moment her father stopped acknowledging her existence or the moment she actually feared Pete was about to smack her in the face, and more just a cool anecdote for her son.

'Do you want me to take a picture of you, to put it on Instagram?' Sonny asked.

Stella shook her head. 'No, not of me. I'll take one of you.'

Sonny shook his head. 'Nah, my hair looks shit.'

Not wanting to upset their fragile détente, Stella quashed her usual comment of, 'Sonny, language!' It was quite refreshing. She wondered then why she cared if he swore or not – he'd be swearing non-stop in a couple of years. If her mother had been with them then Stella would definitely have told Sonny off, simply because she would have known her mother would have been offended. She wondered how often she pulled her kids up because of what she actually believed or because of what was deemed acceptable. It made her think of Jack, his silence about his job had stemmed from whether she would deem him less. It was all insidious, these tightening threads of presumption.

Stella realised Sonny was holding the phone up, waiting for her to say something about what to take. 'Maybe take one of the horizon, there's still some pink left.' She pointed out to the rosy aftermath of the sunrise and the sharp flat line of the sea.

'Nah, it's OK. I've done one,' Sonny said, clearly not waiting for her photographic suggestions. He handed her the phone to have a look.

'Oh God, Sonny!' Stella gasped, looking at the picture, half her back in the shot, her vest, her hair in sodden waves, the caption: *Mum's been swimming*. Three easy words loaded with a lifetime. When she saw the flicker of disappointment on his face, the retreat of his shoulders she forced herself to add, 'He'll like that.'

And Sonny took the phone back, nodding in agreement. Then as they started to walk back towards the steps that led up to the house, he mumbled, voice tentative, 'Can we stay, Mum? You know, stay and find him?'

Stella really wanted to say no. But something about the fact they had had this conversation, this moment together, that they had unwittingly found neutral ground in the unlikeliest of sources; her father, made her say, 'Maybe. We'll see.' And Sonny do a barely perceptible, 'Yes!'

CHAPTER 19

Jack was sitting outside drinking coffee when Stella and Sonny climbed up the steps to the cliff path and along to the garden. A figure as forlorn as the ragged palm tree that stood thin and weather-beaten next to the table. He didn't look surprised to see them together, and Stella wondered if he'd watched them on the beach. He looked knackered – the bags under his eyes puffy like marshmallows, his shirt half-buttoned, his hair as askew as Jack's short hair could be. Sonny ran straight over with his phone to show him the blurry Neptune013 Instagram pic. Stella joined them, slightly more reticent, pulling out the chair opposite Jack.

'Where do you think he is?' Jack asked. 'Do they geotag Instagrams?'

'Big words, Dad,' Sonny mocked. 'How do you know what a geotag is?'

'I'm not a complete dinosaur, Sonny.'

'Dad, you have fifteen Instagram followers. One of them is Rosie.'

'Watch your cheek, young man,' Jack said, smiling, taking a sip of his coffee. One eye all the time on Stella. 'I know what a geotag is.' Then a little less confidently he added,

'I read about it in the paper. It's a thing that shows where someone is, no?'

'Very good.' Sonny nodded. 'But it's not automatic on Instagram, you have to tag yourself. Which he hasn't.'

'Oh,' said Jack, not really sure what Sonny was talking about. 'Right.'

Gus appeared in the doorway. 'Oh, there you are,' he said to Sonny. 'Your bloody game has kept me up nearly all night. It's impossible.'

Sonny sniggered. 'It's not impossible. You're just RUBBISH.'

Gus made a show of mock offence. He was dressed in shorts and a faded green T-shirt with characters made of McDonald's products on the front – a milkshake and a chip packet with eyes and arms and legs – dancing with each other. 'Why are you talking about geotags?' he asked, and Sonny went over to the doorway and held the phone out for him to see. Gus squinted at the screen. 'Is that a leg?'

Sonny nodded. 'It's Grandpa's.'

Gus tipped his head. 'Well that's it then, search over. We have located his knee.'

Stella laughed despite herself.

Sonny thumped him on the arm. Gus winced. 'Come on then, Loser,' Sonny said, stepping just inside the French doors, 'show me your score.'

Gus got his own phone out and pulled up the game he had failed so badly.

At the table, Stella looked at Jack. Jack at Stella.

Jack looked nervous, or rather, sheepish. 'I'm sorry about last night,' he whispered. 'It was unfair to bring parenting into it all.'

The air was all salty sea breeze and apricot sunshine. Stella picked at the flakes of weather-worn paint on the table. 'Yeah.'

They felt like strangers.

'I know you do the brunt of the hard work with the kids,' Jack went on. 'And I know I come in through the door when you've dealt with all the hard stuff, so it's easy to make judgements.'

Stella was listening but none of it was really going in. She had wanted to be all post-swim breezy and say it was all cool and she was all cool and they should just chill and discuss. But now he was talking, little arrows of annoyance were piercing through the walls. She wanted to ask how, without a job, he had still had the nerve to walk in the door at seven thirty, when she'd been shouting at the kids for three hours to do their homework, share the stupid iPad and had cooked dinner.

There was a whoop from the doorway where Gus had just completed some move on the game with the help of Sonny.

Jack glanced up, all big eyes and sad mouth, and it made Stella want to slap him. She wanted to stand up and go inside, make her own coffee and sit on her own.

But when she went to move, hands flat on the table, she saw the once familiar sight of sea salt dried on her skin. And the sudden reminder of her swim made her stay. The adrenaline from the cold and the exertion, the high of endorphins, the rarely acknowledged memories. It had done something to her. She could feel it. It had given her a sense of being alive. She was reminded of Jack last night sighing as he said, 'I think I understand why your dad's gone. It's just for the break from life. From expectation.' If she closed her eyes she could see the view she'd had of the sky as she lay floating on her back, the wide expanse of marbled pink and blue. And she thought briefly that that was how Jack had felt. That was why he had lied. For that freedom.

It occurred to her that she could still stand up and walk inside and this would fester and grow and spread its tentacles through their lives. Or she could do what her dad had never done for her. She could realise that these weren't actions of Jack's normal character. She could remember that she loved him and attempt to give him the benefit of the doubt. She could force herself to stay sitting and try to understand.

'Mummy! Amy let me have a bowl of Coco Pops *and* Nutella on toast for breakfast!' Rosie appeared at the door with a plate of toast balanced on top of her bowl.

Amy appeared behind her looking a little guilty, wearing pale pink velour shorts and a white T-shirt with the Rolling Stones' tongue sticking out on the front. 'I didn't realise you were here,' she said, as if she wouldn't have said it was OK had she known.

Stella knew she would normally have made a comment about daily sugar allowances. But right now it seemed both the least of her problems and to highlight her supposed control issues. Instead she said, 'Well aren't you lucky, Rosie,' distracted, glancing at Jack who was staring glumly down at the coffee cup in his hands. The moment to talk more was over; parenthood was a million interrupted chats.

Sonny nabbed a slice of Rosie's toast as she skipped past him to the garden, then filled Amy in on the Instagram picture. All the while Gus stood lanky in the doorway still trying to decipher the game, head bent, thumbs moving, brows drawn.

As Amy went out to talk to Stella about the photo, she paused and said, 'Morning,' to Gus, who looked up slightly shocked, checked she was talking to him and then said, 'Yeah, morning.' He watched her as she nodded primly and went to sit at the table, before going back to his phone.

'Sonny says we need to have a day of photos,' Amy spoke through a mouthful of Coco Pops. 'I think that's a really good idea.'

On cue Sonny said, 'Say cheese!' and snapped a photo for Instagram. All of them turned in surprise.

'Oh Sonny, I was eating – I look awful,' Amy cried, immediately bouffing up her hair. 'More notice next time. Let me see.'

Sonny held the phone in front of Amy's face so she could look but wouldn't let her hold it.

'Why can't I hold your phone?' Amy asked, trying to take it from him.

'I don't want you to Like anything by mistake.'

'Oh, please!' Amy snatched the handset from him. 'I'm a social media pro.'

From the doorway, Gus snorted.

Amy pretended not to notice.

Stella glanced over her shoulder to have a look at the photo. There they all were, Instagram filtered to the psychedelic max.

Under the pic it said: **Sxnny.x1x2** *Chillin with the fam.*

Looking at the shot, Stella was suddenly taunted by what Mitch had said on the beach – about the lies of normality. About the unsaid. She looked at Jack across the table and raised her eyebrows. Jack cocked his head in question, eyebrows furrowed. She indicated to the 'fam' with a tip of her head. Jack did a little shake of his head. Stella did a wide-eyed nod.

'What are you two doing?' Amy asked, glancing between them like a tennis game. 'Stella, you look like you've got a tic.'

'Nothing,' Stella said, arms crossed still staring eyes-wide at Jack.

Gus had given up playing the game on his phone and was scrolling through Instagram. 'Blimey Stella, you swam in the sea?' He pointed to the waves in the distance. 'You're crazy!'

Jack's brows rose. 'You swam?'

Stella shrugged.

Sonny loped over to his dad and said, 'Yeah, she did, look—' and showed him the photos of Stella, wet by the water.

Jack stared contemplatively at the photo.

He handed Sonny back the handset.

Gus was talking. 'I've never swum in the sea.'

They all looked at him in horror. Even Rosie, stuffing her face with Nutella, paused. 'Never?' she said, mouth full.

Gus stepped back like he was in the firing line. 'No. Blimey. My family were not big beachgoers.'

'Where did you go on holiday?' Amy asked, like she was talking to an alien.

'I dunno.' Gus edged forward again. 'We went places we could walk. My mum likes the mountains.'

Little Rosie was having none of it. 'Why would you want to walk on holiday?'

Gus shrugged. 'Fresh air. Exercise?' He thought some more. 'Thermos of coffee that tastes like someone spat it out? Soggy egg sandwiches? Big red blisters that weep through your socks?'

Sonny laughed.

Rosie frowned. 'I don't understand.'

'He's being stupid,' Amy said. 'Ignore him.'

Gus made a face. 'Come on, that was funny.'

She made a face like maybe, maybe not.

'I don't think it was funny,' Rosie whispered to Amy.

'Me neither,' Amy whispered loudly back.

'Oh, come on, it was funny,' Gus said. 'Now you've ruined it by making it too big a deal.'

Amy scoffed. Rosie giggled.

Jack, who had been sitting a little glassy-eyed since he'd heard about his wife swimming, cleared his throat and said, 'There's erm— There's something you should all know.' He cleared his throat again. 'I've er— been made redundant, which means I won't be working in my job any longer. Sonny, Rosie – it's nothing to worry about.' He caught Stella's eye and added, 'It happened a while ago.'

Rosie, who believed anything anyone told her, so if the message was not to worry she wouldn't worry, said, 'Oh, OK,' and munched the rest of her toast.

Sonny put his hands in his pockets and looked up from under his hair, eyes unable to hide their panic. 'Why didn't you tell us?'

Jack shifted uncomfortably. 'I er— Yes.'

Sonny frowned at the response.

Once again, Gus retreated back within the safety of the French doors, sensing another awkward family moment to avoid.

Amy gave Stella a look. Stella made a resigned face back.

Jack was floundering. He never floundered. He glanced at Stella to bail him out. She almost sat back with a return glance of you're on your own, buster, but even after all their earlier back and forth, she couldn't do it to him. So she turned to Sonny and said, 'Because sometimes people need some time to come to terms with things by themselves.'

Sonny looked down at the floor, scuffed at some moss growing between the paving slabs. 'Are you going to leave?' he mumbled.

Stella frowned. 'Why would he leave?'

'Like Grandpa.'

Jack pulled himself together. 'No.'

Sonny looked up, nervous.

Then Gus stepped forward from the shadow of the doorway and said, 'I got sacked once. From Cineworld. It wasn't my fault – the girls used to go outside for a fag and when they came back in they'd warm their hands up by shoving them in the popcorn. When they got caught we were all given the boot – aiding and abetting.' He grinned.

'That's disgusting!' Sonny said, cheering up immensely. 'Dad, did you do something like that?'

Jack cleared his throat again. 'Well actually, Sonny, being made redundant is very different to being sacked—'

He was cut off by Amy who was still reeling. 'I have popcorn all the time at the cinema. ALL THE TIME! That's the grossest thing I've ever heard. I'm repulsed. I'm—' She pointed to herself and repeated, 'repulsed.'

Gus scoffed, 'Oh come on, that can't be the grossest thing you've ever heard? I know way worse than that.' He looked around his present company and clearly decided against sharing most of it.

Sonny said, 'I've got a mate who unscrews all the caps off shampoo and stuff in Boots and gobs in them.'

'Oh, Sonny!' Stella made a face.

'What? It's not me!' Sonny pointed to himself like he was being hard done by while trying not to crack up.

Amy looked appalled. 'God, I'm not going to be able to buy anything ever again.'

Gus winked at Sonny.

Stella exhaled, unexpectedly relieved by the lightening of the atmosphere.

Amy turned away from them with displeasure, then, stretching her slightly streaky fake-tanned legs out in front of her, said, 'So, go on then, Jack, what have you been doing all that time?'

Stella's head shot up, surprised by the audacity of the question she had barely had the nerve to ask. Jack did another nervous cough. His neck dotted red as a flush crept up to his cheeks.

Even Gus took a step closer.

'I think,' Jack said, his expression shifting, like excitement was edging above his embarrassment and shame, 'it might be easier if I show you.'

CHAPTER 20

The sun had settled in by the time they were heading out of the door, a close, oven-baking heat muted only by scraps of cloud. Aeroplane trails crisscrossed the sky.

Sonny had his red Wayfarer sunglasses on. Gus came out wearing bright blue ones.

'Hey dude, we match,' said Sonny.

Gus paused. 'No,' he said, shaking his head and taking his sunglasses off. 'That's too embarrassing.'

Sonny smirked and went to sit on the front wall.

'Where's the car?' Amy asked, appearing in a giant hat and flip-flops with sunflowers on them.

'Shit!' Stella tipped her head back, staring up at the sky. 'It's miles away and it's got no petrol.'

The plan suddenly scuppered, they all stood around unsure what to do. Everyone too hot.

'Mummy, you said "shit",' Rosie piped up.

'Yes,' Stella said. 'Sorry.'

Rosie shrugged like she'd only been pointing it out and didn't really care. Then she skipped off to play with the swing-ball in the garden.

Fat flies buzzed lazy in the heat. Jack, deflated, tried to

check the coordinates of the nearest petrol station on his phone. 'Sonny, I need your help with this. How do you work out distances?' Sonny ambled over to help his dad.

Gus kicked a stone on the drive then apologised when it hit Amy's flowery flip-flop. Looking up, he nodded towards the picture of a giant tongue on her T-shirt and said, 'I didn't know you were a fan of the Rolling Stones.'

Amy narrowed her eyes at him. 'I'm not.'

'But you're wearing their T-shirt,' Gus said, confused.

Amy looked down at her top. 'Am I?'

'That's their logo.'

'Oh. I just got it in Primark.'

Gus raised his brows then slipped his sunglasses on to hide his mocking expression.

Amy shook her head. 'You're so condescending. "I didn't know you were a fan of the Rolling Stones,"' she said, mimicking his voice.

'That's not condescending.' Gus held his arms wide. 'That's putting facts together. Condescending was the look I gave you afterwards when you said you didn't know it was their logo.'

Amy curled her lip. 'I knew it was their logo.'

'You so didn't.'

Amy shrugged like she didn't care what he thought.

'OK, then,' Gus said. 'Name me a Rolling Stones song.'

Amy paused, looked momentarily stricken, then she said, 'No, I don't have to prove myself to you.'

Gus scoffed and wandered off to have a peer in the dilapidated garage.

Stella watched the exchange from where she stood in the shade of the front porch. She felt unexpectedly sorry for Amy. Could see her flounder without someone there to protect her.

No Bobby to wrap his arms around her and drawl the right answer. No Moira there to tick Gus off.

When they were younger it had been Stella's role to protect her. Taking her away when their dad got mad when the car broke down. Treading water alongside her when she took her armbands off. Explaining her homework. Showing her how to practise French kissing on the back of her hand and letting her borrow her crimpers. But then Stella had left and Bobby had assumed the role so effortlessly. So all-encompassing. And sometimes when Stella visited she would barely say two words to Amy because she seemed to let Bobby do her talking for her. And Stella couldn't blame Bobby for that, he adored Amy. And he was as sweet and lovely as everyone said he was. It was Amy who allowed it to happen, who sank into the mollycoddling comfort of it. Who frustratingly backgrounded herself. And then after Bobby died, still Amy remained protected – when she would run sobbing from the room Moira would immediately jump up to follow, gesturing for everyone else to stay put. Then Amy would return and settle silently in with her dad on the sofa.

Last Christmas Stella remembered thinking the three of them were almost feeding off their dependency – no one in the house stepping out into the world. Fanning the flames of grief in order to stay cosseted from life.

It made more sense now in light of her mother's unhappiness with her marriage. The appearance of Mitch also went some way to explaining the almost shocking fact that Moira had told Amy perhaps it was time to move on.

But however positive Stella thought Amy's ushering back into the world was, she couldn't help feeling sorry for her – like a thirty-year-old teenager struggling with adulthood, completely out of her depth half the time. That was why she leant forward and whispered, 'Satisfaction.'

Amy turned Stella's way, confused.

'Satisfaction,' Stella whispered again. 'That's a song,' she added and Amy suddenly got it, momentarily distracted by gratitude. Stella ushered for her to say it to Gus.

'Satisfaction,' Amy said loudly, really smug.

Gus looked at them over his shoulder, shaking his head with disappointment. 'I heard Stella.'

Amy blushed. Stella tried to hide a giggle. It felt like when they were kids.

Jack looked up from his phone and said, 'The petrol station on the main road is closed for refurbishment apparently, which means we have to go to Sainsbury's.'

'That's miles away!' said Stella.

'7.6 miles,' Sonny said. 'Two hours twenty-one minutes walk or a forty-minute cycle. In the opposite direction to the car. Which is only a fifteen-minute cycle away, if it's where Dad thinks it is on the map.'

The sun chose that moment to dazzle through the clouds.

Gus was peering through the garage doors. 'Whose is this motorbike?' he asked, hands cupped round the crack in the wood. 'We could siphon the petrol.'

'No!' Amy gasped. 'That's Bobby's. You can't touch it.'

CHAPTER 21

Amy felt immediately self-conscious. All eyes on her as she stood flummoxed by her response to the motorbike.

'Sorry.' Gus backed away quickly.

'No, it's fine.' Amy waved a hand. 'I don't know why I shouted. That was silly. Sorry.'

Gus looked awkwardly down at the gravel.

Jack and Sonny exchanged a knowing glance then hid themselves away in the phone.

Stella came over. 'Amy, it's OK. Don't worry. We won't touch the bike.'

'No.' Amy pulled off her stupid hat and lay it on top of the hydrangea bush. She bit her lip. The sun was blinding. She winced. 'I might just—' She was about to say that she might just pop inside for a second, take a moment in the coolness of the living room. But as she thought about it, she realised she didn't want to be in there alone, or even with Stella hovering awkwardly in the kitchen, offering a cup of tea. No one going on the excursion or maybe half of them going. She had been looking forward to it.

Stella was standing with her hand on Amy's shoulder. 'What do you want to do?' she asked.

Amy swallowed. 'I think I want to look at the bike.'

Stella's eyes widened. 'Are you sure?'

Amy nodded. 'Yes.'

'I'll come with you,' Stella said.

'No.' Amy shook her head. 'No. I think I want to look at it on my own.'

'Are you sure?' Stella looked around uncertain.

Amy nodded.

Gus glanced up as she walked towards the garage. He moved himself out of the way, jogging a couple of steps to get over to the grass. Stella sat waiting on the raised stone wall by the hydrangea.

Amy could feel everyone watching in awkward silence pretending they weren't. She bent down to get the key from under a brick by the garage drainpipe and unlocked the big door.

It was a relief to slide inside. The air was dark and cool. Sunlight fought its way through cracks in the walls. It smelt of kerosene and polish and warm wood. Her dad's old boat was suspended from the ceiling along with a couple of surfboards and some rusty old racing bikes. Tools littered the back bench. Years of stuff burst from the shelves. But at the side, leaning propped up on its stand, was Bobby's motorbike. Black and silver. The metal scuffed.

Amy walked over and stood next to it. Placed her hand on the seat. She remembered almost hugging it like a soft toy after he died, pressing her face right up close to the leather. Apart from his board it felt like one of the closest things she had to being with him. She would sit with her back against the garage wall, feet tucked under the bike, toes reaching up sometimes and tracing the pedal, remembering how in the summer he'd ride in a T-shirt and jeans, what it felt like to squeeze the soft fabric of his top tight as he rounded a bend deliberately fast to scare her. The wincing look of pain on his face when he'd been showing off to his mates in the beach car park, skidding on the gravel, the bike sliding out from under him, his arm shredded by the stones. His teeth gritted, braving it out as Amy called her mother all in a tizz to come and deal with it. She smiled now as she thought of Moira turning up with the medicine box from their bathroom, scolding Bobby for refusing to wear a jacket while she patched up his wounds. Amy hovering at his side, panicked that he was going to lose his arm to something like gangrene, not even knowing really what gangrene was, snapping at her mother for snapping at Bobby, but Bobby just shrugging it all off with a wince and a grin.

She edged round the bike and sat, as she had sat before, sliding down the wall, flowery flip-flops resting on the stand. She felt the pressure of time, of everyone outside waiting. She wondered what they were doing. Whether they were talking about her.

She crossed her arms over her chest and stared at the bike. Wondered, as she had countless times looking at something of Bobby's, at the oddity of it having once being ridden by a man it now outlived. How could the bike be here and him not?

Her hands slipped down to rest on her tummy. On the baby. The baby suddenly that felt like an interloper. A thing that took her to a place away from Bobby. Like with her hand on her stomach she was being unfaithful to his memory. For wanting this child. She could see him slamming the wall with his hand if he found out or kicking the door. It all being made worse by the fact they as a couple had never been able to make a baby. She wanted to say that she was sorry, 'I'm—' but as she came to apologise she stopped.

Because if she apologised then she was sorry for this little life inside her. And she wasn't sorry. She couldn't start its existence on an apology.

She swallowed and looked away. Her emotions a confusing cocktail of guilt and defiance. She stared down at the dirty concrete floor next to her where she had sat for hours, sore-eyed, hiding, shivering, the cold numbing her bum.

She pushed herself up, came round the bike and touched the seat again. Her body willing her forward, willing her to bend and rest her face on the worn leather, to press her nose and mouth hard against it. But something was holding her back. It felt like the knowledge of the baby was keeping her upright. Keeping her apart. And it felt sad and scary and, if she dared admit it, strangely liberating.

There was a scratch on the roof. Just a seagull landing and squawking up and down the metal. But the noise made her jump. She backed away from the bike to the door. The light almost blinding, she kept her eyes downcast, avoiding any looks. Clicking the latch, wary of what she had felt.

Stella was waiting. 'Are you OK?'

Amy looked up at her sister, cut-off denim shorts and bottle-blue silk shirt, simple effortless elegance in contrast with Amy's patterns and slogans and big flowery shoes, always a one-upmanship battle between them. A funny, snarky little aside waiting in the wings of any conversation. Except right now. Right now Stella was looking at her like she might look at her kids – worry trumping every other emotion – and in her hand she clutched Amy's hat, holding it waiting, poised to pass it back to her. The simple tenderness of the gesture made Amy stand rooted to the spot and give her head a tiny shake.

A second later she was being hugged by Stella. 'It's OK,' whispered into her hair as she had the tiniest little cry. Sniffing she could smell Stella's skin through the suntan lotion and perfume. The smell of Stella's bedroom growing up. The smell of Stella's bedroom long after she'd left. The smell that never really went away until her mother repapered with the green parrots.

Amy wiped her eyes with the back of her hand and reached to take her hat back. 'I'm OK,' she said.

Stella looked at her unsure as she fished around in her pocket for a tissue.

'No, I am, really,' Amy said, blowing her nose. 'It was good I think. To see it. The bike.'

Stella nodded. 'OK. Well they're all over there,' she said, pointing to the far end of the garden. 'We're going to siphon the petrol out of the lawnmower instead.'

Amy laughed as she blew her nose again. 'That's ridiculous.'

'Gus's idea.'

Amy rolled her eyes as she looked to where Gus and Jack were hauling back the tarpaulin that covered the mower.

They walked together across the grass, at one point Stella put her arm briefly round Amy's shoulders and gave her a squeeze, the action was a touch awkward in its unfamiliarity but Amy didn't care. It was enough. She used to lie on Stella's bed as a teenager, willing her sister back.

Gus looked up as they approached. 'Sorry if I upset you,' he said.

Amy shook her head, embarrassed. 'It's OK, really. Don't worry about it.' Then she looked at the mower, wanting to deflect the attention, and said, 'Who knows how to siphon petrol anyway?'

Gus looked at her like it was obvious. 'Me.'

Amy scoffed, 'Yeah right.'

'I do! It's easy, we used to do it all the time on the farm.'

Little Rosie looked him up and down. 'Aren't farmers all big and muscly?'

Gus sighed. 'I can always count on you, Rosie.'

Amy turned away to hide a smile. It was a relief to feel it.

'Right,' Gus said, puffing up his chest. 'We need some plastic tubing, a petrol canister and an old towel – preferably one that can go in the bin afterwards.'

Ten minutes later Gus was blowing air into one clear plastic tube while Jack stuffed one of the dog's old towels into the petrol seal to make it airtight, the vacuum forcing the liquid to flow into the canister via the second plastic tube which Sonny and Stella were on their knees monitoring. Amy and Rosie watched, unconvinced.

'I don't think this is going to work,' Amy said.

'Me neither.' Rosie shook her head.

They stared, arms crossed.

Then suddenly the air was filled with the sound of liquid hitting the bottom of the old green metal canister that they'd unearthed from the back of the garage. It was impossible not to cheer with excitement. Sonny gave Gus a thumbs up so he could stop blowing into the tube.

Gus stood back to avoid the fumes and inhaled sharply. 'Bloody hell,' he said, catching his breath, eyeing the canister with surprise. 'It worked!'

Amy frowned. 'You said you did it all the time.'

'I said we did it on the farm all the time. I did not necessarily say that I was the one who did it. Semantics, Amy.'

Amy made a face. 'You said you did it.'

'I didn't.' Gus held up a hand, 'I said I knew how to do it. It's all in the phrasing. All in the subtle nuances of word play.'

Amy went, 'Urgh.' Stella laughed. Jack shook his head and tapped Sonny on the shoulder for them to leave them to it and go and get two of the bikes from the garage. Little Rosie said, 'I don't understand half of what Gus says.'

Amy raised a brow. 'It's because it's all rubbish, Rosie.'

Gus rose above it with a deep inhale, then said to Rosie, 'It means I had a couple of big, muscly younger brothers who did a lot of siphoning.'

Rosie still looked confused.

Jack and Sonny came out of the garage, wheeling two bikes. They were in reasonable nick since the pair of them had spent last Christmas doing them up, oiling the chains and pumping up the tyres – something to do to escape the more awkward times when the whole Whitethorn family were together.

'OK pass me the petrol,' Jack said when they got to the road, clipping up his helmet. Gus handed it over.

Sonny snapped a photo for his Instagram feed. 'Gus stealing Grandpa's petrol,' he narrated as he typed, straddling his bike.

'Oh, thanks for that!' Gus got out his own phone to check the post. 'He's really going to like me now, isn't he?'

Amy flicked her hair and with a little smirk said, 'Don't worry, he won't like you anyway.'

'Amy! That's so mean.' Stella thwacked her with the dirty old towel Jack had been using to block up the petrol hole.

'Ow!' Amy rubbed her arm. 'That towel is gross. It stinks.'

'OK, we're off,' Jack called.

They all stood by the front wall.

'Take care,' Stella said.

Jack nodded. 'See you in about twenty minutes.'

Amy noticed that they didn't kiss goodbye, Stella just held up her hand in a wave.

Then everyone shouted, 'Bye.'

Amy hoisted herself up to sit on the wall. Stella sat next to her, watching them go.

Gus stood in front of them. 'Don't worry, your dad'll like me,' he said, smugly cocky.

'You think?' Amy raised a dubious brow.

Gus shrugged. 'Parents like me. I have that thing.'

'What thing?'

Gus paused. 'I'm charming.'

'Oh, please.' Amy crossed her legs, perching on the wall next to Stella who was smiling to herself at Gus. Rosie jumped up to join them. Gus sat down next to her and, with Sonny gone, pulled his blue Wayfarers back on.

The four of them sat side by side like birds on a wire. The moment passed for anyone to say anything. The sun beat down. The telegraph pole hummed. Rosie kicked the wall with her heels. Birds danced back and forth on the road.

After a while Stella asked, 'How long have they been gone?'

Gus looked at his watch. 'About fifteen minutes.'

Stella exhaled, long and slow. Amy glanced across at her. Gus leant forward to check up the road for the car. Building in the air was a strange jittery excitement, like they were sitting waiting to find out what the end of the world looked like.

CHAPTER 22

The car turned onto a suburban backstreet. All bungalows and mums pushing prams. Stella frowned at Amy who made a face back like she had no idea where they were either. Outside it was getting hotter. The sun beating down on the hot pavement. Mirages flickered on the side roads. Stella, Gus, and Amy were squashed into the back seat, Rosie in the boot and Sonny up in front where he had stayed when he and Jack had pulled up with the car, bikes from the roof hastily deposited back in the garage. Stella had been quite pleased not to have to sit next to Jack, currently at a loss for how to act around him. It was like a glass wall separated them. They were no longer two halves of one whole.

'OK, we're here.' Jack put the indicator on and turned into what looked like a barren wasteland at the side of the road.

Stella squinted at the surroundings. In the distance she could see a building – maybe some sort of cricket pavilion. If he'd taken up cricket that would be a massive let-down. He already played cricket sometimes in the summer.

She stepped out of the car, pulling on her sunglasses, fanning herself from the frying heat magnified by the scrubland surroundings. It was like the Outback.

Amy was not impressed. She peered out from underneath her giant sunhat. 'Where the hell are we?'

Sonny was watching with amusement as Gus liberally applied suntan lotion. 'I burn very easily,' he said, face streaked with white.

Amy winced at the sight of him.

In the distance was a sad-looking playground. The big bucket swing had broken off the frame and lay in a heap, the seat for the zipwire had been removed and graffitied swear words decorated the little wooden huts. Unfazed, Rosie trotted off to investigate.

'What are we doing here?' The brim of Amy's hat bashed Stella in the face as she leant forward to whisper.

Stella shrugged.

Jack was busying himself in the boot.

Gus chucked the suntan lotion back in the car and came to join them. He'd rubbed in ninety per cent of the white – face still streaked like a tiger.

'You've missed a bit,' Amy sighed.

'Oh thank you, my love,' Gus replied in a saccharine voice, rubbing his face to get rid of the missed bits.

Amy rolled her eyes. Gus made a face back. Then Jack appeared from behind the car and she laughed out loud.

Stella looked up to see why Amy was laughing. 'Oh my God.'

Gus held his hands wide. 'Brilliant.'

Jack didn't make eye contact with any of them. Just strode past like if he was going to do this he was just going to get it done. On his head was a green helmet. On his feet were turquoise Adidas skater shoes. Black pads were strapped to his elbows and knees and he had fingerless glove supports on his wrists. Under his arm was a plain wooden skateboard.

'Jesus Christ,' murmured Stella as they followed. The only thing she hadn't noticed on this barren field was the skatepark at the other side of the playground.

'Dad's a boarder?' Sonny jogged to catch up with them. Heat almost visible as it rose from the boiling concrete and sizzled beneath their feet.

'This is the strangest thing I've ever seen.' Amy was trying not to giggle as they walked through the gap where a gate had once been into the skatepark full of ramps and giant slides. A couple of kids on the far side looked up from something they'd been watching on their phone. They eyed Jack warily.

Jack didn't stop. He kept on striding till he got to the top of the highest ramp. The others paused at the concrete bench.

Stella didn't quite know what to do as she watched Jack poised on the lip of the half-pipe, eyes closed and deep breathing. Part of her was relieved that he hadn't taken up something really weird or deviant, but staring up at him now she couldn't help thinking this was absolutely ridiculous. He was a grown man. And he was up there in his special skater shoes, his face crammed into his helmet, all his little pads and his brand new board. He looked like a complete wally.

'It's very high,' Gus said, shielding his eyes from the sun glancing off the steel ramp.

'Do you think he should start on something lower?' Stella said. 'Surely he's going to break his neck on that one.'

Gus shrugged. 'I don't know. I'm no skateboarding expert.'

'Jack!' Stella called. 'Jack, honey! Are you sure that's not a bit high?'

Jack seemed to pretend he hadn't heard.

'Mum, you're kinda ruining his cool,' Sonny cringed, gesturing with a nod of his head towards the gang of kids in the corner watching with clear amusement.

Stella just wanted the whole thing over. Jack hadn't been going to work, he had been skateboarding?! She shook her head with slight despair.

Next to her Gus smiled. 'It's good,' he said. 'Exciting.'

'Easy for you to say,' Stella replied.

Amy settled herself down on the bench. In her big hat she looked like she'd taken a wrong turn for Ascot.

Rosie was watching from the swings.

Jack teetered on the platform.

Stella held her breath.

Then suddenly off he went. Zooming down the ramp. Flying up the other side. Stella gasped. 'Please don't die,' she said under her breath. But he stopped safely on the other side.

Gus clapped. 'Go Jack,' he shouted.

The kids on their phones were laughing at this old guy trying to skateboard. The sun shimmered on the ramp. Sweat trickled down their backs. Jack was doing deep centring breaths.

Sonny, trying his best to maintain his cool in front of the other kids, winced at his dad's deep breathing, but still his eyes shone with intrigued amazement.

When Jack dropped again, this time he flew a foot into the air on the other side of the half-pipe in a move usually reserved for cool kids in Coke adverts. Stella's eyebrows shot up in surprise. Gus whistled, 'Wow.' But then the board landed slightly off-kilter, thwacking down on the glaring metal. Jack couldn't quite get his footing, all his weight on the back wheels, the board tipping up in front of him, like slipping on a banana skin, panic swept across his face and suddenly he was down, shoulders slamming hard against the ramp, board clattering, helmet ringing against the metal.

Stella's hands flew to her mouth. 'Oh my God, Jack are you all right?'

Amy jumped up from the bench, Gus took a step forward. Rosie ran from her swing to the railing where the playground edged the skatepark.

But Jack was already standing. 'Fine,' he said, holding his hands up, a gesture for them to back away. 'I'm fine.'

The video kids were heads down, shoulders shaking as they sniggered.

Jack gathered up his board, checked one of the wheels, and then climbed straight back up to the top.

'He's not going to go again?' Stella said to Gus. 'He can't. Jack,' she shouted, 'don't go again, it's OK, we've seen it. You don't need to do this.'

But Jack wasn't listening. This time there were no deep breaths and centring of self. He just put the board down and went. Dropping into the gleaming metal. He did another jump at the top, a little fast, a little unsteady on the landing but this time when he lost his footing just at the last minute he managed to right himself. The look of panicked concentration relaxing when he stopped shakily on the deck.

Stella put her hand on her chest in relief.

Sonny whooped. Rosie cheered from where she was sitting on the playground wall to watch. Gus punched the air. Amy whistled, two fingers in her mouth. Gus glanced over impressed that she could whistle. Amy pretended not to notice.

Jack did a tiny bow.

The skater kids' laughter was still mocking.

And then Jack went again. This time higher. This time with more finesse. This time with his arm out as he paused midair at the top, showing off, this time landing all smooth on the transition. This time smiling. Grinning. Ear to ear. Wiping his brow with a faux-phew when he reached the top. Laughing. Them all laughing. Amy whistling again. Gus clapping. Sonny cheering and taking photos on his phone.

The skater kids were bored now Jack was getting better, their attention back on YouTube.

But Stella watched. Watched as Jack went again and again. Better and better. Less awkward in his helmet and his knee pads. More relaxed. And as she watched she started to see him differently: like when someone comes back from holiday with a tan. His legs looked like legs rather than Jack's legs – calf muscles tense, thigh muscles bulging a little. His arms like arms, his neck like a neck. All the composite parts one notes in a stranger rather than just the familiar limbs and body parts of her husband. She looked at his face, his chin, his cheeks as he smiled. His eyes as the wind of the movement whipped at his skin.

When was the last time she had actually looked at Jack? Even the other day, when they'd been side by side in the mirror she'd been mostly studying herself.

She stared up at him as he paused at the top. He had a nice jaw. A good nose. A little dimple. Ridiculously neat sideburns. He was good-looking, always had been. Jack wiped the sweat off his face with his T-shirt. He was grinning. High. Eyes sparkling. Looking only at the shimmering slope of metal in front of him.

Stella got a sudden rush of panic that she was about to lose him. That he would go off all hip and cool with his skater buddies. Given the kids slumped over their phones at the end of the park this was irrational, she knew, but she imagined her skater-chick usurper. 'You're kidding right? You didn't even know he'd lost his job? That is In-Sane.'

Gus clapped at the end of every ride. Amy watched, wide-eyed and bemused. 'He's good, isn't he?' she said to Stella.

Stella nodded but didn't say anything. She felt odd. Vulnerable. She felt on the outside of Jack's life. She wanted to be happy for him but couldn't summon it up over the hurdle of feeling both duped and forgotten.

Gus came over. 'He's a dude.'

Stella slipped her sunglasses on. 'Yeah,' she said. But Jack wasn't a dude. Jack had never been a dude. Jack wore Crew sweatshirts.

They stood watching in silence for a bit. Then Stella said, 'Why do you think he didn't tell me?' She wouldn't have asked had it not been Gus – he was neutral territory.

Gus frowned. 'Like you said earlier,' he said, 'some things you've gotta do on your own.'

He said it like he'd been impressed with her rational cool-ness when it came to Jack's deception. Like she'd nailed the perfect answer in one fell swoop. His expression now was hesitant like he worried he'd been too quickly impressed. That she was about to let him down by responding with run-of-the-mill annoyance.

And he would be right. Stella hadn't meant it. It was just some bullshit she'd spouted to keep Sonny happy. But the look on Gus's face made her pause. Made her remember her promise to give Jack the benefit of the doubt.

She thought of her morning swim again, imagined how different it would have been had Jack been standing on the shore saying something like, 'You can't go in in your clothes. Why don't we go back to the house, get a towel and change? I don't want you to get upset out there on your own. Maybe I should come in with you, just to be on the safe side ...'

Stella had to swallow down a wave of frustration just at the idea of this fake conversation. Then Rosie's high little voice cut in on her musings. 'Daddy, can I have a go?'

Jack was catching his breath at the top. 'OK Rosie,' he said. 'Wait there, we can go on that smaller one.' He jogged down the steps.

Stella wasn't sure about Rosie going on any of the ramps, they looked like death traps, but Jack was giving her a little lesson on the flat ground first.

'Can I have a go?' Along went Sonny.

Stella watched Jack with the kids and realised that was what it would have been like had he told them – there'd be Rosie and Sonny in tow. She corrected herself, it wouldn't have been like that at all because there was no way she would have agreed to him going off and skateboarding rather than looking for another job. And she doubted, had he ever voiced the desire to learn to skateboard out loud, it ever would have got further than a throwaway comment, she and the kids would have laughed him down – made the tentative notion scuttle back into hiding.

Admittedly Jack's secret time alone had been a little longer than her morning swim – but how nice would it have been, she thought, to have held her swimming close to her chest for a few weeks, what a luxury to have been allowed to explore it completely without comment. To sneak out every morning undiscovered and unmissed. She suddenly envied him his brief sojourn of aloneness.

Rosie was attempting a ramp, Jack holding her tight around the waist. 'OK, no steady, Rosie. Lean into it, not on me. Concentrate. Almost.' His feet straddling the board, Jack looked like a waddling duck as he ran down behind her. Halfway, Rosie slipped and fell on her bottom.

Stella watched realising that, whatever the simmering under-current regarding his decision to keep this adventure from her, she wanted to give him more of his moment in the here and now. Had the situation been reversed, she would have wanted him to take the kids for an ice cream as she was lying on her back in the sea staring up at the pink-skied sun.

So Stella stepped forward and said, 'Rosie, Sonny – come and sit over here. Let Daddy show us a bit more of what he can do.'

Rosie came bounding over, almost relieved that she didn't have to do any more. Sonny sloped after her. 'Can you do any tricks?' he asked, kicking a can across the concrete on his way to the bench.

Jack nodded. 'A couple,' he said, but his eyes were on Stella, looking at her quizzically, surprised that she'd called the kids away and encouraged him to do more.

Stella did a nonchalant little shrug. Jack raised his brows, she raised hers back. He frowned like he was trying to figure her out. She looked down and smiled, turning to walk away and sit on the scrubby grass at the side. She stretched her bare legs out in front of her, resting back on her hands, the sun shimmering off her skin.

Jack strode to the top of the ramp.

Stella looked away, down at the grass, thinking how this notion of him needing a break from life, to be alone, tied up tightly with the feeling like she might lose him – not to someone else necessarily but to himself, that he had found contentment without her. The thought that he wasn't comfortably, sedately hers, while terrifying, was also strangely exciting. That she had to continue to work at this. She flicked her hair from her face, toyed with her necklace, did her best to look sultry. Inside feeling giddy like a teenager.

There was a cough. She looked up and saw Jack waiting at the top of the ramp for her attention. Wanting to impress her. And she realised the feeling was mutual.

Stella bit her lip, held her hair up from her neck, and watched languid with faux-indifference as Jack dropped into the ramp. Who knew middle-aged skateboarding could be such an aphrodisiac.

CHAPTER 23

Moira was at Mitch's yoga class in the village hall. She usually enjoyed it very much but today it was too hot. Stuffy even with the windows open. The label on her new leggings itched. She glanced at the clock which made her lose her balance mid-Warrior Pose. Mitch appeared by her side. 'It's because you lost your breathing, Moira. The focus comes from the breath,' he said, elongating the word breath and raising his hand in the air to emphasise the point.

She blew out her bloody breath, rolled her shoulders, and tried to get back into position, surreptitiously glancing round the room to see if anyone in the class had watched her fall. They hadn't, they were all now bent double, left elbows pressing on the inside of their left knees, staring up at the ceiling, while Mitch wandered round the room calling out more about 'breath' and carefully adjusting various arms and shoulders.

Moira followed suit, staring contorted up at the cracks in the ceiling. Mitch had said that yoga would help her let go of some of her anger. He said that she carried it all in her upper body, tight like a ball of fire. She had told Mitch that she wasn't angry. He had smiled and told her to use her breath to connect with her heart.

Moira didn't go in for things about hearts and love being all you needed and more often than not let her mind wander to what she needed from the supermarket when they were doing all that kerfuffle.

But today she didn't seem to be able to get into any mood whatsoever – not even zoned out enough to think of her shopping list. She kept thinking of how everyone stepped forward after they'd unblocked the septic tank and claimed responsibility for Graham's disappearance. And then the girls sitting round her at the table telling her she couldn't leave. Stella this morning saying that she wanted it all back to normal – as if their family was a jigsaw puzzle to be slotted back together if only they could find the missing piece. No one saying – maybe it was him. Maybe it was his fault. Maybe the lost piece of the puzzle had been vacuumed up and thank God for that!

And so when, at the end of the class, Mitch made them shut their eyes, cross their arms and place their hands around their backs to give themselves a good hug – 'Let yourself know that you think you're OK' – Moira burst into tears. She couldn't think of the last time anyone had hugged her. She had hugged – she had hugged Amy when she'd wept over Bobby and she had hugged little Rosie hello – but it had been years since she had been given a good squeeze just for being herself.

She wiped her eyes on her Sainsbury's Tu yoga wear – just like Sweaty Betty but half the price – and said, 'Goodness me, I don't know what came over me,' as Mitch smiled encouragingly, then she nipped off to the loo all embarrassed.

She only ventured out again when she knew everyone else had left. She'd heard all the 'cheerios' and the car engines starting up. Her bag and sandals were still in the main room.

She crept in. Mitch was leaning over one of the long tables pushed to the side of the room, used for the OAPs' Wednesday lunch, reading the paper.

Moira grabbed her bag and clutched it over her shoulder. 'I'm sorry about that.'

Mitch glanced round, white hair slicked back, big smile on his face. 'Never be sorry, Moira. It's good. It's a step forward.'

'I haven't cried in years.'

He tipped his head. 'I cry all the time.'

Moira found herself smirking.

He raised a brow. 'You think men shouldn't cry?'

'Well no, I just, I don't—' She stopped herself. He always made her feel like this. Got to the root of everything she believed and then yanked the whole thing out in one fell swoop.

Mitch smiled.

Moira sighed.

'Would you like to come back to the van for a coffee?' he asked.

Moira hesitated. She'd never been to his van before. As he had never been to her house. They met on the beach to walk the dogs. They sometimes had a cup of tea at the beach café, but never at the other's territory. The idea was quietly thrilling. Especially in contrast to the muddle at home. 'Yes, I'd like that,' she said.

Mitch nodded, pleased, like he could tell she'd finally acquiesced to her own instinct.

The walk from the village hall to the campsite that housed Mitch's van wasn't far. It was a straight line down towards the sea, along a grey stone path lined with fir trees that smelt sweetly of pine in the sunshine. The dogs trotted along about three feet in front of them at all times. There was a tiny bakery open just in the summer months on the right before the fence to the field. Mitch stopped to buy freshly baked bread and a couple of croissants. The girl at the counter knew him by name, he'd been there months. Then tucking the paper bag under his arm he unlatched the gate and beckoned for Moira to go in ahead of him.

She could tell she was blushing, felt like she was doing something illicit, coming here to have coffee. All her other male friends were part of a couple and, on the rare occasions she and Graham went out together, she predominantly spoke to the wives.

'Are you OK?' Mitch asked, hand on the gatepost, waiting.

'I'm just a bit worried people might, you know, talk.' Moira glanced back at the girl in the bakery who wasn't paying them the slightest bit of attention.

Mitch guffawed. He stood with his arms wide. 'Moira, it's the middle of the day. We're two adults having coffee. Good Lord, you have a lot of rules.'

Moira felt immediately foolish. She gave a little nod and scuttled through the gate, followed by the remnants of Mitch's laughter.

His van was an old mustard VW Westfalia T3. It had a high-top with a little slide-out bed in the roof and downstairs was a faux-wood laminate kitchen and a green and orange tartan sofa. Crystals sparkled at the windows alongside feathered dreamcatchers and a stone Buddha's head was propped up against the back wheel. The van was parked almost on its own under a canopy of pines, with a secluded view over a daffodil field and then out to the sea. Moira walked round the van and waited as Mitch unslid the side door, lit the gas for the kettle and flipped out two purple floral deckchairs fraying at the seams that must have been at least thirty years old. Mitch's dog 'Dog' curled up on the velour sofa while Frank Sinatra stretched out on a patch of grass next to Moira who tentatively settled herself into a threadbare deckchair. Tucked away from the world, surrounded by nature, she felt unusually relaxed. If she mentioned the fact, Mitch would say it was the healing energy of his crystals but Moira knew it was the escape from herself, her responsibilities, her rules as Mitch so bluntly put it.

As she sat, she closed her eyes, listening to the laconic movements of Mitch making coffee – no hurry, no fuss, pausing to scratch Dog behind the ears – the radio soft in the background. Then, in ten times longer than it would have taken Moira, there were two cups of exceedingly strong coffee and a croissant each on a rickety, fold-out side table.

Mitch took the seat angled beside her, legs outstretched so his tanned feet reached the parched long grass in front of them. He wore a shirt open halfway down his chest with a circular pendant stamped with an Om just visible, and loose yoga pants with elasticated ankles. Dog came out to sit by his feet.

Mitch took long slurps of his coffee while he stared straight ahead at the sun shimmering on the crests of the tiny waves.

Moira drank more neatly. Taking a sip then putting the cup back on the table.

Frank Sinatra gently snored.

'It was good to meet Stella,' Mitch said, rolling his head to glance at Moira. 'Nice girl. Bright. Similar issues to you, here—' He patted his chest a couple of times.

Moira swallowed. Felt suddenly ashamed for passing on her angry repression.

'Vivacious though,' he added. 'Knows what she wants. I liked her.'

Moira had another sip of coffee, wondering if he would ever describe her as vivacious. She looked up to find Mitch watching her like he could tell exactly what she was thinking and was mocking her for it.

'She is a credit to you,' he said.

'Oh no,' said Moira. 'Not to me. I don't think Stella owes anything to me.'

'No?' His mouth turned down.

Moira shielded her eyes from the sun, looking out towards the sparkling waves. 'I don't think I was a very good mother when it came to Stella.'

'I'm sure you were.'

'No honestly.' She gave a little laugh as she turned into the intensity of Mitch's gaze, bright like an interrogation light. 'Graham had a couple of affairs you know, when we were younger.' She turned back to the sea, watched a yacht in the distance, its huge white sail billowing gracefully. 'Always came back, never serious,' she said. 'But you know—' She paused. 'I was never as jealous of them as I was of Stella.' She looked round at Mitch and smiled. 'Horrible, isn't it? Horrible for a mother to say.'

Mitch shrugged.

'She just commanded so much of his attention. And she did it so effortlessly, as if she didn't even really want it. Next to her I think I looked very desperate. Very uncool,' she said in a voice Amy might use, then picked up her coffee with a sigh.

Mitch waited, silent, like time was of no consequence. A dragonfly swooped and Dog lazily lifted his head.

'Stella was ever such a good little swimmer,' Moira said, feeling an urge to continue. Like in this hidden tranquillity she had started to get something off her chest and now couldn't stop, because if she did she would never say it again. 'It's a shame really, they pushed her so hard. They were so tough on her. I think that was the way back then. Maybe it still is? I know top athletes have to be pushed, but, well, you have to enjoy it, don't you? I think that was their mistake really, she was so good they forgot she was just a young girl. For Stella it was all she knew so she just did what they told her and then suddenly she spent some time being normal—'

Mitch laughed at the word normal.

'What?' Moira asked.

'Nothing.' He shook his head.

'Well, anyway,' Moira said, 'maybe not normal. Ordinary. She got injured, went out with her friends, lots of parties, festivals, that kind of thing – and I think suddenly realised what life could be like.'

'You didn't ask her?'

Moira felt her cheeks warm. 'We didn't talk much about things like that. Stella does what Stella wants to do and off she went. Gave it all up in an instant.'

Mitch frowned. 'And no one said anything? What did Graham do?'

Moira scratched her head, awkward. 'Graham stopped speaking to her for quite some time.'

Mitch whistled.

Moira put her cup down on the table again, she felt a little got at, didn't want to talk about the past any more. Didn't want to feel criticised.

Mitch picked up his croissant and tore off a strip to feed to the dog. 'Were you still jealous of Stella after she left?'

Moira had forgotten she'd started this by saying she had been jealous of Stella. She remembered as well that she'd mentioned Graham's affairs. She wondered what had come over her, she never aired her dirty laundry. Standing up she went and untangled two stalks of grass that had been annoying her. When she sat down again she hoped the conversation might move on.

But Mitch wasn't going to let it go. 'Come on, Moira,' he pushed. 'What happened? Tell me.'

She pursed her lips. Glanced across at him and said, 'Nothing happened when Stella left. That's the stupid thing.' She shook her head. 'Nothing changed.' She had always pre-sumed that without Stella and her remarkable talent in the picture, Graham's gaze might fall back on Moira herself. 'What I didn't realise, I suppose, was that Graham and Stella were the great big fireworks of the family. Me and Amy were those little ones on the ground that everyone says are nice but really they're waiting for the rockets that explode with all the pizzazz.' She ran her finger along the frayed edge of the chair. 'No one wants to see just the boring little ones, do they?'

Mitch's eyes crinkled up with a smile. 'I don't know, I've always been pretty fond of a Roman candle.'

Moira smiled. 'That's sweet of you to say.'

Mitch shrugged like it was his honest opinion.

After a moment of silence, Moira said, 'It's terribly hot in the sun, isn't it?'

'So, move into the shade.'

'Oh right, yes,' she said, as if she hadn't really thought about moving her chair. But more that it never felt her place to take the lead on such things, years of always fitting in with what the stronger character might do. She repositioned herself under the dappled shade of the pine tree.

Mitch got up and moved his chair as well, then went back for the table. After that he disappeared into his van and came back with a small wooden box stencilled with cannabis leaves.

'Do you want to get stoned, Moira?'

Moira snorted into her rapidly cooling coffee. 'Absolutely not.'

Mitch smiled to himself. 'It'd do you some good, I think. Loosen you up.'

'No.' She shook her head vehemently. 'I don't do drugs. I've never done drugs.'

'It's not drugs,' he said, all lazy and a touch mocking as he sat back in his chair and lifted the lid on the box. 'It's legal in Holland.'

'Well that's the Dutch for you.' Moira felt herself sitting all prim and rigid.

Mitch barked a laugh. 'Come on, Moira, live a little,' he said as he started rolling a joint.

'No.' Her lips were tightly pursed.

He looked her straight in the eye. 'What are you so afraid of?'

'Besides being arrested?' she asked.

'We're in a field, down a lane, in the middle of nowhere. You aren't going to be arrested.' He kept his eyes on her, wouldn't look away. 'What else are you afraid of?'

She swallowed. She frowned. 'I don't know. Maybe losing control?'

'And what would be wrong with that?'

'I've never done it before.'

'Well, shall we see what happens?' Mitch said, running the edge of the rolling paper across his tongue.

There was absolutely no way Moira was going to say yes. Absolutely no way. She got her phone out of her bag, hoping suddenly that one of the girls might have texted and she'd have an excuse to leave. She felt like a prude. Mitch was lighting up, a big grin on his face. There was no text. Only a WhatsApp message letting her know that Graham had Instagrammed. She frowned, clicked on the app that Sonny had downloaded for her the previous week to have a look, and there indeed was Graham's leg. What was he doing? And next there was a picture of Stella after her swim. When she'd seen her that morning Moira hadn't thought much about the fact Stella had been swimming, she'd been more focused on keeping her and Mitch apart, but now she saw the picture she realised it must have been quite monumental. Stella never swam any more. Then there was a picture of Gus doing God knows what with the lawnmower. And Jack on a skateboard? And Amy whistling in her big sun hat. Wasn't everyone busy! And where was she? Feeling guilty about murky details of the past, dealing with septic tanks, and worrying about her daughters who had no trouble unloading their burdens on her but wouldn't dream of letting Moira move on and live her own bloody life.

So, when Mitch leant forward and passed her the glowing joint, instead of a quick wave of decline, she thought why the hell not? Why not. Maybe I will get arrested and then they'd all have to do a bit of soul-searching to work out what sent me off the rails.

But as she took her first daunting acrid puff, Moira crossed her fingers that she wouldn't get arrested because she couldn't imagine anything worse than a night in their local jail. The Travelodge looked bad enough.

She had a few quick cautious inhales, checking left and right that no one was coming, Mitch watching her, amused. She coughed, waved the smoke from her face, coughed again, and then handed the joint back so she could settle herself more comfortably in her chair.

'I smoked a bit at school, you know?' she said. 'Gauloises. We all did. All for show. Thought we were the bee's knees. Never one of these. Never a reefer.' She smirked when she said the word. Feeling a little like she was back at school. Also wondering about that expression – did bees have knees?

Mitch was reclining, all lazy and sated in his chair. Moira couldn't quite put her finger on how she was feeling. Completely normal to some extent. But then she lost her train of thought watching the sun flicker through the pine needles and the shards of light dancing on her skin.

Mitch handed her back the joint.

A couple more puffs and she felt like a ragdoll. Like someone had plucked her from the confines of her packaging; from the bits that cautioned her about what was the right thing to say next. In fact, she didn't give two hoots about what she might say next. 'I was quite a looker in my time.'

Mitch gave a wry smile. 'I have no doubt.'

Moira sighed, her arms fell to the armrests, her hands flopped, she gazed at Mitch in his white linen shirt. 'Oh to be young again. I had this bright red hair and tiny little figure. And I'd go into work all strutting about in my high heels and pretty dresses. That's where I met Graham, on set. I was a weather girl on *West Country Morning*, did you know that?'

'I didn't know that.'

'Well, I was. And one day the sports man was off sick – it was a Tuesday – and they couldn't get anyone and I was drafted in. What did I know about sport? Well, nothing. Suddenly I'm on the side of the pool with a microphone thrust at all these men in tiny pants,' she giggled. Mitch handed her the joint. She was more careless this time, inhaling more deeply, coughing, laughing. After passing it back, she lifted her feet up on the chair, curling them under her like she was a girl. 'Graham was a young hot shot of the swimming world at the time. Their rising star. And I didn't know who he was.' She gave another little giggle. 'I was just blushing like a beetroot because he was dripping wet, all muscles – very good-looking – and his trunks were so small. I could hardly get a word out, said something like "Good swim?" when he'd just won the British Championships by half a length of the pool and broken about three records. I think that's probably why he fell for me in the end: that first meeting, me all giggly and blushing while he was puffed up like a gloating peacock.' She turned to look at Mitch, he was watching her, listening, joint dangling in one hand, the other stretching down to scratch the dog's ears. 'When Graham was swimming he wasn't anything like Stella was. They could shout blue murder at him and he'd just shake it off. Did his own thing half the time. Skin so thick. Arrogant bugger, always was,' she said. 'I don't even think it was the swimming particularly that he adored, it was the winning. Swimming, winning. Does that rhyme?' She frowned.

Mitch laughed. 'Maybe Stella liked to swim and Graham liked to win.'

'Yes.' She nodded. 'Yes. That was his problem really, always has been. Do you know just before his last Olympics one of his teammates hurt his back. Couldn't race. They asked Graham to take his place in the two-hundred-metre freestyle and you know what he said?'

Mitch shook his head.

'He said no.' Moira did a pursed-lipped look of disapproval. 'And do you know why? Because he didn't think he'd win it. He knew it would be his last Olympics. He had four events that he knew he could win, and he didn't want to take on that last one and risk going out a loser. Worried he'd be remembered for being the man who lost one rather than won four. He's never told anyone that. I'm not even sure he knows I know. But I was listening on the other end of the phone. It was good in those days – being able to listen in. Well not good, clearly, because of course it's wrong to eavesdrop.' She stopped. Mitch was looking at her, brows raised. Moira reached up and reclipped her hair, a little flummoxed, trying to grasp some thread of a train of thought so she could gloss over that last bit.

'Graham loved to win,' Mitch prompted.

'Oh yes,' Moira agreed. 'Yes, that was it. He couldn't bear the idea that no one stays at the top forever. That younger, better people come up. It infuriated him. He was terrified of getting beaten. I think that's why he retired – no question. Wanted to go out while he was still at the top. And it was a mistake, definitely, because when he started coaching none of his athletes were ever quite good enough for him. Always thought he could have done it better. Which he probably could have done, but well, he couldn't change his mind and come out of retirement, could he? Couldn't lose face.' She shook her head, despairing. Mitch handed her the joint. She smoked as she spoke, quite casual with it all now. 'He moaned constantly that he was fobbed off with the bum end of the squad to coach. But he was too much of a maverick. Didn't toe the line, enough. To be honest, they were the athletes I would have given him if I was them, but Graham couldn't stand it. He wanted the stars. He wanted the medals. And, well, then Stella started showing promise. Real promise. She was so fast. Like a little fish. And you could see Graham's eyes light up. He was going to make her his star.' Moira took a last drag, huffing out her breath, reaching forward to hand the joint back to Mitch. 'It was never about Stella, was it? It was about proving a point. It was about the buoyancy of Graham's own greatness. Buoyancy?' she said. 'Is that the right word?'

Mitch shook his head like it didn't really matter. 'I know what you mean.'

'Yes,' Moira said, aware she would normally feel foolish for her confused aside, but not really caring. His outline was a little blurry. 'Well, anyway. I don't know. I suppose in retrospect all of us – me, the women he slept with, Stella – we were all the same, just extensions to make him look better. Don't you think?' She paused.

Mitch shrugged. 'Possibly.'

'I was what you might refer to as a "trophy wife".' Moira did little inverted commas with her fingers, then frowned at herself because she'd never done them before in her life. 'I had this very big red hair. Oh, I've said that haven't I? Well, I also had quite fantastic breasts. Everyone thought so.' She peered down at them squished flat by her Tu sports bra. 'They're not quite so fantastic any more,' she added. 'Just droopy.' Then she snorted a laugh, astonished that she was even talking about them.

'They look pretty good to me,' Mitch said with a mischievous grin.

'Oh, you rotter.' Moira guffawed. 'What was I saying?'

'About your fantastic breasts.'

'No.' She shook her head. 'About Graham. About all of us. Oh, I know. What is it they say now? For famous people like David Beckham. And Posh Spice? Goodness, where did that name come from? I'm not sure I knew that I knew who Posh Spice was.'

Mitch shook his head, bemused. 'I have no idea what they say.'

'You know! About them and their brands. Furthering their brands … That's it! It's all about them getting bigger and bigger.' She made the gesture with her arms, blowing up like a balloon. 'It's all about them. Them, them, them. That's what it's like for Graham. That's what Stella winning meant to Graham. It was about his brand. Not hers. If I had realised that at the time, perhaps I wouldn't have been quite so jealous of Stella. Perhaps I would have been more supportive. Perhaps if I'd had another interest, or stayed at my job or filled up those boxes you keep drawing in the sand, I wouldn't have wasted so much time waiting for him to notice me.'

Mitch shook his head.

Moira nodded, a little resigned. 'Or maybe I would.'

'There's no point berating yourself about the past, Moira. You can't change it,' Mitch said, fingers toying with the Om pendant round his neck. 'Only learn from it.'

Moira worried he might suddenly start talking about love

and heart-centres and yogi things again, so she hurried on. 'He did start to be more of a father to Amy when Stella left which was good. That was nice. And then Amy got friendly with this boy Bobby at college who was very very good at surfing and suddenly Graham had a new project. Another rising star to throw all his energies into. To bask in his glory.' She waved her hands in the air, knowing she'd gone a bit over the top but couldn't help herself.

Mitch handed her the joint and she thought it was maybe just to give her a second to dial things back. She took a quick puff, a bit scared of quite how relaxed she was feeling, how uninhibited, and then passed it back. He gestured for her to take more so she did, just a tiny weeny bit.

Mitch took great long drags, like he was sucking all the air from the world. Moira watched him blow well-practised smoke rings as he exhaled, all of which fit perfectly inside one another, expanding as they escaped into the air.

She sat back in her chair, staring at the rings as they disappeared up into the pine trees, and thought about everything she'd just said. She felt a tiny wave of melancholy. Of a past handled badly. 'I wonder sometimes if Graham ever thought about Stella as a person.'

'Or about you as a person,' Mitch said.

Moira stared at the smoke and shrugged.

They sat in silence. More rings drifted up and away.

'I was pretty good at my job, you know?' she said, stretching her legs out, looking over at Mitch. 'I held my own.'

'I bet you did.'

'They sent me off to do quite a lot more of the sport after that first go. I interviewed John McEnroe once.'

Mitch made an impressed face.

'He was my claim to fame,' she said. 'If I'd stuck at it I suppose I'd be like that Sue Whatsername now who does Wimbledon. Or that jolly lesbian who's on everything nowadays.' Moira frowned. 'Is that judgemental? To refer to someone as a lesbian?'

Mitch raised a brow. 'Just say person, Moira. No need to bring sexuality into it.'

'Well, you wouldn't know who I was talking about if I didn't.'

'I think we'd riddle it out.'

Moira giggled. She was rather enjoying herself. She'd never talked so openly to anyone. 'I could quite imagine myself settling down with a nice woman friend, you know.'

'Yeah?'

She reached forward and plucked the joint out of Mitch's hand, ready to go the whole hog now and taking a great long drag before handing it back. 'At least we'd be guaranteed to get things done. Women are much better doers than men.'

'Is that a fact.'

'Without a doubt,' she said, her eye catching on the crisp, fluffy croissant sitting on the table. 'We need less pandering and looking after.'

Mitch was laughing. 'You're funny when you're stoned, Moira.'

'Do you think I'm stoned?' Moira looked up proudly from where she was reaching over for the croissant. Usually she'd cut a croissant in half to eat it more discreetly but today she just rammed it into her mouth with a great big bite. 'It's probably a good thing I didn't stick at the job, by now I'd be making a spectacle of myself on *Strictly*,' she said, mouth full of flaky pastry. 'Or in the jungle eating cockroaches and kangaroo willies.'

Mitch burst out laughing.

Moira sniggered and croissant almost came out her nose.

Dog barked. Frank Sinatra snored.

'I wish I'd done this years ago.' She sat back, holding her croissant lazily in one hand. 'It's bloody marvellous, isn't it?'

Mitch nodded, a wry smile on his lips. 'I think so.'

Then suddenly there was a rip and the fabric of Moira's thirty-year-old deckchair tore completely from the frame and her bottom fell straight down to the floor. Mitch sat up startled. Moira's whole body was sandwiched into the square metal frame, legs flapping in the air, croissant still in hand. She looked at him, him at her, neither of them made any attempt to move. Both of them unable to breathe for laughing

CHAPTER 24

The car home from the skatepark was hot and jolly and filled with an underlying tingling euphoria. Like everyone had experienced a wave of adrenaline. Rosie and Amy were singing along to Beyoncé on the radio. Gus had his head in his hands at how bad they were. Sonny was laughing at Gus's displeasure.

In the front, however, between Stella and Jack was just a big ball of sexual energy. Stella's little finger tracing his sweaty thigh as she changed gear. Jack's hand brushing over her knuckles. He leant back, knackered, eyes trained laconically on her. 'You OK?' he asked.

Stella nodded, no idea how she felt beyond their electric sizzle.

Beyoncé changed to something less energetic, Amy leant forward between the front seats and said, 'So, where did you learn all that, Jack? Did you have a teacher?'

'Sort of,' Jack said, angling his head to talk to her, his hand still on Stella's thigh. 'I actually learnt quite a lot from YouTube. Then these young chaps took pity on me when I had a pretty bad tumble.'

'Don't think they call it a tumble, Dad,' Sonny called from his seat in the boot.

'No, sorry.' Jack corrected himself, 'I totally bailed and they took pity on me.'

Sonny sniggered at his dad saying bailed.

'It was sick,' he added.

Sonny put his hands over his ears. 'OK, stop now.'

Jack laughed. Looked at Stella to check she was laughing. She was. He kept his hand on her leg.

'Why skateboarding?' asked Gus.

Jack shrugged. 'Because they were doing it when I was sitting on a bench near the station and I watched thinking, that looks fun.' Stella glanced across at him, he turned his head so he was talking mainly to her. 'One day I got up and asked a guy if I could borrow his board and have a go. He said no.' Everyone laughed. Jack smiled. 'So I went and bought one.'

'So it was just because it looked fun?' Gus said.

Jack paused. Stella waited. He looked really tired now. But a different type of tired from that morning or last night at 4 a.m. A sated tired. 'No. It looked like a good way to turn my brain off. I didn't want to have to think any more.'

Stella looked down at his hand on her leg and put her own hand over it. The touch lasted just a second, because then she rounded the country lane to find a tractor coming the other way and had to change gear really quickly, but it was enough.

By the time they got home the sun was hovering above the trees and the afternoon light had started to haze. The scent of jasmine trailed through the air like cigarette smoke. House martins darted into the old nest in the eaves watched intently by Frank Sinatra on the doorstep.

'Hey, boy.' Sonny scratched him behind the ears then picked up an old tennis ball in the drive and lobbed it for him across the garden. Rosie sprinted alongside the dog as he ran to fetch.

Almost before Stella had unlocked the front door, Jack said, 'I think I'm going to have to have a lie-down.' His hand was on Stella's back, his fingers scrunching the fabric of her top. 'Me too,' Stella replied and they both disappeared upstairs.

Amy wandered in, kicking off her flip-flops, sticky with heat and desperate for a drink.

Gus strolled in behind her, head down checking his phone. He was just about to walk into the lounge area when he looked up and paused. 'Is that your mother asleep on the sofa?'

'What?' Amy was at the sink, gulping down water. She turned to see Moira fast asleep, flat on her back, mouth open, a huge bag of Walker's crisps spilling out on her yoga top.

Amy and Gus exchanged a look. 'My mother never sleeps in the day,' Amy said, creeping forward to stand next to Gus, 'let alone when she knows we might be coming back. And I've never in my life seen her eat crisps out of the packet.'

Gus went and peered at her, leaning over so he could check that she was still breathing.

Moira woke with a start. Their heads banged. 'Good gracious. What are you doing?'

'What are you doing, more like?' Amy asked, bemused at the sight of her mother, hair askew, eyes all heavy and hooded.

'Nothing,' said Moira, actions all a little shady while looking decidedly off-kilter – hair sticking up on one half of her head, mascara smudged under her eyes.

'Are you OK?' Gus asked.

But Moira was up, brushing the crisps off her T-shirt, smoothing out her hair. 'Where have you all been?' she asked. 'Anyone want a cup of tea?'

Gus looked at Amy who shrugged, bemused.

Moira paused on her way to the kettle. 'Did anyone say yes?' she asked, completely befuddled.

'Yeah, I'll have one, thanks,' said Gus, walking over to lean against the kitchen partition. Then sniffing the air said, 'Can anyone smell weed?'

Amy had a sniff. 'What does it smell like?'

Gus rolled his eyes like he couldn't believe she didn't know. 'Like this,' he said, moving his hands around to enhance the scent of the room.

Moira hurried to the kettle and mumbled something that sounded like, 'I don't know what you're talking about.'

Gus's eyes narrowed and he looked at Amy. Silent puzzlement passed between them, then Amy shook her head. Gus shrugged and went round into the kitchen. 'Let me help,' he said, leaning in and inhaling as he got closer to Moira. Then he nodded emphatically back at Amy. Amy laughed, shocked, then covered her mouth.

Moira turned. 'What's going on?'

'Nothing,' Gus and Amy said in unison.

Moira went back to the tea, self-consciously smoothing her hair again.

Amy tiptoed to join Gus, standing behind her mother as she poured water from the kettle into the pot. She leant forward to try and fully appreciate the aroma. But this time Moira caught her. 'Both of you, I don't know what you're doing, but you can do it somewhere else. Leave me alone,' Moira scolded, cheeks burning red.

'Oh, chill out, Mum. We're just winding you up,' Amy laughed, as both she and Gus were booted out of the kitchen and went to flop on respective items of living room furniture. She in the chair by the bookcase in the far corner because her mother's stuff cluttered the sofa, and Gus in the squishy armchair nearest the kitchen where Moira was still huffing and puffing.

Gus caught Amy's eye and nodded, big eyes, like he was definitely right. Amy shook her head, unable to believe that her mother was a mid-afternoon stoner. Gus leant back in his chair with a nonchalant shrug, expression confirming he was right whether she chose to accept it or not.

Amy looked away laughing, relaxed, pleasantly in the moment. Then her eye caught sight of a photo frame on the second to bottom shelf of the bookcase next to her chair. Her laughter froze as she recognised the familiar silver edges of her wedding photograph. It was like it had been tucked down there to keep it out of obvious sight so as not to upset anyone, namely her, but could still be claimed to be on show. She reached down and tipped the frame up so she could get a clearer look. Her goofy grin, white satin slip, a flower crown in her long sun-kissed hair. Bobby in his pale blue suit, the trousers cut down to shorts in typical Bobby style.

The sight of them standing there together made her insides tighten. Made her synapses fire with panic. She felt foolish for ever being that girl, for believing in the future she had imagined. Amy did a quick glance of the room. Suddenly nothing seemed familiar in the landscape ahead. Her mother was smoking dope. The stranger over in the squishy chair was the father of her child. How easily everything concrete could change. Nothing was as the girl in the photograph had thought it would be. It seemed crazy that a second ago she was laughing. Her life was like a seesaw she couldn't get off.

CHAPTER 25

In the bedroom, Jack and Stella felt like nervous teenagers. She kept staring at the definition of his muscles, the slight narrowing of his waist. All previously overlooked in favour of an examination of their wrinkles in the mirror.

'All right?' Jack asked.

Stella nodded, standing with her back almost against the door.

Jack watched her from where he was, closer to the edge of the bed.

Stella wished she had better underwear on.

She flicked her hair back.

Jack ran his tongue along the bottom of his teeth.

Neither of them knew what to say.

In the end Jack asked, 'So, what did you think? About today.'

'I think you're a tosser,' she said, 'for not telling me.'

Jack looked momentarily less blasé, like he'd completely misread the situation.

'But I understand,' Stella said, walking slowly towards the bed. 'Sort of,' she added, kicking off her shoes.

Jack swallowed. Nodded.

She could feel the warmth of the room on her skin, see the glisten of sweat on Jack's.

'You looked kinda sexy up there,' she said, moving closer to the bed.

Jack's mouth tipped up into a grin. 'Yeah?'

'Yeah,' she said. His fingers reached across and laced with hers. Pulling her towards him so they ended up on the bed. Her hands pressing down on the sheet, either side of his head. She looked him in the eye, her hair falling either side of their faces, a dark veil of glinting sun. 'No schmaltzy movie-style stuff,' she said.

'No,' Jack grinned. Then he reached up and pushed her hair behind his ears. 'I love you, Stel.'

'I know,' she said. 'I love you too. Sometimes.'

He laughed. Hand round the back of her neck, he pulled her down, mouth hard against hers. Less schmaltzy movie style, more unable to stop himself.

***

They lay sweaty and tangled, eyes half-closed, smiling, able to hear washing-up downstairs and children shouting in the garden. The sex had been the best they had probably ever had. Made all the more exciting by the fact her entire family was downstairs and it was mid-afternoon. Stella could actually feel herself glowing and wondered briefly if she looked as young and vibrant as she felt. Jack's fingers trailed up and down her arm. She snuggled into him all relaxed, wondered if she might get away with a little snooze.

Then she heard Jack take a long breath in and out, seemingly readying himself for something really hard to say. She felt her body tense in anticipation.

He moved, propping himself up on his elbow. 'I blamed you last night because I was being defensive. And immature.'

Stella lay where she was, very still, cautiously intrigued. Jack rarely admitted such fault.

'It was cost-cutting, the reason they picked me – I cost them too much, I was too experienced.' He slumped back down, rolled his head her way on the pillow, eyes a little sad. 'I was doing some really shit stuff, Stel. They were taking contracts on that were lucrative but so boring. I was so bored.' He looked back up at the ceiling. 'There's only so many cheap blocks of flats you can design.'

Stella rolled onto her side, watching his profile as he talked. Outside she could hear the dog barking and the kids laughing.

'I knew we needed the money – need the money. And I knew that I could be more helpful at home, I knew all that. But—' He shook his head. 'When it happened, I felt like such a failure. I've never felt like that before, Stel. Completely defeated.' He scrubbed his face with his hand.

She reached across and put her hand on the flat of his chest. Could feel the gentle thud of his heart.

'I wanted to tell you,' he said, eyes pleading. 'I really did. You wouldn't believe the amount of times I lay awake thinking about telling you. But— how could I tell you? The lie just got bigger and bigger the longer I left it and I felt like with the job gone, and the money gone, I wasn't who I was meant to be. And then something kind of took over.' He looked across at her, big blue eyes wide, like he was almost unable to explain. He sat up, arms draped over his knees. 'I think to begin with it was relief – that I wasn't doing the job any more. But then it became kind of exciting. I enjoyed the break.' He glanced back at her. 'Not from you obviously, but from expectation, I think. Pressure. Stella, I have never rebelled before in my life.' He twisted round to face her. She sat up so they were opposite each other, the sheet draped between them. 'When I was growing up, I was good at school and good at home. I worked really hard for my exams. I got a good job. Christ, my dad still rings me to find out my bonus.' He put his hands over his eyes and laughed at the ridiculousness of it all. 'With the boarding, I enjoyed being reckless. I know it wasn't even really that reckless but for me it was reckless.' Stella smiled. Jack shook his head. 'I enjoyed that my days were mine again. It was like I was Sonny's age.'

She nodded.

'I know it makes me sound like a selfish bastard,' he said. 'And I was.' He laughed with disbelief at himself. 'I was being completely selfish. But it was like I'd been given this little window of a life where I was completely free of all responsibility. And it was such a relief.'

'And now?' Stella asked.

'I don't know. I don't know what to do. I'm just glad you know now.'

Stella watched him. Then she moved so she was sitting in his lap, wrapping them both in the sheet, with a view out of the window of the sea stretching almost to infinity as the blue of the sky merged with the horizon. 'I would have tried to fix it,' she said. 'I would have pushed you to get another job. But I really believe, that if you had told me all of this, I would have listened, I believe I would have listened. And I understand.'

Jack tightened his arms around her waist.

She sat up straighter and glanced round so she could see his eyes. 'It was unfair to make someone the proper one,' she said. 'You're not the proper one.'

Jack nodded, quietly accepting.

'I think maybe we just fit the role we have to step into,' Stella said. 'I mean, any one of us could have done what was meant to be done with that septic tank, couldn't we? It's just we waited for someone to say they'd do it first. We're basically a sliding scale of shirkers.'

Jack frowned. 'I don't know if just anyone could have done it.'

She laughed. 'No one would have done it as well as you did,' she said. 'Except maybe me.'

Jack half-smiled. He looked exhausted again. Stella kissed him softly on the corner of his lips then turned to look back out of the window, the side of her head resting against his, his arms wrapped tightly round her waist, the seagulls drifting towards the never-ending horizon.

CHAPTER 26

Stella lay with her eyes open. Jack was fast asleep next to her. She'd heard her mother say she was taking the dog for a walk about ten minutes ago. Downstairs Gus and Sonny were intermittently shouting so must be locked in some battle on their phones and she could hear American-accented talking blaring out of the TV which could have been Amy or Rosie's doing, or both.

So, when she heard the sound of tiptoeing on the landing Stella sat up intrigued. Even more so when the door to the attic staircase creaked open. Someone was trying to be super quiet and failing as the hinges whined and the staircase squeaked.

Stella got out of bed, pulled on a vest and denim shorts, then went to have a peek out of the bedroom door at what was going on.

Amy was creeping really slowly up the attic stairs, the attic door not shut due to the loud creaking.

Stella ducked out of her bedroom and crept across the landing. Downstairs Sonny shouted something that made her jump.

She paused and frowned, wondering why she was tiptoeing, then marched up the stairs. 'What are you doing up here?'

Amy froze by a packing box like a thief caught red-handed. 'Nothing,' she said, immediately defensive.

The attic was sauna hot. A cracked, dusty window in the eaves drank in the sun like a spotlight. The wooden beams above them almost pulsed with heat. The fluffy yellow insulation oppressive like an overstuffed winter duvet. Stella could hardly breathe. 'It's unbelievable up here.' She fanned herself with her hand and tied her hair back with a band on her wrist.

Amy stood with her fingers tapping restlessly on the packing box.

'What's in there?' Stella asked.

'Nothing.' Amy shrugged. 'Just some of my stuff.'

Stella went to say something then stopped. She glanced around – there were maybe fifteen, twenty boxes stacked up, all of them newer, more recently packed than anything else in the musty space. She realised that these must be the contents of Amy and Bobby's house. She didn't know what to say. She walked closer. She'd never thought about what had happened to their stuff. To their mugs, their vases, their books. And here it all was.

Amy turned away, pulling open the flaps on the box in front of her. 'I thought maybe, if Mum's going to sell the house, I should have a look. I don't want to have to do it when all the removals people are here and it's really stressful, right?'

'Right,' said Stella. It seemed to her like a strange thing to be doing amidst everything else that was going on. 'Do you want some help.'

Amy shrugged. Stella weighed up whether that was a no

or a yes. Part of her wanted to scuttle back down the stairs and into the easy cosiness of the bed, but she was pretty sure that if Amy hadn't wanted her there she would have answered no. To say yes was more vulnerable. Stella decided that Amy's shrug was a tacit agreement.

They worked in the heat for about an hour. Sweating as they unpacked boxes of kitchen utensils and old catalogues for sofa companies that Stella couldn't believe had been packed but realising, the more she sorted, that it must have all been swept in at speed. No one in a fit state to sort out the trash. Or perhaps Amy not in a fit state to let anyone throw anything away. Stella paused, kneeling on the gritty wood floor pretending to sort some cutlery, hit by a rush of guilt that she didn't know any of this. She hadn't been here. They had been abroad at the time of Bobby's accident. And her role as the outsider was so entrenched that even at Bobby's funeral, she had felt like the add-on – arriving with her own new family as she watched her old family grieve. There hadn't been room for them in the front row so they had squeezed in near the back, late for no reason other than cajoling the kids out of the bed and breakfast. The majority of the funeral had been spent trying to subtly distract a then five-year-old Rosie with *Frozen* on her phone. And after that she had barely got near Amy, a protective circle around her of Bobby's surfer friends and her parents. Stella and co had milled around at the wake like distant cousins.

That whole period stood out in Stella's head as a time that highlighted, no matter how many half-terms and Christmases they visited, just how isolated she would always be from her family. Rather, she realised, than a time her sister had been walloped by the grief of losing her husband. Stella's judgements of Amy suddenly seemed so unfair when she considered what she'd actually been through, if she took a moment to absorb the fact Amy's whole married life was here, packed up in twenty cardboard boxes.

In front of her, Amy pulled out a green hooded sweatshirt, the cuffs frayed, the colour bleached pale from the sun. Stella watched her hold it momentarily to her face, then sit down on a weird old rocking zebra that they'd been terrified of as kids and never played with. 'I didn't come up to sort it out,' Amy said, holding the sweatshirt in a ball on her lap. 'I came up because I couldn't remember.'

Stella got up off her knees, swiping off bits of dust and sand, and went to sit on a leather trunk adjacent to the zebra. 'Remember what?'

'Enough of the good bits,' Amy said.

The heat magnified as they sat still. A poltergeist of energy throbbing round the room desperate to claw its way out.

Stella frowned and wiped her forehead with the back of her hand. 'What are you talking about? I thought it was all good bits.'

Amy shook her head. 'At the time. But it's all getting muddled. Stella, I feel guilty every time things are better. Like in London, I had this really fun time and I'm laughing and I want to stop half the time and go, "It's OK, Bobby, it's not better." But it is. Sometimes it is.' She folded the jumper on her lap, smoothing out the white, peeling logo on the front. She blew her hair off her face, then held it back with her hand. 'At times I'm happier and I'm having more fun and I think it looks like I'm glad he died, which I'm not, because it's really hard to be happy. But I don't miss him as much, Stella.'

Stella didn't know what to say. She felt herself staring at Amy, slightly overwhelmed by the realisation of what she had been through. By her strength. Stella had always seen herself as the strong one but actually she'd been looking the wrong way.

Amy tipped her head to stare up at the ceiling and sighed, resigned, 'What do I do?'

'I don't know.' Stella shook her head. 'But I do know you can't live the rest of your life in the shadow of a memory, Amy. The worst happened to you – he died – and you coped.'

'Not very well.'

'Yes, but you coped. And you will cope again.'

Amy looked back at her, eyes damp at the corners. 'I'm afraid of being alone.'

If the zebra hadn't been so small, Stella would have gone to sit next to her. Instead she reached over and touched her on the arm. 'You're not going to be alone. You're going to have a little baby to look after. And believe me, that'll get you out and making friends and whatever because you won't want to be stuck in on your own. And we'll all be here, just not necessarily in this house.' Stella stood up. Unable to cope with the heat any longer she went to force open the window. 'And don't forget Gus,' she said, struggling to unstick the years of dust gluing the pane shut. 'He is the dad.'

Amy made a face. 'He's so annoying.'

'He's funny,' said Stella, still struggling with the window catch.

'He's annoying,' Amy replied, rocking the little zebra back and forth.

'I think you're too hard on him.'

The window finally gave way so suddenly Stella almost fell out. 'Jesus!' she cried, righting herself on the sill.

Amy laughed. Then she went over to join her, both of them sticking their heads out of the window into the fresh air. After a moment Amy said, 'What am I going to do if the baby has Gus's nose?'

Stella almost chocked on her gulp of air. 'It's not that bad,' she said.

'It is,' Amy insisted. 'It's ginormous.'

Stella tried to stifle a smile. 'I don't understand why you slept with him if you find him so abhorrent.'

Amy glanced across at her, their faces nearly touching out of the tiny window. 'Have you ever had a unicorn martini?'

Stella shook her head.

'Well believe me, if you had, you'd understand. After half a glass you'd have sex with Shrek if he introduced himself.'

Stella laughed. 'How many did you have?'

'Three.'

'Oh Jesus. Amy!'

'Well, I was nervous. And it was all so weird.' Amy pushed her hair back from her face then clipped it with a kirby grip from her pocket. 'Do you really think this haircut looks nice?'

'Yes,' said Stella. 'It makes you look more grown-up.'

'Old?'

'No. Less babyish.'

Amy frowned. 'Thanks. I think.'

'What was the sex like?'

'Stella!'

Stella turned her face towards the hint of a sea breeze. 'Go on, what was it like?'

'I have no idea,' Amy said, taking her hair down again.

Stella smiled.

They both looked out at the sea, at a chugging fishing boat and the swooping gulls, the paddleboarders, and a family packing up all their clobber from a day at the beach.

'I have a vague idea,' Amy said.

'Yeah?' Stella nudged her on the shoulder.

Amy looked at her from underneath her fringe. Eyes a little sheepish. 'I think it was really good,' she said. 'I think I remember really laughing.'

'Yeah?' Stella felt her face light up with surprise.

'Yeah,' Amy nodded. 'Stella, I never laughed when I had sex with Bobby. I'm not saying I think that's a bad thing. But our sex was really proper. Like … Candles and stuff. I think—' she paused, sighed.

'You think what?' Stella was fascinated.

'I don't know. I wonder if either of us had enough sex before we got together. I think Bobby would have been offended if it had been funny. I'm not saying that Bobby and I had bad sex. It was good sex.'

'Just not funny?'

Amy shook her head, then ducked back inside and slumped down against the rough wood wall.

Stella sat cross-legged under the window. 'I'm having visions of Gus sitting on the bed acting out some kind of stand-up routine.'

Amy thwacked her on the arm. 'Stop it.'

'Sorry.' Stella smiled. 'So it was good, funny sex.'

Amy nodded. 'Don't tell Mum.'

'Unlikely.'

'Or Jack.'

'Equally unlikely.'

'You'll tell Jack.'

'Maybe just the sitting on the side of the bed cracking jokes bit,' Stella said.

'Stop it!' Amy bashed her again, voice whiny and faux-tantrum.

Stella dodged the hit. 'I like that you had funny sex,' she said.

'I don't.' Amy flumped back against the wall, a shower of dust fell from the rafters. 'Yuck.' She moved her legs away, brushing off the debris.

'Why don't you like that you had funny sex?'

'Because of Bobby. It does something. It kind of takes away from him. From his memory.'

Stella made a face, confused. 'Seriously?'

Amy shrugged, then reached over to pull the faded green hoody back onto her lap. 'I don't want to be comparing people to him and it changing the memory of him.'

Stella sat forward so she could look her straight in the eye. 'You've just sat here saying how ugly and awful Gus is, that's hardly negating Bobby's memory.'

Amy tipped her head, like maybe so. Then she held the sweatshirt right up to cover her face.

Stella reached over and pulled it away. 'You have to find a way to stop this. Anything. Put him in a box in your head marked something like, "This was great – I loved this" and then pack it away. Know that it's precious and you will treasure it. But put it to one side, and open a new box.' She paused, stared with big sympathetic eyes at her sister. 'You have to do whatever you can to keep moving forward, because life isn't an either/or, it's an is. And it's OK to live it.'

Stella remembered Jack saying something really similar to her when they'd met at university. When she'd first fled her parents' house. He hadn't said it quite as articulately as she felt she'd just said it to Amy but along the same lines. Telling her it was OK to get on with her own life.

Amy was looking at her, tears she couldn't hold back slipping down her cheeks. Stella squeezed her hand. Amy dabbed at her eyes with the hoody. Then after a second she smiled and said, 'What's an is?'

Stella rolled her eyes. 'Please don't undermine my supremely profound comment.'

Amy laughed.

Stella said, 'It's the now. The mess we're all in; good, bad, OK, indifferent. Hot—' She jumped up seeing something scuttle along the wall. 'Spiders!'

'Spiders!' Amy shot up. 'Yuck.'

Stella shuddered, brushing down the back of her top, and that was when she saw it. A tatty old cardboard box with the word STELLA scrawled in marker pen across the side.

She didn't care about the spiders any more. Amy was still frantically swiping through her hair while Stella ducked down past the beams to reach into the eaves. The box made a trail like a sleigh in the dust as she pulled it towards her.

'What's that?' Amy asked.

Stella shook her head. 'I don't know.' She yanked open the flaps. Then she paused, crouched, staring down at the shimmering contents.

'What is it?' Amy peered over her shoulder.

'It's all my medals,' Stella said. Reaching in, picking up big gold European and World Championships discs with a red, white, and blue ribbon. Underneath were pennants and trophies. More medals. One in a scuffed plastic box for an Under-11 Regional Championships. There were good luck cards she'd never been able to throw away. A crappy teddy bear talisman she'd stuffed in her bag before every race. The clips she used to wear in her hair. Her Great Britain kit. Her goggles. Everything. Buried in the back of the attic. Never marked, "This was great – I loved this", not treasured or precious. But saved. Rescued from the rubbish.

She looked again at the writing on the side. It was her mother's.

Stella wanted to reach in and touch everything, hug it all to her. She owned nothing of her past and here it all was. Photos of herself on the podium staring back at her, hair scraped into a high ponytail, smile as wide as her face – looking like a cross between Rosie and Sonny. Stella felt immediate guilt for this girl who had tried so goddamn hard, for not treasuring it all and not keeping it precious.

Amy plucked the photo of Stella out of her hand and guffawed. 'Look at you! What a doofus.'

'Shut up.' Stella bashed her on the leg.

'Aw.' Amy looked at it again before handing it back. 'I was always so proud of you.'

'You were?'

'Course,' Amy said. 'Then you went and bloody left.'

'I had to leave.'

'Not forever.'

Stella looked at Amy, then at the photo, then back at Amy and felt suddenly as if she'd lived like a horse in blinkers. Trotting through life seeing only her way ahead. Perhaps if she had thought about what the knock-on effect of what happened would be on Amy, even maybe her mother – judging by the fact she'd carefully packed her stuff up in this box – she might have tried harder to nudge her way back in, kept pushing until her father relented. Or even if he hadn't, she might have tried harder to see them all as individuals. Three people under one roof. Instead she had fused them all as one. All in support of him. The enemy was too strong a word, but as good as.

She wondered if that was what being controlling meant – trying to mould everyone to fit your vision of events, having to think less about whether or not you're right.

Amy bent down and squished in beside her, fingers rummaging through the glinting box of gold. 'Ooh look at your shellsuit!' she laughed, yanking out a mid-nineties polyester tracksuit jacket with Great Britain stamped on the back. 'Do you remember Dad had one of these, he wore it all the time. It was so embarrassing. And look, a matching bag!' Amy hauled out the kit bag, bright red with the Union Jack emblazoned on one end from Stella's first European Championships.

Stella, who was still a bit flummoxed by her own seemingly tunnelled-vision view of the world, laughed along as best she could.

Then her brain did a little fizz and she snatched the bag out of Amy's hands. 'This is it. This is the red square in the photo.'

'What red square? Oh, in the Instagram?'

Stella jumped up, bashing her head on the roof beam. 'Shit!' she cried, rubbing furiously at her bump while waving the bag at Amy. 'He has one. Always took it to competitions.'

Amy looked nonplussed, like she'd never seen it before in her life. 'I thought he used to use one Bobby got him from a sponsorship deal.'

'Not then.' Stella thought for a second. 'Has anyone checked his passport?' she said, suddenly incredulous that they may not have done.

'I doubt it,' Amy said. 'He doesn't travel.'

But Stella was already heading down the attic stairs, bag in hand, Amy close behind.

On the landing they bumped into Gus and Rosie.

'Oh my God, Gus!' Stella stopped, hand over her mouth.

'Don't you think he looks lovely, Mummy?' said Rosie. Gus had been done up and adorned from Granny and Grandpa's fancy dress cupboard. An old skirt over his shorts, a strip of fabric tied as a bandana, a red cape, beads, gloves, a chiffon scarf. He'd been given the Rosie treatment.

Amy saw him and snorted a laugh through her nose.

'Is that lipstick, Gus?' Stella asked.

'I believe it is, Stella,' Gus replied, deadpan.

'No one was playing with me, Mummy,' said Rosie, hands on her hips. 'And I said that Gus had spent so long with Sonny that it was my turn for someone to play with me and Sonny wouldn't.'

Stella had to bite her lips to stop from laughing. 'Well, it's very nice of him, Rosie.'

'I think he enjoyed it,' Rosie said, very serious.

Gus folded his arms. 'I'm right here, you know.'

'That's quite apparent, Gus,' said Stella, grinning at his get-up and then walking across the hall to her mum and dad's room.

Amy followed, giving Gus a quick up-and-down before shaking her head like she completely despaired of him.

CHAPTER 27

'His passport's gone,' Stella said. They were all sitting round the garden table, the house too warm even with all the windows open. Lines of pink and orange sunset concertinaed the skyline.

Moira had made Pimm's. Which Stella thought was inappropriate but decided not to comment given the whole controlling thing.

'And up till now, no one's checked his passport?' Gus glanced round the table, incredulous. He was no longer bedecked in Rosie's fancy dress ensemble but a faint trace of hot pink still stained his mouth.

'He doesn't travel!' Amy defended the decision. 'And he certainly doesn't fly. You still have lipstick on, you know?'

'Good,' said Gus.

Amy rolled her eyes.

'I checked the passports,' Moira said, stirring all the strawberries, cucumber and mint round in the jug before she poured. 'There were two in the drawer when I looked.'

'Yes,' Stella said. 'Yours and Amy's.'

'Amy's?' Moira made a face. 'Amy, why is your passport here?'

Amy shifted uncomfortably in her seat. 'Daddy looks after it for me.'

Gus tipped his head back in his chair. 'Oh, good God.'

'Shut up, Gus.' Amy glared at him.

Gus smirked as he continued to gaze upwards.

Amy crossed her arms and legs in a huff.

'So, where is he then?' Sonny asked, zooming in on the Instagram picture for the umpteenth time. 'Somewhere with a staircase and a red bag.'

'Pimm's, Gus?' Moira asked.

Gus shook his head. 'I'm not a fan of cucumber in a drink.'

Moira giggled. 'I can pour it so you don't get any.'

Stella sighed. 'Mum. Can you concentrate for a minute? Where would Dad go with that old red kit bag?'

Moira shared a sneaky told-off glance with Gus as she poured his Pimm's, holding back all the cucumber and straw-berries with a spoon. 'I have no idea, darling. Probably off somewhere reliving his youth!'

Stella tipped her head. 'What – an Olympic site, do you think?'

'Maybe. Yes. That's a good idea,' Moira said. 'Pimm's, Amy? Oh no, you're pregnant.'

The whole table seemed to pause at the mention of it. Moira glanced up, almost as if it hadn't ever really sunk in. She put the jug down and looked at Amy. Amy looked back a little awkwardly at the staring. Moira smiled. Then something seemed to click, like Moira remembered this was her family – all of them sitting round together – and perhaps she could be of a little more use. That even if she wasn't desperate to locate Graham, this was a moment when she could help her girls. She sat up a little straighter in her chair, gave the Pimm's another quick stir and said, 'Well, let's think – his Olympics were Munich, Montreal, Moscow, and LA. And I can tell you one thing, Graham is definitely not in the Soviet Union.'

'Because it's been dissolved?' Gus said, brow raised, sardonic.

'No, clever clogs, because of his stomach,' Moira said. 'He will not be living off Russian food, not a chance.'

Gus was intrigued. 'I think Russian food is pretty similar to our food.'

'Oh no, Gus,' Moira shook her head. 'It's stroganoff and dumplings and things. Graham hates a stew.'

Gus laughed out loud.

Stella put her head in her hands.

Beside her, Jack got his pad out of his top pocket and deemed this the time to take charge. 'So, we've got LA, Montreal, and Munich.'

'He didn't do as well as he wanted in Munich.' Moira dismissed the option and went back to pouring Pimm's for Jack, Stella, and herself.

'Can I have one?' Sonny asked.

Everyone looked to Stella. She was about to reply but instead looked to Jack. Her parental delegation may as well start now.

'Urm.' Jack looked a bit flustered. 'Well. I don't know. Maybe just a little one. With lots of fruit.' He turned to Stella for verification. She would have said no. She didn't know who was right – the law was on her side, Sonny's delight was not. She gave Jack a nonchalant shrug like she wouldn't have minded either way. He was clearly holding in a smile, completely aware of how hard she was trying. 'So,' Jack went on. 'Montreal or LA.'

'He's got a grand, he could get there easily enough,' Gus said.

Moira pursed her lips at the mention of the thousand pounds.

'I've told you, he wouldn't fly,' Amy sighed, exasperated that no one was listening.

Sonny, who had gulped down his tiny Pimm's and now only had a disappointing glass of soggy fruit, said, 'Well, where is he then?'

Everyone looked blank.

'Maybe it's not the racing,' Gus suggested. 'Maybe there's a place that holds more significance.'

'Nothing holds more significance than the racing,' Moira scoffed.

'Maybe he's gone to Portugal?' Amy suggested, a little hesitantly.

'What's in Portugal?' Gus asked when no one else said anything.

Amy shrugged. 'It's where we used to go every year. For our holidays. You know – as a family. There was a big pool near our hotel so Stella could train.'

'They bulldozed the hotel years ago,' Moira chipped in.

'I don't think he's gone to Portugal.' Stella shook her head. 'I don't think he's that sentimental.'

Moira did a little snort of agreement.

Amy sat back, unconvinced but lacking the evidence to argue.

Sonny was doing something on his phone.

Jack had written Portugal on the list. Stella reached over and put a line through it.

'You can get there without flying,' Sonny said. 'To Portugal.'

Stella sighed.

Sonny ignored her, turning the phone round so they could all see. 'Eurostar to Paris. Then down to somewhere called Irun. Then Lisbon. You can be there in twenty-four hours.'

Gus looked impressed. 'Good work, Columbo.'

'Who's Columbo?' Sonny asked.

Gus shook his head as if why did he even bother. 'Don't worry about it.'

'And look…' Sonny was madly googling something else. 'The train to Irun, it's a double-decker. The staircase, Mum. It's a train not a bus. This has got to be it. This had got to be where he is.'

They all turned to look at Stella. All of them, even Moira who paused to look up while fishing a strawberry out of her glass. 'What do you think, Stella?' said Amy.

And suddenly the decision to go to Portugal relied solely on Stella relinquishing control and taking the risk that she might not always be right.

CHAPTER 28

'Come on!' Jack was clicking his fingers nervously, standing beside the revolving doors of Exeter airport. They were waiting for a bike courier who'd accidentally gone to Bristol to deliver the passports that their cleaner had foraged out of the depths of Jack's filing cabinet for them. Incredibly the revelation that Stella had a cleaner had not been commentated on by her mother, who seemed to consciously hold her tongue when the calls had been made.

Now all of them – except Moira who had staunchly refused to come – were hovering by the airport doors. Check-in for Flight 762 to Faro, Portugal, was meant to have closed but the lovely woman from the desk was waiting for them. They were hand-luggage only, having decided three days was enough to work out if their hunch was right or wrong, and once the passports arrived they just had to leg it through security.

Gus was leaning against the silver railing just across from Jack, his bag at his feet. Amy was perched about a metre away from him. Sonny was sitting cross-legged on his rucksack doing something on his phone. Rosie was wheeling the trolley from side to side.

Time ticked by. No one really spoke.

Then Gus glanced over at Amy and said, 'So, have you ever looked after your own passport?'

Amy didn't look at him.

Gus laughed. 'It's a serious question.'

'It's not a serious question,' Amy said. 'It's something that you're saying so you can go on to say something else which will be bad about me, like, "Wow, man, if you can't look after a passport how are you going to look after a baby."' She put on a really deep voice as she spoke.

'I don't sound like that.'

'Yes you do.'

'And I'd never say "Man".'

Amy rolled her eyes. 'A baby is very different to a passport, Gus.'

Gus held his hands up. 'This is so unfair. You're having a go at me about something you've invented for me to say.'

There was a snigger of laughter from where Sonny was sitting on his bag on the floor.

Amy turned away.

Gus tapped his passport on his knuckles.

After a second or two, Amy said, 'That's a really annoying noise.'

Gus carried on tapping.

'I said that's really annoying,' Amy repeated.

Gus carried on.

'Gus!' Amy snapped.

Stella swung round. 'Can you two stop bickering. Jesus, Gus – stop tapping.'

Gus stopped tapping.

Everyone was silent again. Stella looked at her watch. Jack

was still clicking his fingers, peering out into the road constantly checking.

Sonny looked up from the floor. 'How come you had your passport with you, Gus?'

'Carry it with me everywhere,' he said, with a smug raise of his eyebrows. 'Always ready for adventure.'

Amy scoffed in disbelief.

Little Rosie stopped messing with the luggage trolley. 'Do you go on many adventures, Gus?'

'What do you call this?' Gus asked, arms stretched wide.

Rosie looked around at them all, excitement sparking in her eyes at the idea that this was an adventure.

They'd formed a gang and nothing could split them up. Back at the house the day before when Stella had suggested maybe just she and Amy go, Sonny had kicked off that he was the main reason the search had carried on and demanded a seat on the plane. Newly free-spirited Jack had said a holiday might be good for them. Rosie had whooped. Gus had raised his arms and gone, 'Why the hell don't we all just go?' To which Moira had tutted and said, 'If he wants to come back he knows where we are. You won't catch me traipsing half-way across Europe to find him.'

Unable to stay completely out of proceedings, however, Moira had wrangled them a pretty impressive discount at the camp-site-slash-yoga-resort on the Algarve where Mitch was a regular teacher.

At which point Stella had frowned and said, 'Why would Mitch do that for us?'

'He didn't do it for you, he did it for me.'

'Are you sleeping with him, Mum?'

Moira had gasped, 'Stella!' at the impertinence.

Now the clock was ticking. Stella shook her head. 'Adventure or not, I don't think we're going to make it.'

A couple of smokers by the airport door checked their own watches, sharing a look of agreement between them.

Sonny thumped his bag.

But then the dark helmet of the motorbike courier drew up alongside them – four passports in his outstretched gloved hand and Jack almost crumpled on the pavement in relief.

The moment was immediately overshadowed however by the dramatic arrival of Moira, stepping out of a taxi, dressed in black-with-a-hint-of-crazy-fluoro athleisure wear, and unclicking the handle of her snazzy little wheelie case as the driver put it down on the pavement in front of her.

'What are you doing here?' Stella asked.

Moira pushed her sunglasses up into her big red hair and said matter-of-factly, 'Catching the plane with you. I checked in online.'

'Come on!' shouted Jack and suddenly they were all running. The woman from the check-in desk was radioing through to the departure gate. The queue at security glared at them as they squeezed their way to the front full of apologies, expressions anxious – apart from Gus who seemed to be enjoying the drama. The flight attendants welcomed them aboard with raised brows at their lateness. Other passengers audibly sighed as they went past to find their seats. Stella had to look at the floor to avoid any eye contact.

They sat down: Rosie by the window, then Jack, then Sonny, then Gus, then Stella because Amy nudged her forward so she didn't have to sit next to Gus, then Amy. Then in the row in front was Moira, who stuck her head through the gap in the seats and said, 'I don't know why everyone had to glare at us, we're not exactly criminals – just a bit late for a plane, for heaven's sake.'

Gus nodded. 'I couldn't agree more, Moira.'

'Don't encourage her,' said Stella. Then leaning forward to talk to her mother's face pressed between the seats asked, 'Why are you here?'

Moira did a haughty little pout. 'Mitch thought it would be good for me. For closure. His use of the word, not mine; it's a ghastly term.' She was about to turn around when she paused and glanced back. 'And someone has to keep an eye on you all, don't they?'

Stella sat where she was, leaning slightly forward, looking at her mother's hair through the seat gap, strangely relieved that she had turned up. It had concerned her that were they to find their dad, Stella really didn't know what she would say to him, and suddenly the presence of her mother, for one of the first times in her life, felt amazingly comforting.

Stella reached through the gap and tapped her on the shoulder.

'Yes?' Moira asked, her handbag on her lap as she rummaged for her things for the flight.

'You kept my stuff,' Stella said. 'In the attic.'

Moira paused. 'Yes.'

Stella nodded.

Moira twisted round further so she could see if Stella had anything else to add.

Stella sat back in her seat.

Moira looked at her for a second then she smiled and

turned back round. Stella watched as she put her book club book in the mesh pocket, her bag under the seat in front, and then turned and looked round again, catching her eye just for a moment, before reaching for the in-flight magazine.

CHAPTER 29

The camp-site-slash-yoga-resort was situated down a bumpy dirt track at what felt like the end of the earth. Flocks of bright white storks strutted on red legs across the neighbouring farmland. Dogs trotted inquisitively down the centre of the road. A white banner stamped with a huge cross-legged yogi flapped in the gentle breeze as they drew up in the car park late afternoon.

Jack got out of the car, took his sunglasses off, had a look around and went, 'Where the hell are we?'

Wind-chimes tinkled in towering pines. Rows of squat little palm trees lined the walkway like giant pineapples.

Amy got out. 'I can smell incense.'

Gus got out after her. 'It's like my teenage bedroom.' He leant forward and inhaled the smell of one of the incense sticks jabbed in a palm tree trunk. 'Although here it's probably not to mask copious amounts of weed.' He glanced at Moira who was climbing out of the huge SUV with the kids. 'Having said that …'

Moira refused to meet his eye. She was saved by the arrival of a grey-haired man tanned the colour of a walnut and dressed in purple tie-dye, clearly born from the same mould as Mitch.

He greeted them with a hands-together, head-bowed 'Namaste', as they trooped through a lattice archway that marked the entrance to the camp site.

Stella watched her mother bow back. 'Namaste,' she said.

'What are you saying?' Stella asked with a bemused frown.

'It's a yoga greeting.' Her mother's tone was a little uppity.

'What does it mean, Moira?' Jack asked.

'I have no idea,' Moira said, and stalked into the little entrance cabin following the man in the tie-dye with a dismissive toss of her hair.

Stella, Jack, Amy and Gus exchanged a smirk.

Moira stood at the desk pulling printouts of their booking from her bag, her lurid sportswear a sharp contrast to the weather-beaten hut with its wooden veranda and scorched palm trees.

'Ahh, the friend of Mitch,' the man said, his hands aloft as he spoke. 'Our home, his home, your home.'

Moira blushed.

'I am Vasco. Come.' He grabbed some keys on plastic lotus flower fobs from the wall, and led them all out into the piercing Portuguese sunshine.

They wheeled their various cases over the bumpy arid path. Sonny rested his big sports bag on his head. Rosie kept dropping hers to the floor moaning about how heavy it was. All around them the rising hiss of cicadas felt like the sound of the sun burning down. Every few steps a gust of wind swirled dusty tumbleweeds along the scorched red earth. To their left were the campervans. People with their feet up, reading the paper under awnings with cups of coffee in tin cups and dogs lying weary from the heat. To their right was a slope of desert-esque shrubs; cacti, prickly pears, and giant agaves with fleshy green leaves graffitied with carvings of people's names. The land was barren. The earth creaked with thirst.

Rosie stopped midway and wailed, 'I'm too hot.'

'Come on, Rosie,' Stella called, sweat dribbling down her forehead. 'We're nearly there. Give me your bag.'

But Rosie would go no further. 'My legs are tired.'

Vasco paused. 'Problem?'

They all stared towards Rosie, sitting in a heap in the dust.

Vasco smiled. 'The heat is too much for the little ones.' And walking back to Rosie scooped her up and onto his shoulders.

Sonny broke into a fit of giggles at the look of horror on Rosie's face. 'All right, Rosie?' he shouted. But her expression morphed quickly to delight as Vasco strode happily to the front of the group once again, charging up the incline ahead, nimble as a gazelle.

Gus watched, stunned. 'Maybe I should start doing yoga? I'm not sure I could get Rosie up on my shoulders that easily. He must be what? Fifty? Sixty?'

'Seventy-one,' Vasco bellowed.

Gus, surprised he'd been so readily understood, called back, 'Impressive.'

'You want to be strong? You join me for sunrise yoga in the morning,' Vasco shouted.

'What time?' asked Gus.

'4 a.m.'

Gus snorted.

'Yes?' said Vasco, stopping at the crest of the slope and depositing a giggling Rosie on the ground.

'Maybe,' Gus said, unconvinced.

'These are your homes,' said Vasco, as they all stopped next to him. Sonny chucked his bag to the ground, panting.

Side by side, shaded by three looming eucalyptus, were nestled two wooden huts. They looked to Stella like homes for Rosie's Sylvanian Families – tiny slated boxes with neat little windows and three-step stairways leading to a narrow veranda, all pale lime-washed timber with a white sail-cloth roof that sucked back and forth in the wind. Strips of tree bark curled on the ground like crocodiles. A crow scratched at the surface of a long wooden picnic table. The air smelt sweet of warm wood, the sharp tang of eucalyptus, and sea salt drifting on the breeze.

'Very cosy,' said Gus as Vasco led them up the steps of one hut and inside, pointing out the basics of the kitchen living room, the fridge, the candles, the matches, the tiny toilet and shower, and the two bedrooms, separated by canvas. One with twin beds almost touching, the other with a little double.

'Anything you need,' Vasco said, jogging away down the steps. 'I am at the reception. Or I am over there.' He pointed into the distance where, past a few more huts and a couple of yurts, there was a huge concrete square. A group of people were mid-yoga, arms stretched high into the air, and behind them was a wide expanse of bright cerulean sea.

'Wow,' said Stella. Vasco grinned with pride and handed them all a copy of the yoga timetable before jogging to join the group on the stage.

They were all standing in various spots of their new abode. Gus watching Vasco still, saying, 'I can't believe he's seventy-one,' to no one in particular. Moira avidly studying the time-table. Jack was inspecting the construction of the hut, Stella was opening and closing cupboards having a look, while Rosie and Sonny fought over who got which bed.

Amy stomped out of the second hut and said, 'The sleeping arrangements won't work. Where's Mum going to sleep?'

Stella poked her head out of her hut, exhausted from the heat and the journey. She knew immediately what Amy's problem was but wanted to just gloss over it, unable to face a tantrum. 'She can have the double and you and Gus can have the twin.'

Amy gave Stella a death stare. 'I'm not sharing a room with Gus.'

'Oh come on, Amy,' Gus pitched in. 'It's not my dream either but aren't we beyond this? I have absolutely no interest in you and you don't have any in me. We're just two adults sharing a room.' He raised his hands like 'where's the problem?'

Stella watched Amy stumble for a reply. She looked momentarily baffled by Gus's response. The frankness too much for her. As if it wasn't his place to publicly reject her as harshly as she rejected him.

Moira came over. 'What's the problem?'

Amy wouldn't say anything.

Stella sighed. 'Amy doesn't want to share a room with Gus.'

Moira frowned, examined the set-up, then, as if the possible configuration had just dawned on her, said, 'Oh darling, I'm not staying with you. I have my own little yurt, further up the hill.'

'Why?' asked Stella, confused.

'Just for a bit of privacy.'

'Really? Are you sure?'

'Stella, darling, this may come as a surprise but it's a bit of a treat for me – being on my own. Now if you'll excuse me.'

Moira waved the timetable as she started wheeling her snazzy little case up the path, 'I have a session of Jivamukti Yoga to prepare for.'

Stella watched her mother, arms crossed, from the veranda, wishing she too could have reached a point where she could take all this in her stride.

Amy stomped off into the hut. 'I'm having the double bed.'

Gus exhaled, shaking his head. 'Whatever you like.' The limits of his good humour finally breached.

CHAPTER 30

The afternoon had remained fractious, everyone tired and grumpy. Gus had gone off on his own for a walk. Amy sulked in her hut. Jack and Sonny got lost trying to find food, arriving back furious and empty-handed only to be pointed in the direction of the beach by Vasco. 'Why do you not come to me and ask?' he said, all of them traipsing after him in silent exhaustion.

But as heads lifted, and eyes focused on where Vasco was pointing down the beach steps, everything began to feel a little brighter. The collective mood lightened. Jutting onto the sand was a little restaurant; rattan-thatched roof, strings of white lights, long bench tables and in the corner a huge sizzling barbecue. Gus raised a brow. 'Things may have just improved slightly.' Jack's hand tightened round Stella's. Rosie and Sonny scrabbled ahead down the steps. Even Amy's pout tilted up at the corners.

They ate spicy piri-piri chicken charred to black and plump fleshy sardines, they drank chilled rosé, Sonny tried biscuit cake and didn't like it. Rosie tried it and ate the lot. They talked a bit, they even laughed and then Jack said, 'So, what's the plan for the morning?' and everyone suddenly seemed to remember why they were there. Everyone suddenly a little uncomfortable, as if now they were here it all seemed a bit ridiculous. That perhaps they'd got a bit too carried away and gone on an exciting but expensive and completely pointless wild-goose chase.

In the morning, they piled into the huge tinted-windowed SUV – the only hire car big enough to take the lot of them – all except Moira who didn't actually want to lower herself to the search itself, she would talk to him when they found him. But for the others, there was nervous trepidation in the air because as far as Stella knew there wasn't a plan beyond the pool in Portugal. Which, twenty minutes later, when they were lined up along the side of the flashy, newly rebuilt swimming pool complex, seemed a lot like clutching at a straw so tiny it was almost microscopic.

Jack, the only one of them who had a smattering of Portuguese from a gap year volunteering in Brazil, came back from showing the lifeguards a picture of Graham with a solemn shake of his head. 'Nothing.'

Stella sucked in her top lip. 'I knew it.' She reached up and tied her hair in a knot on top of her head. She had expected to feel almost smug when no trace of her dad could be found. She'd known he wouldn't be there.

But as she looked round at the others, at Amy's face screwed up in a weepy frown, Rosie slumped down on the tiled bench behind them kicking her feet against floor, Sonny pulling his Wayfarer sunglasses on, face crestfallen, and Jack putting his arm around his shoulders – 'We always knew it was a long shot,' – Stella found herself equally dejected. And it wasn't just that she felt bad for those around her or that she wanted all this just to get back to normal. The feeling stemmed from the part of her that had lain forgotten like a hedgehog in hibernation, the grinning girl in the regulation swimsuit in the photo in the attic, the Under-11 Regional Champion, the girl from before any of the serious training really kicked in, who had drunk tea from a Thermos and shared Marmite sandwiches with frozen fingers. The part of her that, while she might deny it if asked, had actually been quietly excited about finding him.

Shouts of kids playing in the pool echoed round the giant space. Sunlight glared in through the wall of windows, reflecting in ripples on the white-tiled walls.

Gus looked across at them. 'This is not the attitude. It shouldn't all be doom and gloom. He might still appear.'

Stella shrugged.

'No, Gus is right,' Amy said, hesitating momentarily when she realised what she'd just said. Gus was affecting a bit of a swagger at the statement. Amy moved swiftly on. 'I mean, what do the lifeguards know anyway? When have you ever seen a lifeguard actually look at the people in the pool? Half the time they're all too busy looking at each other.' She pointed to where a pair of exceptionally good-looking Portuguese lifeguards seemed to be flirting at one end of the pool.

Sonny perked up a bit. 'We could come back this afternoon? This might be too early for him.'

Amy grinned. 'Yes, I agree.'

Gus held his hands aloft. 'Maybe the guy likes an evening swim.'

Jack laughed, which in turn made Rosie smile.

Stella didn't say anything. She was thrown by the strange sense of hope she was experiencing. It scared her that it was all becoming too big in her head, bigger than finding her father. Because what if he didn't speak to her still. What if this wasn't about any of them at all? What if he'd just wanted a bit of a holiday or was having an affair and was currently shacked up in some fancy woman's bedroom? What if it wasn't what she was psyching herself up for? She glanced around the pool. All of it unfamiliar, all of it new. Not one memory here of all those years, all those countless lengths. She looked out at the landscaped garden that had once been home to an old silver bullet caravan, the tyres melted into the dry earth, that sold chocolate milk in bottles, Portuguese bread toasted and buttered, and tiny custard tarts. Where she and her dad would sit under the shade of a sun umbrella and stuff their faces, exhausted, hot, calm, before heading to join her mother and Amy at the beach or the hotel. Those were her favourite bits. When the swimming and the shouting and the stopwatch checking were done. Both of them secretly putting the moment off when they would rejoin the family because it would always involve some stress, her mother annoyed that they'd taken so long, them lying and saying that was how long training took. Neither admitting to the little pockets of time they snatched just to sit, the pair of them.

Looking out she wondered if he remembered any of that. He probably just remembered the number of lengths she did or the split times. Or perhaps he'd erased it all, built over it and landscaped it like the silver bullet café itself.

Then another thought took hold. About her mother. About how she must have known they were lying. About how that must have felt. She glanced over at Jack with his arm around Sonny. Tried to imagine what it would be like to know that your husband preferred your child to you. To know you were now second best. Especially in the eyes of someone like her dad, to whom second best was worth diddly-squat.

'So, what do you want to do now?' Gus asked, to everyone but directing the question mainly to Stella because she always had the answers.

Not today though. Stella just looked at him blankly.

'Can we get an ice cream?' Rosie piped up.

'If we're on this trip we may as well make it a holiday,' Amy said. 'Let's go to the beach and get ice cream.'

'Yay!' shouted Rosie. 'Can I get a Twister?'

'What is it with you people and Twisters? They're disgusting,' sighed Gus.

'I think they're gross too,' Sonny agreed.

Rosie swung round. 'No, you don't. You're just saying that because Gus says it.'

'I am not.'

'You are!'

'Shut up.'

Jack cut in, voice firm, 'Don't argue or no one's having one.'

Stella looked over, surprised at Jack's tone of command.

Jack shrugged like it was nothing, like he could be the bad cop given half a chance. Then slightly ruined it as they walked out by saying, 'I'm going to have— Stella, what's that orange lolly I like?'

'A Solero.'

'That's the one.' He winked to say what would he do without her to rely on.

Stella rolled her eyes, wondering if knowing each other's favourite ice creams was on the Marriage MOT list. Then she shuddered at the thought of the article she still had to write, currently bottom of her list of priorities. She wasn't even sure if she and Jack had passed or failed. The temptation to hide behind Potty-Mouth was getting ever greater.

'I like those ice creams that are shaped like a shell,' Gus said as they walked across the car park, sun dazzling on the melting tarmac. 'I always had them as a kid.'

Amy paused. 'An Oyster?'

Gus nodded.

'Are you serious?'

Gus nodded again, this time more hesitant.

Amy glanced incredulous at Stella. Stella shook her head in sympathy for Gus but grateful for the lightness of a laugh.

Even Sonny frowned as he climbed into the car.

'No one likes those,' Rosie sneered with her trademark withering look.

Jack gave Gus a pat on the back. 'You've got a lot to learn, mate.'

CHAPTER 31

As far as they could see was golden sand. The beach had barely changed in all the years they'd been away. To the right were chairs and tables laid out in front of a couple of familiar beach bars, their once flimsy palm-thatched roofs now more permanent constructions. The same slated wooden paths led down to sun-loungers with blue and white striped umbrellas. Chart music mingled with the sound of laughter and kids shouting. There were still the deckchair circles of old women in swimsuits next to men in shorts, shirts, and white socks drinking Coke from ancient cool boxes. The lithe teenagers laughing all golden limbs and ankles inked with stars. The hot pages of magazines flapping in the warm breeze and bright-coloured windbreakers billowing. Out in the ocean, clusters of surfers like black dots waited for the waves. The wind whipped warm. In the distance kite-surfers flew suspended in midair.

To the left was just miles of beach, backed by a wall of pampas grass, palm trees, and prickly pears, the wooden fence posts marking the path white with sea snails. That was the direction they would always troop. Far away from the beach bar music that annoyed their dad but still close enough to get their mother a sun-lounger and umbrella. Stella followed Amy who seemed to head that way out of instinct.

The sunbathers thinned out as they got further from the bars, walking through the shallow water to avoid the searing sand, Sonny and Rosie moaning about whether they could stop yet. Amy finally settled in a spot with the feathery shade of a palm. 'Here, this is perfect,' she said.

The others plopped hot and tired down on the sand.

The sun was ferocious but almost addictive. Stella could feel it pounding on her skin as she laid down a towel and the buckets and spades they'd bought for Rosie. The kids were lathered up with Factor 50, frantically licking their ice creams where they were melting over their hands. Rosie and Amy had zeroed in on the Twister. Gus had been delighted to find that the nineteen eighties classic, the Funny Feet, had been reissued. Sonny had copied him, giggling at the luminous pink foot-shaped ice cream.

Stella had chomped quickly through a lemonade lolly just to get it out of the way. Her brain still muddled and distracted. She felt antsy and irritable, uncomfortable in her clothes and the heat.

As Rosie roped in her brother to build the largest sandcastle known to man, Stella stood facing the water and said, 'I think I'm going to go for a swim.'

Jack looked up from his Solero. 'Can I come?'

'No,' she said too quickly. Feeling immediately mean, but almost spoiling for a fight and not sure why.

'OK, no problem,' Jack said as if he completely understood.

Stella glanced back. She had wanted him to react and knew it. But Jack just smiled.

She fumbled around with a towel trying to change into the cheap yellow bikini she'd just bought from the tourist shop, tying the thin spaghetti straps behind her neck and praying the little triangles would hold her boobs.

'Very nice,' said Jack, supressing a grin, when she emerged from the towel.

Stella looked down at herself, at the yellow frills adorning her like a chicken. She never wore bikinis like this. She wore plain black ones. She closed her eyes and shook her head as Jack laughed. 'Piss off,' she said.

Jack grinned.

She stalked off to the water. Restless and on edge. The waves whacked her, one by one, like punches. Her eyes stung from the salt. Her back burnt from the sun. She breathed in deeply. She knew suddenly that Jack had laughed because he was happier now, less stressed, less quick to react. He had the capacity to see things for how they were. His battle was done. And she envied him. It made her realise, as she dived head down into the searingly cold Atlantic, that what was pumping through her veins was adrenaline, unused. It was all building inside her, bubbling up, desperate to escape. Like it used to before a race, when she couldn't sit still, couldn't sleep, couldn't eat. Muscles firing. This time, however, carving through the water did nothing to abate the restless feeling. She would have to find her dad soon, she realised, pausing to tread water and look back at the group on the beach, because otherwise she was going to explode.

***

Gus came back with yet another bucket of water to aid the building of Rosie's ginormous sandcastle. Jack and Sonny were hard at work digging with cheap plastic spades alongside Rosie, who kept stopping to shout instructions.

Amy was sucking all the yellow swirl off her Twister.

'That's disgusting,' Gus said, pausing to watch in horror.

Amy glanced up from under her huge hat. 'I know. But I like it.'

Gus shuddered. His Funny Feet was long since demolished.

'Do you want to try it?' Amy asked, eyes goading as she held out the Twister.

'Not after you've licked it like that, not a chance.'

Below them Rosie sat back on her heels. 'He's afraid.'

Gus held his hands to his temples in sheer disbelief. 'Why do you do this to me, Rosie?'

Rosie giggled.

'Go on,' said Amy. 'Unless you are afraid. I mean, it's only an ice lolly.'

'Oh, for God's sake,' Gus sighed and snatching the Twister out of her hand took a bite off the end. 'Urgh!' He made a retching face. 'It's revolting.'

Amy shook her head. 'You're lying.'

Gus took another bite. 'Yeah, it's not actually that bad.'

She snatched the Twister back, trying not to smile.

'Gus, we need some shells for decoration!' Rosie ordered.

Gus shook his head. 'You're a hard taskmaster, Rosie.' He looked down the beach, shielding his eyes from the sun, then after a pause said to Amy, 'Do you er— want to come?'

Amy stopped licking the Twister and glanced down the beach to where he was pointing. 'OK,' she said, feeling strangely flattered that he'd asked.

Gus nodded, clearly half expecting to be rebuffed and pleased that he hadn't been.

Amy picked up one of the water bottles they'd bought, Gus took it from her and chucked it into the bucket, then they tiptoed across the burning sand, swearing until they hit the cool relief of the shoreline where the dark sand was ridged and raked by the tide.

They walked, heads down inspecting the washed-up seaweed for shells. There were mainly pine cones and bits of burnt wood, bottle tops, and an old shoe. But every few steps empty shells lay dotted along the water's edge. Gus bent to pick one up, a long razor-clam, holding it over his finger like a talon. 'Imagine if these were your fingernails,' he said.

Amy gave it a glance. 'It'd make being on your phone a nightmare,' she replied.

Gus laughed as if he hadn't expected to, chucking the shell in the bucket.

Amy picked up a couple.

They walked on in silence, just the echoing sound of shells hitting the plastic.

Then suddenly Gus said, 'Watch out!' nudging Amy out of the way of a giant flobby jellyfish that had been washed up on the shore.

'Urgh,' she said, as they peered over to inspect it. Gus gave it a prod with one of the razor shells and it wobbled.

They carried on. Seagulls cruised overhead. The sun beat down. Gus unscrewed the cap of the water, then handed the bottle to Amy before he had a drink.

'Did you know that they think wind turbines and off-shore

rigs and stuff have the perfect surface for jellyfish to breed. That's why there's so many of them nowadays?'

Amy shook her head. 'I did not know that.'

Gus nodded. 'I saw it the other day on a documentary.'

'Do you like watching documentaries?'

'Yeah,' he said. 'Sometimes nature. But mainly depressing ones with subtitles.'

Amy laughed. 'So, do you watch them just because they've got subtitles?'

'Mostly, yeah. It's one of my key criteria,' he said, kicking the surf with his foot and smiling like he'd scored a victory with her laugh. 'And the longer and more depressing the better. What do you watch?'

'Stuff I think you wouldn't like,' she said. 'I watch of lot of YouTube – I like all the make-up stuff.'

'Yeah you're right. I wouldn't like that.'

Amy took her sunhat off, smoothed her hair and then put it back on again. 'I put the subtitles on the TV sometimes, just when I can't really be bothered to listen.'

'Really?' Gus looked to check she was serious.

'Yeah.' Amy nodded, smiling. 'It's much easier to read them than listen.'

'That's the most ridiculous thing I've ever heard.'

Amy shrugged, uncaring, and bent down to pick up a little white shell for the bucket.

They walked on a bit more. More razor-clams went in. The sun went momentarily behind a cloud. Amy stopped, relieved for the shade. 'Can I have some more water, please?'

'Of course,' he said, handing it to her.

She felt him watching as she drank. She swallowed, paused and looked back at him. 'Why are looking at me?'

He bit his lip. Thought for a second about whether he was going to say what he was thinking or not. Then said, 'I heard what you said, you know. When you were in the attic with Stella.'

Amy frowned, taking another sip of water to buy herself some time as she tried to remember what they'd talked about. Then she remembered and did a spluttering gasp, coughing up water onto the sand.

Gus gave her a couple of thumps on the back. 'Sorry, I didn't mean to make you choke.'

Amy was frantically playing the whole attic conversation back in her head. His big nose. The funny sex. She felt herself blushing. Bobby. The guilt. She stood up straight, wiping her mouth with the back of her hand. 'How?' she said. 'You were downstairs with Sonny.'

Gus put his sunglasses on. Pushing his hair back with his hands. 'Actually, I was being dressed up by Rosie in her room which is just below the attic window. And I have really good hearing. It's one of my things. Like really, really good. Weirdly, my dad has a really good sense of smell. We're like sensory superheroes.'

Gus took the water from her and had a gulp, then he screwed on the lid, put it back in the bucket and started walking again.

Amy was dying inside, shuffling along next to him, pretending to focus on the smattering of empty razor-clams.

'All that guilt that you're feeling. It's crazy, you know that?' Gus said, looking out at the beach ahead.

'Sorry?' Amy frowned.

'It relies on the fact that he's watching. Your husband. But he's not watching.' Gus turned to look at her. 'The belief that he is, it's just a comfort.'

Amy looked shocked. 'I don't want to talk about this.'

'Why not?'

'Because.'

'Because what?'

'Because it's got nothing to do with you.'

'I think it does. And no one else is saying it to you.'

Amy bent down and picked up a shell with a huff. 'OK, well you've said it now. Fine.'

'I'm not saying it to upset you,' Gus said. 'I'm saying it to free you.'

'Well, it's not freeing,' Amy snapped back. 'It's just a mean thing to say.'

'Seriously?' Gus said, incredulous. 'It's not freeing? The idea that there's no one watching? That he can't see you? That your every move isn't being watched and judged? Please!' Gus strolled on, gaze fixed on the horizon. 'And it's not mean, it's reality.'

Amy blew out a breath. 'You sound like one of your documentaries.'

'Oh, believe me' – Gus shook his head – 'they are way worse than that.'

Amy stomped ahead to put some distance between them. Then she slowed, knowing he wouldn't try and catch up. She toyed with the razor-clam in her hand, running her finger down the line where the two halves joined. She stared at it, picturing Bobby. Then she tried to imagine nothing. No viewing from above.

She felt a shiver of fear.

There was comfort in the idea that he could still see her. Like her life was a giant Instagram story for him to watch and review like *Gogglebox*.

Without that, it was a daunting path ahead of her. No safe pair of eyes watching, checking.

She threw her shell down, it moved forward in the surf then rolled back in the damp sand.

She thought of the baby. Put her hand on her stomach. She remembered the feeling, when she had been standing in the garage, of his disapproval. She remembered thinking that she had to stand up to it for the sake of the baby. But what if there was no frown of Bobby's upset? What if he could see none of this? She looked down at the sand, all confused.

A huge part of her believed he was watching. And if he wasn't? She squinted her eyes up towards the sun, hand back on her stomach, and found herself overcome by a small flutter of excitement. That maybe the sky held no watching eyes. That she was going to have her baby. Her tiny little baby. That she had wanted for years. And it was OK to be happy about that. The sensation was like clouds parting to reveal a patch of blue sky.

She heard Gus's footsteps speed up behind her, and next minute he was just ahead walking backwards, facing her, feet splashing in the shallow water. 'OK, it was a bit mean, I admit. I could have said it better.'

Amy nodded. 'Yeah.'

'OK, so go with me for a minute. Let's say he is up there' —they both glanced up at the vast expanse of blue above them— 'you really think he's spending his time looking down at you? Really? You don't think he's talking to Picasso. Or Henry VIII. Or' —he held his arms wide— 'Patrick Swayze's surfer dude character in *Point Break*. Or Patrick Swayze for that matter.'

'I don't think he'd be talking to Patrick Swayze.'

'No? Not getting some *Dirty Dancing* tips.'

Amy shook her head, eyes creasing up at the corners trying not to laugh because it was all in really bad taste.

Gus fell into step beside her, pushing his hair back again with his hand, grinning. 'Who would you talk to?'

'I have no idea, Gus!'

'I'd try and find Anne Haddy. You remember – Helen Daniels from *Neighbours*? She always gave sage advice.'

'You talk such bullshit.'

Gus laughed. The waves continued to roll over their toes. The flotsam changed from razor-clams to black pebbles. A couple of aeroplane tracks lined the sky.

Amy realised as she walked that it wasn't really about whether or not Bobby was watching. It was about her clinging on to the thought that he was out of comfort, hiding in the safety of the past. A past and a role she had understood. Really it was about finding the courage to walk head high, eyes forward, straight into the unknown. And if he was up there, well, maybe Bobby could watch if he wanted but as a bystander on the sidelines rather than the guiding light.

They walked on, side by side. On the beach were pockets of people sunbathing, striped umbrellas flickering when the wind blew. Up ahead was a kid running in the surf with a blow-up dingy. The noise of the waves lulled hypnotically. Gus sighed contentedly then said, 'You know a big nose is quite often considered a key sign of wisdom and virility.'

Amy covered her face, wincing at the memories of what she'd said to Stella. Gus turned and winked at her, actually looking quite cool in his sunglasses and navy T-shirt.

Before she could apologise though, she felt something soft and squishy beneath her foot and then a red-hot searing pain up her leg. 'Oh my God, oh my God!' she screamed. 'I've trodden on a jellyfish. Oh my God, Gus. It hurts so much. Oh my God!' Amy collapsed on the sand, clinging on to her foot, red welts appearing on her skin. Her face contorted in pain.

Gus stood frozen to the spot. Eyes wide. 'It's OK,' he said, almost a mutter. 'It's OK,' he said again, then 'Shit!' raking his hair back, looking about wildly for someone to help.

'Gus, it really hurts.' Amy was crying. 'What about the baby?'

Gus squatted down next to her, he took her hand. 'I think the baby will be OK. I don't know.' He looked at the clear glistening jellyfish on the sand. 'Shit, it's massive. OK. Think. We need to get you to a hospital.'

'I can't walk.'

Gus put one arm under her knees, one round her back and started to lift. 'No, I can't, you're too heavy,' he said, dropping her back down into the shallows.

'I'm not that heavy!' she cried.

'You are! You're really heavy!'

'Oh God, Gus. Do something. It really hurts. It hurts so much. I think my leg is swelling up.'

Gus looked down at her leg which was indeed swelling up. She had no visible ankle. 'No, it's not too bad,' he said, disguising a disgusted face as he looked around for what to do. 'Oh!' he said, spotting the kid with the inflatable dinghy who'd paused to stare at the commotion. 'I need that,' Gus shouted, running and grabbing the rope from the child who immediately started to cry. His parents sunbathing down the beach glanced up and started shouting, but Gus was already sprinting back to Amy with the tiny blow-up boat.

'What are you going to do with that?' she cried.

'Pull you!' he said, out of breath, panicked.

'No way.'

But Gus hauled her up again and slithered her into the centre of the inflatable. 'Hold on!' he shouted, and taking the end of the rope started to heave. The boat moved about half a metre. Gus's shoulders slumped with defeat. Then the tide came in and the boat lifted an inch off the sand and suddenly they were moving.

'Shit, Gus!' Amy shouted, holding on tight to the plastic handles as he pulled her further out and the boat tipped precariously.

'It's OK! I've got you. Don't worry,' he shouted without looking back, eyes fixed on the giant sandcastle being constructed in the distance.

'Gus, it's miles.'

The tide retreated, the boat slid heavy on the wet sand. The rope strained against the plastic, not designed for adult weight. 'I can do it,' Gus panted. 'I worked on a farm.'

Amy almost laughed through the pain. 'How long ago?'

'A long long time ago.' Gus was heaving the dinghy, skin scalded by the sun. Then suddenly the rope snapped. The boat stopped. 'Shit. Shit. Shit. STELLA!' Gus shouted as he hooked his arms around the front of the inflatable to keep dragging.

'She won't hear you.' Amy shook her head. 'Please hurry up. Hurry up – it hurts. Oh my God.'

'Why can't they be the ones with the supersonic hearing? I'd hear them!' Gus was muttering. Staggering. Muttering. His back bent double. 'Jesus. I need a distraction.'

'I need a distraction. I've got red-hot pokers on my leg.' Amy winced. 'What about the baby?'

'The baby.' Gus nodded. 'Let's talk about the baby. That's a distraction.' Almost the moment he said it, the moment he realised that it might be in danger from the jellyfish sting, it hit him, square in the chest, that the baby was an actual thing. There was a baby. His baby. There would be a baby. A kid that he would take out at weekends and maybe it would stay over one night of the week and he would take it to school the next day. There would be packed lunches and fish fingers. Gus loved fish fingers. They had that comforting after-school taste about them, always best with tomato ketchup and peas. To him, fish fingers meant family. They meant hectic and chaotic and six kids and two parents and three dogs and baby sheep in the kitchen and cats walking over the sideboard, and shouting and squealing and washing and no one going to sleep and everyone barging into his room and the water going cold during his shower and watching endless television, a lot of it that he didn't want to watch and having to explain the plot of every film he did want to watch over and over again and everyone else always scoffing all the biscuits and all of them being dragged out at dawn to stack the hay when all he wanted to do was sit by himself and read a book. A life that he had loved but had staunchly decided against ever emulating. The selfless hassle more than it was worth.

But this, this was just one baby. He wasn't having six of the buggers. He was having one. One little heartbeat. One that he could tell jokes to and make laugh. One that might love Lego. One that might love comics. One that might understand the films he loved. One that he wouldn't mind so much explaining the plot to because it would be half him. One. That would be his.

He had a sudden vision of his young self finishing the hay stacking at sunrise, lolling exhausted on the tractor, his dad carrying him over his shoulder up to bed. He remembered having his boots taken off for him, his dad tucking him into bed still in clothes that smelt of sweat and hay, sweeping his shoulder-length-huge-mistake-hair out of his face and kissing him on the forehead. 'You're an awkward little bastard, but a great kid, Gus.'

Gus almost welled up at the idea of having his own great little kid. He found he could suddenly barely breathe, and it had nothing to do with hauling Amy's weight along the shore. 'Actually, no,' he managed to splutter, 'let's think about other stuff. What else can we think about?' He glanced over his shoulder to see where he was going. 'STELLA! JACK! SONNY!' he shouted, muscles straining.

'Rosie might be the one with the supersonic hearing,' Amy said, one hand clutching her leg, the other clinging on to the boat.

'ROSIE!' Gus hollered. 'Oh my God, she's looking up. ROSIE!' Gus let go of the boat with one hand and frantically waved. He saw Rosie stand and look then hit her dad on the arm. He saw Jack spring up. 'Oh, thank God,' Gus almost cried. 'He's much more suited to this type of thing than me.'

'Come on, Gus,' Amy chivvied him along. 'You worked on a farm.'

Up ahead Jack was yelling at Stella who started swimming hard to get back to shore. Rosie and Sonny were running towards them, then Jack. Really fast.

Amy was crying. Holding her leg. Gus thought his back might snap in half. Sweat was dripping from his brow as he pulled. 'Remember the hay,' he mumbled. 'Stacking the hay. That was really hard work. Harder than this. Remember the hay.'

'The baby, Gus.'

'I know the baby.' Gus was starting to really panic. He couldn't fail. His legs were burning. Save the baby. Save the baby.

And then suddenly Jack was there, a hero hoisting Amy out of the little boat and into his arms. 'What is it?'

'Jellyfish,' Gus huffed out the word, trying to catch his breath, trying not to collapse on the sand.

'What type?'

'A massive one.'

'Colour?'

'See-through with brown veins.'

And then Stella was there, breathing fast, cheeks flushed. 'Do we need to pee on it or something.'

'No.' Jack shook his head, carrying Amy with effortless ease. 'We need to check there are no bits of tentacle on the leg.' Stella peered to examine Amy's skin and shook her head. 'We need heat on it for the pain and to get her to a doctor just to be on the safe side,' he said, striding back in the direction of the car park. 'Sonny, run and see if you can get a warm towel or similar.'

'On it.' Sonny legged it to the beach bar.

Stella was already starting to jog away, holding Rosie by the hand. 'Rosie and I will grab the stuff and meet you at the car.'

'What about the baby?' panted Gus, walking fast, still trying to get his breath back.

Jack was all straight-backed and super calm. 'I think it'll be OK.'

'How do you know?'

Jack looked at him and smiled. 'Because I carry a lot of useless useful information in my head.'

CHAPTER 32

The doctor at the hospital was very dismissive. By the time they'd got there the swelling on Amy's leg had started to subside and the hot tea-towel Sonny procured had knocked the worst of the pain on the head. When they were actually seen, Gus had to back Amy up about how bad it had been, doing a big exaggerated spread of his arms to emphasise the hugeness of Amy's ankle. The doctor peered unimpressed at the now much more normal-sized joint and packed her off with some cream for the red welts.

It felt so fine that Amy even insisted they pop into the pool on the way home to see if there was any sign of their father – which there was not.

'Well, that's enough drama for one day, I think,' Jack said as they pulled up outside the huts so Amy didn't have to walk as far. He stayed in the driver's seat, engine ticking over and blocking the path, ready to turn round because they were going out again to find a supermarket.

Gus and Stella helped Amy out of the car even though she was probably fine to walk. Sonny followed. Rosie stayed in the car.

A van drew up behind him. Jack leant out of the window, 'Sorry mate, I'll just pull in.'

Above them the eucalyptus rustled like waves in the wind.

The van drove past. 'Afternoon,' said a voice out of the open window.

They all looked over to see Mitch cruising past in his mustard-coloured VW Westfalia T3.

Stella took her sunglasses off and stared after him. 'Mitch? You have got to be kidding?'

Amy was open-mouthed.

'She doesn't mess about does she, your mother?' said Gus, arm round Amy's waist, Amy's arm over his shoulder.

'That's why she wanted a yurt.' Stella shook her head. 'I can't believe he's here,' she added, supporting Amy on the other side from Gus.

'I think it's a mid-life crisis,' said Amy.

'That'd have her living till about a hundred and thirty,' said Gus.

'God help us,' Stella sighed.

They sat Amy down on the veranda deckchair, moving the small wooden table round so she could rest her foot on it. Gus folded up a towel underneath it.

'Comfy?' Stella asked.

Amy nodded. 'Fine, thank you.'

'Right, we'll leave you to it then,' said Stella, jogging down the steps. 'Come on, Sonny. In the car.'

'Can't I stay here?' Sonny asked from where he'd positioned himself on the neighbouring veranda with his phone.

'No,' Stella said. 'You'll just be on your phone the whole time. Come on, it'll be interesting. Loads of different stuff to look at.'

'Nah.' Sonny shrugged.

Jack called from the car, 'Come on, mate,' his eyes almost pleading.

Heat seemed to permeate from the wooden huts, the sun dazzled on the white roofs, the crow that lived in the nearby pine screeched loud. The cicadas buzzed, a manifestation of the mounting tension.

'I don't want to come, all right?' Sonny shouted. 'I just want to be on my own.'

'Sonny! Get. In. The. Car.' Stella snapped, tone exasperated, already wound up to the brink.

Just then Moira appeared, fresh from mid-morning yoga, sipping on a lurid green smoothie. 'Careful Stella, you sound just like your father.'

Gus and Amy watched, silent, from the veranda.

The crow screeched.

Stella turned to look at her mother completely dumbfounded. She looked back at Sonny. Then she swallowed, glancing down at the floor.

No one quite knew what to do.

Moira took a slurp of her smoothie.

Gus leant over the balcony and said, 'We'll keep an eye on him, Stella.'

And Stella said, 'OK.' She nodded. 'Thank you.'

Over at the hut, Sonny's eyebrows shot up, clearly never for one moment thinking he'd get his own way.

Jack leant over and pushed open Stella's door, wanting to get away quickly, before anyone changed their mind. 'Be good, Sonny,' he shouted.

Sonny was leaning against the veranda balcony rail, nodding like he'd do a tap dance right now if asked.

The car U-turned and cruised away, Stella's arm on the open window, her straight-ahead gaze visible in the wing mirror.

Moira trotted over to where Amy was propped up and said, 'What's going on here? Are you all right?'

'Fine, just a jellyfish sting but it's better now. Mum, why is Mitch here?' Amy asked.

'He's teaching.'

'That's a lucky coincidence.' Amy raised a brow.

Moira stood with her hand on her hip. 'I don't know what you're implying, darling, but there's no funny business going on between myself and Mitch. I'm still married to your father – whether I like it or not.'

Amy scoffed.

'I like Mitch, we're friends,' Moira went on unabashed. 'He makes me feel good about myself – which you may find hard to believe, but hasn't happened in a very long time.'

Amy sighed like her mother was overreacting, then said petulantly, 'Well, I just wish our Mum would come back.'

Moira stared at her, astonished she could say such a thing. 'Well, young lady, you'll be wishing for a long time,' she said, 'because she won't be coming back. Because she is me. I am a person, Amy. A person.' She jabbed her chest. 'My name is Moira. And I have a right to be happy.'

Amy rolled her eyes as though her mother was having some airy-fairy, yogi-inspired dramatic episode. 'All right, Mum, calm down.'

'I will not calm down. One day Amy, you'll realise I am not just here to be at your beck and call. You wait till you have that baby, then you'll understand.'

Amy pulled a 'whatever' face.

Moira turned away with a huff.

The cicadas hummed.

Moira paused halfway across the scrubby lawn. 'And do you know something else?'

'What?' Amy spat, arms crossed.

'I hate Emma Bridgewater china.'

Amy looked horrified. 'You do not.'

'I do,' Moira snapped. Then she paused. 'Well no, I don't hate it. I just don't want any more of the bloody stuff,' she said, before stalking away up the path.

Amy turned to see Gus looking at her, expression derisive as though she'd behaved like a child. 'Don't look at me like that. You know nothing about it.'

'I know enough to see that was out of order. What do you want her to do with her life, Amy? Stay at home and look after you?' He rolled his eyes as if realising then and there that Amy would never change.

Amy looked away, across at the arid dune. She nibbled on her fingernail, sulking and silent.

Gus stood up and leant over the balcony. 'You all right over there, Sonny?'

'Yeah!' Sonny yelled back.

'OK, good.' Gus glanced at Amy and then disappeared into their hut. His disappointment in her radiating like the heat.

As Amy wondered if he was going to come back out again, he appeared with two glasses of water.

'Here,' he said, handing her one.

'Thanks,' she snapped.

Gus was stony-faced. He sat with his glass cradled between his hands, elbows on his knees. 'You know, today was the first time that I actually realised properly that we're having a baby. I think before it was this thing that might go away, but today, when I thought everything was about to go wrong, I realised that I actually might like it.'

Amy kept pouting.

Gus rubbed his face with his hand, looked out at the dune then at Amy. 'I would never have chosen this for my life—'

'You've made that perfectly clear, Gus,' Amy snapped.

Gus ignored her. 'But now it's happening. And I acknowledge it's happening. I thought today that it might be quite cool.' He leant back, his expression a little softer as he exhaled. 'But the thing is, Amy, if we're going to do it, if we're going to bring this kid up, I want to do it with you. I don't want to do it with your mother or your sister. I appreciate they will be involved but this will be our kid. We have to work this out together, but I'm afraid that you're just going to relinquish all responsibility when it's born. I look at you and I think her husband died, she moved away and lives in London and seems to have quite a cool job. And I'm actually quite awed by your resilience. You're even quite funny. And then other times I look at you – like just now with your mum – and I think holy shit, who is this girl? Did she really go through all that or is she making it up because I have no idea how?'

Amy swallowed. No one had spoken to her like that before. No one had ever been so clear about both her achievements and her faults. His capacity to make her feel ashamed of herself knew no bounds. But what she hadn't experienced before was the rush that came with his compliments. They were hard-won but unquestionably sincere. 'You think I'm resilient?' she said.

'Yes,' he said.

She thought about what they'd discussed earlier. About Bobby. About the comfort of his memory. And she knew that when she considered walking the path ahead, it wasn't just with Bobby watching, she had secretly squirrelled her mum and dad alongside as well. Her courage shamefully propped up by her parents.

She took a deep breath. 'I don't know what to say.'

Gus shrugged. 'Just say you'll try.'

Amy thought about it and nodded. 'I'll try. I promise I will try to try.'

He laughed. 'And apologise to your mother.'

Amy made a face.

'It'll make you feel better,' he said.

'I feel fine,' Amy retorted. Then as he gave her yet another condescending look she said, 'I really don't understand why you picked me, on Tinder.'

'I didn't,' Gus replied flatly. 'My friends set it up as a joke.'

'Oh.' Amy flushed with mortified shock.

'Oh, come on! You're not upset. Why did you pick me?' Gus pointed to himself, to his face, to his nose.

But she was upset. It hadn't occurred to her that he wouldn't have wanted to pick her. That he hadn't been desperately reaching up out of his league. It was only now that she wondered if she was in fact out of his league. He was funny, as funny as she was good-looking, and that was currency. Maybe his funniness outweighed her prettiness? She imagined him and his bunch of acerbically witty friends having a good laugh over her picture. Maybe, she flinched at the thought, she was out of his league.

'Well?' Gus pushed. 'Why did you pick me?'

'I don't know,' Amy said, her cheeks going red. The rug swept from under her by this possible reversal of fortune.

'Yes you do.'

She looked away. 'It was the same,' she admitted. 'My friends thought you'd be a good person to ease my way in with.'

'Like use for practise?' Gus clarified.

Amy winced and nodded.

'I can't believe you could be upset that I was set up with you when you were using me.' Gus shook his head, laughing in disbelief.

Amy didn't have an answer for it. Only that maybe she wasn't used to not stealing the show – to not being granted a free pass to the top based on looks alone. 'It's different when you hear it about yourself,' she said.

'Well, now we're even,' Gus joked.

Amy only half-smiled. She drank some water. She felt suddenly a bit awkward and self-conscious around him. When the towel under her foot slipped as she moved and he went to put it back she didn't want him to, didn't want him to look at her gross swollen foot.

Completely oblivious, Gus stretched himself out and said, 'I take it Bobby was a man like Jack? The kind of guy who could carry you down the beach?'

Amy nodded.

'That's your type,' he said.

She paused. 'It always has been.'

They both sipped their drinks.

'I'm not sure Bobby would have stolen a dinghy from a small child though.' Amy smiled.

Gus laughed. 'No, probably not. I did have to check his dad out first – looked like a real wimp. I knew I'd be OK.'

Amy sniggered.

Gus put his hands behind his head, pleased with himself. 'Sonny, you still there?' he shouted.

'Yeah.'

'Good.' Then rolling his head her way, Gus said, 'I was thinking Algernon. As a name. If it's a boy.'

Amy raised a brow. 'You'd better be joking.'

Gus shrugged, face blank, eyes possibly smiling.

'It doesn't matter anyway,' Amy flicked her hair, 'I'm calling it Apple. I've known it's what I'm going to call my kid since the moment Gwyneth Paltrow called hers Apple. I love it.'

Gus swallowed. 'I was only joking about Algernon. Please don't call it Apple,' he said, voice rising in panic.

Amy grinned. 'As if. I'm not going to call my kid after a fruit, for goodness sake.'

Gus exhaled. 'Thank God for that.'

'I can be as funny as you, Gus,' Amy said. 'When I want to be.'

Gus snorted as if that was highly unlikely. 'If you say so.'

'I do,' Amy replied with certainty, fluffing her hair, raising her chin slightly in the air and feeling happily like she'd rectified the balance, a momentary lapse in confidence on her part back to normal.

CHAPTER 33

The afternoon brought with it clouds from the sea, drifting in a lazy blanket over the bright red sun, the sky marbled in veins of colour.

Jack had dropped Stella back at the hut and taken Rosie to a nearby playground with a skatepark that they'd spotted on the way home. Amy was napping. Sonny was sitting at the picnic table on his phone. Gus was helping Stella unpack the shopping. In the distance Moira, Mitch and Vasco were sitting cross-legged on the platform meditating towards the wind-licked sea.

'How was Sonny?' Stella asked, pulling bread and a bunch of bananas out of one of the shopping bags.

'Fine,' Gus replied, putting milk in the fridge, a little hesitant of Stella's coiled-spring mood. 'No problem at all.'

Red and white plastic bags dotted the tiny floor space. There was barely room to open the fridge with two of them in the room.

'He's so silly not coming.' Stella shook her head. 'The supermarket was really cool. We ended up stopping for ice cream.'

Gus paused as he took some yoghurts from the bag. He could totally understand not wanting to go to the supermarket and stay at home playing computer games. He would love to be able to sit around all day playing computer games. 'Stella, you know that Sonny loves what he does?'

Stella glanced up from where she was rooting about in one of the bags. 'What? Playing on his phone?' she said, tone belittling.

'Yes,' Gus pressed. He put the yoghurts in the fridge and was about to shut the door when Stella handed him a block of cheese. 'Would you have a similar problem if he was into a sport or chess club or something?'

'What?' Stella was tipping peaches into a bowl. 'No.' She thought briefly about what he'd asked. 'No, because they're—' she searched for the right word.

Gus waited, arms crossed.

'They're real,' she said. 'If it was sport he'd be outside in the fresh air.'

'He was outside.' Gus pointed to the veranda.

Stella made a face as if he was being facetious.

Gus sighed. He couldn't win so he went back to unpacking. When he'd done his last bag he stretched and said, 'You know he's really good at what he does? Yeah?'

Stella was walking over to the table with the fruit bowl. She paused. 'What do you mean – good?'

'Like he's just really good. I can't beat him.'

'But it's computer games,' she said dismissively, placing the bowl down and walking away with a shake of her head. 'I just don't understand the appeal.'

Gus sat down at the table and picked a peach from the bowl. 'It doesn't matter if you understand it.'

Stella frowned.

Gus chucked the peach in the air. 'It's a multi-trillion-pound industry. It's probably the main growth market of the entertainment sector. By slagging it off you're just marking yourself out as a different generation.'

She gave him a warning glance.

Gus smiled. She didn't scare him, well only a bit. 'And it's a shame that you don't try and understand it because your kid's got talent.'

Stella slid herself into the seat opposite him. 'But there's so much more to life than a screen.'

'Not to him.' Gus took a bite of his peach. He'd chosen poorly – too hard and not very juicy. 'I always pick substandard fruit.'

Stella picked up a peach, taking her time to select the ripest. 'So, why do you think he's got talent?'

Gus watched her bite into her super-juicy peach, it looked like a really good one – yellow flesh, lots of juice, red around the stone. He shook his head with jealousy. Stella smirked.

Gus narrowed his eyes. 'Ever asked Sonny about that game he's playing on his phone right now?'

Stella shook her head.

'You know he designed it? You know he built it?'

Stella looked a little less smug about her peach. 'No.'

'It's rough around the edges but it's pretty addictive.'

'I didn't know that,' Stella said.

'No.' Gus shook his head. 'People play it. It's free and popular.'

'How did I not know?'

Gus shrugged.

'Oh God, Gus.' Stella let her hand holding her great peach

flop to the table, resigned. 'I'm a dreadful person.' Then completely letting go of the peach she put her head in her hands. 'I think I'm turning into my dad.'

Gus looked at her head bent forward. Felt a little out of his depth. 'Er... Why?'

'Because I'm just doing to Sonny what he did to me. I push him too hard. I clearly don't know anything about him. I don't listen to him. Shit.' She sat back up, hair everywhere. Eyes pleading.

Gus was way out of his comfort zone. He couldn't really relax until Stella had sorted her hair out which thankfully she was doing right now. She smoothed it back and then rubbed her face with her hands, looking more normal, less desperate.

'I don't think it's that bad,' said Gus. 'I think maybe it's that you're both really stubborn. My dad always said that he was the hardest on me because I reflected back the things he was least proud of in himself.' He paused. 'That sounds less good when repeated but at the time I kind of got it. I just frustrated him because he knew I was wasting my potential – which I was because I was in my room getting stoned all the time.' Gus smirked. 'But he hadn't gone to uni for similar reasons – not because of the weed more because he wanted to make money and got a job on the farm straight out of school. I think it worked out OK for him in the end – he likes it – but he knew I wouldn't like it and if, well, if I hadn't got my act together he knew that's what I would have been doing.'

Stella looked up. 'But I see Sonny loafing about on his phone and compare it to how hard I trained and worked and was pushed and it makes me mad that he's just wasting his time.'

Gus frowned. 'Did you enjoy that pressure, Stella?'

'No, I hated that pressure!' Stella said, then she covered her face with her hands again and sighed like she'd just answered her own question.

'I think what I was getting at with that whole my-dad-story thing,' Gus said, 'is that it's good to push people, just make sure you're doing it in the right direction.'

Stella opened her eyes, peeking through the gaps in her fingers. 'Yes,' she said, tired and hesitant. 'Yes, you're right.'

Gus nodded, pleased with himself. Stella moved her hands from her face and sat more normally. He shook his head and added, 'Your family, you're all nuts.'

'We're not nuts,' she said, defensive. Then taking a bite of her peach added, 'You're just the outsider so you can see it all more clearly.'

Gus laughed. 'Well, go on then. There's Sonny...' He nodded towards where Sonny sat outside at the long picnic table. 'See him how I see him.'

Stella glanced behind her, looked where Gus was looking. 'How do you see him?'

'I see a cool kid, a little too grown-up for his skin – he looks like the Hulk when he's mid-change. I see shaggy hair that he thinks is great and you probably think needs a cut, but he should be left to grow it because he's gotta have his long hair years—'

'But it'll look terrible!' Stella covered her eyes for a second.

'So, it looks terrible, who cares!' Gus laughed. 'Imagine him not as your son, get rid of the expectation and I think you might start to see it all as funny. Let him off the hook, Stella. Let him just be and like him for it.'

CHAPTER 34

Outside the clouds had torn into ribbon strips. Around the huts the eucalyptus blocked the glare of the emerging sun, occasional shafts of light breaking through the branches like magic in a Disney film. The crow was watching from his pine perch as Stella crossed from the front door to where Sonny was sitting at the picnic table. In the distance someone was chanting an 'Om'.

'So I've been hearing all about this brilliant game you've invented,' Stella said, sliding onto the bench next to her son.

Sonny looked up, surprised. Then he pushed his hair out his eyes with the back of his hand. 'It's nothing,' he said, shifting along the bench to put some distance between them.

'Can I see it?'

'You don't want to see it.' He shoved his phone in his pocket.

Sitting this close, Stella could smell him. She tried to feign normal breathing when really she was inhaling him. She wanted to put her arm around him.

He sat arms braced either side of him on the bench.

Stella pressed her lips together. She wasn't sure how to proceed. Through the open door she could see Gus pretending not to watch them, but then she caught his eye and he gave her an encouraging thumbs up. She tried again. 'Why didn't you tell me you'd built a game?'

'Dunno.'

The light from the trees flickered over the table.

Sonny sat forward, started to scratch with his fingernail into the lichen-dotted surface of the table. 'I didn't want to. You'd say it was a waste of time.'

'I wouldn't,' Stella said, knowing that she would have done.

'You would.'

They sat there, side by side.

'I would have done,' she admitted. 'I'm sorry.'

'The whole world knows you think it's a waste of time. How annoying you think I am.'

'What are you talking about?' Stella asked, sliding across to close the gap he'd put between them.

'It's always in your column,' he said, head hung, still scratching lines in the table top.

'You read my column?' While horrified that he'd read everything she wrote, there was part of her surprised and proud that he took an interest.

'When it's lying around. Gran had a copy.' He shrugged.

'Sonny, the Potty-Mouth column's just venting. It's not what I think, it's just meant to be funny.' She tapped the table with her fingers. 'You are quite annoying sometimes,' she tried for a joke, he glared at her.

She sighed. 'Sonny, it's just how you are about me in the playground.'

'I'm not.'

'You are.'

He managed a smirk in his sulk.

She smiled. She rested her forearms on the table, hands clasped, the sun criss-crossing her skin. 'When you have kids, Sonny, it's pretty full-on.'

'I'm not having kids.'

'Well, if one day you change your mind, what you'll realise is that while you love that you have those kids, sometimes you just need to share some of the shit bits with people—'

'Yeah, yeah, whatever.'

Stella ignored him and carried on, 'Well, most people do that with their friends. But sometimes it's easier to hear it from someone else. And to laugh about it. So some people, like me, share it with the world. Or the 800,000 circulation. If only it was the world.'

Sonny flicked his hair. 'I sound like a real disappointment in them.'

Stella inhaled, brain furiously trying to work out how best to play this. 'I know.' She nodded. 'But that's because the bad bits are the funniest.'

Sonny shrugged.

Stella watched him, thinking how she'd always made those bad bits a little bit worse for better ratings, a little bit naughtier and perhaps in her head Sonny had morphed into the kid that she wrote about. She wondered if maybe occasionally she'd written about the bits she was proud of, they might have magnified in equal proportion.

A butterfly landed on the edge of the table, she nudged him to look at it. He glanced. It flew away. Stella ran her hands through her hair and sighed, 'The thing is Sonny, Potty-Mouth Me is much funnier than Me Me. Much more laissez-faire and sardonic.'

'I don't know what laissez-faire means.'

'Well, you should do your French homework, shouldn't you?'

Sonny rolled his eyes.

'It means relaxed, letting life take its course.' Stella sat back against the bench. 'Sonny, I'm just hiding behind Potty-Mouth, really. In real life I'm not quite as relaxed.'

Sonny did a snort of agreement.

Stella went on regardless, 'I've discovered that I have much more set ideas about who I want you and Rosie to be and what I want you to achieve. But I'm beginning to realise that my expectations aren't necessarily your expectations.'

'Mum, this isn't like therapy or something.'

'Just shut up and listen,' Stella bashed him on the arm. 'This is important stuff. I think that I have projected my dreams for your future on you. And I apologise for that.'

Sonny glanced up at her, big young eyes.

'In some ways it's natural for a parent to do it,' Stella carried on, 'and I really don't want you to settle too early. I don't want you to miss out on football camp or taking up Spanish or something because you want to play video games. I just really want you to have options.' She was going to say how she'd narrowed her own options at his age but stopped herself, it was just another example of the pressure of her dreams. Instead she said, 'But I realise that maybe you have to find your own options.'

The butterfly came back. Sonny stretched his hand out to try and get it to walk up his finger. It flew away again. Sonny turned to look at Stella. 'Thanks,' he said.

She nodded, twisting round so she could face him, resting

her arm along the back of the bench. 'I also have really high expectations, Sonny, I can't help that. And I actually think it's not a bad thing, but I do concede that a lot of them are placed on you. And perhaps not so much on Rosie, just probably because you're the first – paving the way. I know, before you say it, it's really unfair. But' —she paused and thought about what Gus had said— 'it might also be because you're the most like me.'

'I'm not like you.'

'You are like me.'

'I don't think I'm like you.'

'Well, just take it that you are like me.'

'No.'

'See – that's being like me. Your dad would have agreed by now just for the peace and quiet.'

Sonny shifted in his seat.

'Well anyway,' Stella said, 'I will always have high expectations because I know inside myself how much potential you have, but I will try really hard to make them your expectations rather than mine.'

Sonny stared straight ahead.

The wind swirled the dust track. A lizard darted through the wisps of dry grass. Stella let her arm slip down from the back of the bench and around his shoulders. 'I am proud of you, Sonny.'

Sonny shook his head. 'That's just because you know I built the game.'

'No,' Stella said. 'But yes, I'll admit I am quite amazed by the whole game-building stuff. Gus says you're very good – and I know it shouldn't be Gus telling me, I should know for myself.'

'It doesn't matter.' Sonny shrugged. It clearly really did.

Stella squeezed his shoulder. 'I love you very much, Sonny. You're very frustrating at times but I know I am as well. So—' she paused. 'I don't have an answer for that, we'll just have to muddle through. I'll try very hard to let you find your own way in life. And you can do it however you like – as long as it doesn't involve not doing your homework or any form of substance abuse.'

Sonny sniggered.

'Or calling me a bitch,' Stella added.

He did a little nod down at his hands. 'No,' he mumbled. 'Sorry.'

'Unless,' Stella said, 'it's in some kind of cool down-with-the-homies fashion – like, "My mum's da bomb. That bitch is killer."'

Sonny squirmed.

Stella frowned. 'No. Actually, having said that, even then no.'

He looked despairing of her.

She swept his shaggy fringe to the side and kissed his fore-head. He wiped it with the back of his hand. She squeezed him into a hug. He let it happen for a second then pulled away, but not too far away, enough that he was still sitting right close up next to her.

'OK then,' she said, 'are you going to teach me how to play this bloody game or not?'

CHAPTER 35

It was pitch black, the middle of the night. The air was filled with the steady sound of distant waves and the wind at the windows. Amy felt it as soon as she woke up. A weight on her hand as heavy as a mouse but with furry great scuttling legs. 'Shit!' she shouted, smacking her hand onto the sheet as she jumped from the bed. 'Gus!' she yelled. 'Gus, help me!'

In an instant, Gus was in the room, hair all on end, boxer shorts on, no top, narrow skinny chest. 'What? Are you OK? Is it your leg? Is it the baby?' He was right next to her, holding her by the shoulders, eyes imploring. 'Are you hurt? What's wrong?'

Amy pointed to the bed and said, slightly sheepish, 'I think there was a massive spider on my hand.'

'What?'

Amy felt like a fool. She expected him to push her away with a laugh. But when he said, 'A spider?' quite softly, taking a step back, she thought actually he was really annoyed with her for waking him up over something so petty.

'Yeah,' she said. 'Sorry! It was massive though!' She tried to justify the commotion, pushing her hands self-consciously through her bed-hair. 'I could feel it, like a mouse or a rat walking over my hand.'

'A rat?' Gus gasped. 'Serious?' He looked pale in the sliver of moonlight.

Amy realised suddenly that he wasn't annoyed with her at all. 'Gus, do you not like spiders?' she asked, trying not to giggle as he backed further against the wall.

'I hate spiders,' he said. 'I really f-ing hate them.' He shuddered, brushing at his arms quick and jerky. 'Shit, I can feel it on me. Where did it go?'

Amy laughed. 'I don't know.'

Gus looked horrified. 'You mean it could be on the floor?'

'Turn the light on.'

'You turn the light on.'

'You're closer.'

Gus wouldn't move, back against the wall.

Amy rolled her eyes, stomping round him to get to the light switch. 'Some protector you are,' she said, flicking the overhead on full beam.

'This is the age of equality,' Gus muttered, lips taut, eyes darting around the room. 'We should protect each other. Can you see it?' he whispered.

She shook her head. 'Maybe it's still on the bed?'

'Pull back the sheet,' he said.

'I turned on the light. You pull it back.'

Gus closed his eyes, took a breath, then stared at the crumpled white sheet. 'Like a rat, you say?'

Amy nodded, lips twitching in nervous amusement.

Gus reached forward and yanked back the sheet.

Amy screamed.

Gus's eyes widened. 'No!'

In the middle of the bed was a spider as big as a pint glass, legs crumpled, head squashed.

'Is it dead?' Amy asked.

'Decidedly,' Gus replied, both of them peering over the giant black body.

'That's disgusting,' said Amy.

Gus agreed.

'I can't sleep in here.'

Gus shook his head. 'I can't sleep in this whole damn camp site.'

Amy laughed.

Gus looked up. 'I know you find the idea abhorrent, but you are welcome to sleep in my room.'

'I don't find it abhorrent—' she started, meeting his eyes then having to look away, awkwardly aware again like she had been earlier on the balcony. 'I just— I just wanted my own space.'

Gus shrugged. 'Well, the offer's open.'

Amy nodded. 'Thank you.'

'You're welcome.'

'Should we just leave that there?' She pointed to the spider.

'I think so,' he said. 'Rosie can get rid of it in the morning.'

Amy laughed.

As she followed him through the eerie stillness of the kitchen she wondered if she'd ever been made to unexpectedly laugh so frequently before. Like almost as if she steeled herself not to he'd still somehow get through.

'You OK?' he asked. 'Cold?'

'No.' She shook her head.

Gus pulled back the curtain door of his room, ushering her inside then jogging round the bed to flick on the side light. 'Welcome.'

She had to hold in a smile.

His bed was chaos. Sheet all in a bundle, pillow haphazard. Clothes chucked over the chair. Glasses on the tiny side table, a book, a bottle of water, his passport, a watch.

'You like to keep that with you,' she said, pointing to the passport.

'Always ready,' he quipped while making a futile attempt to tidy up.

Amy perched on the side of the unslept-in twin, the white sheets still taut, the pillow plumped.

'So, have you been on many spontaneous adventures?'

Gus sat down opposite her. 'No.' He shook his head. 'This is actually the first time I've ever needed it with me.'

She laughed. Then she tried not to laugh but her mouth disobeyed.

Gus smiled. He leant back over the bed to look at his watch. 'It's three o'clock. We should probably go to sleep.'

'Only an hour till sunrise yoga,' she said. 'Didn't Vasco invite you?'

Gus lay back on his bed, hands behind his head. 'I think it's safe to say I will not be getting up for sunrise yoga any time in the near future.'

Amy lay back on her bed, curled to face him, hands tucked under her cheek. 'You'll be getting up at four soon. When we have the baby.'

'No.' He shook his head. 'We're gonna have one of those

306

textbook babies that doesn't make a sound and sleeps all the time.'

'You think?'

'Without a doubt. My mum says I was perfect.'

'That's just what mums say.'

'No way?' His expression was mock horror. 'You're saying I'm not perfect?'

She laughed again, turning her face into the pillow embarrassed that she kept laughing.

He rolled to face her. 'I think perfect is pretty overrated anyway.'

'Oh yeah?'

'Nothing perfect is ever interesting.'

Amy thought of her previously perfect life. It had been wonderful. It had been loving and adoring, generous and perfect. But she couldn't honestly claim it to have been interesting. Probably because there had been so few surprises – no moments beyond her comfort zone. Bobby would have got rid of the spider.

Gus rolled away from her to turn off the light. 'Good night,' he said.

'Night.' She stared at his back in the darkness. Lying this close, she remembered snippets of the night they'd had sex. The drunken giggling. The lip-clashing kissing. The laughing stumbling. The unexpected heat. The smell of his skin.

Before Gus she'd only ever had sex with Bobby and Bobby always smelt of Acqua di Giò Homme.

Amy inched her way forward on her bed as quietly as she could, stretching her neck so she could smell him better.

'What are you doing?' Gus's voice filled the darkness.

Amy shot back on her bed. 'Nothing!'

Gus flipped over. 'Do I smell? You were sniffing.'

'I was not!' Amy's cheeks felt like a flashing beacon in the dark.

'You were.' Gus propped himself up on his elbow. 'Remember, I have excellent hearing.'

Amy lay completely still. She could see the vague outline of his face as her eyes adjusted to the dark.

'Why were you sniffing, Amy?'

'No reason.'

Neither of them said anything. There was just the noise of the wind whistling and the fridge humming.

Amy whispered, 'I was smelling you.'

Gus paused. 'You were?'

Amy nodded.

Neither of them said anything.

Gus cleared his throat. 'Why were you smelling me?'

Amy swallowed. 'Because I remembered liking how you smelt that night, you know?'

'The night we got blind drunk and had sex?'

'Yes.'

'Right.'

The silence hung in the air.

Amy felt weird. The darkness seemed to magnify her every tiny emotion. She wasn't sure if they were flirting or if she just wanted someone to put their arms round her. She wasn't sure if she found him funny or if she fancied him. She didn't know if she wanted him to fancy her just to prove that she had the one-upmanship of the relationship or because it would genuinely make her feel good if he did. She was one half neediness and the other half needing to prove that she wasn't. As she stared at him in the darkness she found herself saying, 'You can kiss me if you want,' almost like she was offering him a reward.

Gus frowned. Shifted his position. Scratched his head. 'Urm. I don't think that's a good idea, Amy.'

'Oh.' Amy rolled onto her back, immediately humiliated, wrapping herself tight with the sheet, stinging with the sense of rejection. 'You don't want to kiss me?'

'No, it's not that.' Gus winced. He reached to the floor and pulled on a T-shirt. 'But we're just starting to be friends. And we've already established that I'm not your type and you're not mine. So, you wouldn't want to mess that all up for a quick shag, would you?' He laughed as he said the last bit, trying to keep the tone light.

'It was only a kiss,' she muttered.

'Well a kiss then.' Gus shook his head, exasperated and amused. 'Come on, Amy.'

But Amy was floundering, she couldn't come on. She couldn't laugh it off. Because part of her had wanted him to deem her irresistible. She wanted his feelings to be as confused and muddled as hers. She wanted him to struggle not turn her down outright.

'We might not have messed it up, you know,' she said a little sulkily, rolling away from him to face the wall. 'We might have made it better. And then we might have been a family. For the baby.'

'Oh my God. Are you serious?' She heard Gus flop back on the bed. 'As if having a baby wasn't bad enough, now you want me stuck in a bad relationship because of it!'

Amy felt her bottom lip tremble. Wishing suddenly that

she hadn't said the last bit. It had been a mistake, tipped the balance. All Gus's good humour gone. She wasn't even sure if she had meant it, simply talking out of dejection. Heaping on to the moment all her wishful fantasies of the past.

Gus was bashing his pillow, more out of frustration than to plump it up, then he thumped his head down and hoiking up the sheet said angrily, 'Goodnight, Amy.'

'Yeah. Whatever,' she replied, quiet and spiteful.

He didn't reply. Not even a sarcastic quip about how grown-up she was.

Amy curled herself up into a little ball on her narrow single bed, facing the wooden slatted wall.

After a minute or two Gus's breathing changed to sleep.

The sun came up and the darkness of the room faded, and Amy watched the grain of the wood appear before her eyes.

CHAPTER 36

In the next door hut, Stella woke up at sunrise. She couldn't get back to sleep, too many thoughts in her head. As quiet as she could she got dressed. Outside the early morning mist hung in the air like Spanish moss dripping heavy from branches. The camp site was glass quiet. Completely still. The sun red. A huge hare lopped across the path as Stella walked down to the beach where she sat on the highest dune watching the dawn kite-surfers whipping through the waves.

She wanted this over now. She wanted her dad found. She wanted to be able to breathe properly again. She got her phone out and looked back at the Neptune013 Instagram picture to see if there was anything she'd missed. Nothing.

Then scrolling absently through the rest of her feed, she found herself looking at picture after picture by Sxnny.x1x2 she hadn't realised he'd posted. After the lawnmower-petrol-stealing shot was Jack skateboarding '*Gnarly old man!!!*', Sonny's empty Pimm's glass at the table '*#wasted*' – Stella winced – and then a host of shots from the plane window, the wind-chime palm trees, Vasco carrying Rosie, Amy's swollen ankle, even one of Stella trying and failing to master his game which she could only assume Gus must have taken. The final one was of last night's magnificent sunset taken from the beach café – a giant sinking orb and a river of red on the sea – '*Missing out, Grandpa!*'

She scrolled through the Instagram feed again, this time trying to imagine herself as her father. Not as hard as she might have thought. Maybe they were more similar than she allowed herself to believe. She remembered Sonny vehemently denying any resemblance to Stella the afternoon before, but it was plain as day to everyone else.

So she sat there, toes buried in the sand, eyes fixed on the wave-licked horizon, trying to embody her dad. Trying to imagine what it had all been like. Imagining the loss of Bobby dying, imagining the wide-open nothingness on his own horizon, imagining the disconnect with her mother, the fresh gap left by Amy, the old gap left by Stella, the realisation that there was no one left for him. His world had shrunk to one.

Then Sonny turns up. A little ray of hope. Stella put her hand on her chest, thinking of the sweet little relationship that had formed over Sonny's two-week banishment that would soon be back to awkward, fleeting visits with the black-sheep daughter.

Stella thought about how she'd felt when she first got to Cornwall, when she was almost afraid of seeing her own son and her husband had announced he'd been living a strange double life – how she would have gladly upped sticks and fled.

The sun shimmered bright and blinding through the sea mist. Stella closed her eyes. She tried to imagine, were she to have fled, how she would have felt discovering Sonny posting all these Instagram pictures for her, to show her the life that she was missing. To show her that she was missed, not just by him but by everyone. That they had crossed countries to try and find her. That her world was not one.

It brought a lump to her throat.

But she knew also that he might now be in a bit of a catch-22. Go home and it all stops. Ring one of them up and feel like a fool for causing such a fuss. Pride was at stake, and he certainly wasn't the type to willingly feel like a loser.

Stella looked out at the huge, choppy white waves, watched them crash and tumble to the shore. She wondered if he'd pick up if she called him. She never called him. She wasn't even sure if his number was in her contacts.

In her head, her calling him would be different to her mum or Amy because it would be a show of appeasement. It would bring with it the possibility of him building a proper relationship with Sonny. If nothing else it would be her pride on the line rather than his.

She blew out a breath, considering whether she was the bigger person.

She screwed up her hands. Why did it have to be her pride? 'Damn it,' she said out loud. Then she thought of the pitifully disappointed looks she would get from Sonny, Jack and Rosie, Amy, maybe her mother, even Gus if they saw her battling such a petty loss-of-pride-based decision.

Reluctantly she reached into her pocket and scrolled through the contacts on her phone. There it was: 'Dad Mobile'.

She called. It went straight to answerphone.

On the second attempt he picked up.

CHAPTER 37

Stella scrawled a note on piece of paper and left it on the table in the kitchen. She grabbed the car keys and, without pausing in case she changed her mind, she started to walk to the car park. At the far end of the path she noticed all the yoga lot, arms raised to the sun, and the glint of her mother's copper hair as she looked round and saw her.

Stella waved and walked on. She was beeping the car unlocked when she heard running footsteps behind her and turned to see Moira, her cloud of red hair swept back as she jogged.

'Where are you going, Stella? Is everything all right?'

Stella walked back to meet her. 'Fine. Everything's fine.' She fiddled with the car key. Her mother was out of breath as she stopped, hands on hips. Stella thought about lying but didn't have the energy. 'I called Dad.'

'And he answered?' Her mother frowned.

Stella nodded.

Moira shook her head in disbelief. 'Well, I should have known.'

Stella remembered the realisation at the Portuguese pool – of being her dad's favourite at her mother's expense – and worried suddenly that Moira was going to go mad, get really angry like she had in the past.

But she didn't go mad. Instead her mum took a big breath in through her nose and said, 'Don't let him bully you, Stella. You make sure you stand your ground.'

Stella frowned. That was not what she was expecting.

The sun flickered through the mist, hazing outlines and casting long shadows.

Moira glanced back to the yoga, thinking for a minute. Then she turned back to Stella. 'Do you know what, I'm coming with you.'

'No, Mum, you don't have to.'

Someone else had stood up from the yoga platform and was walking their way. It was Mitch. Striding purposely in his white flowing trousers and shirt.

They both waited for him to reach them, shielding their eyes from the glare of the morning sun.

'Everything all right here?' he asked when he drew near. 'Do you need any help?'

'No we're fine, Mitch,' Moira said. 'Stella has located her father. I think I'm going to go with her.'

'Mum, seriously, I'm OK going on my own.' Stella could just imagine her dad's face if she turned up with her mother in tow.

Moira shook her head.

Stella glanced at Mitch for support.

'If she wants to go on her own, Moira—' Mitch started.

'No!' Moira shook her head. 'Just no. I know you think I should let them all do stuff on their own. But no. I didn't stand up for Stella before so I'm damn well going to now.' She turned to Stella. 'You are not going on your own.'

'Going where?' A voice said from further back up the path. Amy appeared at the top of the hill wearing her pyjamas.

'Stella's found your father,' Moira called. 'We're going to meet him.'

Amy frowned. 'Well, I'm coming.'

It was too much for Stella, who was still reeling from her mother's declaration of support. 'No.' She shook her head.

'Don't tell me no,' Amy said. 'You're not the boss. I can't believe you were going to go without telling me. Wait while I get changed.' Amy dashed away back to the hut.

'Oh God.' Stella looked away.

Moira stood with her arms crossed, braced and ready.

Mitch looked like he was trying not to smile. 'It's good,' he said.

Stella rolled her eyes. She heard the hut door shut. 'OK, that's Amy. Let's go.'

But it wasn't Amy. It was Sonny. 'I just saw Amy,' he said, jogging down to join them, wearing hastily pulled on shorts and a T-shirt. 'I can't believe you were going to go without me.'

Stella covered her face with her hands.

There was another slam of the door. 'No, you can't come,' she heard Amy say, and then both she and Gus appeared on the little hill. Gus was yawning, yanking on a T-shirt as he walked, paying no attention whatsoever to Amy.

Next came the thumping patter of Rosie, zooming across the scrubland in her nightie, clutching her dress and flip-flops. 'This is it!' she shouted. 'This is the adventure!'

Jack appeared behind her looking half like he'd just woken up, the other half cringing slightly for Stella, having deduced what had happened and knowing exactly how she'd be feeling.

'Looks like you're all going,' Mitch laughed.

'I'm glad you find it so funny,' Stella said, turning her back on him to walk away.

'It's always better to laugh in situations like this, Stella,' Mitch called after her.

She shook her head without looking back.

***

The drive was predominantly silent. Everyone on tenterhooks. Everyone a little nervous. Moira sat in the front next to Stella, suddenly like her bodyguard. 'Are you all right?' she asked at intervals.

'Fine,' Stella replied.

Sonny was directing from the back on his phone. 'Left here!' he shouted.

Stella indicated and turned down a side street that was all little white villas and big red hibiscus flowers. Standing outside one was her dad. His tall frame leaning stiffly against the stone wall, dressed in grey sweat shorts and a white T-shirt. She hadn't seen him in shorts for years, or flip-flops for that matter. His arms were tanned. His black curly hair smattered with more grey than last time she'd seen him. The lines on his face deeper.

'Well, look what the cat dragged in,' Moira muttered under her breath.

Stella parked the giant tinted-windowed SUV and jumped out. Her dad stepped forward. 'Everyone's here,' she said quickly, before the side door slid open and the whole lot of them spilt out on to the pavement.

Her dad's eyes widened. He looked for a second like he might flee, then Sonny shouted, 'Grandpa!' and ran towards him, about to hug him then pausing, not quite sure what to do, so instead stood where he was and said, breathless with excitement, 'Did you see my Instagrams?'

Stella watched her dad as he took a deep breath, unclenching his hands.

'I did. I enjoyed them,' he said.

Sonny nodded, grinning, then reached forward and gave him an awkward, tentative hug and she saw her dad's shoulders relax. Then he opened the gate and walked through first, Sonny by his side.

Inside was a big lush garden, more hibiscus bushes fringed the lawn alongside towering palms, there were odd white statues, bougainvillea-draped window awnings and luminous green grass. To the right was a wide mosaic pool. Behind that was a low haphazard bungalow – a glimpse through the fly-screen of the open door showed a TV flickering and dark wood furniture covered in bright-coloured throws.

Amy squeezed to the front of the group to get closer to her dad, throwing her arms around him tight. 'Daddy! I'm so pleased you're all right. I was scared someone might have kidnapped you.'

Her dad did one of his laughs reserved just for Amy, humouring her. Enabling her dippiness.

'Daddy, things are awful,' she carried on, whiny. 'I'm pregnant, and Gus there is the father and we're not a couple.'

Gus froze in horror.

'And he's only slightly sure if he even wants the baby,' Amy added, looping her arm through her dad's, holding him tight to her.

Gus looked like he could barely hold it together, spitting rage that Stella didn't think him capable of while having to swallow and reach out his hand in an awkwardly polite attempt to shake her dad's. 'Nice to meet you,' he said, tone expressionless, like he actually couldn't care less whether this guy was about to smack him in the face, he was done with it all.

Stella watched her dad size him up, look at the hand. He gave it a second's worth of a shake, if that, then reached round and stroked the side of Amy's hair. 'It'll be all right, Pumpkin,' he said. 'You can come back and live with me. I'll look after you.'

'You'll do what?' Moira stalked forward from the back of the group. 'You'll do no such thing. Since when have you known how to take care of a baby?'

'I know how to take care of a baby, Moira.'

'Graham, we had these two when we did so they could fit in with Olympic Games years. I could count the times you changed a nappy on one hand.'

They stood glaring at each other.

Gus tried to get Amy's attention but she stayed where she was, pouting. 'Are you really doing this?' he said.

Amy turned her face into her dad's sleeve.

Gus exhaled, long and slow, expression appalled. Then he held his hands up to the sky and said, 'You know what? You do what you like.' And turned and walked away.

'Gus, where are you going?' Sonny shouted.

But Gus didn't turn around.

Stella watched her dad frown. 'What is going on here? Who is he?' he asked. 'How do you even know him, Amy?'

But no one answered.

It felt to Stella exactly like it always did. Her dad was back and the little gang they'd formed had disbanded in one fell swoop. Like their old familiar roles were too ingrained. Too alluring. She could already imagine Amy handing her passport back at the end of the trip.

Stella was about to say something but she was stopped by her mother's voice. 'No,' said Moira. 'No, you won't do this, Graham. You won't do this. Whatever is happening here, don't you dare hide behind Amy. She has a life to lead and it's not with you.'

Graham looked wounded. 'I was just offering to help.'

'No you weren't, you were dragging her back in. Well, it's not going to happen. I won't let it.'

Amy was aghast. 'Mum! Why are you being so mean?'

'Oh Amy, grow up!' Moira shouted. 'You need that man,' she said, pointing to where Gus had disappeared out of the gate. 'Your child needs that man. Don't throw it away because you're being a spoilt brat.'

Amy's cheeks pinked, enraged.

Moira folded her arms. 'Go on,' she said.

'What?' Amy spat, hands on her hips.

'Go after him, you silly girl.'

'I will not.'

'You damn well will. Now go!'

Amy stomped off, fuming, slamming the gate hard behind her.

As this was going on Jack looked at Stella and made big

eyes down at Rosie who was watching the drama like it was *Real Housewives* of wherever. He angled his head towards the pool. Stella nodded and gestured to Sonny as well. Jack tiptoed round and yanked Sonny on the arm, dragging both the kids reluctantly over to the poolside.

That left Stella, her mother and her father, standing in the middle of the lawn.

Little birds fluttered in and out of the tree next to them. The filter on the pool opened and closed as the water lapped in the breeze.

Stella didn't know what to say, but it didn't matter because suddenly her mother was taking the lead on everything.

'Right,' said Moira, rubbing her hands together. 'Are you going to make us a cup of tea, Graham?'

CHAPTER 38

Graham came back from the kitchen with three cups of tea.

Stella and Moira had settled themselves into a couple of old wicker chairs with yellow and blue striped cushions under the shade of an awning. As she'd sat down, Moira had given Stella a wink.

Now, as Graham handed her a tea, Moira said, 'Thank you.' Then inspecting the colour of it and taking a quick sip added, 'It's amazing what you learn when you're left to your own devices, isn't it?'

Graham mumbled something.

Stella raised a warning brow at her mother who looked away with a smirk.

In the background the kids were messing around by the pool.

'What is this place?' Stella asked as her dad sat down with his tea.

Graham looked around. 'I found it on Airbnb.'

'Airbnb?' Stella was surprised he knew what the website even was.

'Your son made me quite proficient on the Internet,' he said.

Stella nodded. She looked around, saw a woman watching

from the screen door with a bowl of cereal in her hand, a man behind her having breakfast at the table. 'How many people are staying here?' she asked.

'A lot,' he replied. 'And they play music. Very loudly.'

Moira snorted a laugh. 'Serves you right.' Then, after a sip of tea, said very matter-of-factly, 'So, go on then, why did you leave?'

Stella was relieved once again that her mother was here. On her own she'd have been pussyfooting round the issue, the pair of them immediately at a stand-off.

Graham shifted in his seat. 'I don't know really.'

Moira puffed an exasperated breath. 'Course you know.'

Graham looked up. 'I felt like I was surplus, I suppose. No one needed me,' he said. 'You'd gone off with your Mitch—'

'Er, excuse me, but I haven't gone off with him.' Moira plonked her tea down on the table. 'He's a friend who I like and who challenges me to be my best self, Graham, rather than his teasmaid. And I don't believe for one minute that's why you left. I think you were afraid. You suddenly looked around you and were frightened you'd ballsed it all up.'

'Mum!' Stella tried to stop her from being so harsh.

'I don't know why you're defending him, Stella.'

They were all quiet.

Graham exhaled. He sat forward in his seat, rubbing his hands together. 'You're right,' he said to Moira. Then glancing at Stella said, 'Your mother's right. I probably was afraid.'

Stella felt uncomfortable under his gaze, big dark eyes like Sonny's, unused to him looking at her.

He sucked in his cheeks before speaking again, the lines on his face deep as cracks. 'I saw you all on that Instagram, living your lives, and I felt like I was on the periphery which isn't somewhere I was used to being. I knew I had to do something, even before Sonny visited.' He paused. 'I like your kid,' he said.

Stella watched him rubbing one thumb back and forth over the other. She wanted to say, 'What about me? Do you like me?' But she stayed silent, just nodded.

'You were all getting on with it. Your mother was off with her new man.' Moira sighed heavily in the background. 'And I realised the only one stopping me was me. I'd forgotten what it was like to be out in the world.' He sat back in his chair, a little more confident now. Getting into his story. 'So, I tested it. Picked up my passport and gave it a go.'

Stella saw her mother roll her eyes.

'And withdrew a thousand pounds of our money,' Moira added. 'And packed a bag. And managed to research a route that didn't involve any flying. Don't make it sound quite so romantic, Graham. You were lonely and you realised you'd be lonely forever if you didn't get up off your bottom and do something.'

Her dad cleared his throat. 'Well,' he said, a touch more coyly. 'I don't know if I'd put it quite like that.'

'Why didn't you come back?' Stella asked.

'I don't think I thought anyone would miss me. But then I saw you were all together, looking for me and I didn't want to have caused such a fuss so … I was embarrassed.'

'Oh fiddlesticks,' Moira scoffed. 'You loved it.'

Graham looked at her perplexed.

'Don't look at me like that.' Moira shook her head. 'I know you, Graham Whitethorn. You love nothing more than a bit of attention.'

Graham frowned. 'That is not true.'

Moira sighed. 'You loved the fact they were all trying to get you to come home with their photos. Just admit it.'

Her dad sat back with a slight smirk. 'OK, maybe I was flattered. It was nice. It's nice to be missed. Saw you all coming here, saw you swimming,' he said, nodding to Stella. 'Better late than never,' he quipped.

Stella looked away. The sun had risen higher in the sky, red fading to yellow. All around them the palm trees swished in the ever-present wind.

'Graham!' Moira warned.

'What?'

'Don't wind her up.'

'I'm not winding her up. It is about time. Would have been better if she'd never stopped in the first place. But—'

'Graham,' Moira warned again.

He held his hands up. 'OK, fine.' He picked up his tea, blew on it, took a sip and muttered, 'You could have been so good. It was such a waste.'

Stella narrowed her eyes. She couldn't believe he would say it, still. 'What did you say?'

'Ignore him, Stella,' her mother said.

But she couldn't ignore him. She couldn't slip back into their familiar caricatured relationship. She thought about Mitch that day at the beach. If it's normal you're all lying. 'Dad, it was twenty years ago. It's over. It's so over it's not even a thing any more. I didn't want to do it. Do you understand that? I didn't want to do it.'

'You just got distracted, that was all, by a bit of time off and a load of parties. You just thought you didn't want to do it. That was always your problem, you thought too much,' he said with a disapproving shake of his head.

To Stella that bit of time off, that freedom, was like a ray of sunshine through the clouds of her memory. 'I didn't think too much. I just started thinking for myself. That was the only problem. Maybe if you'd seen me as less of a project and more as a person then I would have had more balance and would have dived in the bloody pool.' She realised she was starting to shout. Sonny and Rosie were looking up, worried. Stella waved her hand and smiled to show she was fine.

Her dad drank his tea. 'Doesn't matter now, anyway.'

'Oh Graham,' Moira exclaimed. 'You can't say that and just shut it down.'

Her dad jutted out his jaw.

Stella wasn't used to her mother sticking up for her. She found it was giving her the confidence to carry on – knowing that if he shouted her down there was suddenly an avenue of support. 'It does matter,' Stella said. 'It matters because I want you to see that what I did was right.'

Her dad looked across at her. 'Why?'

'Because it matters to me,' Stella said.

He thought about it for a second, swatted a wasp away that flew near his face, and said, 'I see that you think it was right for you.'

'But not right?' Stella said.

'Graham, you're being a bully,' Moira snapped.

Her dad ignored her. 'I think you regret it, Stella.'

'You're so annoying!' Stella stood up and started to walk away.

Her dad wouldn't let it go. 'You do regret it, don't you?'

Stella paused.

Moira held her hands up. 'Does it really matter?'

Graham shrugged.

'Do I regret it?' Stella turned to face him. 'Yes,' she said. 'Yes, I do. I regret not diving in.'

Her dad's mouth tilted up ever so slightly in victory.

But Stella hadn't finished. 'Do I regret not going to the Olympics? No.' She shook her head like it was the stupidest most minor thing in the whole world. 'No, I couldn't care less about that. Not one jot. I have a really lovely life. As you say I have a really lovely kid. And another one, Rosie, I don't think you know her at all. I have a really lovely husband. Jack.' She pointed towards the pool without taking her eyes off her dad. 'I don't think you know him at all. I have a really good job that rewards me for thinking too much. You've probably never read anything I've written. And do you know, I also have a really lovely sister, who when she's not being mollycoddled by you, is a really great person. As is that guy, the father of the baby. The one you wouldn't even look in the eye. You want to know why I regret not diving in? Because of all that. Because if I had, you would know my family. I would know my mother and my sister and you. You would know me.' She swallowed.

Her mother was staring at her, fond sadness in her eyes.

Her dad was looking down at his hands.

'It's ridiculous.' Stella shook her head. She could feel the slight sting of tears behind her eyes. Sonny, Rosie and Jack were watching her from the pool but she couldn't stop herself. 'It's ridiculous that it ever got to this. You want me to say I regret it? Fine – I regret it. Does that make it better? You want me to say sorry? Fine. I'm sorry,' she said, then again really loud and drawn out, 'I'm S-O-R-R-Y.'

Then silence.

Not a word from anyone. Just the hiss and suck of the pool filter. Even the people in the breakfast room were staring.

Stella went and sat back down again. Cheeks flushed a touch with embarrassment at her outburst but feeling surprisingly relieved that she'd done it. She picked up her tea. Took a nervous sip and then glanced across at her dad. He seemed suddenly old and small, like an ageing stag in the herd. His power depleted.

He sat staunchly silent.

'Stella, darling—' her mother started.

'Mum, it's fine.' Stella shook her head.

It all seemed so insignificant. So pointless.

She felt suddenly annoyed with herself for how much she craved his forgiveness – or at least a shouldering of some of the blame. She had waited so long to be forgiven that the thing she was being forgiven for was meaningless anyway. She was annoyed that she hadn't been strong enough to put herself in control, believe her actions were good and, as he said, right for her. Who else should they be right for? She felt frustrated that through his alienation of her she had lost a certain sense of her belonging. Her confidence in herself. And that had trickled down into everything – her parenting, her relationship, even Potty-Mouth was an amalgamation of what people wanted her to be.

It all just felt like a giant waste of time, and put how she had just ranted it – like a giant loss of what could have been.

Sitting looking across at him, she was reminded of what

Gus had said the afternoon before when they had been looking out at Sonny sitting at the table: 'get rid of the expectation'. And she had to smile because next to her was really just a man afraid of being alone. A father who made mistakes he could not admit to. The same as Stella was a mother who made mistakes she couldn't admit to – just she had the benefit of Gus's seemingly infinite wisdom.

Her dad took a sip of his tea, staring straight ahead.

Stella watched his profile. Watched the bob of his Adam's apple as he swallowed. Under her breath she whispered, 'I forgive you.'

He turned. 'Sorry?'

'See, it wasn't that hard,' Moira quipped.

Stella grinned.

Graham looked even more confused. 'What wasn't?'

'You just apologised,' Moira said, wriggling down in her seat, amused with herself. 'Now, say it again with a bit more conviction.'

'I don't think—' he started.

'Graham,' Moira cut him off. 'Just apologise to the poor girl and we can all move on.'

Stella watched her dad squirm in his seat. 'I don't see what I have to apol—'

'Graham!' It was Moira's turn to shout.

'Oh, for God's sake.' He sat up all shirty. 'Fine, I apologise. For what, I'm not sure, but I apologise.'

Moira opened her mouth, visibly more enraged at his useless attempt at saying sorry, but Stella stopped her. 'It's fine, Mum,' she said, almost laughing. 'It's fine.'

Moira narrowed her eyes. 'You're a stubborn old fool, Graham Whitethorn.'

Stella looked over to the pool, at Jack with the kids. Jack gave her a thumbs up. She nodded. He winked at her.

She thought about when her dad would wink at her on the side of the pool. How amazing it felt. How it spoke wordlessly everything she ever needed to hear. She glanced across at him, sitting slumped in his chair, a little sulky like he did back home. Then she nodded towards the pool. 'I'll race you for it.'

'For what?'

She shrugged. 'An apology. An acknowledgement that it wasn't all my fault.'

She wasn't sure it was something she even needed any more, but there was something in the fact he couldn't say it that made her worry this wouldn't be the end. A race felt like a language he understood, something with a clearly defined beginning and end. She was interested to see how he would play it.

Her dad was silent for a second. She waited, knowing however old and unfit he was, he couldn't turn down a challenge.

He clicked his neck and rolled his shoulders back. 'How many lengths?' he asked.

'Just one,' she said, unable to stop the hint of a smile that he was considering it.

'Not worth it for one.'

'Two then.'

Her mother was watching, intrigued.

He nodded. 'Let me go and get changed.'

Stella only had the frilly yellow bikini, left in the car after Amy's hospital trip the day before. She went and got it and changed in the bathroom off the kitchen. Nervous, excited, adrenaline making her hands shake as she knotted the ties. When she came out her dad was standing on the edge of the pool, flexing up and down on his toes, wearing his tiny red Speedos with the Olympic crest. Stella had to stifle a laugh when she saw them.

Her dad made a face when she came to stand next to him. 'Can you swim in that thing?' he asked, nodding to the bikini.

'Don't worry about me,' she said.

The couples who'd been having breakfast came outside to watch. Sonny and Rosie were whooping on the sidelines. Jack was waiting at the far end to check, as her father had insisted, that they touch the wall before turning. It was all very serious. Her mother was behind them ready to call the start.

Her dad did some more warm-up exercises. 'My legs are a bit stiff because it's so early.'

'Are you just saying that in case I win?' Stella asked.

Her dad's gaze fixed on the water as he did a final stretch and said, 'You're not going to win.'

Her mother reached forward and placed her hand softly on Stella's shoulder. The briefest of touches. Stella glanced round and caught her eye.

'Good luck,' Moira mouthed.

Stella took a deep breath. 'Ready when you are.'

Her mother moved round to the edge of the water. 'On your marks!'

Her dad glanced across at Stella. 'And you're definitely going to dive in? Not leave me splashing about like a fool?'

'Get set!'

'Oh, I'm definitely diving in,' Stella said, rubbing her hands together, readier than she'd ever been.

'Go!'

And Stella dived. Easy as anything. The taste of the chlorine on her skin. The blue of the water stinging her open goggle-less eyes. She swam fast. As fast as she could possibly go. 'Go Mum! Go Grandpa!' she could hear muffled through the water, neither kid having any idea why they were racing.

She knew she was ahead but could sense her dad next to her. Even with two years off he was fitter and stronger than her and she knew it. She made it through two-thirds of the first length before the pain hit like a hammer, lactic acid burning her muscles. She was unfit. She felt him pull away. Her arms seared. The water like a net pulling her back. She could see the red of his trunks now as he got further in front and she could feel her strokes shorten as she got annoyed. She couldn't work out if she'd wanted him to let her win – but knew how infuriating it would have been if he had.

At the end of the first length she came into the turn all over the place. Her dad ahead and gone. She imagined Pete, fag on the go, heaving himself up from his chair to bellow, 'Stop thinking! Just get on with it, you stupid girl.' And she tensed again. Then as she turned she glimpsed Jack. The bubbles off her dad's kicks rippled her water. She looked to the side when she shouldn't have done and saw Rosie and Sonny waving their arms. 'Go Mum!'

Imaginary Pete hollered, 'For crying out loud, don't get distracted!' Her brain shouted, 'Piss off, Pete,' and he disappeared, poof. And Stella smiled underwater. Her muscles screaming while bubbles of air rose as she laughed. 'It's always better to laugh in situations like this,' Mitch had said – maybe he was a bona fide guru.

'You really do have to stop thinking, Stella,' she warned herself, her dad slipping further and further away. And so she concentrated only on the twitching smile on her lips. Focused. The pain starting to energise, the thrill starting to spur her on and suddenly the adrenaline kicked in. She hit her stride. The red shorts got closer. He was getting tired. There was a tiny inkling of a chance she might be able to take this. But she no longer cared about the outcome. She didn't need his approval or his forgiveness. She needed her own, and that would come from giving it everything she had. Knowing she could have done no better. All the while grinning as her lungs threatened to explode. She felt like a fish having the time of its life. This was her, racing for herself. Fast, graceful, happy. Then it was done. Two lengths. Over.

He won. She was close. Gasping to catch her breath.

Her dad slicked his hair back. 'Not bad,' he said.

Stella was panting, holding onto the side. 'Quite good actually, I thought,' she said, looking him square in the eye. Then with a wink and a smile she hauled herself out of the pool.

CHAPTER 39

Amy had made it look like she was going after Gus but instead she skulked around on the corner, moping, kicking fallen bougainvillea leaves with her flip-flops, waiting for them all to finish what they were doing so she could position herself, leaning up against the car, all hard done by and misunderstood.

So when she glanced round the corner and saw Gus walking back in her direction, she found herself in a half-crouch by the wall trying to work out which way she could dart.

'I saw you,' he shouted.

'Shit.' She peered back round the brick wall of the house on the corner, bougainvillea like a curtain around her.

Gus approached. 'What are you doing?' he asked, lips in a permanent sneer.

'Nothing,' she said.

'Why aren't you with the others?'

'No reason.'

He made a face like he couldn't be bothered with her and carried on past in the direction of the car.

'I don't know why you're annoyed with me,' she called out.

'Yes you do,' he said without looking round.

Amy stared down at the kerb. At the little pink bougainvillea cups that had scattered to the floor in the breeze.

Gus stopped and turned, doubling back so he was a metre or two away from her. 'You can't be so stupid that you don't know why,' he said, as if he was on the cusp of actually wondering whether she was.

Amy swallowed. She didn't look up.

'That was pathetic, that little show back there with your dad. And what? Because I wouldn't kiss you last night?'

'Shut up,' she muttered.

'You're pathetic, Amy.' Gus stood where he was. 'You said you were going to try and the first thing that doesn't go your way, you run back to your dad. What are you playing at anyway? You didn't actually want me to kiss you.'

'Yes I did.'

'Why?' He raked his hair back, dumbfounded. 'You don't want me. This' —he pointed between the two of them— 'is incompatible.'

'I know,' she said.

'Then what's the matter?'

'I don't know,' she shouted, looking up, trying not to cry. She'd wanted him to kiss her last night, now in the light of day she wasn't so sure. She had seen the look of uncertainty on her dad's face when he'd seen Gus – even before the baby revelation – he'd never looked at Bobby like that. Gus was right, they were completely incompatible, she didn't know what she'd been thinking – clutching on to some sort of comfort and stability amidst all this change. And then her pride had been hurt and she'd flipped. 'I'm pathetic,' she said, covering her face. 'I know I'm pathetic.'

Gus stayed where he was. 'Are you crying?'

'No.'

'I think you are.'

'I'm not.'

Amy sniffed. Then she had to take her hands away from her face to do something about the snot and the tears. She searched around in the pockets of her skirt for a tissue. Gus reached over and handed her a clean one.

'I think I should be the one crying,' he said.

Amy laughed through the tears and it came out as a little snort. She wiped her face with the tissue. 'You made me snort.'

Gus shrugged.

Tiny dots of sunshine like stardust flickered through the trees.

'Why are you crying, Amy?'

'Because I feel bad. Because I know we're incompatible but I got scared, I suppose, of what's to come. I get scared of doing it on my own and I know it's stupid but I can't help it.'

'I don't think you're stupid. I shouldn't have said that.'

He moved to lean against the wall. She leant next to him.

'Aren't you scared of anything? Of being lonely?' she asked.

'No.'

'Not at all?'

Gus thought about it. 'No. But it has been nice, this.' He gestured towards the big black SUV at the end of the road. 'I've enjoyed being with everyone more than I thought.' He glanced at her. 'I've quite enjoyed being with you. When you aren't like this, though.'

Amy stuffed the tissue back in her pocket. 'I've enjoyed being with you,' she said, glancing up and across at him. 'I think that's the problem.'

'Liking being with me is a problem? That doesn't sound good.'

'No.' Amy shook her head. 'I like who I am around you. You make me try harder. You push me. And I need that. I really am not stupid, I know what I get away with,' she added, tugging at one of the bougainvillea flowers spilling over the wall.

Gus gave her a wry look. 'I knew it was all an act.'

'It's not an act,' she said, plucking at the hot pink leaves. Then she paused. 'Maybe it was an act, I don't know. It didn't feel like an act until I met you.'

'I don't see what the problem is.' Gus shrugged. 'This all sounds very good to me. I sound like a hero.'

Amy thwacked him on the arm. 'You're not a hero.'

'I am a hero.' Gus pointed to himself. 'A hipster hero.'

Amy rolled her eyes. Then she chucked the flower on the floor. 'And what's going to happen when you go off with your new hipster girlfriend and be all cool and funny together in your horn-rimmed glasses – you'll forget about me and the baby.'

'No I won't.' Gus kicked the wall.

'She's not going to like me.'

'Who? My mythical hipster girlfriend?'

'Yeah. She'll wear dresses from charity shops.'

It was Gus's turn to snort.

Amy smiled.

'Well, what about you when you're off with your new beefcake? You won't want me and my desperate wisecracks hanging around.'

'I'm not going to go off with a beefcake.' Amy sighed. 'I'm going to have a baby to look after.'

Gus rolled his head along the wall to glance at her. 'Oh, I reckon you'll find yourself a beefcake. Some topless hunk to cradle the baby against his bare chest.'

Amy giggled.

'See, you like it already.'

She smiled. Then she sighed. 'Our dinner parties together will be really stilted.'

'Dinner parties?' Gus looked horrified. 'Do people still have dinner parties?'

'You know what I mean.'

'I'm not sure I do,' he said. Then when she gave him a look, he nodded. 'I know what you mean.'

They both kicked the wall.

Gus looked up at the bright blue sky then after a second gave Amy a bash on the arm. 'Well, how about we have designated together-time? What would you think about that?'

Amy pushed herself off the wall so she was facing him. 'What like every Saturday?'

'Well, that's a bit keen, but yeah OK.'

'What were you thinking?'

'I was more like one Saturday a month but no, I'm game. Every Saturday.'

'Or maybe every Sunday might be more practical. People don't do things on Sundays.'

Gus tipped his head in agreement. 'Every Sunday it is. You, me, and Apple.'

'He's not going to be called Apple.'

'You, me, and Orange.'

Amy laughed.

'So, does that make you feel better?' Gus asked.

'Yes.'

'No need for any kissing?'

She shook her head. 'No need for any kissing.'

CHAPTER 40

Stella came back out into the garden after getting changed. The kids were still splashing about at the edge of the pool. Sonny shouted, 'Hey Mum, do you wanna race me?'

Stella shook her head. 'No thanks, I'm exhausted.'

Moira was taking a tour of the garden with one of the women who'd been having breakfast when they arrived, nodding profusely as various plants were pointed out to her and described in Portuguese. 'Lovely, just lovely,' she kept saying.

Stella watched with a smirk, knowing her mother didn't have the faintest idea what was being said.

Her dad appeared next to her, freshly showered and back in his sweat shorts and T-shirt. 'Here,' he said, handing Stella a bottle of water from the vending machine, 'I got you one.' His own bottle in his other hand.

Stella paused, staring at the bottle for a second before taking it from him. 'Thanks,' she said.

He shrugged like it was nothing. But to Stella it felt like the closest she would get to his apology.

Then Sonny and Rosie called him over to show him some game they were playing flicking water. Stella watched, sipping her water, feeling as though for the first time in years she was finally allowed to relax. Her frown had lessened. Her baseline was happier.

Jack came over and put his arm around her. 'Are you OK?'

She didn't even need to think about it. 'Yes,' she said. 'I'm OK.'

Jack nodded. His eyes smiling. She realised how much calmer his face looked, too. All this lessening of tension was working wonders for their wrinkles.

Amy appeared at the gate. 'What's everyone doing now?' she called, walking in Stella's direction.

'I don't know.' Stella shook her head, watching as Gus ambled a little slower behind Amy, eyes wary as he looked across at their dad.

'Well, maybe we should all go back to the camp site?' Amy said. 'Dad, do you want to come back to our camp site? There's a nice beach, and I think I saw something on a flyer about a full-moon party.'

Her dad looked dubious.

'It'll be fun.' Amy trotted over to him adding in a whisper, 'And you have to be nice to Gus, OK?'

Graham nodded, slightly bamboozled.

Moira was watching, hands on her hips.

He turned to her for clarification. 'Would you be all right with that?' he asked.

Moira shrugged. 'Nothing to do with me. I have yoga anyway.'

'Come on, Grandpa, you have to come!' Sonny said, bashing him with his shoulder.

Graham put his hand on Sonny's head. 'OK then.'

Sonny whooped.

Amy linked arms with her dad. They started to walk together, closer to Gus who was standing with his hands in his pockets.

Graham looked him up and down. 'So Gus, what is it that you do?'

Gus swallowed. 'I, er, work for the Ministry of Defence.'

Amy frowned. 'No you don't, you said you work in computers.'

Gus said, 'I work in computers for the Ministry of Defence.'

'Do you now?' Graham said, impressed.

'You're lying,' Amy said. 'What do you do for them?'

'I'm not actually at liberty to say,' Gus said, eyes starting to smile.

'I always quite fancied the military myself,' said Graham, 'if the swimming hadn't worked out.'

Moira laughed out loud. 'Since when?'

Graham blustered a vague response, then marched on ahead firing questions at Gus to distract from Moira's sniggers.

Amy hung back, falling into step with Stella and her mum.

'Am I allowed to ask if you two made up?' Moira asked.

'Yes you are,' Amy replied. 'And yes we did, thank you.'

'Good.' Moira nodded.

Ahead of them Jack beeped the car open and the kids climbed in. 'Do you want to sit in the back with us, Grandpa?' Sonny asked.

'No, I think I'll take my car,' he said, pointing to the snazzy red sports car parked in front of them. 'Gus, would you like to drive with me?'

Amy nudged Stella with a grin, both of them holding in smiles as they watched Gus roll his shoulders and stammer slightly as he said, 'Yes, absolutely, sir.'

'You don't have to call him sir,' Amy called over.

'He can call me sir if he likes,' Graham said, beeping the locks of the flashy rental.

Gus looked back, a plea for rescue in his eyes.

Amy just waved. 'Have fun.'

Stella shook her head. 'You're so mean.'

Moira watched a little worried. 'I hope he's OK.'

'He'll be fine,' said Amy. 'He's the one always going on about how charming he is.' Then she paused. 'Stella, did you know that Mum doesn't like any of her Emma Bridgewater china?'

'No?' Stella gasped.

Moira did a big sigh. 'Oh, I knew this would come up again. I didn't say I didn't like it. I just—'

Amy giggled. 'Mum, we don't care if you don't like it. We're just winding you up. It's only mugs! Just tell us next time.' She fluffed up her hair with a grin. 'Sorry about yesterday by the way. I know you're a person and all that,' she added before hopping in the car.

Stella stood next to her mum. 'God, if only every apology was as easy as that.'

Moira laughed.

Her dad's red sports car zoomed off.

'He does love you, you know,' her mum said.

Stella shrugged as if who knew.

'He does.' Her mum nodded, then she looked across at Stella. 'You did very well today. What you said. I felt dreadful hearing it all but it needed to be said.' She paused. Amy tapped on the window of the car to hurry them up. Moira said, 'I'm sorry I wasn't there for you, Stella.'

Stella swallowed. 'I'm sorry for how often we cut you out.'

343

Moira looked surprised. 'You didn't—' Then she paused, as if allowing herself to acknowledge that they did. 'Well, it's all water under the bridge now, isn't it?'

Amy tapped on the window again.

Moira hesitated for a moment, then she reached across and squeezed Stella into a hug. Stella almost pulled back with shock but Moira was clutching her too tight, enveloping her in a cloud of red hair and Estée Lauder. 'Oh, you were wonderful today. So wonderful,' she said.

Amy was at the window all wide-eyed at the fact they were hugging.

Moira stepped back, holding Stella by the shoulders. 'I almost jumped in the pool and held him back but I thought you might get cross that it wasn't a fair race.'

Stella laughed.

'It was all very dramatic wasn't it? I think we did well.'

'I think we did well, too.' Stella nodded.

Her mum smiled, then she pulled open the car door and said, 'Let's get going. I could murder a G&T.'

CHAPTER 41

The rest of the day was spent at the wild sparse camp site beach. Gus's relief was palpable when they'd arrived back at the car park and Rosie had yanked him to join her to build a whole village of sandcastles. Jack and Sonny messed around on some new-fangled skimboard bought at the supermarket, throwing it in the surf and jumping on, and while presumably they were meant to glide along the shallow water both kept falling off. Amy had taken Graham for a tour of the camp site, while Stella and Moira had a drink in the beach bar.

'This is nice, isn't it, darling?' Moira said, turning to look at Stella. The sea breeze buffeting the awning. The heavy warm air and the energy of the morning making them sit languid and relaxed. 'I'm not sure we've ever had a drink before.'

'No, I don't think we have.' Stella shook her head, lifting her drink to take a slow sip.

Moira looked at her watch. 'I should be going to yoga.'

At the mention of yoga Stella frowned. 'Mum?'

'Yes, Stella.' Moira drained the dregs of her G&T.

'What are you going to do about Mitch? Don't you think it'll be a bit awkward with him and Dad if they bump into each other?'

'Mitch has gone, darling. Left this morning. He's heading to another retreat just north of Lisbon,' Moira said. 'I'm going to join him on the way home, but not for long, I want to get back for the dog.'

'Oh right,' Stella said, surprised. She swirled the remains of her drink in her glass. 'Mum?' she asked hesitantly.

'Yes, Stella.'

'Are you and Mitch in a relationship?'

'Why are you girls so keen to label everything?' Moira frowned. She ran her finger round the rim of her empty glass. 'Let's just say, I'm keeping him on his toes. Something I never did with your father,' she added with an insouciant little smile.

Stella rolled her eyes. Then as she finished her drink said, 'Do you want another one?' pointing towards Moira's empty glass.

'I really should be going to yoga,' Moira said, but then she seemed to take in the moment, sitting there with Stella, and changed her mind. 'Go on then, what the hell,' she said, lifting her legs up to rest on the chair opposite.

Stella was just coming back from the bar with the fresh round when Graham and Amy appeared, glowing from the scorching sun.

As soon as Moira saw them she looked at her watch and made to stand up. 'I really should be going, you know. Yoga starts in a minute.'

'But I've just got you a drink,' Stella said, holding the two

G&Ts in her hand. 'You can't go.' Graham and Amy walked over to the table. 'Do you two want a drink?' Stella asked.

Graham glanced at Moira a little sheepishly, aware that he was the one making her want to leave. 'I'll go if you want to stay,' he said.

Moira tutted. 'Don't be so silly,' she said, clearly saving face, not wanting to be seen as pettily running away. 'We can all stay.'

'OK.' He looked at Stella. 'Yes thanks. I'll have a beer.'

Amy was just settling herself down when Stella said, 'You can help me, Amy.'

'Me? I'm just sitting down.'

'Amy!' Stella said, cajoling eyes wide.

Amy realised what was going on and jumped up to help Stella.

Moira tutted again, sighing at their unsubtle tactics to leave her and Graham alone.

Graham toyed with a beermat on the table. 'So,' he said.

'So,' Moira said.

'I take it you're going to marry him,' Graham said. 'This Mitch character.'

'Oh, for pity's sake.' Moira sat back in her chair, arms crossed. 'Is that really what's bothering you? Graham, I'm sixty-five, of course I'm bloody not, I'm just going to live a little.'

Graham pulled at the neck of his T-shirt, uncomfortable.

Moira shook her head. 'Graham, we had some lovely times but we don't love each other any more. We're one another's comfort blanket. Gosh, when was the last time you and I did anything? When was the last time we had a holiday? Or even a chat for that matter?'

'I can change,' he said.

'Yes,' she said, leaning forward. 'I should hope so.' She studied his face, catching a glimpse of his handsome, charming former self but still with that familiar neediness in his eyes as he gazed back at her – a lazy helplessness that believed she might once again prop him up. But she wouldn't. Looking at him sitting there, a little boy and an old man, she felt the freedom of it not being her responsibility to prop him up. Her fear that she would slip back into old routines silenced by her ever-growing inner strength, the strength that was making her stand up for what she believed and giving her the courage to defend not just what she wanted but what she knew was right. The strength that said – just because he is back, doesn't mean you have to take him back. If she could save herself, then he was old enough to do the same.

'What do you think I should do?' Graham asked.

Moira snorted a laugh. 'Oh Graham, that's not up to me.' She took a sip of her drink then looked up to see him waiting for more of a response. 'You just have to do a few more things outside your comfort zone,' she said, taking the lime out of her glass and squeezing it then giving her drink a quick stir with a teaspoon from the flower pot of cutlery in the centre of the table. 'Join some new things.'

He made a face. 'I don't like joining new things.'

Moira shrugged. 'So stay lonely,' she said, swigging a big gulp of her drink before standing up. 'I really do have to go to yoga.' She had another quick sip and was about to walk away when she paused. 'It's in your hands, Graham. Remember you got to Portugal easily enough. You've taken the first step.'

He looked a little forlorn.

She pointed to Jack and Sonny on the skimboard. 'There's something new you could try,' she said with a cheeky little grin, then she strolled off out of the bar, high on her own bravery and courage.

CHAPTER 42

As the sun began to dip on the horizon the others strolled up to the beach shack with its strings of white lights glowing against the pink-tinted sky and the sardines sizzling on the grill. Everyone except Amy, and even Graham, had had a go on the skimboard in the shallows. Everyone falling over. Rosie the closest to mastering it. People had started gathering on the beach now, building a bonfire for the full-moon party. Music drifted up from the sand backed by the melodic crash of the waves. The evening yoga practise was coming to an end up on the hill, all of them standing tall like silhouettes of trees reaching for the dusky sky.

Gus and Amy were at the bar. Sonny was playing pinball. Jack, Stella, and Graham were talking.

Graham was sitting back, relaxing into being with the family, ankle crossed over his knee, greying curls a bit wild from the sea salt. 'You know the Pemberton farm is for sale,' he said to Jack. 'If you're looking to change jobs for good.'

Gus came over, plonking a tray of beer bottles down on the table. 'Don't do it. A farm is a nightmare.'

'I reckon I could be a farmer,' Jack said, rolling his shoulders, testing it out for size. 'Get a dog. I like tractors.'

Stella frowned but didn't say anything, just listened.

Rosie was hovering by Sonny at the pinball machine, hopping up and down for her turn.

'You're chained to a farm,' Gus added, picking up his beer. 'You have to be there all the time to make sure everything's OK. And get up at four.'

'Oh no, I wouldn't like that,' Jack backpedalled.

Stella held in a smile. Amy appeared with her tomato juice and a small colourful bowl of olives.

'Or what about a pub?' Graham asked.

At that point Moira arrived, trotting down the wooden steps, fresh from yoga and a little glammed up in white jeans and an off-the-shoulder striped top. 'The Coach and Horses is for sale,' she said, picking up the thread of the conversation as she came to the table.

'You took the words out my mouth,' said Graham, immediately standing up to get her a chair, clearly trying to be on his best behaviour.

Moira settled herself down like a movie star, relishing the attention.

'A pub!' Jack sat up straight. 'I like that.'

'Stella's not going to live in a pub!' Amy laughed, popping an olive into her mouth.

Stella shrugged, poker-faced, taking a sip of beer. 'I'd think about it,' she said, while inside itching to shout, 'This is ludicrous!' But she had sworn to herself she wouldn't take control and bulldoze any of Jack's ideas.

'It'd be fun,' said Jack. 'We'd be near the sea, the kids could go to the village school, it'd be perfect.'

Sonny swung round horrified from the pinball machine.

'I don't want to go to the village school. I like my school. Mum, tell him we're not going to the village school!'

They all looked at Stella, who was peeling the label off her beer. 'I'm not telling him anything. He can do what he likes. Although' —she paused, unable to stay out of it completely, however hard she was trying— 'I'm not sure I want to move to the country. I like the city.'

Jack looked at her, beer bottle paused at his lips, first with surprise that she was being so amenable, then with a smile. 'Me too,' he said.

'Me too!' said Sonny with relief.

Jack sighed. 'So, what am I going to do?'

'Do you know, darling, you could start by ordering me a G&T,' Moira chimed in, still perfectly poised on her chair. 'If you wouldn't mind.'

Jack frowned as if that was not the answer he was looking for.

Moira raised a brow. 'Well, you're the one who wanted to work in a pub.'

Graham guffawed. Moira looked very pleased with herself.

Jack hauled himself up, despondent, and went over to the bar with his beer.

Stella slipped away after him, leaving Amy sharing cringing looks with Gus over the table about her parents.

The sun was setting now, the waves a strip of white against a vermilion horizon, the sky above still glowing blue. More people had gathered over by the water, building up the bonfire with armfuls of sun-dried wood.

Stella sat on a bar stool next to Jack, their knees touching. She tucked her hair behind her ears. 'Jack, a rebellion doesn't mean you have to change completely. It's just a pause to find out what you really love.'

Jack looked at her. 'But what do I really love?' he said.

'Well, that's what you have to think about rather than clutching at bizarre ideas offered by my father. Have fun with it. Work out what you enjoy.'

He nodded.

Stella looked back towards the table where the waiter was setting out candles, everyone illuminated in the flickering dusk. Her mum and dad were laughing at something Gus was saying. Amy was gesticulating about something. Rosie was trying to beg a euro for the pinball off anyone who was willing to spare her some cash. Graham dug in his pocket and gave her a handful of change.

Stella shook her head. 'I don't know about the Marriage MOT but it's certainly been a Family MOT.'

Jack glanced to where she was looking, then back at her. 'What do you mean? I think we were pretty tremendous with our MOT. Look at us, all good as new. Discovered the brake pads were in order.'

'Jack, please!' Stella shook her head at the dreadful analogy.

'What was next on the list?' he asked.

'I'm meant to pretend to be your mistress.'

Jack almost choked. 'Are you serious? How exciting.'

'Don't get your hopes up, it's never going to happen,' Stella said. 'I'm just going to make the whole article up I think. It's easier.'

Jack frowned. 'That's a shame.' The waiter brought over the G&T. Jack was about to stand up when he paused and said, 'What would it take for you to pretend to be my mistress?'

'Are you serious?'

'Deadly.'

Stella thought for a while. 'You have sex with me in that field, I'll pretend to be your mistress.'

Jack winced.

Stella grinned. 'Well?'

'What – you actually want to do it?' he said, a touch taken aback.

Stella rolled her eyes. 'Jesus Christ, Jack.'

'Oh right. Wow.' Jack stared at the G&T on the bar a little petrified. Then he seemed to warm to the idea. 'OK. Let's do it. May as well go the whole hog with this rebellion.'

It was Stella's turn to look terrified. 'Really?'

Jack narrowed his eyes. 'You don't want to.'

'Yes, I do.'

He laughed. 'No you don't.'

'OK, maybe I don't actually want to have sex in a field. I suppose I just wanted you to want to have sex with me in a field.'

Jack looked bemused. 'Stella, if you want to have sex in a field, I'll have sex in a field,' he said. 'Personally, I'd just prefer it in a fancy country hotel that we could book into instead.'

'That's not very rock and roll, though, is it.'

'Stella,' Jack reached forward and put his hands on her shoulders. 'Who are you trying to impress with this? We've never been rock and roll. Ten years of marriage hasn't changed that,' he laughed, shaking his head at her, then he picked up the G&T and stood. 'Look, this MOT thing was good. It brought us back to us. But I'm sorry to say, I'm proud that I have never had sex in a field and never will be someone who has sex in a field.'

Stella nodded, resigned to agreement.

Jack walked away. Then almost immediately he came back. 'But if you still want to, I will. If it would make you happy.'

Stella shook her head. 'No, it's fine.'

'Phew!' Jack did a mock swipe of his brow and went to join the others, delivering Moira her G&T.

Stella stayed at the bar a little longer. Sipping her beer, looking out at the last of the sun patterning the water and the waves as they crashed and frothed on the shore.

Suddenly Jack was back. 'Now I feel like a real fuddy-duddy,' he said. 'Come with me—' Grabbing her hand he dragged her off past the bar, in the opposite direction to her family, and down onto the darkened beach.

'What are we doing?' Stella asked, a little breathless.

'What do you think? We're having sex on the beach.'

'Oh God!' Stella was laughing as he pulled them behind a huge rocky enclave. 'Who are you trying to impress, Jack?'

'You, Stella,' he said. 'Always you.'

CHAPTER 43

The evening wore on, the sky got darker and the stars brighter. The bar filled out. The barbecue smoked. Stella and Jack returned giggling and sand-swept. More drinks were bought. More pinball played. After dinner, Rosie was almost falling asleep on two chairs pushed together but then Vasco beckoned them all down on the beach. 'We are going to light the bonfire.'

Rosie's eyes opened immediately and, yawning, she jumped down from her chair.

The crowd gathered on the beach. Flame torches touched the dry branches and the wind did the rest: light and sparks shot up to the sky. Bursts of bright orange crackled and popped, shimmering like petrol on the water.

They stood, mesmerised. Vasco got out his guitar, one of the yoga women sang. Drinks were carried down from the restaurant. There was dancing barefoot in the sand.

The fire raged. The moon glowed. Stella asked Jack if he wanted to swim with her in the dark, black sea. He said yes.

Rosie forced Sonny to dance, whirling around with the yoga lot. Amy tried but failed to get Gus to dance.

Moira and Graham sat side by side at the table, half-drunk

356

drinks in their glasses, looking out at the water and the fire reflected in the ripple of the tide.

'So, what are you going to do?' Moira asked.

Graham sucked in his breath. 'Not sure.' He looked across at her. 'You were right. I need to do more.'

'Yes.'

'I thought I might stay away for a bit longer – carry on round into Spain. I've enjoyed this trip. But I'm not sure what I'll do when I get back…'

Moira took a sip of her drink. 'There's lots to look forward to, Graham,' she said, pointing out towards the beach.

They watched Jack splash Stella as they swam. And Sonny, Rosie, and Amy drag a very reluctant Gus to join them on the sandy dancefloor.

The fire hissed as new branches were thrown on the dwindling flames.

Graham took a quick, almost nervous, gulp of his beer before saying, 'When I get back Moira, would you like to have dinner with me?'

Moira's hand stilled on her glass. She smoothed her hair. 'Well, actually I won't be back for a while either. I have another retreat in Lisbon then I'm off on a Tuscan painting holiday.'

'Oh right,' he said, looking dispiritedly at his beer bottle on the table. 'Busy then.'

'Very busy,' she agreed.

'I didn't know you painted.'

Moira laughed. 'Don't be daft, no one goes on these trips to actually paint.'

Graham looked confused.

'I'm sure I'll paint the odd tree but really it's for the wine and the chat,' Moira said, feeling smugly seasoned in the art of joining new things. 'What you'll learn, Graham, is that half the point of going to these classes and things is the thrill of bunking off them.'

'Right,' Graham said, trepidation visible on his face at the possible activities to come.

'You'll be fine.' She tapped his leg. 'It'll be good for you.' Then after another sip of her drink added, 'Dinner was it you said?'

Graham nodded. The bonfire sizzled and cracked down on the beach.

'Maybe,' said Moira. 'Maybe, when *I* get back.'

CHAPTER 44

It was midnight when they all lined up in the car park. Like the von Trapp children, waiting to say goodbye.

The air was still warm. The wind had dropped. The sky a gauze of stars.

Amy was the first to step forward and give her dad a hug. 'You will come back, won't you? You won't disappear again?'

Graham shook his head, almost embarrassed by the reminder that he had disappeared in the first place. 'No.'

Amy sniffed. 'You'd better not, you're going to have another grandchild to get to know!'

Graham nodded, as if that were exactly why he would never disappear again.

Then he moved on to Gus, his arm outstretched. 'Don't mess it up,' he ordered as Gus stepped forward and Graham gave his hand a bone-crunching shake.

Gus's face blanched. Graham snorted a laugh. 'I thought you were a military man.'

'I'm not actually in the military—' Gus started but Graham had already moved onto the next in line.

Stella.

They stood silently face to face. The wind rustling through the giant palm trees and clinking the wind-chimes.

'That was good swimming,' Graham said.

'You too,' Stella replied. 'You should go back to coaching at the pool when you get back. Pete's even more of a menace than he was.'

Graham tipped his head. 'I thought you thought I was the menace.'

She shrugged. 'You don't have to be.'

He cleared his throat. Ran his hand round the neck of his T-shirt. Then he nodded, seemingly considering whether that was their goodbye done.

Stella rolled her lips together. Then she smiled.

And Graham sort of smiled. Then he leant forward and gave her a kiss on the cheek. Surprised by the closeness, she put her hand on his arm. He smelt of her dad.

'I acknowledge some responsibility,' he mumbled in her ear, so quiet she almost asked him to repeat himself, it only dawning on her just before she did what he had actually said.

She stood, stunned, as he moved along the line to Sonny.

'Work hard and listen to your mother. Yes,' Graham barked.

Sonny gave a begrudging nod. Graham ruffled his hair. 'And you'll set up the blog?'

'Yes.'

Amy poked her head forward. 'What blog?'

'Sonny is going to build me a blog,' Graham put his hand proudly on Sonny's shoulder, 'so I can write about all my adventures. And you can all read it. It's called Gone Dad.'

They all collectively rolled their eyes.

'It's a good name, yes!' Graham looked really pleased with himself.

Sonny said, 'I've already changed your Instagram. And remember, it's double tap to Like, the square in the middle to load and the little speech bubble to comment.'

Graham did a slow salute. Sonny grinned.

Graham moved along to Jack who had Rosie asleep on his shoulder. They shook hands.

'Get a job,' Graham said.

Jack nodded. 'Will do.'

And then finally, at the end, was Moira. They smiled at each other. She said, 'Good luck, Graham.'

He said, 'Thank you.'

They kissed demurely on the cheek.

He inhaled. Closed his eyes. Then he stepped back. 'I'll see you for dinner?'

Stella and Amy gave their mother wide-eyed looks behind his back.

'If you're lucky,' she said with a coy flick of her hair.

'We can talk about putting the house on the market,' he said, as if adding another incentive to make sure she agreed.

From the other end of the line Amy gave a little yelp then silenced herself after a look from Gus.

Moira nodded.

Graham gave a final wave and strode round to get into his flashy car. 'See you,' he called before starting the engine and roaring away in a cloud of dust.

They all watched him go. Stella went to stand next to her mother. 'Dinner?' she said.

Moira narrowed her eyes as the car disappeared out of the main gates. 'We'll see,' she said. Then she glanced across at her daughter. 'Got to keep them on their toes.'

CHAPTER 45

Everyone walked back to the huts. Everyone except Amy, who hung back.

Gus was strolling with Sonny and Rosie and almost halfway to the hill before he noticed Amy wasn't with them.

He paused and looked round. She was standing in the middle of the path. He jogged back. 'What are you doing? What's wrong?'

Amy frowned, deep lines across her forehead. 'I think I'm jealous of the hipster girlfriend.'

'Sorry?' Gus laughed.

'I'm jealous of the hipster girlfriend,' Amy said again. 'I think about her and I hate her. I hate her charity shop dresses and ugly flat shoes.'

Gus was looking at her, perplexed.

Amy scuffed the floor with her flip-flop. 'I don't want you to go out with her. I don't want you to hold her hand.'

'Amy, she doesn't exist.'

'I know, but she will. And all I can see is me with my beefcake sitting across the table from you and your annoying girl with her blunt cut fringe and being jealous.'

'You really know what she looks like, don't you?'

'Yes. And I don't want her to exist. I don't want her to have you.' She looked up. 'Believe me, I don't want to want to have you either but that's the situation I'm finding myself in.' She put her hand on her chest. 'I do not want to want you, Gus.'

'This is very flattering, Amy.'

Amy narrowed her eyes. 'I know you don't want to be tied in an awful relationship for the sake of the baby, but what if it wasn't awful? I mean, wouldn't that be good for the baby if we could be more than friends? So what if we did split up all acrimonious? Isn't that what happens with lots of couples with kids anyway?'

Gus didn't say anything, just watched her a bit bewildered.

'Well?' she ordered.

'I guess so.'

'There you go,' she said.

'There I go, what?'

'Well there you go, your argument is ruined.'

'Right.' Gus inhaled, crossing his arms over his chest.

'So?' Amy said, staring straight at him.

'So what?' Gus frowned. 'I don't know. I'm slightly afraid of you.'

'Why?'

'Because I think in your ideal world I'd drop down on one knee now and propose.'

'No you wouldn't.' She shook her head. Then she paused, caught out.

Gus laughed.

Amy suddenly felt really exposed. She blew her hair up out

of her face, kicked the sand at her feet, realising she'd kind of expected them to be kissing by now. She put her hands up to her cheeks. 'You don't fancy me, do you?'

Gus didn't say anything, just looked down at the dusty path.

Amy screwed her eyes tight and leant back against one of the fat palm trees. 'God, I'm such an idiot.' She opened one eye. 'I shouldn't have said it.' She opened both eyes and slumped against the jagged palm trunk. 'I just—' she sighed. 'I did want you to kiss me the other night. I really did. It wasn't because I was scared of being alone. I've been alone for two years now. I know how to be alone. I'm quite good at it.'

She bit her lip, reached and pulled at one of the overhanging palm fronds. 'And I know I said just now that I didn't want to like you, which wasn't very nice, but that's because if I'd said what I thought it was just all too embarrassing. If I'm honest, I literally can't stop thinking about you. I like you more than I thought I would ever like you. Things I couldn't bear about you I now find attractive. I like that you like Rosie. That you looked out for Sonny. When you make Stella laugh, I get this rush of pride. It's ridiculous. And I don't even care if the baby inherits your nose because now I just think it will inherit your kindness and your humour. Your stupid logic and your laughter.'

She pushed herself off the palm tree trunk. 'And it's all wasted now anyway because you don't even fancy me, which I think I knew anyway.' She started to walk away. 'You've got your stupid hipster girlfriend to go home to.'

Gus walked next to her, hands in his pockets.

Up ahead the giant eucalyptus swayed in the wind. The clouds darkened over the moon. The highest flames of the bonfire were just visible on the horizon.

Gus said, 'I do fancy you.'

Amy looked across at him. 'You do?' She frowned. 'Why didn't you say so?'

He shrugged. 'I wanted you to work a bit harder.'

'Oh my God, you arsehole. You made me say all that stuff.'

'Too bloody right.'

She thwacked him on the stomach.

He laughed, doubled over. 'We all like a bit of romance, Amy. Me as much as the next person.'

'What about me?' she said. 'I like a bit of romance, too.'

'You'll get romance, don't you worry.'

'Fat chance. You'll be all: "Now, Amy, no happy ever after for you."'

'You're going to have to stop doing that voice for me because I don't sound like that at all.'

She laughed, 'You do.'

'I do not.'

He reached forward and caught her arm. She stopped. He pulled her back towards him. 'Amy,' he said, 'I'm never going to promise you happy ever after because it doesn't exist, it's unpromisable. All I can offer you is what we have right now.'

Amy felt his hand on her arm, was close enough to smell him, to look up at the whites of his eyes in the dark. She could see the moonlight dancing off the eucalyptus, the flicker of the fire, the glow on the wild waves through the trees, and she didn't know what else would be worth asking for. So she nodded, tentative at first and then a proper real nod and a huge wide smile. 'That's good enough for me,' she said. 'I'll take your right now.'

Gus grinned.

He put his hands on either side of her face, tilted her head ever so slightly and, when he was just about to kiss her, she jumped up on tiptoes so her giggling lips met his first.

CHAPTER 46

The night ended round the little table beside the hut. Lots of smirking glances across the table as Amy and Gus appeared hand in hand. A delighted clap from Rosie. 'She is your girlfriend. I knew it!' A bottle of chilled Portuguese Mateus Rosé poured into the hotchpotch of camp site glasses. Some more chat, some more meaningful gazes at the beautiful trees, a snigger from Amy when she demanded to hear word for word Stella's outburst round the pool. 'Her face went red and she was really shouting!' Rosie again. A pause to listen to the pop and hiss of the fading bonfire embers. A rummage in Amy's beach bag and then she held a little brown mug painted with white flowers aloft. 'Here you go Mum, to start your new collection. It's Portuguese.'

'Oh, I love it.' Moira was touched. 'Where did you get it?'

'I nicked it from the bar.'

'Amy, you didn't?'

'Course I bloody didn't.' Amy grinned. 'Gus did it for me.'

'Amy! You said you wouldn't say anything.'

Moira looked both appalled and quite delighted that such a heist had taken place in her honour.

Then Gus said, 'Hey Sonny, I got to the next level on your game last night.'

'You didn't?' Sonny couldn't believe it.

'I did.' Gus got his phone out to show him.

Amy said, 'Will someone show me how to play this game?'

'I will,' Stella offered.

'Show me, too,' said Jack.

'What about me?' asked Moira.

Rosie said, 'You don't want to Granny, it's very boring.'

'It's not boring,' Sonny scoffed. 'You just can't play it.'

'I can!'

'Go on then.'

And that was how the evening ended. Everyone heads down, locked into Sonny's game. The competition intensifying as their names on the scoreboard rose and fell with every attempt. Laughing. Shouting. Bashing the table in frustration. Together. As the clouds drifted across the moon and the eucalyptus leaves shook and the crow watched from its perch.

Then, after everyone had gone to bed, Stella sat up and wrote her article. About everything that had happened with her and Jack over the period of time her dad had gone missing. Not under the Potty-Mouth pseudonym but her own name.

And so I conclude, that along with all the extra sex, the shared grievances, the dates, the pretending to be mistresses, the time outs to speak honestly without judgement, for any relationship to work it's about remembering that the people in it once existed quite happily without the other. They are people in their own right. Not simply cut-outs of predictable reactions to walk alongside. Be nice to each other. Be open to surprise. To

369

change. To argument and apology. But most of all, don't become one. Don't lose the side of yourself that shores you up, and you alone.

Ours was less an MOT more a swap the car for two bikes. A realisation that marriage doesn't come with an automatic right to the other's pocket. But instead an invite if you want to pop in every now and then. Our MOT got maybe a C+. Our bikes are brand spanking new.

Share any comments you have with @StellaWrites Potty-Mouth is away.

When it was done, Stella sent it off to her editor, snuggled under the sheet and fell asleep.

CHAPTER 47

'Ow! What are you doing?' Stella opened her eyes, disorientated. It felt like the middle of the night. 'What's going on? Is it the kids?'

'No, it's not the kids, don't worry, nothing's going on,' Jack said. He was sitting up next to her, T-shirt rumpled.

'What time is it?'

'Four o'clock,' Jack said.

Stella winced.

'I've decided what I'm going to do,' Jack said with a grin, all eager. 'I'm going build skateparks! Don't you think that's a good idea?' He nudged her for a response. 'I have to go miles for mine. There should be more. It's no wonder teenagers don't go out of the house, they have nothing to do. Anyway, that's what I'm going to do. What do you think?'

Stella was still squinting in the early morning light. Her eyes stung, her body ached. 'You woke me up at 4 a.m. to tell me this?'

Jack looked immediately dejected. 'I wanted to be upfront with you. I thought you'd be excited.'

Stella rubbed her eyes. 'I am excited. But could you please be upfront with me between the hours of 8 a.m. and 10 p.m.?'

Jack laughed. 'So, what do think, though? About my idea.'

'It sounds great. Good idea. Lovely. Can I go to sleep now?'

'Yes.'

Stella yawned, lay back down and closed her eyes. She was just dropping off when Jack nudged her again.

'What?'

'Do you really think our marriage only got a C+?' he asked.

Stella's eyes flew open. 'Did you just read my article?'

'Maybe.'

She sighed, plumping her pillow. 'No,' she said, 'I think we got an A but a C+ makes better copy. Now I'm going back to sleep.'

She closed her eyes.

Jack nudged her again. 'Do you really think we got an A?'

Stella groaned, her eyes opened in slits. 'No, probably more like a B+.'

Jack smiled. 'Yeah, that's what I thought.'

Stella put the pillow over her head.

Jack couldn't sleep. He got up and went outside.

There was a mist over the entire camp site, drifting in with sharp fresh air and catching the rising sun like glitter on candyfloss.

A voice said, 'What are you doing out here?' startling him.

Jack looked across to see Gus leaning over from his veranda. 'I'm going to build a skatepark,' he said, walking over to join him.

'Nice one.'

'What about you? Why are you up?'

'Amy snores.'

'Does she?' Jack said, surprised.

Gus nodded, unimpressed. 'Like a train.'

Jack guffawed.

Amy woke up, stretched and looked out of the window. Gus and Jack were standing on the veranda. Jack was laughing. She wondered what was so funny. Then she saw her mother walk past all spritely and ready for yoga, she gave the guys a wave. At the same time Stella came schlepping out looking half-asleep, 'Why are you all awake?'

Behind them the sun was just rising: big, round, and red above the mist. Amy yawned and picked up her phone, snapped a picture for Instagram.

She thought about writing something really poignant. '*A new day begins...*'

But she didn't.

Instead she wrote: '*The sun looks like a Strepsil.*'

And snuggled back down under covers that smelt of sleep and suntan lotion.

Stella stomped back to her room.

Gus asked Jack if he fancied going to yoga.

Jack guffawed again.

And a heart popped up on Amy's phone screen. GoneDad likes your photo.

ONE PLACE. MANY STORIES

Bold, innovative and
empowering publishing.

FOLLOW US ON:

@HQStories